GALAHAD

I THOUGHT OF DAISY

BOOKS BY EDMUND WILSON

Galahad
I Thought of Daisy

BY EDMUND WILSON

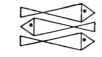

FARRAR, STRAUS AND GIROUX
NEW YORK

FOREWORD

I Thought of Daisy, first published in 1929 and written much under the influence of Proust and Joyce, was intended, like *Ulysses* and *À la Recherche du Temps Perdu,* to be a sort of symphonic arrangement. The main theme is of course the relationship between the narrator and Daisy. This narrator is supposed to be a typical example of the American intellectuals of the twenties, who is always attempting to formulate an attitude toward life in the United States, and Daisy the American reality, which is always eluding his grasp. By shifting the elements of the situation in each of the five sections, I aimed, in each one of these, to produce a different mood and to bring out a different point of view. In each of them except the third, the mood and the point of view were to have as their representatives, the personality of one of the characters, which would dominate the mind of the narrator and preside over the section as a whole. In the first, it is Hugo Bamman, with his revolt against bourgeois society and his social revolutionary ideas. In the second, it is Rita, the romantic poet. In the third, the narrator is adrift in the void, with no planet to gravitate about: the world in which he finds himself now appears to him anarchic and amoral, and the point of view is more or less materialistic, with an emphasis on animal behavior. Here the place of the interpolated character sketch that figures in the first, second and fourth sections is taken by the disquisition on literature regarded as a desperate effort to create an illusion that the world makes sense. In the fourth section, my hero recovers himself under the influence of the metaphysician Grosbeake, who instils into him a certain idealism and induces in him a certain serenity. In each of these states of mind, he has made a different image of Daisy, has tried to fit her into a different system; but in the fifth and final section, she herself becomes the dominant character. Since he effects a real union with her, there is here no interpolation—disquisition or character sketch—that sets off the point of view from the narrative and is not assimilated by it: Daisy simply tells about her own life. The point of view—or state of mind—here is instinctive, democratic, pragmatic. My hero has at last, for the moment, made connections with the common life. And just as this narrator is shown to slip from orbit to orbit of a series of planets, so Daisy is shown to pass from one to another of a series of partners, in each of whom she tries to believe. Phil Meissner, Ray Coleman, Pete Bird were intended as pygmy specimens of familiar American types.

I Thought of Daisy is thus very schematic, and the scheme does not always succeed, for it is sometimes at odds with the story. In rereading the book for the first time since I wrote it, I have sometimes been rather appalled by the rigor with which I sacrificed to my plan of five symphonic movements what would normally have been the line of the story. There is no very full account of the narrator's relations with Rita, though the reader must have been led to expect it—since, though Rita is more interesting than Daisy, her role had to be kept to

proportions that would not prevent Daisy from playing
the central role; nor could I, for similar reasons, allow her
to be too sympathetic. Yet, in spite of this, she otherwise
upsets the scheme by attracting too much attention when
she appears in the opening section, which is supposed to
be dominated by Hugo.

Nothing annoys me more than to have the characters
and incidents which figure in my works of fiction represented as descriptions of real people and events. In a study
that is supposed to be scholarly, this is, of course, inex-
cusable, and no one would be guilty of it who had any
grasp of the rules of scholarly evidence; but it is equally
irritating to have facile guesses made at supposed orig-
inals. In the case of a still living writer, such guesses are
something of an impertinence, and, besides not allowing
for the freedom with which the writer of fiction may combine and transform and fantasticate suggestions from different sources, they are likely to be wide of the mark. The
identification of these elements can hardly become desirable or feasible till after a writer's death, when his letters
and other papers and the memoirs of people who knew him
have become accessible to the student. It has taken Mr.
George D. Painter many years to disentangle the real cir-
cumstances which were laid under contribution by Mar-
cel Proust to produce the creations of his novel, and even
so his findings are questioned by persons with some independent knowledge of the people whom Proust knew.
Though I sometimes, in *I Thought of Daisy,* used the
sayings and traits of real people, the story is an invention
from beginning to end. What has misled these amateur
detectives is that the only two novels I have published
are told in the first person. But *Daisy,* as I have said
above, suffers not from sticking too closely to actual
experience but to having been subjected to a precon-

ceived scheme. So the narrator of my *Memoirs of Hecate County* was identified with myself not only by the representative of the District Attorney's office who prosecuted the book in the courts and treated the narrative as a brazen confession, but also by reviewers who ought to have known better.

The shorter story included here, *Galahad,* was written in the early twenties and first published, in 1927, in *The American Caravan,* a miscellany of current writing edited by Van Wyck Brooks, Lewis Mumford, Alfred Kreymborg and Paul Rosenfeld. It was suggested by an actual incident which reached me at second hand. The speeches at the Y.M.C.A. are more or less accurate reports of speeches I have heard myself. I very soon in my own prep-school days, came to think such performances funny or disgusting. An alumnus of this same school has told me lately that he once laughed out loud when one of the reformed bums who were supposed to put the fear of God into us declared that he had "first met Jesus in a box-car." As a result, he was had on the carpet by the committee from the Sixth Form which was supposed to deal with cases of misconduct. The punishment decreed was his banishment from further Y.M.C.A. meetings, which were compulsory for everyone else. He was delighted. I wish this had happened to me.

The intensive evangelism to which we were subjected at school was entirely the affair of the Headmaster's wife, a very strong-minded woman, who was something of a religious fanatic, especially obsessed with sex. I am told that, after I left, she went so far as to show, for the benefit of the "bids" who took care of our rooms, a film designed to fortify them against temptation and to put them on their guard against rape—a fate of which I should say, from my memory of them, they stood in little danger.

My impression is, in fact, that she had carefully screened these women with a view to having them as old and as unattractive as possible. But with her retirement, all this lapsed and vanished, and it had never very seriously disturbed the humanistic tradition represented by the excellent faculty. For the purposes of my story, I have called the school in question St. Matthew's; but it has occurred to me since that a New England school—the real one was not in New England—which was named in this way for a saint would probably have been Episcopalian and not to that degree evangelistic. So we shall have to assume that, at some recent date in the history of this school, the conservative Headmaster had married an intemperate New England Calvinist. The trustees had not yet intervened. Our actual Headmaster's wife *was* a product of New England Calvinism, which at the date of which I write was continuing to play a role in even the higher domains of American education. I found it behind even the institutions of gay and easy-going Princeton, though in a less aggressive form than I had known it at school. But I was never plagued again by this branch of religion in its evangelistic form. At Princeton, after all, Billy Sunday was not allowed on the campus, and Frank Buchman was banished from it.

Both these stories are here presented in a very much revised form.

1967

CONTENTS

GALAHAD

CASALINO

I

It had just been brought home to Hart Foster that he was probably certain of being elected to next year's presidency of the Y.M.C.A. of St. Matthew's School. The officers were always members of the Sixth Form, but when the Sixth Form secretary had been obliged to leave school, as the result of a mysterious nervous breakdown, Hart, who was still only a Fifth Former, had been asked to take his place. Tonight, before dinner, when he had mentioned to his room-mate that Boards Borden, the Sixth Form President, had invited him to visit him during the holidays, Eddie O'Brien had observed, as if with a chill of alienation: "Well, we'll all have to reform next year when you're President of the Y!" Hart had noted the change of tone, which already implied both the gulf between the layman and the consecrated priest and the inequality between the commoner and the heir to some position of prestige, and it had somewhat worried and distressed him. As he had dressed for the evening meeting, plastering his hair down glossily on each side, stretching his watch-chain with Y.M.C.A. tautness between the two lower pockets of the vest of his immaculate blue suit, he confronted the situation for the first time. The Fifth Form was notoriously below standard in moral character:

3

three Fifth Formers had recently been suspended for a
nocturnal escapade to Boston, and almost a whole floor
of the Fifth Form Flat had been deprived of their priv-
ileges—from going into town on Saturday to visiting after
evening study hour—for having been caught smoking
in their rooms. The only other member of the Fifth Form
who had been as active in the Y as Hart had a stutter
which would make it impossible for him to preside at
the weekly meetings. But Hart wondered now whether
he were really prepared to assume the responsibility of
of the Y. He would enjoy this position of importance, but
he doubted whether he possessed the qualifications for
it. He would, he felt, make a good executive; and, from
some points of view, a good speaker. But he was far
better as a debater than as an inspirational orator: he
felt more confident of his ability to achieve distinction
in the big inter-school debate. When his room-mate had
spoken with that edge of grimness, Hart had felt a little
like a hypocrite. Did being President of the Y.M.C.A.
mean denying the jovial roughhouse, the nonsense and
bawdy jokes, of the Fifth Form Flat? Did it mean becoming like Boards Borden? His own temperament was
severer and more restrained than that of most of his
companions, but he thoroughly enjoyed their society and
shrank from the prospect of being isolated from them.
One of the great sports of the hour before lights-out
when life so rapidly became heightened and riotous—
as soldiers soon to return to the front make the most of
their last hours of leave—was putting people under the
bed. Could he continue to participate in such diversions
if he were President of the Y.M.C.A.? Yes, he told himself, he certainly should: he would show them that he
was still a good fellow. But would his presence discourage their fun? Would his former companions feel at
liberty to put *him* under the bed? And would it be right

for them to do so? Yet, without equality of privilege, the roughhouse game would be spoiled; the situation would become impossible. Hart wondered whether he really lacked faith: he knew himself to be capable of an earnest kind of moral enthusiasm, but he had noticed that, though he had prayed with the best masters, he had never seemed to catch their exaltation, and that Holman Hunt's *Light of the World,* which was hung behind the platform in the Study Hall, had obstinately remained for him a beaconless symbol which never flashed its revelation.

Tonight, therefore, at this most important of all Y.M.C.A. meetings, the last before the Christmas holidays, as he sat behind his desk on the platform, watching the room gradually filling and making accurate business-like gestures in connection with the minute-book before him—his glowing cleanness, but lately issued from the shower, gilded richer by the powerful droplight which illuminated his desk—he felt an unaccustomed self-consciousness and, as it were, an imperfect harmony with the ritual at which he was officiating, such as, before his final realization that the mark of his call was upon him, had rarely caused him embarrassment. Where he had hitherto been able to enjoy the sensations that were the accompaniment of presiding at a Y meeting, the deeply gratifying sensations of a pure and well-washed consecration, of a competent noble maturity, which, though still on terms of admirable good-fellowship with the juvenile student body, bears the seal of having passed from among them to receive the Tables from Sinai, and smiles down upon them now for the moment with the cordiality, a little too ready, of the heroic Christian leader who is but the servant of all—though he had hitherto enjoyed these sensations, he seemed this evening to have partially lost contact with them. He tended to scrutinize and reflect on himself—even, before his own conscience, to judge.

The meeting had been well advertized and the attendance was particularly good. In his belief that the Christmas holidays were a period of peculiar temptations, Mr. Hotchkiss, the patron saint of school and college Y.M.C.A.'s, who kept them all under supervision and was usually present on occasions of importance, had especially provided, to warn them against Vice, a professional reformed debauchee; and perhaps a third of the school had turned out in the eager, if apprehensive, hope of being treated to gamy details of this sinner's abominable life. They swarmed along the rows of seats, with flurries of restrained rioting, in the hard electric light and the plain woodwork setting of the Study Hall; and, above them, in a plaster garland, were ranged the busts of the great men of antiquity—of Homer and Socrates and Plato, of Thucydides and Euripides, of Seneca and Virgil and Augustus.

Boards Borden at last rang the bell and called the meeting to order.

He was a tall square-shouldered youth, blond, handsome and without distinction, whose white collar stood so high that his neck seemed encased in a pipe and whose watch-chain and plastered hair followed the same convention as those of Hart. When he stood up to open the meeting, a vast solemnity paralyzed the audience—as if the barren robustness of his spirit had had the effect of making even emptier that great bare box of a room, as if the crude steady light of his zeal had been able to render even harsher that unshaded electric glare. It was apparently not merely his family name, but something in his appearance and character, which had earned him the nickname of Boards.

First, *Onward Christian Soldiers* was sung with a certain amount of gusto, and then the President offered up a short prayer requesting divine support during the holidays. Then Hart read the minutes of the last meeting with creditable distinctness and gravity.

Now Boards Borden stood up again and haltingly addressed the assembly. Hart reflected that, though he himself might perhaps somewhat lack inspiration, he would at least be able to speak more coherently.

"Fellows, we have to talk to us tonight both Mr. Hotchkiss and Mr. Bergen. Mr. Hotchkiss hardly needs an introduction among St. Matthew's fellows. His work among the schools and colleges is—well known throughout the country—and especially at St. Matthew's—as is also his work in connection with China—with the missionary work in China. —And I want to say, by the way, in regard to this work, that the response we've been getting has been pretty disappointing. Now, fellows, we're pretty lucky! We have about everything we want. And it seems to me that we ought to be able to spare a little more to help this work along. It seems to me that each of us ought to be able to spare something—for this work in China. The first meeting after the holidays is going to be especially devoted to the work in China, and I hope that we'll make a better showing then than we have so far.—Mr. Hotchkiss will now speak to us, fellows."

Mr. Hotchkiss arose and came behind the lectern. He was a big broad-shouldered man with a florid solemn face and the sonorous fluent voice of a natural orator.

"Fellows," began Mr. Hotchkiss, "there are certain things that I want especially to speak to you about tonight. Next week, you will all be going home for your Christmas holidays. You are all very eager to get away from the restraints of school and to see your dear ones at home and to have a chance to play. Now that instinct to get away and play is a perfectly healthy and normal

one. You have all heard the old saying: 'All work and
no play makes Jack a dull boy.' Well, that is perfectly
true. Without the right amount of play—and *the right
sort of play*—we should not be able to do our work or to
be of service to God. Play then, for all you are worth!
Play to your heart's content. Go to the theater; go to
dances; go sleigh-riding; go skating. Enjoy yourselves in
every clean manly sport that the town or the country
provides. But be sure that the amusements which you
choose *are* clean and manly and wholesome. There will
be other kinds of amusements that will not be so clean
and not be so wholesome; and you will perhaps be
tempted to indulge in them because you are no longer
at school and because there is no one there to watch over
you. In the carelessness and gaiety of the holidays, you
will perhaps be tempted to forget yourselves; you will be
tempted to drink a cocktail or to go with a loose woman;
you will be tempted to abuse your body and your soul—
perhaps to ruin them for ever—all for a moment of so-
called pleasure. I believe that the Christmas vacation
—which will begin for you next Wednesday—is the most
dangerous period of the whole year!"

The boys, who, for the most part, had found their
vacation a harmless, though agreeable, experience, asked
themselves how they had ever overlooked the peculiar
snares with which it appeared to abound. It was no doubt
by reason of their youth that they had so far managed
to escape them; but they told themselves now that in the
future they would be on the look-out for them. The
younger and more timid boys were a little frightened by
the news; it seemed to put such an ugly mask on the
dear and looked-forward-to holidays, which had hitherto
smiled from afar to them, with the joyousness of freedom
and the kindness of their homes.

"Now," continued Mr. Hotchkiss, "I want to take these

temptations up one by one. I want to show you that, far from bringing happiness, they can also bring degradation. First, let me say a word about gambling. Now, gambling has always seemed to me the most foolish of all the vices: if you win the other man's money, you are taking money that doesn't belong to you, that you have no right to keep; if you lose, why then you lose, and you're poorer than you were before." (The audience, enslaved by his spell, were heard to give an abject giggle.) "I cannot conceive how a rational man can be willing to waste his time and his money in gambling!"

He proceeded to the other vices—smoking, drinking and swearing were all discredited—and at last he arrived at the culminating vice of which they had all been waiting to hear.

"And finally," he began, "there is the most dangerous of all temptations—the temptation from which perhaps none of us is free. I mean the temptation which has its basis in the sexual instinct."

At these words, the whole room became perfectly still: not a coat sleeve was heard to rustle; scarcely even a breath was drawn.

"Fellows," proceeded Mr. Hotchkiss in his ponderous droning voice, like some flat and monotonous organ that swelled now to a fuller strain with the speaker's mounting emotion, "I'm not going to handle this subject with gloves on! I'm not going to handle this subject evasively! I believe in calling things by their right names; and I believe in telling the facts! But before I do anything else, I'm going to show you two photographs." He came to the front of the rostrum and handed them down to the audience. "They are two pictures of the same girl—the first one taken when she was living decently, earning an honest living in a soap factory, and the other after she had fallen and had been practising for a number of years the trade of a woman of the streets. You wouldn't know it was the same person, would you? Slovenly, debased, diseased!

"Fellows! Suppose someone came to you and said: 'It was you who did this thing! It was you who changed this decent and happy girl, with the whole of life before her, with the hope of a respectable marriage and the sacred joys of motherhood—it was you who changed this decent girl into this miserable degraded creature dying of poverty and filthy disease!' You might laugh at the person who told you this. You might think it was impossible. You might think it was impossible for you, for you a St. Matthew's fellow, to have had anything whatever to do with such a hideous tragedy. But somewhere, fellows, somewhere that girl *took the first false step.*" (Here his voice began to grow lachrymose, as it always did at the climax of his sermons: he had acquired, among the irreverent, the nickname of Weeping Fred.) "Perhaps some evil-minded fellow—or perhaps only some careless fellow —because carelessness is the cause of almost as much evil in the world as wickedness—perhaps some careless young man offered her marriage and then took advantage of her trust in him; or she may have been tempted into drinking too much and may have made her first fatal error when she didn't know what she was doing; or she may have craved luxury and fine clothes and become the mistress of some wealthy man, who cast her aside as soon as he was tired of her. But it wasn't you, you say. How do you know it wasn't you? You go into a bar or café, let us say, where there is a young girl serving drinks. She allows the men to talk with her familiarly as she waits upon them. All day she is obliged to listen to the profanity and the filthy talk of the men in the bar or the café. One day some drunken fool puts his arm around her waist—perhaps he tries to kiss her. It may even be you who do this;

you may forget that she is a woman; you may forget St. Matthew's School and all that it has meant when you were here; you may think that because she talks slangily, because she has never been educated like you, that she is any the less worthy of respect than your own sister or your own mother. She smiles at you when you joke with her. You may ask her to go out with you, to go to the movies. For a girl in her position, that will be a temptation hard to resist. She may allow you to flirt with her and you may take advantage of her folly. Now think, fellows!—think a moment!—what you could do to that girl!"

His appeal thundered out over the room with lugubrious vibrations and the audience sat stunned and gaping, petrified before the abyss. It had never before occurred to most of them to think what they could do to that girl. Even Hart, who, in his present mood, had tended at first to sit through this classical set-piece with the composure of a conjuror's assistant looking on at a levitation act, found himself both stimulated and scared by the vision of this imaginary seduction. He feared that he might be capable of taking advantage of this girl—after somebody else had seduced her and made her more easily accessible. But the description of venereal disease which followed disinfected his erotic imaginings.

When Mr. Hotchkiss finally sat down, with a tear in either tragic eye, and Boards Borden stood up again to announce Mr. Bergen as the next speaker, there was a shuffling of frozen feet and a clearing of phlegmy throats, a rustle of moistened lips and relieved respiration. They looked up at the figure before them with expectation and awe.

He was a bloated red-faced man with a wild alcoholic eye, who had assumed the youthful blue suit and the white zinc-cylinder collar appropriate to the Y.M.C.A.

But not even that rigid uniform, nor the gold chain across his bulging paunch, not even his fierce glaring dignity could impart integrity to that countenance, which had spoiled like an old pumpkin-lantern that a child has left to rot. He carried with him a pile of papers.

"Before I start to talk," he began, in a loud raucous voice, "I just want to show you boys a few pictures and tell you a few facts. You can draw your own conclusions from them! —Now here's a picture of a man that you've all heard about!" He held up a photograph which nobody could see. "Quarter-back on the Yale eleven! The best all-around athlete of his time! As fine a fellow as you could wish to see! And where is he now? Where is that fine young fellow now? Boys, that young fellow is in jail!—in jail for forging his father's name to a check for five thousand dollars! —Here's Jack Sheldon—I don't want to tell you their real names—here's Jack Sheldon—the most brilliant man at Harvard—Captain of the Debating Team and President of the Dickie. —Duh yuh know where he is now? Duh yuh know where Jack Sheldon is now? Jack Sheldon is in the insane asylum with a loathsome social disease! —Here's Bill Davis, the half-mile runner! You've all heard of Bill Davis—a man who was famous for years in intercollegiate sports—voted the most popular man in his class! Boys, here's a telegram I received from Bill Davis's father, begging me to come quick, for God's sake, because Bill is in Roosevelt Hospital with a fractured skull where he was hit on the head in a drunken brawl and found unconscious in the street.

"Now that's just to show you what vice can do to a man, when he hasn't got Christ in his heart! A man may be the greatest athlete in the world or the brainiest student in the world, but if he hasn't got faith in Christ, temptation will drag-um in the mire. —I see them all at Fantoni's and Charlie's! I know which of yuh go there!

—And duh yuh know where I was once? Duh yuh know where Bergen was once? Boys: Bergen was down! Bergen was down in the depths! You could see him coming out of a low saloon over on 4th Avenue, with a hiccough on his lips, with bleary eyes and a sodden face, begging the passers-by for a nickel to buy him another drink! Boys: *Is Salvation real?* —When my father heard the life I was living, it almost broke his heart. He sat down in his office one day—the fine old Southern gentleman!—and he took out his will from his desk and he crossed out his son's name from it and he broke down and wept because Bergen was a prodigal and a bum! I'd wasted my father's money in the saloons and the low dives of New York. Some nights I hardly knew my own name! You couldna told me from the tramps and the bums that you see laying around in the street. Oh, Bergen's been in the depths, boys! —*Is Salvation real?*"

He proceeded to disquieting details of his life in the underworld. The boys' hands sweated in their pockets or clasped the arms of their seats. At last, Bergen staggered into a mission and was suddenly and miraculously redeemed.

"Well, one day my picture appeared on the front page of a New York paper, and when my father saw that picture he took the train straight up to New York and he came to see me at my hotel. I put on a silk-hat and a frock-coat—yes, Bergen put on a frock-coat!—and I walked right down into the lobby of one of the swellest New York hotels. And when my father saw me there, when my father saw me dressed like that, he threw his arms around my neck, and he said, 'My boy! my boy! My God! forgive me!' —*Is Salvation real?*

"Now, I'll be in Mr. Clarkson's office," he concluded, "tonight and tomorrow morning. If any boy wants to ask me any questions or talk over any of his problems with me, I'll be glad to have him come and see me. I've been able to help hundreds of young men who were struggling with secret sins and temptations."

He sat down amidst deathly silence, and the President arose.

"Do you want to say anything more, Mr. Hotchkiss?" he inquired.

"Only this," said Mr. Hotchkiss smiling. "A merry Christmas to you all!"

"We will close the meeting," continued Boards, "with as many short prayers as possible and afterwards the singing of Hymn Number 508."

The audience collapsed into attitudes of prayer, and the President started them off with a dull and correct invocation which bore witness to long practice. This was followed by a strange vacant moment of shyness, broken at last by several voices which all tried to begin at once and then pulled themselves up in a panic; then two voices were heard to begin and again strike a deadlock of silence—till, at last, one, bolder than the other, persisted and prayed his competitor down. But when he had finished, little jets of prayer, lifted sometimes in plaintive trebles, were heard rising one by one. They had been taught to feel the stirring of the Spirit. When the President, peering at his watch, decided that they had prayed enough, he cut them short with a prayer of his own, like a wooden plug in a leak; and the audience, blinking, disturbed and moved, found their places in the hymn-book self-consciously, so solemn that they did not know what to say nor how to look at one another.

And Hart, as he watched them disperse, felt stiffened and sterilized. There was something, to be sure, about Bergen which he had not entirely liked, which had affected him unpleasantly at first, which had embarrassed him as he had been embarrassed by the billowing breath of a saloon belched obscenely across his path when he had been walking in New York with a lady. But Bergen did make vice seem poisonous—though perhaps at the same time alluring, a crapulous and fascinating power. As he had listened, he had lost his detachment: gambling and drinking meant nothing to him, but day-dreaming about women he had to admit and, as Bergen talked, Hart had felt a kind of dizziness, a vertigo at the edge of the abyss, a perverse desire to plunge, to succumb to its iridescent waters. Yet that lasted only a moment. Yes: the Y.M.C.A. was right! It stood for clean thoughts and clean living; and clean living was the only way! He told himself that now forever he must be master of those sinister lapses: no longer would he look through the cheap magazines for the buxom breasts and legs of actresses; no longer should a line from Virgil set him chasing white nymphs in a wood. He remembered the bawdy little boy who had once told dirty stories, who had sneaked into his uncle's library to read *The Decameron,* and he felt nothing but hatred and contempt for the creature he had once been.

He knew now that there were only two courses in dealing with one's sexual desires: one way was to sink and to drown in the morass—prostitution, syphilis, shame; and the other was to accept the revelation handed down by the Y.M.C.A.: to preserve one's self-discipline, stay clinically pure. It was a sort of scientific idealism, a mixture of pathology and holiness. He felt as if his soul had now been dedicated to some chivalrous religious order, a combination of the Round Table and a Trappist monastery, in which the brothers wore the white robes of doctors when they worked in contagious wards, and washed their hands, as regularly as they prayed, in a solution of carbolic acid. And now he had been chosen as their Leader. He felt a thrill of consecration—and yet also a cramp of fear.

II

Hart Foster had never visited Board Borden's family and was astonished to see the scale on which they lived. For almost half an hour, the glossy limousine glided along among landscape-gardened lakes and groves and finally drew up at the door of a prodigious, an apparently limitless house, which lifted its vast white façade in the naked winter dusk. It was as if some simple colonial cottage had been blown to enormous dimensions and its grace become stupid and gross, being swollen beyond man's measure. Hart had known that Boards's father had been rich but he had not realized how rich. Rather like a hotel, he reflected, as he gazed up at the tiers on tiers of windows.

Boards opened a shadowy door on an interior of warm rich light, and they were saluted by a crash of barking, as if they had invaded a kennel. Hart found himself surrounded by dogs, most of them very large; a Great Dane, as big as a calf, nearly knocked him down. Boards ordered them to be still, but they only barked louder than ever, and when he tried to placate each in turn, the dogs that were being neglected were aroused to frenzies of jealousy. At last, a tall young girl rushed up and, with the ruthless authority of a lion-tamer, succeeded in beating them down. Hart saw that, besides the Great Dane, there were two collies, a Russian wolf-hound, an Airedale and a spotted coach-dog.

"This is my sister," explained Boards. "Barbara, this is Hart Foster."

"Hello!" said Barbara.

She was a handsome girl, with fine brown eyes, wilful and superb, and a heavy clot of brown hair arranged at the back of her head: she bulked strangely on Hart's gaze, almost with a physical impact. The smooth robust mask of her face, which smiled with conventional cordiality, seemed to shield some formidable power, which challenged him and asked him a question; she was charged with some magnetic current which might almost have galvanized him as he took her frankly-given hand. In her presence, he suddenly became aware, not merely of his Christian manhood, but also of his smartly parted hair and his brown eyes that were returning her cordiality.

As he was trying to shake hands with Barbara, one of the collies got between them and jumped up on her.

"Get down, you big clumsy boob!" she cried. "You'll ruin my dress!"

"What a lot of dogs you have!" said Hart.

"Yes," she answered. "They're all mine."

"The new Dupont has come," she said to Boards. "Let's go out in it after dinner. It's got a new kind of gearshift." Hart watched her with an admiration not untempered by fear and disapproval. She seemed to Hart as different from her brother as possible: Boards was conventional and stiff, moving slowly and speaking weightily, but his sister followed vigorous instincts with natural and rowdy movements, as imperious, yet as little formal, as a young barbarian queen. . . .

They had got into a curious room, a paradise of pink and gold, which suggested the gilt cord and ribbons of an expensive box of candy. It made Hart uneasy to see the dogs ranging unrestrainedly about this room among the fragile furniture and jumping up with ruthless paws on the satin sofa cushions. The Airedale and the wolf-hound, which had jumped onto the couch, were barking out the window behind it.

"The old Baxter stalled on me again yesterday," Barbara was saying. "It just fell dead in the ditch. I was so sick of getting the darned old thing fixed that I just went away and left it in the road. The man in the barber-shop at Greenwich came out and tried to fix the clutch, and I told him he could have it, if it was any good to him."

"You ought to have sent somebody to get it," her brother objected, shocked. "You oughtn't to throw away a perfectly good car like that. We could have given it to the McFadden Street Settlement House."

But here the Great Dane knocked over with his tail an enormous Japanese vase, which crashed like an egg-shell on the floor.

"Oh, my God!" exclaimed Barbara, "there goes something or other! —Now, look what you've done, Goofo!"

She gave him a terrific smack.

"Still," she reflected, "he never knows where his tail is going—do you, Goofo?" She patted him and put her arm around his neck. "Poor old Goofo," she said.

"Oh, Barbara!" cried a voice. "I've told you not to bring the dogs in here!"

Hart, who had been picking up the pieces, beheld a broad, rather handsome lady, who combined a majestic presence with an air of bewilderment and uncertainty. Her dark hair, parted in the middle, made two smooth low bands along her temples in a manner both becoming and plain.

"I'm sorry, Mother," said Barbara, "but we were just

going through this way. And besides, I never could see what this room was good for, anyhow!"

Hart, looking about him in the lull that had followed the appearance of Mrs. Borden, saw a salon which somehow reminded him of the "parlors" of old-fashioned houses. The scale was infinitely greater but the style was unmistakably the same. On the walls were portraits of the children, painted badly but invested with the air of young princes; a portrait of the late Mr. Borden, with the masterful brow of Barbara; a water-color of a group of blue-birds perched appealingly on a bough; and a great gilt-framed placard which said "God is Love." On a little stand stood a silver model of the first Borden Motor Truck —Mr. Borden had made motor trucks—and on a pedestal an enormous bust of Barbara modelled at the age of twelve, with the blank white pupils of the eyes, the hair-ribbon and lace collar, all precisely reproduced in the marble; on the table were books by Raymond Fosdick and Dr. Henry Van Dyke, and two richly bound volumes, with clasps, of a work called *Picturesque Florence*. Hart felt that the shades should perhaps be pulled down and the room preserved in darkness.

"That was the vase your father brought from Japan," Mrs. Borden explained to Barbara. "Oh, don't bother about picking them up," she stayed the helpful Hart.

"It must have been a beautiful vase," he said politely, holding up a flowery fragment.

"Well, we were very fond of it. My husband brought it home from Japan. They make such beautiful things in Japan. It's all imitated from the Chinese, of course, but they make beautiful things. Have you ever been to Japan? . . . It's such a beautiful country. Of course, you don't think the women are beautiful, at first, but after a while you get used to them—the Japanese type of beauty. My husband never would admit that a Japanese

woman could be beautiful, but I really learned to like
them. And then their little feet seem so queer at first—
as if they were deformed. We had the cunningest little
Jap girl to wait on us at the hotel. . . ."

After dinner, which was eaten with simple manners
amidst impressive surroundings, the new Dupont was
tried out. Accompanied by unheeded admonishments on
the part of Mrs. Borden, Hart, Boards and Barbara all
three wedged themselves into the front seat, and Barbara
drove, at a terrific rate. Without slackening speed, she
would wrench the car in a masterful way around wooded
curves. There was an arrogance about her which dis-
quieted Hart and at the same time compelled his admiration. She seemed to be riding above ordinary life; she
lifted them into a new world.

In the town, they stopped for a soda.

"I believe," Boards advised Hart, as they imbibed straw-
berry syrup through straws, "that you ought to do everything you can to reach Butts Bigelow and that bunch
when they get back to school next fall." (Butts Bigelow
had been the ringleader of the dissipating group of Fifth
Formers, and one of those suspended for taking a
night out in Boston.) "They'll be Sixth Formers next
year, and I think it's a darn shame that the younger fellows should see Sixth Formers behaving the way they
do."

"I think Butts Bigelow is cute," said Barbara. "I danced
with him and he was awfully funny."

"I heard that Butts Bigelow was seen drunk in New
York," contributed Hart.

"You don't mind my drinking your water, do you?"
asked Barbara, smiling at him delightfully.

"No—not at all," replied Hart, with a responsive smile
which he somehow felt did violence to the spirit of the
conversation.

"You heard that he was drunk," said Boards. "Well, there's more to that!"

"What?" asked Hart.

"I'll tell you sometime."

"Oh, tell now," demanded Barbara. "I won't tell anybody!"

Boards shook his head. "It wouldn't be fair to the man," he explained. "It might hurt him some day when he's trying to be decent. If a man has a bad reputation, very often he's unfairly handicapped later on when he wants to lead a clean life. Nobody will believe any good of him. I always make it a point not to tell anything I may know about the the fellows."

"Oh, bull!" said Barbara. . . .

But when Barbara had gone to the back of the store, in order to buy some flea soap, Boards laid bare the shame of Butts Bigelow in a low grim voice, which nearly made his companion's heart stop beating. "Well, there's a place in New York called the Prince Edward Club, which is really nothing more than a brothel. And it seems the people who go there have to sign names in a register. Well, Butts Bigelow has been seen in this place, and, you mustn't let it be known at school, but instead of signing his own name, he signed Dr. Durham's name!"

Hart gaped before it aghast: to make light of the Headmaster was like blasphemy. Yet a sinister fascination summoned up for him a muffled ambiguous front, then a narrow electric-lighted room with a glittering bar at one side, where Butts Bigelow, entering with rakish aplomb and hideous sophistication, wrote sneeringly in a register and then went upstairs—to what?

"How do you know?" he faltered.

"Bergen saw him and told us."

"How can you reach a fellow like that?" Hart wondered in dismay.

"You must try to pray with him," said Boards.

Then Barbara returned and swept them off to the car.

"You drive going back, Boards," she commanded, "and Hart and I'll sit in back. It's too crowded three in front."

"Let's put this big robe over us," she said to Hart. "It's cold as blazes tonight." And she wrapped them up close together.

As they cut through the winter night, mowing down the shadows with their headlights—beneath a cold high-riding moon that left the thickets of the roadside black— Hart, setting his face against the wind, with his head thrown impressively back, felt the combined exhilaration of rapid movement, spiritual nobility and power, and the presence at his side of an exciting girl who was evidently disposed to like him. He saw himself reasoning with Butts Bigelow, saying, "It's not fair to the girl, Butts. It's not fair to the girl." How clean, how handsome, how firm, and withal how human he was! Butts thanked him and shook his hand—frank and wholesome, a fine fellow now. It nearly brought tears to Hart's eyes: he was a Helper, a Leader of Men!—And he turned an earnest and exalted face to the handsome girl at his side.

When they were back in the inflated house, eating apples in front of a fire, Boards's sober decision that it was time to go to bed brought a vehement protest from Barbara. She insisted that Hart should stay up and play a bout with her in the bowling-alley. But Hart, much in awe of his friend and invariably following Boards's lead, excused himself and went up to his room.

But they bowled the next afternoon, and Barbara scored against Hart so heavily that, embarrassed, perspiring and flushed, he was moved to muster all his skill and energy for a smashing succession of strikes. "You'd make a good bowler," said Barbara, "if you had a little practice." The close, sweaty, woody smell of the bowling-alley, which, as he knew it in the school gym, had always seemed stale and unpleasant, now took on a rank and heady savor from Barbara's moist face and bright eyes. The crash of the falling pins fed a nervous accelerating excitement.

When that night they went again for a ride, he and she sat behind all the way, and Hart tried to sing tenor to her popular songs, a refinement which did not seem to impress her. Once his hand, beneath the robe, was shifted against hers as they rounded a curve, and he noticed that she did not draw her hand away, as he should have supposed a well-bred girl would do. Then he wondered why he did not draw his own away, and immediately did so. She began a kind of ballad about Frankie and Johnnie which he had never heard before, and he sat in stupid silence. Its rowdy sound—like her reckless driving—seemed again to raise a barrier between them. . . . Now her head was flung back in drunkenness; she was riding down the night with ribaldry. She glanced at him from under lowered eye-lids with gaiety and a challenge. It would be nice to kiss her, he thought. Then he felt her snuggle against him, and he pressed against her. So they sat, singing *Harvest Moon, My Yellow-Jacket Girl* and *The Girl I Love Is on a Magazine-Cover*. Before long, they were holding hands, and he found himself embarrassed by the evident eagerness with which she squeezed his.

Alone in his bedroom later, his gratification overflowed the bounds by which it had been restrained during a visit from boring neighbors and a very confused billiard match: it flooded the enormous room and became the element in which he swam. The high ceiling, the magenta curtains, the abundant purple-shaded lamps, the serviceable tables and bureaus set about at enormous distances, with nothing on them except a few of Hart's neckties and his military hair-brushes, seemed to make an appropriate setting for the present state of his soul—they reinforced a conviction of power, of moving through the great scenes of life. He struck a kind of noble pose in a great gilt-framed oval mirror; then slicked down his hair a little and looked at himself again. In the bathroom, of a candor like smooth glazed snow, he was humming *My Yellow-Jacket Girl* along with *Who Follows in His Train?*

He was thinking of himself again now as a Master and Leader of Men, but with Barbara for a wife. He was imagining the scene between them when he should tell her first of his love. He would say, "Barbara, I have loved you for a long time now. . . . Will you share with me my life and my work?" . . . She was evidently a great woman, whose extraordinary energy and strength needed only to be shown the path, to be turned to the service of Christ. What a spiritual companion she would make! At the end of the busy day, when he would come home utterly exhausted—exhausted, strong as he was—from his administrative duties and his speaking; and she from her settlement work, deeply moved by the condition of the poor, they would console and sustain one another, they would kneel down together and pray. . . .

He knelt now by his bedside alone and prayed to be made worthy of her—to be clean, to be wise, to be upright, to be a tower of strength to the weak. . . . Then he turned out the silk-shaded lights and opened a window by the bed. Below it lay the phantom grounds, like the floor of a tranquil lake—all brimmed full to-night by the moon with a limpid bluish-gray water, where the trees stood up like water-weeds and the grass seemed just to show green with a faint silver luminosity. He thought for a moment of Romance, of magic in German forests, of monstrous castles cracked asunder and black-armoured foemen beaten down, of a lady riding behind him on the back of a great white horse. . . . Then he snuffed out these childish fancies and got in between the fresh crisp sheets. From the window fell a shaft of moonlight which threw long silver panes on the floor.

He thought of the first time he should kiss her—on the cheek it would be, of course—when they had told one another of their love—and then, later, they would kiss on the lips, like the people on the covers of *Life*. It must be wonderful to kiss on the lips!—wonderful and very sacred. It seemed almost the last satisfaction, the ultimate moment of intimacy—an incredible realization of the fact that two people understood one another. . . . And then the first kiss at the altar, when the ceremony was over, and the bride, in her long robe of white, took her husband's lips with closed eyes, with face tenderly yielded . . . Then these visions began to dissolve and to float away on dark waters; dim irrelevant shapes reëmerged and were whelmed by the dark again, till he drowned in the swell of that warm and pleasantly benumbing sea. . . .

He became aware that somebody was in the room—somebody in a vague dark gown, who was closing the bathroom door with a gentle and stealthy click. Someone had got into the wrong room. Hart called out: "Hello!"

"Hello," replied a woman's voice in a deep cordial whisper. Hart recognized the voice of Barbara.

"I—I'm sleeping in this room!" he tried to explain.

She came forward without answering into the moonlight.

He saw her now in her kimono, with her thick hair about her shoulders, shrouded palely in shadowy silver and with shadows under her brows.

"Did I wake you up?" she inquired.

"Oh, no," he answered, uneasy and puzzled. "I wasn't quite asleep. It's perfectly all right."

She sat down on the bed beside him, so that the panes of silver light from the window were broken across her lap. It occurred to him that she might be in need of some immediate spiritual guidance, that she might have come to confide to him some struggle or some agony of the soul. . . . He noticed that her thin silk kimono was molded to the roundness of her thighs and that her feet were clad in little slippers with round puffs of silk at the toes.

There was a momentary silence. Then, "I thought I'd come and visit you. I didn't want to go to bed so early."

He was embarrassed and could only say, "What time is it?"

"Oh, it's early," she replied and bent toward him, as he sat up in bed, her dark hair falling about her face. She whispered, "You can kiss me if you want to."

But a proud and virginal shrinking made him hesitate a moment. Then he leaned over toward her quickly, and his lips, which would have found her cheek, were drawn to her swiftly proffered mouth; he touched it in a brief clumsy kiss. As her own lips were still parted and she seemed to expect something more, he kissed her again and again, embracing her with awkward arms.

And in that timid self-conscious embrace, those dry half-terrified kisses—at the touch of her warm wet mouth, the smell of her clothes and skin, he suddenly became a lover, a new personality had been brought into being—a much more exciting one. His old self had shrivelled in the blast to a brittle and hollow shell. His shyness was melting away.

"I love you, Barbara!" he breathed, and pressed his mouth against hers in mounting intoxication. Her mouth was something unexpected, an enormous physical fact, something brutal and overwhelming, of an almost indecent intimacy. He had never known that kissing was like that!

Then she disengaged herself from his arms and swiftly slipped off her kimono. As she bent over for a moment, Hart had a glimpse of her firm round breasts; he was surprised to find them so big: he had always supposed that girls' breasts were little low dotted things. He was shocked and recoiled from the sight, as if from something indecent; it drove him back into himself.

She slipped into bed and whispered, "It's better in bed like this."

"Oh, you mustn't do that!" he objected.

"Why not?" she asked. "Don't you like it?"

"I don't think you ought to," he said.

"I thought you said you liked me."

"That's just why I don't want you to. I don't want you to—to compromise yourself."

"Nobody'll know."

"Somebody might.—And besides, it's not the right thing to do. We—oughtn't to do like this." His protestations sounded childish.

"I don't see why you say you like me then!"

He could feel how warm she was as she lay beside him there, her face half hidden in the pillow. But he now sat upright and prosaic.

"I do like you," he replied and tried to assume a correcter tone, tried to bring the conversation closer to his ideal standard for such scenes. "You're the only woman I've ever loved." In his attempt to achieve his end, he bent to kiss her forehead gently, but again she offered him her lips and again they overwhelmed him. In a moment, he was down beside her, with one arm about her back. She came up close against him, and he slipped his other arm beneath her; then she came to place with her arms about him and he found himself embracing her body,

which, solid, soft and very warm, lay against his thighs
and breast. So this was the real Barbara, this solid living
body!—not merely the face at the top of a dress that one
knew in ordinary life. How wonderful—he could not
have imagined it—it was to lie against another person's
body! All the pains and constraints of his life seemed to
melt in a sudden blaze; he was flooded with a gratitude
that was close to tears. That warm breathing body was
everything—all happiness, all satisfaction! It was not an
embrace, but a different world, a different kind of life!

"I love you! I love you!" he repeated, and she turned
her mouth for more kisses. . . .

But, as they lay, he felt the waking of desire in a now
unmistakable form. . . . In horror, he drew away. How
base that that should have happened! How dreadful if
she should have noticed!—She was lying with eyes closed
and lips parted, her cheeks all flushed and hot.

He wanted to rouse her and warn her: "We mustn't
stay here like this!"

"Why not?" she demanded softly, half opening her
eyes and half smiling.

"Because—because it isn't right. We mustn't, honestly.
You really ought to go now. We—we can see each other
tomorrow."

"You don't need to be afraid," she said. "I know what
to do."

"Please go, Barbara!" he insisted, half pleading, half
assuming the tone of an older person reasoning with a
child about matters it does not understand. "You and I
mustn't . . . till after we're married."

"Married?" she replied. "I'm never going to get married!"

This brought him up against a blank wall, and he did
not know what to answer.

"Won't you marry me?" he asked at last and was aware that it sounded foolish.

"I'm not going to marry anybody. I don't want to be married! You'll have to wait a long time if you wait to have me marry you!"

He was silent again for a moment, then he doggedly returned to his point: "You and I oughtn't to be together like this without being married."

"Oh, why shouldn't we?" she retorted. "Everybody does!"

"No, they don't."

"Yes, they do. Look at the débutantes!" she continued with indignation, turning over now on her back. "You don't think they're all so pure, do you?"

"I certainly think they all ought to be," he replied, driven back into priggishness. And he noticed how beautiful her throat was, as her head, thrown back on the pillow, uncovered its smooth firm bow. He would like to kiss her there, he thought.

"Why?" she demanded. "Why should they be?" And she delivered this terrible judgment: "Do you know why girls stay pure? It's just to get themselves married! They just hang on to their old purity so that the man'll still want something from them. They won't let him have it unless he marries them. That's how they get married! If they didn't, a whole lot of girls would never get married at all. But I don't care! I do whatever I want and there's lots of men who are crazy to marry me just the same!"

"I don't think that's true at all!" he protested. "Everybody ought to—try to keep clean—because—"

"Oh, you talk just like Boards!" she cried—she seemed nervous and irritable now. "I thought you were a good sport."

"If it's being a good sport to let you—"

She suddenly sprang up, cutting short his righteous

declaration, in which he had been converting his note of complaint into the authentic high tone of the Y.M.C.A. She determinedly threw on her kimono and shod her bare feet with slippers. He noted how cunning the puffs were.

"Don't go," he said. "Look a minute—"

"I thought you wanted me to go. You just said I *had* to go!"

"Oh, please don't be sore!" he pleaded. "I didn't mean to hurt your feelings. I only—"

"Hurt my feelings!" she flung at him, wrapping the kimono across her breast. "*You* haven't hurt my feelings!"

She turned to the bathroom door.

"Oh, *please* listen a minute!" he begged, jumping out of bed. "*Please* don't go away like that!"

She stopped without turning around.

"It's simply that I don't want you to think that I—that I don't like you—or that I think there's anything necessarily improper—"

She went out and shut the door with a bang that shocked his nerves. He remembered that the bathroom had another door—it must lead into another bedroom.

He stood for a moment in the darkness, staring at the closed door. Then he found that he was trembling all over and weakly sat down on the bed. He was much relieved that she was gone; his soul had been disordered to its depths. . . . After contemplating the moonlight a little, he got back into bed again. All night his thoughts continued to churn with the violent throbbing of his head. He was sometimes the Christian Leader saving a foolish child from herself; sometimes the conqueror of life to whom the splendors of love came easily; but the picture too often collapsed in a treacherous doubt and confusion, a terror before unknown facts, an uncertainty of himself. . . . Yet, for all his bewildered distress, her kisses and her embrace had drenched all of life with a wonder which he had never known before. It was a feverish breathless romance in which mighty emotions ran high! It was a drama which dwarfed the setting and where everything but emotion was the setting. . . . When he looked out, at early morning, on the slow gray winter dawn, where the lawn lay unreal and silvered with the whitish bloom of the frost, it was now upon a grimmer, less familiar world, a world full of mystery and danger, but a world where great men and women lived and died by the grace of great passions.

III

"AND THERE IS ANOTHER THING I should like you to say a word about," Mr. Hotchkiss continued to Boards Borden. They were having a conference in the Bible class room just before the first meeting after the holidays, and the boys sat about on the benches in all their official solemnity. Only Hart seemed haggard and distrait: he sat drawing little circles with a pencil on the arm of his seat. The bookcases were black with hymnals and on the walls were a portrait of Christ and a photograph of Mr. John Mott. "Something which has been particularly called to my attention during the holidays. I mean the behavior of young girls at dances and, in short, in all their relations with young men. I believe very warmly in dances and in sports of all kinds—I believe in every sort of 'clean mirth,' as Kipling says; I believe that young people should be jolly and free together, and I think that for the ordinary wholesome boy and girl a chaperon is ridiculous; but it seems to me that the modern young girl is coming dangerously close to the line which separates freedom from license. I don't speak only of the clothes which are worn and which are hardly proper even for older women, nor of the open sensuality of the new dances—'cheek to cheek,' as I believe they are called—but it seems to me that when it becomes tolerated, when it even becomes fashionable, for a well-bred young girl, or a young girl who is supposed to be well-bred, to smoke cigarettes, to drink cocktails and to tell risqué stories without provoking any surprise or losing caste among her companions, then it is time to begin to consider where this thing is taking us!"

"Well, but Mr. Hotchkiss," retorted Hart, much to everyone's consternation, "do you really think it's up to us here to say what the girls ought to do? I should think they ought to deal with that at the girls' schools."

"Tell me," propounded Mr. Hotchkiss, with weighty assurance, "who do you think is responsible for the moral standards of the fast young girl? Where did she first learn to drink the cocktail, to smoke the cigarette, to tell the questionable story? Is it not the *young men* with whom she has associated who must have encouraged her in these things! Who taught the girl the unclean story? She can hardly have imagined it herself: she is not yet so corrupt as that. She can hardly, in the first instance, have learned it from another woman. No: some young man must have told it to her—some young man with whom she is on terms of friendship and whom she perhaps innocently thought to please by exhibiting an interest in such stories. But no friendship can long remain pure which indulges in such impurities as these. The girl may think it only a joke—something which exists only in words—but the thought is father to the deed. The thing which you imagine today is the thing you perform tomorrow. The next time they dance together, she may perhaps permit him to hold her more closely; the next time, she may consent to drink with him and may allow him to flirt with her a little—though he may not really be in love with her nor have any sincere intention of marrying her. The next time. . . ."

"Do you think," interrupted Hart, a little acidly and terribly constrained, "that she ought to make him promise to marry her before she lets him begin to make love to her?"

"I think," replied Mr. Hotchkiss, adopting a more direct severity, and bending upon Hart his great creased and heavy face, saddened by the sinfulness of the world, "that if we lose our reverence for womanhood, we shall lose the keystone of our civilization, and I believe that it is the duty of the Y.M.C.A. to warn the fellows against allowing their ideal to become debased. They should certainly not be willing to see a young girl do anything which they would not be willing to see their sisters do. If you put that argument to them, they will see the point every time! Without reverence for womanhood, without chivalry and chastity, there can be no clean and enduring love, there can be none of that adoration which you find expressed so beautifully in Browning's lines—

'Oh, lyric love, half angel and half bird!'—"

Hart found himself regarding Mr. Hotchkiss with hostile and angry eyes, which were also guilty and shy; he had flushed with his last retort and kept his hands pressed against the bench arms to conceal his trembling tenseness. But his defiance broke out abruptly in all its naked insolence. "I don't see why a girl should have to make a man promise to marry her before she lets him begin to make love to her! I think that a good deal of this modesty—" (Barbara's verdict hung in his mind, but in that company it seemed impossible to repeat it, and the inhibition, robbing him of his point, brought his climax down with heartbreaking lameness) "—is—false modesty!" he concluded; and with the collapse of this speech, his voice broke.

"You ask me," replied Mr. Hotchkiss, with magisterial composure, while the others sat in the stricken silence which always follows a breaking voice, "you ask me if a young girl should let a man make love to her without promising her marriage. I answer that there's all the difference in the world between clean and unclean love and that any decent wholesome girl knows which kind is being offered her."

"Listen old man!" said Boards, coming over to Hart. "You're not feeling very well, are you? You don't have to come tonight. Somebody else can read the minutes."

"That's all right," snapped Hart irritably. "I'm all right!"

"Have you any fever?" asked Mr. Hotchkiss, feeling his forehead and pulse. "I learned how to be a doctor among the lumberjacks," he explained, as he took out his watch, smiling in proud gratification at feeling himself rough and ready, a man among men. "The only regular doctor in the woods lived about a hundred and twenty miles away, so I had to be doctor and druggist and trained nurse all in one!"

"No, I don't think so," answered Hart between anger and the temptation to flee. "I've just got a little headache."

"Too many dances during the holidays?" inquired Mr. Hotchkiss, smiling, in an undeceptive attempt to speak of these things as other men.

"No," said Hart, "I'm just out of sorts."

"Look here, my boy," said Mr. Hotchkiss, "you'd better go to bed right away. It's a losing game in the long run to use up all your nervous force by trying to keep on working when you're sick. When I was up in the lumber-camps, I rode a hundred and sixty miles and conducted five services and a 'sing' one Sunday, when I could hardly stand up with chills and fever, and I've never got over the effects of it. I've never been able to do the same work. Now you'd better go to bed right away and see the doctor the first thing in the morning."

Hart left the room on the verge of tears; but, as he walked out across the frozen campus, Mr. Hotchkiss and the Y.M.C.A. passed swiftly beyond the limits of his consciousness, outshone by the splendor in his heart.

Nothing else in the world was real except his overwhelming longing! The school itself, but a few weeks ago the scene of his whole drama, a drama which he followed with excitement, had shrunk to a stage for amateurs, whose triviality enraged him. His school-fellows were children; the masters were fogeys and pedants. He was humiliated by these pygmies.

He knew what passion was! They knew nothing of passion! The word thrilled and terrified him and filled him with a kind of drunkenness. Now he understood the conduct of the people in the stories of Maupassant; now he understood why Marc Antony had behaved so badly about Cleopatra. Now he found himself living the lurid dream which had seemed so fantastic and remote! He shuddered at its rank carnality, yet it conquered him and made him proud. He knew himself a man now at last.

In his room, he found Eddie O'Brien doing Greek with another boy. He had hoped there would be no one there so that he could write another urgent letter to Barbara, and he regarded them with undisguised disgust.

"Thought you were at the meeting," said Eddie.

"I'm not feeling very well," he explained shortly. "I've got a headache."

"That's a darn shame," said Eddie. And they went on doing Greek. "οὐ γάρ πώ ποτέ μ' ὧδέ γ' ἔρως φρένας ἀμφεκάλυψεν"—'For never this desire concealed my mind' —now wait a minute: this ὥς must be the end of it, that

must mean 'as'—ὥς σεο νῦν ἔραμαι καί με γλυκὺς ἵμερος
αἱρεῖ."

"Say, look: we don't have to do these lines: I've got
that passage marked to omit."

"There must be something dirty in it then. λέχοσδε,
that means something about a 'bed.'—Say, I've got to read
this passage: it's got something about a bed in it!"

"Oh, pshaw!" (shutting the book) "you couldn't hire
me to read any more of that stuff than I have to—bed or
no bed!"

He hated their slipshod work; he hated their imbecile
jests. What did they know about Paris and Helen? He
had worked the passage out himself—and now he saw the
beautiful couple, not merely smooth and white like Greek
statues, but flushed and made drunk by desire. *"It's better
in bed like this,"* she had said. . . . What right had such
creatures as these schoolboys to chatter and brawl in his
room? . . . He opened the window and looked down
from their hill on the snow-laden roofs of the town. A
spell had been laid upon it: its sordidness was effaced;
the dreary life that one knew had been utterly purged
away. The very streets were blank pages on which no
one's name had been traced. But from the yellow lights
in the windows he knew that life there was still warm.
He pictured pleasant family scenes—young couples, just
come back from their honeymoons, settling down to the
intimacy of winter. He saw in his imagination a fresh
young woman in a silk kimono, with brown hair un-
loosed about her shoulders, who sat happy, before a fire,
with a clean-cut young man at her side. He envied that
clean-cut young man. . . . Through the frozen air, from
a distance, came the brisk jingle of sleigh-bells. And he
thought of how lovers rode out on moonlight nights like
this; he had heard that they revelled in a moon. They

would make a safe little world of warmth in the icy night through which they moved. He would put his arm about her and with the other arm drive the sleigh through the empty country roads, terrible and lovely beneath the moon, through the stiff-standing pines of the mountains that walled their path about with black. And he would feel how warm she was and how he guarded her against the night, against the snow and the lonely moon and the shadows that lurked in the pines. They would be reckless and gay together and conquer the cold road with songs. But stay! there are wolves behind us!—you can hear their faint yelping in the distance—they drew nearer—Don't be afraid!—They are all about us now, barking hungrily— Bang! Bang! Bang! they are dead!—their blood lies black on the snow. He would put his arm about her again and feel her warm bulk against his side. What a brave staunch partner she was! And when they were back at last, he would take her in his arms altogether; he would kiss her once warmly on the lips, and then she would go up before him. . . .

"Say, do you want to freeze us out?" came the voice of the visiting friend.

"Yes, for Pete's sake," yelled his room-mate, with the superior harshness of intimacy, "put that damn window down!"

He remained at the window a little longer to indicate his contempt for them; then he withdrew and threw himself on the bed.

"Hope we don't disturb you," said the visitor. "We'll be through before long."

"How long will it be?" asked Hart with authoritative distinctness.

"Oh, we'll be done pretty soon!" said Eddie.

They turned the lamp-shade around so that the bulb would not shine in his eyes, and he detested them for their attentions, which seemed to him insincere—since it was evident he couldn't rest with them talking in the same room. . . .

Oh, he was in agony to possess her! He could think of nothing else night and day. To hold her in his arms again! He had once held her in his arms! It was incredible—it must be a dream. How could he ever have lived through that rapture—so prosaically, so calmly? In retrospect, it had become for him the central experience of his life. It was a burst of illumination which blazed like a pillar of fire on the horizon of the past, and the further he receded from it, the more magical and amazing it seemed and the more pressing became the necessity of getting back to it and finding it real. . . . And it had been so different from what he thought!—not a bit like the covers of *Life*. His mind was no longer divided into two not very well policed compartments—a compartment for lecherous longings and a compartment for ideal love: the dyke had been broken down and the turbid waters of desire had been loosed on the chaste embraces, the aquiline kisses, of *Life*. The plump wanton ladies of Boccaccio came romping into the love scenes of Booth Tarkington, and the two were being founded together into something which was terrible, which was real. . . . *"It's better in bed like this,"*—the words seemed to reach him electric with the life of another world. Oh, to find it, to enter it again! To find the world where that language was spoken!

He must write her a letter at once to show her he knew now how to speak to her. And yet wouldn't that perhaps be an error so soon after his other letter? He had had no reply to that, and it would make him ridiculous to write again; it would put him at a disadvantage. But if he made it an ultimatum on a high and decisive tone?—in that case, she must let him know definitely that she was really in love with him or wasn't. But what if she should become indignant and perversely declare that she wasn't when actually she was? Suppose he should spoil the whole thing by approaching her, as he might, too clumsily?—If he could only go down to Greenwich and talk it all over with her!—he would put his case so eloquently, so nobly, with such fire and compelling force, that she could not but be moved by his love and respond with the gift of hers. . . . How intolerable that it would still be at least three weeks before he could get away from school!—And as a makeshift in his bitter privation, he pictured himself running off to see her—getting out by the fire-escape, making a dash for the back fence, catching an early train to New Haven. . . .

The students shut up their books and slammed down the roll-top desk. The sound of slippers was heard in the corridor. The roughhouse was about to begin. Hart was sickened as he thought of tearing off people's pyjamas, of pushing them under the bed. He withdrew to the shower-room and took a very long hot shower which lasted until lights-out. As he ruminated in the steam, the fancy of escaping from school presented itself as a possibility; and, in a moment, his will had seized on it and made of it an overmastering purpose which beat down all opposition and filled him with excitement and panic. After all, why shouldn't he go? It would perhaps be betraying the Y, the confidence and respect of the masters; it would mean, if he ever returned, a trying scene with Dr. Durham; but, in the end, they would take him back on the strength of his excellent record. He could say that he had been worried about something, some personal matter he couldn't explain, and they would have to treat him sympathetically. He thought of Butts Bigelow's escapade to Boston, and it terrified him for a moment to reflect that his own conduct might have something in common with his. . . .

But what were such qualms to the anguish of three more weeks endured at school? With this racking uncertainty and anguished desire, he was unable to interest himself in anything; he could not even do his assignments. If he only knew that Barbara loved him, he could be more brilliant than he had ever been. With the support and stimulation of Barbara, he could be happy and clear-headed and strong! He would win the interschool debate!

Perhaps, when he came back to school, he would be able to announce his engagement—in which case he would be certainly forgiven. In any case, he must go! He knew about a 4:30 train on which boys who were expelled were bundled off so as not to be seen by their fellows; and he now chafed more fiercely at five hours' delay than he formerly had at three weeks. . . .

At last, it was three o'clock. He got up and took his clothes from the chair and cautiously made his way to the bathroom, looking furtively down the hall to make sure that the hall master's room was dark. This movement set going again the painful rhythm in his head. When he had dressed, he returned to his own room, where his room-mate, breathing heavily, was entombed in a heavy comforter. Hart had tied the laces of his shoes together and slung them around his neck, and he made his escape through the window in a pair of noiseless wool-lined slippers.

The fire-escape steps were narrow and coated with frozen snow, and the hand-railing was also slippery; he had to descend very slowly. At the bottom, he crunched through a snow-crust and had a terrible moment of fear when he half-expected a blast from the Headmaster's house to stop him in his tracks. But once he had left the

school grounds—among the sleeping streets of the town—
he breathed deep of the strong cold air and lifted his
head in release. How clear-minded he felt! How dynamic!
—If he could only talk to her now—walk into a house and
find her! He felt himself a dashing fellow who had just
claimed a daring freedom—but at the same time a level-
headed hero with the situation well in hand, who in
breaking the rules of the school had not sacrificed his
responsibility nor his fundamental seriousness. His Barbara was no longer a rowdy wanton, but a noble and
passionate woman—a Guinevere. And he, in his illicit
love, was still knightly and dignified. Where he had
formerly pictured himself as Galahad, he now figured as
Lancelot. . . . The houses were dark and faceless. People
lying in each other's arms, he thought. . . .

At the deserted desolate station, he half-expected the
ticketman to challenge him: "Say, you're leavin' pretty
early, aintcha?" or to ask for his card of permission, but
the old man seemed quite indifferent and went back to
doze against the stove. . . . Hart paced the cracks in the
station platform back and forth past a squad of milk-
cans, and at last, at 5:15, the 4:30 train appeared, loung-
ing along in a tranquil somnolence as if the nervousness
and haste of men had not yet waked up to excite it.

In the train, he tried to think exactly what he should
say when he found himself with Barbara, but he went to
sleep against the window. . . . The train stopped joltingly
every fifteen minutes at unfamiliar stations with irritating names—East Walsheim, Bloodgood, Medill. He could
hardly believe they existed; he had never heard of them
before. They intensified in Hart an uncomfortable feeling of having rashly broken through into an unfamiliar
world. He had somehow lost his grip on his project, and
now, when he thought of it again, it had come to seem
quite ridiculous in the raw and livid winter light which

harmonized so much better with the thawing snow and the unloading of morning milk-cans than it did with declarations of passion and vows of compelling devotion. Had that all been a feverish fancy of the evening, a vision of late hours and electric light? On one occasion, when Hart had dozed off and abruptly waked up again, he was utterly unable to believe that he had ever undertaken this errand. In the air of that dreary dawn, romance was thawing out like the snow. The ache he had felt for days reappeared as a hopeless blueness, which kept brimming up toward tears. . . .

At New Haven, he partially revived by the aid of a cup of coffee and a very old thick chicken sandwich, lined with something like a pale slice of rubber, which seemed to have been preserved for years under a fly-blown glass cover, as if it had been the sandwich of some distinguished person. . . . He told himself that he now felt fit to go on and play his great scene. He would be serious, earnest, yet charming. He shuddered in violent revulsion when he imagined the figure he had made. How insufferably priggish he had been! With what stupid obstinacy he had sent her away! But this time he would make no mistakes. She should quickly understand and forgive. Had she not once held him in her arms? Were they not pledged, deeply, supremely?

And yet there was something about the whole affair which made him apprehensive and uneasy. The day after she had come to his room, she had refused either to bowl or play billiards, and he had left the following day. It was as if his conception of their personal relations were founded on some insecure base. Was there really something wrong about it? Did he fear to find out what it was? . . . His impatience was diluted now with a complacency in delay: he clung tight to, he cherished, the security of the hours that stretched ahead before he should arrive at his goal, and he gazed out at the skeleton landscape between New Haven and Greenwich with a kind of morbid relish for every dry winter meadow mottled with melting snow, for every long flat factory building, for every black ice-glazed stream, for every hard square-angled town with its hollow-looking boxlike houses, because they were still recognizable things untransfigured by that terrible spell.

At last, with a dreadful sinking, he beheld the outskirts of Greenwich, littered with dead-looking cottages that seemed all to be closed for the winter. But with a rapidly awakening excitement, he descended the steps from the train. He felt that all the people in the station must notice that he was getting out.

He went first to a small hotel and called up the Bordens' house. Barbara was not at home but was coming back later to tea. It was now not yet noon; he had five hours to wait. This at once annoyed and relieved him. He looked at himself in a glass and was sickened by what he saw: instead of a handsome and determined young man full of passion and determination, he beheld a pasty puffy-faced child with a pitiful hangdog look, whose shirt collar was smudged with soot and whose derby seemed much too big for him. Perhaps it was just as well, after all, that he should have enough time to refresh himself. He took a room at the dreary hotel and lay down and slept for three hours. . . .

At a quarter past four, when he woke, the overcast January day was collapsing as a total failure: the world seemed dirtily melting away in drizzle and slush and mist; the very daylight seemed dissolving in a fluid gray like the snow. Hart took a bath, dressed and brushed his hair; then summoned a rickety taxi and curtly bade the driver to take him to the Bordens'.

At the door-step, the Great Dane and the collies assailed him with a deafening clamor, and as soon as the door was opened, the others came eagerly to join them. Damn the dogs! He had forgotten about them. It was impossible to keep one's dignity among them!

Then Mrs. Borden appeared and explained that Barbara was not back yet, but wouldn't he come in and have some tea?

By a lamp in the monumental gloom of the heavily oak-panelled sitting-room, she presided with her slight unintimidating air of not quite knowing what to do. She was glad it was thawing at last: she hated cold weather, she said. Her husband always used to say that she might have been born in the South, though she had really been born in Illinois. They had very severe winters sometimes out there. Perhaps that was why she hated them so. She remembered how when she was a child they used to tap the maple trees in winter. She had thought there was nothing so good in the world as eating maple-syrup and snow.

Hart sat at a strain of attention, saying "Yes" and "Really" and "No."

Then Barbara burst into the room, and his fate was upon him at last. As he got up to shake her hand, he felt his knees quaking beneath him. She took it with a casual "Hello," in which he thought he saw a studied indifference.

In her wake came a tall young man with enormous hands and feet, who, when he talked, displayed horse's teeth. He was introduced as Mr. McGuffy, and Hart, in consternation, recognized him as "Runt" McGuffy, the celebrated Yale tackle. The effect of this recognition was instantaneously crushing. Hart, in spirit, crawled under his chair and asked only to be left there in abjection. In the first place, McGuffy was at college, which made him a man instead of a boy. College was the great world beyond, to which a school-boy ascended trembling; in it men triumphantly "made good" or catastrophically went to pieces. McGuffy had perhaps encountered those temptations of which Hart had heard so much, had perhaps even yielded to them. No doubt Barbara liked him better for that! And then, further, McGuffy was a football star, just the sort of man—he saw it all—that the spirited Barbara would admire. Hart kept up a brave pretence of enjoying the conversation, but he sat there watching the others as if it were all something in which he had no real part, something distant and inconsequential, but, paralyzed thus by emotion, he thought it must be plain to everyone how he felt and what he had come for.

McGuffy, from behind his legs, which as he sat were mountainously crossed, talked clumsily, amiably, of the team, with the knowingness of sophomore year—while Barbara turned his more moderate strictures upon certain of the Princeton players into a venomous attack on the whole Princeton team, which she seemed like a carnivore to worry in her teeth as she pointed out their lack of guts, their laughable fumbling with the ball, their abysmal bad sportsmanship. It made Hart shudder to hear her; he felt out of it in the presence of such savagery, and uneasy, as if for his own skin.

At last McGuffy moved to go. "Well, I guess I better ease," he said.

"I must go in a minute, too," Hart murmured.

"Can I take you anywhere?" asked McGuffy genially. "Drop you in town just as well as not. The roads are pretty rotten now. I wouldn't advise you to walk."

Hart stammered out something lame about not going for a minute or two. Barbara accompanied her friend to the door and left Hart with Mrs. Borden again.

"Won't you stay and have dinner with us?" Mrs. Borden suggested.

He hastily declined, embarrassed by the fear that she might have thought he was staying in order to be asked.

Barbara came back, and the conversation dragged. She talked with her mother about the washed-out roads which ought to be repaired in the spring, and he felt himself helplessly shut out. At last, it was half past six: he was keeping them from getting dressed.

He got up and took his leave of Mrs. Borden, then turned in desperation to Barbara. "May I speak to you a minute?" he pleaded.

She led the way out in silence.

"Well, what can I do for you?" she asked, as he felt her father might have done.

They were among the Japanese umbrella-stands and the comic hunting pictures of the hall. She stood before him in a bright red jersey which displayed the roundness of her breasts. Her color was very high. She had assumed a rather snippy manner.

But it was not her snippy manner which turned Hart to a helpless child before her. It was the terrible prestige of her sexual experience. In its presence, all Hart's school authority, his intelligence, his superior age, had shrivelled and dropped away and left him naked in inane virginity.

When he commenced to talk at last, he thought he sounded gasping and tearful like a little boy. "I wanted to tell you, Barbara," he blurted out, "that I'm sorry about the other night. I'm sorry I was such an awful prig. I don't wonder that you were mad about it—but—my ideas about a lot of things have changed since then."

"They have?" she checked him up with irony.

He went on, gaining courage with his passion. "And I want to tell you, Barbara, that I'm in love with you. I think about you all the time. I can't work or sleep or do anything now, because I'm thinking about you all the time." He tried to give her his whole rebirth in one stupendous revelation. "Life has been entirely different since I've been in love with you!"

"Lots of people are in love with me," she answered.

"But you don't know how I love you! I love you the way Lancelot loved Guinevere! I could stand with you against the whole world! I don't care about—about public opinion. I want to be with you—to face life with you! I want to be with you—forever!"

She smiled at him mockingly. "I think you better go and get some nice little girl that won't scare you."

"But I don't want a nice little girl! You've spoiled all the nice little girls for me. I hate everybody else. The other girls make me sick. All I told you in my letters was absolutely true!" He was sick and giddy from the shock. He felt like crying out, "Oh, Barbara; don't you remember where we've been together?" But he only began to reproach her: "Why didn't you answer my letter?"

"I never write letters," said Barbara.

"I don't think that's fair!" he replied. —"I wish you still liked me."

"You reminded me of a boy I like who's away in Canada."

He was dazed as by a cannon's loudness.

She stood before him like a princess, her hands in her jersey pockets. The dogs, who had just been fed, came trooping back into the hall, tails waving and jowls agrin, delighted to rejoin their mistress. He looked at them for distraction. He knew that he had no place there.

In his desperate agitation, he had begun to wrench on his overcoat and, as he did so, there fell from his pocket the shapeless wool-lined slippers which he had used for the fire-escape.

Barbara laughed. "Did you bring those along," she said, "for fear you'd be getting cold feet?"

"I left school last night," he tried to explain. "I'm never going back again."

"What are you going to do?" she asked.

"I'm going out into the world. I'm going to work on a paper or something!"

"You'd better go back to school," she said, smiling suddenly with genuine friendliness. "Of course I do like you. Come down again with Boards sometime."

He brightened. "Maybe I could see you sometime during the Easter holidays. Couldn't you come to New York —and see a show?"

"I won't be here then."

"Where will you be?"

"I'm going to Montreal for the winter sports."

"Well, good-bye," he said, shaking her hand. "I'll see you sometime later maybe."

He pulled open the big door and strode off down the night of the drive, burning face set against the cold, as if with the energy of some sturdy errand. But the further he plunged among the bare black trees and the shapeless bush-masses of the grounds, the more he felt like some captured seaman marching bravely toward the end of a plank. Even if he should come for a visit, he felt that his love was futile. And now he was advancing into emptiness, into a universe divested of meaning; and all about him, in the winter desert, the darkness seemed to ache.

I THOUGHT OF DAISY

I

IT WAS A LOW RED-BRICK HOUSE with a white door, a brass knob and brass name-plates, and new green-and-white awnings and green window-boxes: the sort of place which, in those days, downtown, seemed particularly smart. We rang, and, after a moment, the electric clicking began—with its quick and ready profusion, plucking distinctly the string of excitement which could still be set vibrating for me at the prospect of meeting new people in Greenwich Village.

They were Hugo Bamman's friends: I had never met them. Rita Cavanagh, the poet, was to be there—and other persons reputed to possess genius or to whom I vaguely attributed romance. The stairs were soft-carpeted in green. The host, tall and smiling, in a dinner jacket, met us at the door. The rooms were very bright and well-kept: I saw lettuce-green cocktail glasses, a bruised-mulberry batik behind a divan and, on the wall, a set of framed designs for the costumes of some ballet, vivid tinselly golds, blues and purples. And there were girls, like the colored sketches, in the brightest make-ups and clothes, with red silk roses of Cuban shawls and silver turbans and red hair and black arching Russian eyebrows beautifully penciled on.

The host waylaid the hostess, who had a cocktail glass in each hand and appeared preoccupied. I thought her adorable—she was quite short and had very small gold slippers and Buster Brown blond bobbed hair. "Oh, how do you do!" she said, stopping. "How about putting down the glasses and shaking hands?" said Ray Coleman. "Here, you take this, then," she said, making him hold one of the glasses: I thought he looked a little severe as he stood with the cocktail in his hand. "There's so much traffic," she remarked, "that it's hard to receive people right." She smiled charmingly with a little mauve-rouged, moist and lovely American mouth. Her hand, which she gave me now, was fragile and small, and, with her thin round bare arm, seemed like some soft little tentacle. "What a nice apartment!" I said. "It's the apple of our eye," she replied. That wasn't quite right either, but, as it evidently was the apple of Coleman's, he smiled with satisfaction as he demurred that they were "a little cramped for space."

A bulky woman in green—the one with the silver turban—blazed upon my vision. She recognized me and we shook hands. She was one of those plain elderly ladies who do something or other and whom we meet at parties, but whose names we have difficulty in remembering. I had a drink, which Mrs. Coleman had given me, and I asked the lady with the silver turban whether I couldn't get her one. She said: "A little of that Scotch—straight," and we sat down, at her suggestion, on a large ottoman in front of the fireplace. She had the hearty manners and broad speech of an old *vivandière*—an old *vivandière* of the social revolution, I thought, and approached her with a special respect.

"What we have in America," she declared—we had arrived, through Prohibition, at politics—"is government by headlines! What's the actual explanation of these booms for Cox and Wood? Neither one has the brains of a rabbit. But their names are one-syllable words. They're one-syllable words! I'm a newspaper woman and I know!" "So is Debs," I suggested. "Yes," she replied, "but he's out." I felt that I had said something stupid. I had let her see that I was only an outsider.

My whole point of view at this period was still largely taken over from my old school-friend, Hugo Bamman: he had come, after the War, to live in Greenwich Village, and I had been brought there by his example. It was Hugo who had taken me around and who had told me what to think of what I saw; and I had seen through Hugo's eyes. The people whom Hugo thought important seemed important to me, too: he and they, I believed, were leaders, leaders of the true social idealism which cut under capitalistic politics. To them the social revolution seemed as real as their love affairs; and I had often a guilty consciousness that it was not quite real enough to me. This plain-spoken woman, for example, to whom I presumed to talk of politics, might, for all I knew, have just returned from Russia—might have fought on the barricades. Her bad language and her great bare chest might represent the heroic braveries of some heart-breaking campaign—the devotion to some anarchist lover, deported or sent to prison; the shouldering of some burden of poverty; or perhaps some point-blank vindication of basic human rights in the teeth of the mounted police and the mob.

In that company I had always felt humble: beyond publishing a few satiric verses in a radical magazine, I had never myself struck any blow in the war for humanity (Hugo Bamman was a free lance and a Communist, whereas I professed no political faith and had a tame and respectable job in a publisher's office); but, like Hugo, I had served in the other war, and had served as an enlisted man, and after seeing all the nations of the West tempo-

rarily scrambled together and the social order turned up-
side down, I had come away with a new conviction of the
necessity of human solidarity. *Ten Days That Shook the
World*—they had given me pause when I had read about
them one morning, among the inanities of the Paris *Her-
ald,* after a night spent sleeping in a puddle. In college,
I had read of the Russia of the Tsars as one reads about
the Middle Ages; but now I had been forced to recognize, even among Americans, and as one of the strongest
instincts of society, that horrifying contempt of a dominating class for the lives of those they dominate. So
that, by the time I had got out of the Army, I had acquired a scorn for the pursuit of money, position or rank:
the people who cared for such things seemed now to me
sinister or childish. It appeared impossible ever again to
accept conventional values complacently, to acquiesce in
the prosperous inertia and the provincial ignorance of
America. One could never go back again now to living
indifferently or trivially; one was afraid of lending oneself
to some offense against that unhappy humanity which
one shared with other men.

"Yes, of course," I replied, "he's out.—And Wood is
such a gentlemanly fellow!—he hasn't any of the Regular
Army mannerisms—he's surprising in that way. You think
he's going to be awful, and then he turns out to be quite
a relief after listening to the regular West Point line. You
can perfectly see why Roosevelt got on with him. Neither
one was an ordinary ruffian. Yet both, at bottom, were
stupid men. Roosevelt was only just civilized enough to
know and remember more facts than his neighbors. But
all his imagination was good for was habitually to make
a melodrama out of the most serious affairs of the world
—a melodrama with himself as hero."

Her eye had strayed, she hailed a young man with a
slit-eyed impassive gaze, who, his hands in his trousers-

pockets, had stationed himself near us. I felt abashed—
what I had said had betrayed me as a young bourgeois
trying to play up to her: it had given me away as never
having been at the barricades!—"Oh, Bobby!" she exclaimed, "your ballet was marvellous! Those divine Chinese whites!" The young man accepted the compliment,
with no attempt to turn it off or to pretend embarrassment. He seemed serious and complacent: I wondered
whether he were Jewish—he was blond, but had a hooked
nose. He replied without change of expression and bending over with his hands in his pockets: "It's the first time,
so far as I know, that Chinese white has been used in
the theater. I have two different kinds of white con-
trasted." "How did you ever do it?" said Sue Borglum
(that, it turned out, was my companion's name). "I was
experimenting for two years," he replied. I could tell from
his accent that he was Scotch; and his eyes remained
narrow and solemn, when a Jew, no matter how serious,
no matter how relentlessly preoccupied with the importance of his own activities, would have veiled with some
irony of politeness his human and earth-bound ambitions
in this Valley of the Shadow under the eye of a Jealous
God. "I don't see," she protested, emphatically, "how
people ever have the patience to go on experimenting for
effects they may never be able to get! In the newspaper
game, it's different: we never experiment—we know how
to get our effects and we get them right off, the same
day. And they're forgotten the same day!" He answered,
without smiling: "There's going to be a photograph of
my set in Bradley Foster's book on the ballet." He looked
around as someone grasped his arm.

Daisy Coleman was talking in a corner with an anomalous slight little man; they were drinking the cocktails
she had been carrying. She seemed appetizing in her
lobster-bisque dress, her paler flesh-colored stockings and

her little gold slippers. She was talking over the back of a chair, with one knee on the seat and with both hands clasping the top, like a little girl at school, chatting between classes; the conversation was accompanied with sympathetic movements of the elevated foot. As I watched her, I saw Ray Coleman, smiling in a curious fixed way at nobody in particular, go over, interrupt the conversation, detach Daisy from the little tadpole and launch her again on the company at large. She came forward rather blankly and, it seemed to me, a little sullenly.

Ray Coleman had left Hugo Bamman standing huddled against the mantelpiece and staring out through his thick myopic lenses; and it occurred to me at once that he could talk better than I to Sue Borglum. He would be sure to have the right tone—and besides, he never seemed to care whether women were young or old, attractive or plain. "Ah, there he is!" I cried—I disloyally used to kid him—"Bamman: The People's Friend!" He looked about, smiling vaguely, then, locating us, craned forward, and bubbled and beamed over Sue. I got up and intercepted Daisy.

She began by making an earnest effort to discharge her obligations as hostess, but I could see that her heart wasn't in it. "Don't you want another cocktail?" she suggested. "I'm afraid the one you got was all water. Ray has just made some new ones."

"You were in *Patsy*, weren't you?" I asked: I knew that she had been a chorus girl. "I think that that was about the best musical show I've ever seen—I went to it four times!" "Well, we couldn't complain," she said (it had had a phenomenal run). "Which one were you? I don't recognize you." "Oh, I was just in the chorus," she said. "And then I was one of the pages that came down the steps with the candles in the *Honeymoon Moon* number." "Oh, were you one of those pages?" I exclaimed.

"You were awfully cute! I remember you well!—and that set with the lavender drop and the orange moon was marvellous! Do you ever miss the stage?" "I'm beginning to now. Of course, it's an awful lot of work—so you don't get very much fun out of it." With the intention of documenting myself—in those days I shared Hugo's enthusiasm for sociological documentation—I questioned her about the theatre. I was delighted by her candor. "By the time the show opens," she told me, "everybody is groggy. When we were rehearsing for *Patsy,* I drank so so much to keep myself going that I finally got some kind of d.t.'s: I saw a horse sitting beside my bed." I expressed interest. "It was sitting by my bed with its hoofs on its knees—this way: like hands—it's hoofs were painted blue. It was sitting there leering at me." "Were you able to go on?" "Yes, the doctor gave me a great big drink of something bitter and I went to sleep and slept it off." "It must be a terrific thing to rehearse one of those shows!" "It's a lot of work to be beautiful—especially when you aren't," she added. "Oh, come!" I replied, "I was just thinking that you were one of the very few actresses I had seen who were as pretty on the stage as off!" She made a gesture of burlesque demureness, putting a finger in her mouth. I inquired about the hardships of the stage. "Once, at the Winter Garden," she told me, "I was in one of those living curtains: they left us up there for an hour and we nearly got roasted with the lights. When they let us down again, half the girls fainted.—Oh, yes; us girls," she concluded, parodying us girls, "us girls has our trials!" I found her interesting, attractive, amusing, and profoundly sympathetic. "What a lovely color your hair is!" I told her. "Just the color of honey!" "Mm-Mm!" said Daisy. "More! I eat that stuff up!"

Ray Coleman, smiling, came up behind her and put his arms about her, with his hands over her breasts.

"Don't you think he looks like Ned Grover?" Daisy inquired of her husband. "No: not a bit," replied Coleman. He explained to me humorously: "She always has these insane ideas about people looking like each other—and there's never the faintest resemblance!" I seemed to make out that Ned Grover raised an issue.

"Won't you let me fill your glass?" he suggested. "I've got some real bonded rye over here that I've only just opened. I thought at first I wouldn't open it tonight, because when you have a lot of people like this, anything special is lost on them—you might just as well give them plain bootlegger's stuff." "I thought your cocktails were splendid!" "Well, I know you'll appreciate this rye: it's the real Old Overholt, bottled in bond."

"Is Rita Cavanagh here?" I asked over the glass-topped drinking caddy. "Yes: she's here somewhere"—it gave him pleasure to feel himself master of a company among whom distinguished names might be casually mislaid. "Haven't you seen her?" "I've never met her." "I'll introduce you to her." He lifted his tall amber glass with an air. I saw that his dark eyebrows, which he was always raising in conversation with the air of a man of the world, nearly met above his nose.

He led me over to the divan. Rita Cavanagh was a sharp-nosed little thing with mousy bobbed hair; she wore a shabby black dress. She was so small that I hadn't noticed her. But, as I shook hands with her, she gave me, from eyes of a greenish uncertain color, a curious alert intent look, as of a fox peering out from covert. She was curled up in the middle of the divan and evidently the center of its company. I told her how much I had liked her poems.

Ray Coleman, with smiling politeness, requested her to recite. "Did you know I'd been asked to read in public?" she said. She spoke in a rather dry staccato voice, and with something like a British accent, which seemed to me artificial.—"Where is that?" inquired Ray Coleman. "At the Poets' League."—"Well, you're going to do it, aren't you?" said a young man who looked like a baseball player. "Well, would you? Do you think it's the thing to do?" She took a brief puff at her cigarette—staccato and precise. "Do they offer you money?" asked the man. "Yes." "Then do it!" "But they come up and talk to you afterwards, and you're supposed to answer their questions. What would you *say* to them?" "Say to them?" said the young man. "What did Shakespeare say to the horses? *Whoa! Get over there! Back up!*" She laughed, puckering her eyes, and again raised the cigarette.

This young man, I felt, was a good fellow—his hulking frame, his jutting brow and his prognathous jaw seemed to mask some gentleness and modesty—but I had the impression that he was jealous of Rita and was straining toward her with a maximum of nervous effort, was almost, in fact, on the point of seizing her; and I felt that all the three other men about her were bent in the same direction; and that I myself, though I had only just met her, was about to become involved in the competition. And, since I had told her that I liked her poems and since she had turned to me, acknowledging my compliments, as if they had gratified her especially, I began to find that I myself was resenting the other men almost as rivals.

She laughed—on distinct, impish, economized notes: "I might take an apple with me," she said, "or a lump of sugar." "Couldn't you rehearse a little for us?" Ray Coleman suggested, inclining and smiling again. "You'll find us an appreciative audience!" "This is one that I wrote today," she said, taking a last puff at her cigarette "—This very day!" And, sitting back against the wall behind the couch, straightening her neck and throwing up her head, she began to recite.

The effect was, at first, to embarrass me: it was a little as if a Shakespearean actor were suddenly, off the stage, to begin expressing private emotions with the intonations of the play. The only girl I had ever known who had been able to write respectable poetry had been in the habit of reading aloud—when she read aloud at all—as if her poems had been compositions which she had never seen before, poems written by some other person and by someone of whom she disapproved. But in the gradual silence of the room, amid the respect with which all seemed to turn toward her, those deep sonorities of sorrow and wonder began to move me as much as a play. I had admired, in reading her lyrics, the uncounterfeitable force of sincerity which, in dealing with classic themes—themes in other hands commonplace—the longing for home, the shortness of life, the transience of love—with an effect both of boldness and austerity, had not hesitated to clothe them in an imagery drawn directly from ordinary life. But I had not known, till I heard her recite, to what music these things had been tuned: all her art was in her ear; her words had little color for the eye. Now, in the poem which she had told us she had just written, she described a bonfire built on the beach, which shut out for those around it the empty weight of the waters and the desolate litter of the shore, where a poor disfeatured corpse lay, worried by unresting waves, among the seaweed, bleached boards and dead dogfish— as the joy which we know to be doomed may seem yet to overflow the moment. And in a second poem, the sight of two children—one blotted from birth in face and mind, the other creeping on wry spider legs—yet dressed and fed and sent out every morning by the mothers of wretched streets to play with the other children, was made to shake us with that despair—the damned anguish of our own frustration—which, in the presence of some pitiful human failure may overcome us with the sudden conviction that no satisfaction can be real beside the humiliations of life. And on her lips, the barrenness of the shore, the dingy images of the streets, were a kind of song.

In the pause after the second poem, dramatically tense and distinct as every syllable she had spoken, a smooth-faced and girlish boy, whom if my attitude toward all the company had not been so much one of respect, I should certainly have considered a fool, said, "That *does* something to me—that last one!" The baseball player shook his head and said: "Gosh! that's a knockout!" Rita said, "Yes: I've written that one since I've seen you! You haven't heard that one! I'm *so glad* that you like it!"

Somebody suddenly turned on the phonograph, which began jigging a popular fox-trot. Ray Coleman went over and stopped it, and I saw him engaged with his wife in what looked like a restrained altercation. Then he returned to us, bringing Daisy. "I'm sorry," he explained, smiling—his smile was beginning to get on my nerves. "Daisy has the phonograph habit: it's like a drug—she can't keep away from it! It was unpardonable to jar on those lovely poems!"

"Yes," said Daisy, "I hope you'll forgive me, but I thought you were all through." "We had hoped that you weren't," insisted Ray. "I wish you'd let us hear some more!" Rita replied, puckering up her eyes, "Oh, I think that's quite enough of me for one evening!"

"How sweet she looks in pink!" said Sue Borglum: Daisy had been standing by like a bad little child reproved. "She looks like one of those big pink bonbons on the top of a box of candy." "Melt in your mouth," said Daisy, with her frank and charming grin. "Speaking of clothes," said Rita, "has anybody seen Myra Busch since she got back from Paris?" "*Have* I?" returned Sue Borglum. "She says she bought it all with what she got from writing for *McMoony's,* but if she did, *McMoony's* must pay her a damn sight more than they ever paid me. She's so wide-eyed about it, too! I asked her if she hadn't been able to find a night to go with that lace nightgown." "Oh, Myra Busch is a pushover!" said Daisy, a little snappishly. "She's got round heels!"

Sue Borglum's pleasantry had been in the vein of the Village; Daisy's was in the taste of Broadway—I do not know which, at that period, enchanted me the more. Since I had come back to America from France, I had been noticing with a new attention the way the Americans talked. I had read, with astonished gratification, the first books of those American writers who seemed to be making a new kind of literature out of that sprawling square-syllabled speech where the words had been like colorless frame-houses on the outskirts of an American town, a language fit only, it had seemed, for the uses of a prosaic trade or of a plebeian extravagance and irony. And I noted American slang with an interest self-conscious and pedantic.

I felt, however, that Daisy's husband disapproved of her coarseness and sharpness, and I resented his failure to appreciate her.

"I understand you caught a thief," said Sue Borglum, addressing Ray. "Yes," said Ray, with satisfaction. "Caught him, convicted him and sent him where he'll do no more thieving." "Burglar or sneak-thief?" asked Sue Borglum. "All kinds of a thief!" replied Ray. "He got into the house in broad daylight. Somebody rang the bell last Sunday afternoon, and I pressed the button to open the door, but nobody came up. Now, I always make it a rule, whenever that happens, to go down and find out what's up!"

I had often in my own apartment responded to these false alarms, but checking up on them, I reflected, was like Crainquebille's prison stool chained to the leg of the bed—an idea which would never have occurred to me.

"I went down," Ray Coleman continued, following Daisy with his eyes, as she quietly detached herself from the group and went back in the direction of the phonograph, "but there was nobody in the hall—and nobody on the floor below. Then I went to all the other apartments and asked whether anybody had just come in, and they all said that nobody had. Then I went back and got a gun and a flashlight, and I went down into the basement. I held the flashlight out to one side, so that if he fired he wouldn't hit me. And lo and behold! there was Mr. Thief hiding in the coalbin! I covered him with the gun and asked him what he was up to, and he began telling me a long sob-story about how he hadn't any place to sleep and had just come in to spend the night." Smiling steadily, he gazed at Daisy, who had gone back to the corner again to talk to the anomalous little man with the dark amusing eyes, the natty blue suit and the belling sailor's trousers. "I said, 'Well, you just wait here awhile till we find out a little more about that story,' and I locked him in the basement and telephoned the police. When we searched him we found all the jewelry hidden away in his shoes!—two stickpins, a ring and a wristwatch, and five dollars in bills and change. He'd stolen them from a man in Eleventh Street!" "Oh, they weren't your things, then!" said Rita, who had been listening with that odd tension with which she seemed to react to everything, whether, as I thought, of intrinsic interest or not.

"Oh, no," Ray heartily reassured her. "He didn't get anything of ours. He didn't have any chance! I've got some etchings and some valuable firsts—so I can't afford to take risks. And Daisy has an ostrich-feather evening wrap that's worth three hundred dollars. The fellow on Eleventh Street had missed a lot of other things, too; but they

couldn't get the little bastard to tell them what had become of them. They beat him up at the station, but they
couldn't get him to tell—he was just sullen. A West Indian
boy. We ought to have some way of keeping such scum
out of the country. If they'd only do with all the criminals"—he spoke with a sort of exaltation and his eyes were
rapt away to Daisy—"if they'd only do with all the criminals what they do with the regular gunmen! They're
not supposed to beat a man up more than just so much,
you know—but the way that they get around that in the
case of the big thugs is to send them around from one
police station to the other. As soon as they get done with
them in one place, they just send them along to another
—so that the men in any one station can always say they
haven't beaten 'em up more than just so much, and yet
they can give 'em all they want. If they'd been able to do
that with my West Indian friend, we might have found
out about the silk bathrobe that he'd stolen from the man
on Eleventh Street."

"Yes," said Hugo, whose eyes, behind his spectacles, I
had felt beginning to glow with antagonism. "They might
even have made him confess to stealing the towers of
Notre Dame!" "What do you mean?" asked Ray. "I mean,
if you torture anybody long enough, you can make them
confess to anything. That was what the Inquisition did,
wasn't it?"

I perceived that, although Ray Coleman enjoyed entertaining poets and radical journalists, he was far from shar-
ing the humanitarian feeling which at that epoch pervaded
the Village. I had thought, when I first came in, that his
dinner jacket struck for the Village an unfamiliar and
incongruous note; and I was growing more and more sympathetic with Daisy. I began to concoct an ironic short
story, something rather in the vein of *Crainquebille* or of
Maupassant's *Boule de Suif*, in which a vulgar but charm-

ing little wife was to be patronized and bullied by her husband—who would be editor of a popular newspaper. One day when the husband had gone out, the wife was to find in the basement a poor starving tailor's boy, who would tell her of the petty tyrannies of the presser for whom he had worked. And, remembering her life on the stage—the cruelties of the living curtain; remembering the harshness of her husband—all that money-grubbing anti-human world in which she had always found her own life so harassed—she would listen to the boy with sympathy, and would be just on the point of offering him some clothes and something to eat, when the husband would appear with the police; the boy would turn out to be a thief whom the husband had caught and locked up!—But there would have to be something more to it—I would think about that later.

In the meantime, Hugo's skirmish with Ray had ended in an evasion, emphatically disguised, as Ray became aware that his attitude toward criminals might be considered bad form in the Village. I inquired of Hugo, aside, where Daisy Coleman came from. "From Pittsburgh, I think," he replied—then still chafing with repressed resentment over his argument with Ray, he added: "You never seem to be able to take people for granted!—you always want to know where they come from!" I answered that those things interested me.

And I brooded a little on Pittsburgh—I had been there as a boy—my mother had had a school-friend who had married and gone to live there, and we had visited them once. They had lived in a massive and formidable house, with dingy Ionic pillars, and with blue and green stained-glass windows which, far from adorning the interior, had seemed to me at the time merely somber, forbidding and blind. There had been a boy about my age called Junior, and he had a great many expensive toys; an Indian costume and a military costume (which I had thought a good deal of a bore) and the most elaborate toy railroad that I had ever seen outside a toy store—a labyrinth of signals, switches, turntables and tunnels; it had covered the floors of several rooms and rendered them uninhabitable. This boy had also had fencing foils; a real rifle; a thing that he told you to look through but which squirted water into your eye; and a device of rubber tubes and bulbs, which made plates jump up and down on the table. These luxuries had strongly impressed me and they now presented themselves to my mind—as well as Junior's egoism and arrogance, the arrogance of an over-indulged child, which had kept me from quite getting on with him. Now, as I remembered it for the first time in years, I found that I detested that household. There had been a Pennsylvania Dutch father, who had made money in the coke business and whose domineering silences had oppressed the dining table; and there had been a mother who had been always playing the piano, and singing, with inexhaustible vivacity, the scores of old musical comedies—from *The Sultan of Sulu* to *Forty-five Minutes from Broadway*—which she had heard on visits to New York. I had, at the time I came to live in the Village, developed something of that inverted snobbishness which, in Hugo's case, had impelled him to go to all the garment-workers' balls at the same time that he would grimly decline a dinner where he knew he would be expected to dress; and I had at that moment the kind of emotions which I thought Hugo would probably have in connection with a large heavy house inhabited by a Pittsburgh capitalist. Thank heaven! I said to myself, spurred no doubt by Hugo's rebuke, if I ever go to Pittsburgh again, I shan't have to be visiting there! Here, in Daisy, is the real vital Pittsburgh: frank, humorous, vulgar, human!

"She married some fellow from Pittsburgh, I think, be-

fore she married Ray Coleman," added Hugo, after a
moment during which he had gulped his drink, self-consciously and hurriedly—he was excessively sensitive and so
haunted by the fear of hurting people's feelings that his
sharpness was invariably followed by a spasm of special
affability. "They made a honeymoon trip on a motorcycle
from Pittsburgh to Atlantic City. They had all kinds of
fantastic accidents. She told me about it once. It must
have been awfully fine!" I, too, thought that it must have
been fine. That was the real, the live America—where our
bravery and freedom lay! I drank my highball up. I saw
them, skidding breathtakingly in the ditches—skinned,
bruised and mud-beplastered! Dodging motors and trucks,
shaking off towns and cities, like twigs that had been
caught in their wheels and had scraped the mud-guard a
little, and had then been whipped away!—masters of that
new and American and almost superhuman sense—the
sense of motor traffic! Till, at last, after boiling hot baths,
they had lain clean in Atlantic City, in their clean-sheeted
hotel bed, with the ice water in the pitcher and the room
as warm as a hothouse. In the morning, they would have
breakfast in bed!

Hugo had turned away to bubble, giggle and gasp to a
radical journalist with a harsh western accent and extraordinary personal charm. I rose to talk to the theatrical
designer, who, with deep-lodged slit-eyed self-satisfaction,
stood near me, his arms folded, unmoved by what went on
about him. "Are you doing any shows," I asked, "this
spring?" "Just the ballet in the *Merry-Go-Round*," he answered. "Next year," he went on to explain, "I want to
stage the *Iliad* and the *Odyssey*." "The *Iliad* and the
Odyssey?" I repeated a little blankly. "I want to do them
in a cycle," he said—"something like Wagner's *Ring*."
"How long would it take?" I inquired. "Not more than a
week," he replied. "I shan't try to have everything, of

course. I'll have to leave out a good many incidents—
though I believe that, when the public have been interested, I'll be able to put it on in an outdoor stadium and
do it on a bigger scale—there would be a week for each.
My production next fall would be an experiment with
that in view." "That would be awfully interesting," I said:
the air then, especially in the theater, was so full of high
novelty and striving that no project seemed impossible.
"What sort of text are you going to use?" "Fritz Fishbein
is making an adaptation of Butcher and Lang—it's in a
sort of free verse that will be chanted to music. Boulomé
is working out the old Greek modes, so that we'll have
music that will be really Greek." "That sounds extremely
interesting," I repeated.—"Come in here," he said, "and
I'll show you the drawings."

He led me into a little study with a desk, a window-seat
and some bookcases, and opened on the desk a large portfolio—I don't know how he happened to have it there.
"How," I asked, "are you going to do the clangor of
Apollo's silver bow?" "I'm not going to do it," he said,
"that is, I'm not going to make the attempt to reproduce
the sound. I'm not going to do anything realistically.
There'll be no sound at all. You'll just see Apollo off on a
hill—just a little silhouette, perfectly black but awful, you
know—with a bow in his hands. And then everyone will
cover their ears and sink down to the ground, and the stage
will turn green-black, and then everything will be black."
I turned over the water-color drawings, so beautifully and
lovingly covered with large clinging sheets of tissue paper.
"What's this one?" I asked. "That's the slaying of the
suitors in the *Odyssey*." "They look a little like white
rats," I commented. "Yes; I meant to give that suggestion
—those are masks that they're to wear throughout the
play." I had never heard before of using masks.

Rita Cavanagh had come up behind us, and I made

room for her to look at the drawings. I had been aware of her voice in the next room saying: "Oh, Bobby McIl-vaine's showing his Homer designs!—I want to see them!"

"Oh, what a beautiful Pallas Athena!" she cried, as she stood over the portfolio beside me. I noticed again how shabby her black dress was: she must be very poor, I thought. "Almost like a man!" she continued. It was a figure all in silver-gray, spare, upstanding and clean, like some male heroic woman of the Village—with a helmet that shaded its eyes and with an owl perched on its shoul-der—rather an odd-looking owl, I thought: thin and long, like Athena herself, but like her, austere and impressive. And I found myself delighted—especially now that Rita Cavanagh was admiring them—with McIlvaine's designs for Homer. I seemed to see that, for all their eccentricity, they were closer to the spirit of the poems than the sobri-ety and smoothness of conventional representations: they had something of the unclassical stiffness of archaic Greek sculpture. Rita Cavanagh smiled, and I smiled, at Venus caught in the net with Mars, her little rose-dotted breasts a charming pink behind gold meshes.

Hugo suddenly blundered into the room in his pur-blind big-booted way and took down his old felt hat from the bookcase—where he had carefully put it, I real-ized, in order to get at it quickly and without searching among the other hats. I wondered how he could bring himself to leave so enchanting a party so soon. He sig-naled to me a friendly, but detached and remote, fare-well—stooping, stuttered and bubbled good nights over Rita and Bobby McIlvaine—and abruptly was gone. I heard him ask in the next room: "Where's Daisy?" and the host reply, as if with humorous frankness: "I don't know where she is!"

"Oh, what *lovely* browns and grays!" breathed Rita, before the autumnal smock of Eumæus. "I never saw such lovely browns!" Her italicized "lovely" was not gushing, but had a sort of disinterested and passionate conviction. That was the sort of thing that impressed me about her. She seemed to feast upon the color, eating it with her eyes. I should myself have stopped at something brighter, and I felt guiltily that I should have been wrong. But she lingered over Eumæus: "Like the leaves in October!" she went on. "Like the leaves in the autumn mud! Such delicacy and such color standing out against something neutral—and common!"

The baseball player, or whatever he was, whom I had noticed on the divan, was now standing in the doorway, with his hat in his hand. "I'm going along, Rita," he said. "Take you over if you're ready to go!" I saw that he was unsure and self-conscious. "I'm not going for a long time yet," she answered—her voice had the tautness, the distinctness and the metallic quality of wire—though of a wire that twanged with the vibrations of some strong and superior temper; yet she tried at the same time to smile at him with a definite effect of good-will, at once elfin and sharply registered, as she added for his consolation: "I don't want to be taken home to-night, anyway. I came alone, and I want to go home alone! I'm an independent woman, I am!" "Well, go ahead and have your old single standard!" he met her, putting humorously his best face on it, and disappeared from the doorway.

She turned over to a group of nymphs, the wild girls of some northern loch. "Some people think they're not graceful enough for nymphs," said McIlvaine, without expression. "People who say they're not graceful," said Rita, "don't know anything about grace!" She spoke with a heated vehemence which seemed to me rather excessive—yet I felt something of the awe of the infidel who overhears the prayer of the believer. "They think that grace has something to do with round bodies and Greek dancing! These nymphs of yours *are* beautiful—they have the natural beauty of country girls—they're graceful even when they're gawky and awkward!"

The pretty boy—the one who had asserted that Rita's poem had "done something" to him—glided behind her in a sinuous newtish way and slid one arm about her waist. His hair was glossy and parted in the middle, and he was scarcely taller than she: his tapering and shapely hand, which I saw—and saw with distaste—lying against her black dress, would have seemed too small for a man's if her own hands had not been so tiny—not with the American thinness of Daisy's, but with a miniature complete beauty, at once childlike and mature, as of some muse or magic being. He did not speak at once, but looked with her. The next picture presented Penelope, who had an unexpected proud angularity.

"Won't Ulysses get hell," said the boy, "when he comes back home from his trip!" "No," said Rita, "she's noble!" "Yes," the boy acquiesced at once, "she's beautifully done! Great austerity! Great restraint!"

She had come to the blank cover at the back and slowly turned it over, almost as if with reverence. "I think they're beautiful!" she said, *"beautiful!"* I had heard people say that the flowers were beautiful, or that the front room was beautiful, or even that the view of the Hudson or the painting of Renoir was beautiful—but I had never before heard it said with such authority and such simple intensity. Though still shy of her unconvincing accent and suspicious of a pose, I was, in regions just beneath the surface, excited by this authority and intensity—I found myself heated, too, by the fire which the drawings had seemed to kindle in her. Bobby McIlvaine accepted her tribute in silence distended by pride and tied up the strings of the portfolio. I said: "I must go to see your ballet!" "It's not really much," he replied, "but the white is something to see."

"Well, Princess," said Rita's friend, the boy with the in-
sinuating hands, "are you ready to sail away?" I realized
that her role of princess was a part of some romance which
they had spun together, and I divined, in another moment,
that it was a romance of which she was tired. "No," she
said, "I want to stay a little longer," and added, with her
elfin smile: "Send the boatman back at twelve!"—He
swept low an invisible plumed hat.—"Leave the outside
bolts open: I can push the door myself!"—He bowed again
and backed away, and, as he retreated, she became more
amusing, entering more willingly into the spirit of the legend which they had evidently elaborated, which they had
perhaps lived, together.—"But shut the watchdogs in their
kennels, so that they won't bay at me when I come. Tell
the old woman who makes the fires that she shall have her
snuff on Thursdays, and that I shan't wake her from sleep
tonight, when she's dreaming of the little stony river of
her girlhood in the North.—Tell her to mind the fire,
though," she added, giving good measure to her friend,
who now impressed me rather disconcertingly as perhaps
not a boy at all, but a man of mature years whose coquetry
was wearing stale.—"Though sleep is sweet, the sparks are
always flying, even after the faggot is dead!"

I felt that an original imagination had led her to create
this old woman, who seemed to have nothing to do with
the plumed hat which her partner was pretending to doff,
and this interested me and made me like her, just when I
was beginning to be rather sickened by this business about
the princess and the boatman.

I could hear the voice of her admirer, as he left, just outside the study door, saying good night to Ray Coleman and
asking him where Daisy was, and Coleman's voice replying, as if in frank humorous confession, disclaiming all
responsibility: "I don't know! I haven't the slightest idea!"

—Bobby McIlvaine, who had put away his drawings, and, having finished his own performance, was not disposed to attend to the comedy which Rita and her friend were enacting, had also gone out of the room.

"That river your old woman dreams about," I began, hoping to keep Rita there, "sounds like something in up-state New York." She looked up at me in her unaccountable, quick, nervous, searching way: "Do you come from there?" she asked. "No," I said, "but I've been there a good deal." She had a way of scrupulously following, of checking up with a special exactitude which suggested anxious conscious effort, all the moves of social intercourse, at the same time that she seemed always preoccupied with something different and more absorbing; she now nodded and lifted a moment a brief interested stare.

"Let's sit down here, shall we?" she proposed, moving toward the window-seat. She curled up in one of the corners. "Do turn away that light—it's so bright!" I turned aside the adjustable desk light which was the only illumination in the room so that it lit only the farther wall; then I sat down on the window-seat, leaning up against the opposite corner.

Below the window lay Washington Square: it was still smooth and gleaming with wet. When I had come home before dinner to dress, idle, happy and vaguely expectant, breathing in the rainy sidewalks of the last day of May, I had seen the sky, above the bulk of office buildings, high-piled with white banks of solid light, and in the Square, had found the pavements swimming with milky pallors and lightened by tenderest green. When I had gone to the Brevoort to meet Hugo, I had seen a pale peach-silver sun dissolving the light tree-fringes at the corner of the Avenue. Now new wonders were springing out of that delight—so long and so varied the days were! It was dark —there were the lamps and the taxis with their impudent brisk honking—spinning away through rainy May in the wet relieved freshened freedom.

Rita was looking out the window with her same strange tranced seriousness. I asked: "Don't you like the city just after it's been raining? Hear how happy the taxis sound!" She smiled and said simply, "Yes." I wondered whether she were still thinking of the drawings of which I was almost becoming jealous. "Don't you feel a little, though," I ventured, "that it robs Homer of his own kind of subtlety to deliberately make him exotic by translating him into terms of the Russian ballet?" "Why—I hadn't thought of that," she said. "I hadn't thought of the Russian ballet. I thought those drawings were beautiful in themselves— quite apart from Homer perhaps." Then she added, after a pause: "That figure of Pallas Athena—so slender—so strong—so grave—so lightly built—as strong and yet as light as her spear! No *man* could ever combine that power and that lightness!" "Yes," I said, "that's true, isn't it?" "And then they talk," she went on, "about women never having done anything really important! When the Greeks made the goddess of wisdom a woman! And just as important a woman goddess as the goddess of love!" I tried to assure her that I understood: "Yes, I know," I replied. "Men are always expecting the wrong things of women, aren't they?"—while before my mind there aligned themselves, in the guise of long slender javelins, the long slender sentences of John Stuart Mill on the Subjection of Women. "It's so *false* of them," she went on. "You know, some people who pretend to admire independence in women really want to prevent them from doing things! They think that a woman's work is something she can put aside, as if she were laying down her knitting—or her embroidery! Whatever they may say, they can't really believe in their hearts that her work is the thing she lives for, that she puts above everything and everybody!"

I assented briefly, but with earnest emphasis: the generous flow of my feeling had been perhaps a moment impeded by the "above everything and everybody"; my mounting moral exaltation lapsed for a space into a brooding happiness which hovered outside the window over the rain-refreshed Square—those romantic lamps that burned all night, while all night the speeding taxis, plying in happy privacy to a thousand dark addresses, took people, took lovers, home. To that part of my mind, however—the part that had been talking to Rita—from which my attention had been withdrawn, there presented itself a stupid remark: "I have read John Stuart Mill on the Subjection of Women!"

But it was Rita who, after a silence, went on with the conversation: "I'm so *tired* of people"—she spoke with violence—"who pretend to understand what women feel about things!—and then behave like any stupid stockbroker, who keeps a wife just as he keeps a car!—The stockbroker would really be more sensible, because he'd expect to give his wife certain things in return for what she gave him—she'd at least be paid in comfort and money for what she lost in independence!" The figure of the baseball player rose in my imagination: a good fellow, no doubt, but dull and boorish, with no subtlety and no high honor, no doubt, in his relations with women—quite unworthy of Rita! I was all on Rita's side now. How I could share her fierceness against fools!—"I don't believe *any* man can understand!" But this seemed to shut me out again, and again I gazed out into the Square.

I was, however, after a moment, on the point of attempting to convince her that she might find that *I* understood, when of a sudden, so peremptory and clear that we looked at each other startled, we heard from the next room, which we now became aware had been silent, the voice of Ray Coleman demanding: "Well, what have you got to say?"—and then Daisy Coleman, replying in a voice which sounded constrained, "Where's all the party gone to?" "You can see for yourself they've all gone home: I suppose they saw that the hostess had left and decided that they didn't want to stay!" "We weren't gone so long, were we?" said Daisy. "I just went around the corner with Pete to get a glass of beer." "You've been gone for an hour and a half!—And you!" he went on vehemently, evidently addressing Daisy's late companion—the little man with the large eyes, I imagined. "You weren't invited here to-night and you can leave right away!" "I invited him," said Daisy. "Well, I asked you not to invite him!—Now, get out of here right away! No: your things are not in there! —There's your coat in the fireplace!—and there's your stick in pieces over there!—and I threw your hat out the window! Maybe you can find it in the street!—Now, don't stand there staring at me like that, but get out!" We heard him slam the door.

Rita and I got up quickly from the window seat, but the tirade which followed checked us. "You humiliate me in my house!"—now that Ray Coleman had Daisy alone, he opened upon her his fiercest fire. "You drive my friends away! You send C.O.D. packages home!" "I had to have some stockings for tonight!" "Well, why didn't you ask me for them? I won't have you running up bills!" "Well, I can't see what's the idea of this big third act!" "I told you not to bring that little rat here!" "Well, you have all *your* friends—I don't see why I shouldn't have mine!" "You sat in there on the window seat and let him see your legs!" "We were just telling jokes in there—Gus Dunbar was in there, too." "I don't mind having Gus see your legs—he's a friend of the family, but—" "Well, will you just let me have a list of all the family friends that you're willing to have see my legs?" "Don't be vulgar!" he replied.

Rita determinedly and swiftly broke into the lighted room, and I followed her. "I must really go," she said. "It's been such a marvelous party! I've been having such a marvelous time that I've stayed much too late!" I made my apologies, too, and got Rita's coat out of the bedroom. "Why, it's not late at all," said Ray Coleman. "I'm afraid it's we who haven't been very entertaining!" When we said good-bye to Daisy, she merely met us with a pale drunken gaze, and remarked: "Well, I opened cold!"

Outside, I caught a taxi and asked Rita where she lived. "Oh, dear," she demurred, "I don't think I want to go home. I think I'll go to somebody's house—let's see, whose house shall I go to!" I asked her if she wouldn't come to my house. "But you want to go to bed, don't you?" I assured her that I didn't, for hours.

"Pretty painful scene that was!" I remarked when we had started in the taxi. "I shouldn't think she'd stay with him." "No," said Rita, but assenting, it struck me, from some different point of view than mine. "She's such a dear, isn't she?" I added. "Yes," she said. "She's so beautifully made, isn't she?—her ankles and wrists." I thought of Daisy under the guise of Bobby McIlvaine's little blond Venus caught in the net with Mars. "What do you make of him?" I asked. "He's pretty poisonous, isn't he?" She looked up at me with a little appreciative smile, as if my saying that Coleman was poisonous had been an original deliberate joke instead of a familiar cliché. Then, "He's very jealous of her," she said; and then: "Yes, he *is* poisonous!" Her way of agreeing that he was poisonous made it neither a cliché nor a joke, but something convinced and bitter. "All jealousy is poisonous: it poisons the woman as well as the man—it makes both of them suspicious of all that has ever been between them—and even when they want to be nice, they sound hateful to one another!" I remembered some novel of Wells in which the hero had overcome jealousy along with a number of other ignoble and anti-social emotions; I reflected that it was very foolish and very base to be jealous. However: "I suppose," I said, "that working for the *Telegram-Dispatch* makes him hate himself, and so makes him awfully irritable. How can people who are really sensitive and intelligent—as I have no doubt he is—but who are obliged to spend all their working hours feeding the public libels and lies—how can they possibly be amiable at home?" "Yes," she said, "such lies they print!—such cowardly lies! And even if the facts are true, they cheapen the emotions behind them—and to cheapen human passion, human suffering, is to lie! Like poor Lina Lemberg's letters." (Lina Lemberg was a young Polish girl, who had recently murdered her husband, and been much on the front page.) "They may have been illiterate and clumsy, but they meant something real. To tear people's hearts to pieces for all the grinning crowd to see—and pick up a bit of it and finger it, and perhaps wish they had one, too, and hate the people who have—and then throw it back in the gutter again!" Her passion had not ceased to surprise me. She still seemed a little theatrical, but I had never heard a woman speak so eloquently. "Yes: that's just what happens," I said—it was all that I could say: I felt that I could never express myself so well nor feel what I said so intensely.

I lived in Bank Street then, and the taxi had stopped at my door. Rita waited on the sidewalk while I paid the driver: her little face seemed thin and narrow—almost nunlike.

When we had climbed to my apartment and I had turned on the light, I was ashamed of the prospect disclosed. There were a large and comfortable couch, sets of books in glass-doored bookcases, Whistler's *Battersea Bridge* and a drawing by Leonardo, which I had brought up with me from college, a small mahogany desk, a green carpet and a French clock. Besides, the maid had been there that morning and everything was swept and neat. I was afraid that Rita would see at once—if she had not already guessed—that I was not really one of them, that I had never paid their price. The luxurious couch seemed vulgar; the sets in the bookcases pedantic; the pictures unbearably banal; and the little mahogany desk appropriate kindling wood for the social revolution. I attempted to call attention to the only feature of the place which might be considered Bohemian and raffish: "That's not the right time," I pointed out. "That clock hasn't gone for years!"

"Oh, isn't this nice!" she exclaimed, looking searchingly and quickly about her. There was an alcove off the sitting-room which I used as a study, and she stood looking into it, as if entranced. "Do you work in there?" she exclaimed. "What a *wonderful* place to work!" She came back and sat down on the couch: "Oh, it's so *nice* here!—so *nice!*" She smiled in an ecstatic childlike way.

I felt at any rate that she meant it, and that I possessed an unexpected advantage. None the less, I was a little diffident about offering her some peach brandy, as I had seen her drinking whisky straight at the Coleman's party. I brought out both liqueur and Scotch, and deprecatingly remarked that I didn't suppose she'd care for the former. "I'd love some!" she said.—"What a lovely label! It looks like lace, doesn't it?—like lace made out of wire!"

"You know," she went on, "I have no place of my own to work in now—and I miss it so! I'm living with my mother and sister, and the apartment is so small! I have to write with the sewing machine going in the next room," "Oh, what a pity!" I said, "I should think it would drive you crazy. I know how nervous it makes you to have something going on to a different kind of rhythm from the one you're writing to!" "Do you write?" she asked. "I try to write poetry—but I'm not any good." "I'd like to hear your poems," she said, looking up with an intent gaze which seemed to pierce the politeness of her remark. "No," I replied. "After hearing yours tonight, I wouldn't have the nerve to show you mine. I don't suppose you'd recite again the ones that you recited at the party." "I'm so glad that you like them," she said, again with that incongruous intensity which gave sincerity and significance to even her formulas of courtesy. "I just wrote them, and I like them myself," she smiled with her funny grin, which left her as serious and as strangely pressing as before. She sat back against the couch, dropped her cigarette to her lap and recited the poems again—more beautifully, it seemed to me, than the first time: her voice, in the silent room, sounded lonely, and I was stirred and awed to be alone with this living voice of poetry.

All to me was a marvel then—her old dress, her mother's sewing machine, her formidable dignity, her wide gamine's grin and her feverish preoccupation with some unexplained disturbing reality which I was coming more and more to feel underlay everything she did. It was, I came to see, the same thing—a kind of moral agony, unremitting and exalted—which made it possible for her, in her poetry, to deal with commonplace ideas—as she worked often with the tritest figures, the old debased currency of verse, which poets had then begun to pride themselves on ceasing to try to pass—making them carry whatever passion and whatever strangeness she chose.

Her cheeks were fiery now—all her face was suffused with fierce pink, and I saw that there was red in her hair. I saw now for the first time that she was beautiful. Her brow was very high and wide, and the resonant voice with which she recited—so different from her quick dry speech, a mere pizzicato of those strings—seemed the full-toned

and proper music of what I saw also now for the first
time was a long and lovely throat of a solidity and complexity of symmetry, like some harmoniously swollen musical instrument, almost incongruous with her tiny body
—and through which now the lonely beach, beyond the
meager moment of fire, and the futile devotion of the
mother to the blemished and dim-witted child, sounded
the chords of some mode of feeling more profound than
our human sadness, some ground-tone where human emotion becomes merely the process of life, of life in its labor
through the universe. I knew, what I had never really
felt in my intercourse with friends who had written, that
literature could be reality—as natural as conversation, yet
as deep as life itself.

In another poem, which I had never seen, and which
she had also recently written, she had some image of a
swift upcountry river lacerated by rapids, where a smooth
and lovely flock of stones forever tumbled and crashed
into splinters the black-silver mirror of its deeps, dis-
missing it, fiercer at first, then thin, querulous and shred-
ded, divided in the threads of feebler streams that drip at
last over slimy mossy banks among the last orange drops
of the jewel-weed, and lose themselves in the fields. I
have turned it all into ordinary literature, over-animating
the water, describing the jewel-weed too exactly (it is I
who supply the drops: she had only named the flowers).
I have used too many adjectives; she had only the barest
verbs and nouns, but she woke through them the resonant ache of the throaty sound of the river, so noble in its
dwindled fall. And I, knowing enough of literature to
enjoy the consummate art, but not yet enough of life to
assent with my heart to the terror, the terror mastered by
the mind, and clutched and wrenched into beauty, which
I could only half divine, but which troubled me and made
me solemn, could only tell her how wonderful I thought

it, as if it had been merely a dress she had been wearing or a garden she had grown. And I sounded even sillier and lamer when I added: "I've seen those upstate rivers: I know exactly what you mean!" "Yes, I knew you did," she replied, "when you said that something I said this evening sounded like a New York State river. I come from up there, you know, and I've been getting homesick lately. That was why I was talking about rivers—and why I wrote that poem."

I was silent, and she looked beyond the lamp, through the little dark study, to where the moon seemed imbedded in the pane like a flaw of pearl in dark blue glass. "How lovely the moon is!" she exclaimed in her nervous alert way. I looked out and answered: "Yes: it looks like a bubble in the glass." She noted the accuracy of this, checking it up: "Yes, it does exactly!"—so emphatically that I felt pleased at having said something clever. We stared at the moon without speaking—I thinking, a little dazedly, of the perfect felicity of the moment, full of brightness and freedom and peace—of the beauty of stony rivers, of the pearly moon in the pane, of intoxicating coldness and poetry—of stones, of lovely globes of a lunar fluidity of yolks, lodged unbroken below the translucence of a limpid vitreous stream.

Then I recalled my wandering senses and suggested another drink. "Oh, if I have another drink, I'll be drunk!" she said, screwing herself down in her corner and with a sudden rictus of her grin which transmogrified her grossly in a strange tense glee.

But I could talk to her only of poetry—of those terrific images of the commonplace by which the greatest poets can move us and which her own poems had brought to my mind—the Roman street corners of Catullus, the prison window of Verlaine, the race for the green flag at Verona which Dante remembers in Hell. She had read very widely for a woman, and she talked about the poets as only a master can talk of the masters of his craft and with the fierceness with which only a woman, when woman's narrow concentration has been displaced from its ordinary objects, can concern itself with art—isolating in familiar poems phrases I had never thought of: some armor-joint of a preposition which rang with a solid sound or some unobtrusive adjective which troubled the whole line.

It was cold: she put on her cloak and I wrapped her legs in a blanket—but still we talked, and drank the peach brandy sip by sip. At last, as I was gazing toward the window, I became aware of an indigo deepness which deeply delighted me, like some full triumphant staining of emotion and thought. It was the blue of dawning June, through which presently, as brooding I watched it, green and red began darkly to appear. The blue brightened and now was translucent, now limpid, now dissolved. And, still talking of poetry, still quoting, still eager and glowing with the images of that life of literature which rejects or suppresses nothing that goes to make our common life, but where all is passionate, noble and rich, I saw, as it were with incredulity, that the brightening green and red were the rain-revived trees and brick walls of my own backyards in Bank Street. Now even the poor soiled yellows of the downtown tenement houses, the leaves of the flaccid ailanthus swaying their fingery clusters in the stir of morning air, through that first distinct light of day were seen washed with libations of light—till it seemed to me that I had waked—or rather that, without sleeping, I had passed—to the happier, more living hues of a different world. And I knew, and knew with amazement, that we had talked the night through, and only sunk deeper in spring.

"Good gracious! it's morning!" she cried. "Oh, no: it's

not so late," I assured her. "The nights are getting shorter." She laughed and put out a cigarette. "I must go home!' she said, springing up.

We found a taxi in Greenwich Avenue. She gave the directions to the driver in her precise and compelling fashion. I invited her, in the taxi, to come with me to see McIlvaine's ballet. "I'd love to!" she replied. We made an engagement for Tuesday (it was Sunday morning). Then, with hesitation, I explained that I was never at home in the daytime, and that if she needed a place to work, I should be glad to have her use my apartment. She demurred, but I thought not unpersuadably.

I left her at an incredible address beyond the Ninth Avenue Elevated—on Twelfth Street, almost at the docks —one of two or three red-brick houses among warehouses and sordid saloons. We parted, she quite tired and pale, but with a queer tense final vibration even as I left her in the doorway, just before, quickly closing the door, she seemed to disappear in a flash.

It was day. I walked home through a little open square —Abingdon Square, I saw with surprise: I had never heard of it before, though it lay almost around the corner from where I lived. I gazed vaguely at a statue of a man in a little triangular park and wondered who it was— some legislator or some patriot, perhaps—some patriot in the old style, like Garibaldi in Washington Square—some great man I had never heard of in that region I had never discovered. Farther on, I became aware of a kind of monumental stone pergola—it seemed to me then to be in marble—which I didn't understand and which in my weariness, my happy weariness, I made no effort to. Some downtown equivalent of Grant's Tomb—but who was buried in it? It was almost like a temple. I was still moving in that strange daytime world into which, by staying up all night, I seemed to have been translated. Now the

Village was at last revealed to me; it had that day come alive about me, and I felt myself part of its life. I, like them, had turned my back on all that world of mediocre aims and prosaic compromises; and at that price—what brave spirit would not pay it?—I had been set free to follow poetry!

In Bank Street, as I passed a presser's shop, it occurred to me that it would be, after all, a difficulty about the story which I had had the idea of writing when I had heard about Ray Coleman's thief, that the presser's boy would probably have got away as soon as the wife opened the door.

When I climbed to my rooms again, they seemed no longer, through the drowsy eyes of day, my own familiar husk. There was the couch upon which she had sat—there was the ash-tray full of ashes—there were the glasses from which we had drunk. I poured out the last sweet dregs of peach brandy.

It was Sunday—I did not have to work. I dumped the Sunday paper on the couch. I pulled down the shades in my bedroom—the sun made them glow dull orange. I pulled out the *Divine Comedy* and read the lines about the green flag at Verona—and the scene with Beatrice that began, *"Dante, perchè Virgilio se ne vada—grieve not, thou needst must grieve for another wound!"*—but, having hardly paid attention to the words, I pushed the book away on a table and turned over on the pillow on my cheek. Something or other I had come for, I had found.

*   *   *

It was characteristic of Hugo Bamman—whom I had early known at prep school (though we had afterwards gone to different colleges), and whose point of view, up to the night I met Rita, had, as I say, so much influenced my own—that, at the height of a convivial evening, he

should take an abrupt and determined departure. Even at
parties in Greenwich Village, with which he was in principle more nearly sympathetic than with parties anywhere
else, he would carefully isolate his hat or hang it up in
some specially conspicuous place. He was never sure, even
in the Village, when he might not feel that it was ur-
gently needed, as had been the case on that evening, after
his argument with Ray Coleman. And when he once had
his hat in his hands, it was impossible to make him stay. It
was at the same time as if he had become suddenly
frightened, and as if he were under some obligation of
reporting for duty elsewhere.

And it was true that he did become frightened, and that
he was, in a certain sense, at the orders of a higher obligation. Hugo's father had been a well-to-do lawyer of a
Philadelphia Quaker family; his mother, a Bostonian. The
elder Bamman, after serving with distinction through
three administrations at Washington as Solicitor General,
had been dislodged by the advent of the Democrats; and
had thereupon retired from public life and occupied himself with writing books. He knew Shakespeare and Milton by heart and was given to quoting them in conversation, and he already had a reputation for unconventional
political views; but nobody had been quite prepared for
the opinions which he now made public. His first book,
which was called *Representative Government, and the
Way and the Light,* began with an extremely realistic,
and even cynical, discussion of American public life and
ended, with quotations from Isaiah, on an unexpected
note of religious clairvoyance.

It was said sometimes that Mr. Bamman had been embittered by his enforced retirement; sometimes, that he was
insane. It was not that he had prophesied good of the
Democrats: on the contrary, he had predicted the worst;
but he had also discredited the Republicans. He had as-

serted that, between the two parties, there was not a
pin to choose—that both were lost in corruption and error;
and, what was worse, that one could hope for nothing better from the society which accepted their leadership and
from the religion which allowed them to survive. The book
excited a certain amount of interest, was made the subject
of editorials; then was completely forgotten by everybody.
If I had not happened to know Hugo, I should never have
looked it up and read it. Thereafter—his wife having died
and his sons gone away to school—Mr. Bamman left
Washington altogether and secluded himself on a lonely
island in an Adirondack lake, where he lived on fish and
game, cooked all his own meals and struck off another
book even more realistically pungent and even more apoca-
lyptic than the first. He had vowed to stay the winter out
in his cabin, but in February he caught a bad cold which
developed into pneumonia, and, despite his protests, he
had to be removed to a town where he could have medical
attention. His sons were telegraphed at their school; and
Hugo, blinking at his sudden release from the agonizing
life of prep school, where the boys made fun of his ebul-
lient stuttering, his inability to pronounce *r*, his stiff in-
tractable black hair, and his clothes, which were bought
for him by an aunt and which always looked too young for
him, lifted his goggles from the frozen ground and gazed
about him with singular relief at the ice ponds and white
houses of the north; read nervously half a chapter of Mere-
dith; and, at last, heard his father, dying, mingle texts from
Isaiah and Ezekiel with anxious queries about the pump at
his camp, which he seemed to be afraid was irremediably
frozen, and with the names of his sisters and his wife.

Hugo Bamman, after his father's death, had spent his
vacations with the aunt in Philadelphia who had selected
his neckties and suits, and he had rebelled against her so
violently that he soon found himself under suspicion of

having inherited his father's "queerness." But the more the aunt, who was an admirable person and felt her responsibility acutely, tried to inculcate sound principles in Hugo, the more resentfully did he shy away from them. Save for an occasional peevish outbreak, however, he remained generally docile; and his own docility increased his resentment. While he was still at school and college, his heresies were mostly confined to matters of literature and of minor social convention. But during the third year of the War, though he was to graduate the following spring, he suddenly left college and enlisted in the American Ambulance. In spite of his Quaker tradition, he was at that time full of romantic enthusiasm for the cause of the Allies, and had composed, for the college magazine, an eloquent editorial which began with Joan of Arc and ended with Villiers de L'Isle-Adam. When America joined the Allies, he went over to an American medical unit. Hugo served throughout the War; but he came out with different emotions from those which had carried him in. He never told me much about his adventures, and never indeed, at this time, talked much about himself, so my account of his experience in the Army is mainly derived from the well-known novel which he afterwards wrote on the subject and which seemed such a striking contrast with the precious and exotic little poems, reminiscent of the eighteen-nineties, which he had published in the college magazine.

From Hugo's novel, then, it would appear that through the first months of his ambulance-driving, he was still sustained by his romantic faith and preoccupied with proving to himself his own capacity for courage and endurance. He tells us of the hero of his novel that though most of the wounded men he had been carrying turned out to have died on the way, he had never felt so happy in his life as after successfully bringing his ambulance through the craters and geysers of a bombardment. At that time, after his first physical sinkings of nausea and fear, he had been able to line up corpses on the floor of the field hospital with less emotion than he had once arranged books on the shelves of his bookcases at college, and had incinerated amputated legs with less of real regret than he had once burnt discarded manuscripts.

But after America had entered the War, Hugo enlisted in the American Army and found himself posted, with the rank of sergeant, during the dull and disheartened winter of 1917, at an American base hospital in the Vosges, some distance behind the lines. One afternoon, he had gone for a walk in the hills and come out finally in the public square of a tiny mountain village. A circle of people were standing about the body of a wild sow which had been killed by a hunter and which, bristled like the piny ridges of her northern forests and with her jaws asnarl in death, lay flat, her belly ripped open and her little ones, brightly striped and in a day or two to have been farrowed, stretched out limp beside her on the ground, while the hunter bargained over the carcasses and the dogs sniffed at the blood. A deep tenderness and sadness overwhelmed him for the little wild pigs; and he looked on with horror at the nonchalance of the hunter; he began to rage within himself against the violators of life. Then he was chilled with self-contempt. He took refuge in a little café and fortified himself with brandy. Then he went back to the base hospital.

There was a major of the medical corps who kicked and cuffed his patients, and who was in the habit of amusing himself, on his evening rounds of the wards, by tearing the zinc-oxide bandages off the raw and running wounds of the gas cases. Hugo complained of this major to the commanding officer of the unit. He had always feared his superiors more than any amount of shell-fire.

Soon thereafter, returning in the morning, just before reveille, from the local château, where he often went to dinner and sometimes, by private understanding with the other sergeants and the guards, was able to spend the night, he was picked up, to his surprise, by the military police, put under arrest, court-martialed and convicted, and sent off under guard to a prison camp. As a sergeant he had been lax with his men; and, at the court-martial, he was accused of having abetted all their misdeeds. Of these misdeeds he had never even known, but when he tried to explain this to the court-martial, the effect was equally unhappy.

On his arrival in the prison camp, all his belongings, including private letters, his money and his watch, were taken from him. He saw the photograph of another man's sweetheart torn up before his face. The first morning, when he was led out in lockstep with the other prisoners, the ranks fell into disorder, and the sergeants set upon the men and clubbed them with what were known as "dizzy-sticks" while the officers looked on. This was repeated every morning, and Hugo learned that the confusion in the ranks was brought about by the sergeants themselves: the sergeant at the head of the line would order the prisoners to hurry up while the sergeant at the end would order them to slow down. Hugo was struck in the mouth one day and two of his teeth knocked out (he had the scar across his lips all his life). After this ceremony, which the sergeants called "morning exercise," the prisoners were drilled before machine-guns.

The food was scant bread and thin soup; and on the third day of Hugo's imprisonment, two colored boys got into the kitchen and tried to steal something to eat. One of the boys was caught, blackjacked, beaten and dragged bleeding to solitary confinement. When he had sufficiently recovered, an attempt was made, by order of the officer in command, to induce him to reveal the name of his accomplice. The boy was chained for four hours to a wall, while the sergeants threatened and cursed him, beat him on the soles of his feet and singed off most of his hair. In the meantime, however, the accomplice had cut his own throat with a razor blade. Two days afterwards, a big Texan, who had tried to strike one of the guards when the latter had assailed him with a blackjack, was shot down, in the presence of the men, by the camp's commanding officer. At the end of three weeks, however, Hugo was finally released through the intervention of his elder brother, who was a major in the adjutant general's department and with whom Hugo had managed to communicate before he had left his unit.

The participation of Hugo in the War then came to an embittered end. It was no longer now the Germans who were the enemies of civilization, but the governing classes of the world that were frustrating human progress.

By the time that Hugo was discharged from the service, he had become a social revolutionist; and his reaction against the complacent and conventional, the capitalistic world from which he came, reached lengths that were in some ways grotesque. He hated this world because he feared it, and he feared it because he knew how much of it there was still left in himself. He was haunted by veritable hobgoblins which wore the aspect of doubles of himself. A visit to any of the members of his family was enough to throw him into a panic. He would afterwards describe it in terms which would almost have been excessive on the part of one resuscitated from drowning. "On a Sunday afternoon in Washington," he would gasp, "you go out into the street—and you see all those little bwick houses—and the weather is suffocating—and you look at the people on the stweet and they don't seem to be going anywhere—and you think that, if you stayed there long yourself, you'd probably get like that, too—and yet you haven't got the mowal stwength to leave!" Or, "I was staying with a cousin of mine at Cambwidge—my cousin is being gwoomed for some big job at Harvard, and it weduced me to such a state of depwession! Did you ever know any of these young men who are being gwoomed for big jobs? Well, first their hair falls out—then they have to buy glasses—then they have to appear at certain times and places wearing a silk hat—then their teeth go and they get false teeth—false teeth are almost as important as a silk hat, and it isn't everybody who can make his teeth drop out just by auto-suggestion—if they can do that, they've got the stuff! I'd said I was coming back to Cambwidge, one night after I'd gone in to have dinncr in Boston, but I couldn't face it! I couldn't get a berth at the station, so I sat up all night in the day coach!" (This sort of thing was possible for Hugo, because he purposely never traveled with a suitcase, but only with an old muscttc bag, which he had brought back from France.) Yet I have heard him, when Boston was disparaged, unexpectedly come to its defense with eulogies of Thoreau and Garrison.

Whenever he introduced into his novels representatives of the "cultivated" class to which he himself belonged, he would never allow them to figure save in hideous caricature—the result of his having discerned, seized upon and isolated in them, those ignoble middle-class qualities which they shared with the families of the *nouveaux riches* manufacturers and railroad magnates whom they ridiculed. And, on these occasions of visiting his relatives, by the very force of his fixed intense belief in their incurable perversity and prejudice, he had a faculty for trapping them into absurdities which did not at all represent their real views. These Hugo would make careful note of, as he returned to New York on the train, leaving the cousins and uncles a little blank. His aunt in Philadelphia, for example, with whom Hugo had spent so much of his boyhood, had been, by reason of her Quaker tradition, strongly disposed to admire his war book, though she was offended by the bad language of the characters; it always appeared, however, when she attempted to talk to him about it, that, in deploring this particular feature, she was damning the whole book.

Hugo's elder brother, especially, though, unlike the other members of the family, he did himself profess progressive views, affected Hugo in a fatal way. This elder brother had studied for the ministry, but had found himself unable to accept the doctrines of the Episcopal Church save in a highly rationalized form: as a consequence, he had gone in for sociology, and, after the War, had become a professor of sociology in a small New England college. When Hugo went to visit his brother, the latter would remonstrate with him severely and unremittingly. He would, for example, point out to Hugo the serious impropriety of the latter's having published certain scurrilous verses in a radical magazine. He would argue along lines of social responsibility: the real purport of the objectionable metaphors would be understood by very few readers, whereas the rest would see only obscenity and unpatriotic sentiments; this would hurt Hugo's reputation and weaken his influence as a publicist, etc., etc. Such discussions infuriated Hugo all the more because his brother always went on the assumption that he recognized the same evils with which Hugo was so passionately preoccupied and that he had it as much at heart to discover the proper way of remedying them: Hugo's brother's social ideas and Hugo's, when stated by the former in a certain way, appeared to be indistinguishable. These visits were further embarrassed by the apprehensions of Hugo's sister-in-law: she seemed always on edge for fear Hugo might advance, in the presence of the faculty wives, with whom she was closely allied, some indignant and shocking opinion.

Another bugaboo which lurked behind Hugo—another

monster which he lived in terror of allowing to swallow
him up—was the college dilettante—that is to say, the superior undergraduate who takes tea with the snobbish
Latin professor, plays Debussy at the club after the girls
from the house party have left, and goes about with a
small group of friends who gossip over the politics of the
dramatic club and giggle over the mustache of the brunette who waits on the counter at the pastry shop where
they buy cinnamon buns. These friends, like Hugo himself, had been affected by their experience in the War;
but, in their case, it had had usually left them, not re-
bellious but merely dispirited, writing fragmentary learned
poetry, full of resignation and gall, in imitation of T. S.
Eliot. They used to make fun of Hugo for the obstinate
persistence with which—inordinately fastidious and shy—
he had trained himself to speak in public (overcoming his
tendency to stutter, though not his inability to pronounce
r), and had even attained a certain reputation as an orator
at strikers' meetings and demonstrations for civil liberty.
Hugo's friends, as a rule, disparaged the admirable literary
gifts—the logic, the solid imagination and the feeling for
pungent language—which were disguised by the deliberate
plainness and the colloquial carelessness of Hugo's novels,
pamphlets and appeals.

And Hugo would himself have been the last person
to call any attention to his merits. Since the War, the
discussion of literature had affected him like his memories of college, and the specter of the modern literary
man, whom he had encountered at New York parties
and in Paris cafés, came to accompany, and to merge
with, the specter of the aesthetic undergraduate. Though
in his youth he had been carried away by literary enthusi-
asms, he now habitually treated the great writers—including those whom he most admired, from Plato to James
Joyce—in a manner almost flippantly cavalier. It was

partly, I suppose, that Hugo had never forgotten young country boys from Arkansas and Georgia who could neither read nor write, bewilderedly drafted into the army and pitted against young Germans who had studied Goethe in the gymnasia—the accumulated masterpieces of literature having apparently not in any way affected the fates of either. But it was also that he continually tended, by some natural gravitation which enraged him, to find himself comfortably at home among the sallow-faced reviewers and the review-writing poets and novelists who relieved the mediocrity of their days by the gin drinking and ribaldry of their evenings. At these gatherings, they were able to convince themselves that they were not merely dreary hacks and bookworms, but men of taste and wit, citizens of the world; and it was partly this anti-academic pose which made Hugo—himself violently anti-academic—at first eager to attend their parties. But he soon divined the pit of ashes at the bottom of the bootleg gin, and shied off as he had done from his family and from the companions of his college days; and this kind of literary society was soon added to his index of phobias.

When Hugo put himself into a novel, it was always in caricature—as the little Johnny Boston-Beans of the comic papers of his youth, or as some incredibly fatuous and inept young college intellectual who died of tuberculosis or fell into a subway construction. I have seen him shudder at the sight of a handful of volumes of Max Beerbohm, whom he had himself enjoyed reading at college, which I was unpacking in a new apartment; and I have rarely heard him use bad language (though he admired it on the part of others) save when the name of Henry James was mentioned. This continual shying away made Hugo a little difficult, since he was constantly flaring up to object, not merely to what you had said, but to what he thought you were going to say. Thus, if you remarked to him of W. Z. Foster that Foster had the barren rigid strength of a piston in a steel mill, he would interrupt you with, "Well, I'd rather see an effective and hard-hitting machine like Foster than a jerry-built ornamental bank building in a phony classical style, like Harding!"—and so plunge into a spirited tirade against the industrial system, which you vainly tried to avert with explanations that you did not admire Harding, that you did admire Foster, etc. Or if you were going out to dinner with him and complained that the sentimental Yiddish soloist at Zincovitz's restaurant was beginning to get on your nerves, he would be off with, "Well, I can't stand those little tea-rooms where they have copies of *Town and Country* lying around!"—little tea-rooms of whose existence you had never even known.

He was rather afraid of women, and seemed never to fall in love. I suppose he regarded women as the most dangerous representatives of those forces of conservatism and inertia against which his whole life was a protest; but I am convinced that he cherished, in his heart, the most romantic expectations. I believe that he was always hoping for some straight, dark, spare realistic girl revolutionist, who would be to him a comrade and a partner; but that in fact, he was invariably alienated from the types of emancipated women whom he now encountered in the Village, by an unconfessed but ineradicable instinct which rejected them as not being ladies. He would, of course, shy away from this instinct and overwhelm them with politeness, with sympathy, with determined goodfellowship; but this effusion masked a retreat. I think he was affected, in this connection, by the same peculiar and incurable isolation which had made him seem to himself, during the War, almost indifferent to the sufferings of the soldiers till he found himself brimming with tears at the sight of a slaughtered sow. So he would flee from even parties in the Village, when any situation arose which seemed to suggest a love affair, and go home to write with passion, almost with amorous feeling, of some girl bandit who had been harshly sentenced and brutally denounced by a stupid judge—of whom he had read in his evening paper.

For Hugo was really on close terms with no one. As soon as he had sampled the conversation and caught the social flavor of a household or a group, he would simply go straight away and bottle a specimen for his books, in which he would assign it to its proper place in the economic structure. He distrusted his family and his early associates, because he believed that they had sold their souls to capitalist institutions; but though he chose to live exclusively with outlaws, in whom he was always discovering qualities heroic and picturesque to the point of allegory, he never managed really to be one of them and perhaps never trusted them, either. So tough remained the insulation between himself and the rest of humanity— the insulation of his Puritan temperament and his genteel American breeding, reinforced by his artist's detachment and his special situation. Hugo once told me as if with pain of an illiterate Arkansas boy, lying wounded in a field hospital, who, thinking Hugo a superior person, had been unwilling to ask him to write a letter, and who had finally had to beg the favor of another wounded man nearly as helpless as himself.

So Hugo walked among us like a human penance for the shortcomings of a whole class and culture—of the society which, in America, had paralyzed in his friends and himself half the normal responses to life; which had sterilized its women with refinement; which had lived on industrial investments and washed its hands of the corruption of politics; which had outlawed its men of genius

or intimidated them with taboos; which so strangely had
driven his father to his Adirondack lake and, on the rare
and brief occasions when he returned for a wedding or
a funeral, had seemed to Hugo's eyes to sadden him, as,
to the latter's heartiness and wit, the other members of
the family had returned only so much that was energetically arid, so much that was self-confidently timid
and so much that was cheerfully cold; and which had
desolated Hugo's own soul, when, through empty after-
noons of boyhood, he had wondered why he seemed so
impotent to break the spell of his tutoring in the morning, the nap of his aunt after lunch, the people for tea in
the afternoon and his late luxurious reading in bed, to work
on a paper, to ship on a whaler or to live on a ranch in
the West; and which had finally inflicted on him the
shame of that day when he had found the crippled
Arkansan dictating his letter to his wife to a man half-
flayed with mustard-gas—the shame of knowing that a
fellow sufferer and one who had suffered more than he,
had been afraid to ask him to render what was perhaps
the only service for which his education had fitted him.

I have said, a whole class and culture; but Hugo had
one other memory of his father, which was afterwards,
he told me once, to take on for him a special significance.
They had been lunching at the New York club of the
university from which his father had graduated and to
which Hugo was soon to go, and the elder Bamman had
commented during lunch with humorous disapproval and
imperturbable surprise on the inferior quality of the men
whom he observed in the dining-room about him. On
their way out, as Mr. Bamman was getting into his coat,
he had been disconcertingly jostled by a young man in a
blue suit and bone glasses, who was evidently in a great
hurry, but who hurriedly apologized. Mr. Bamman was
broad-shouldered and well set-up, and he still wore a

fine Olympian beard and one of those flat-crowned der-
bies which were fashionable in the eighties (he continued
to be something of a dandy even after he had become a
recluse); but, at the moment of the impact, as Mr. Bamman looked dazedly around, Hugo had caught on his
father's face the shadow of feebleness and pain. And he
had realized then for the first time that his father had no
longer the prestige of an acknowledged leader of any
community, nor even of a distinguished person: he was
a figure of isolation, bewilderment and fatigue.

In the America where Hugo came to manhood, there
was, in a sense, only a single class and a single culture;
one found it behind every façade, one felt it through
every uniform—and not merely among those members of
society whom it had already become fashionable to ridicule: the small business man, the hired reformer, the
windbag politician—but in the cramped mind of the
clever lawyer, for whom intellectual dignity and freedom
had been forbidden by the interests which he served; in
the grandeur of the medical specialist's waiting-room and
the impoverishment of science which it masked; in the
educated clergyman turned evangelist and vying with
the mountebanks of Methodism; alike in the silk hat of
the labor leader and the homely and hollow plain-spoken-
ness of the self-made industrial boss; and even in the
universities, with their presidents held in subjection by
millionaire trustees, with their middle-class timidity about
raising, in class or conversation, the real political, moral
or aesthetic problems implied by the conditions of the
time; even in the best of the theater, where incompetence
and indifference almost invariably betrayed the beauty of
the noblest text; even in literature, where an ignorant
criticism was ready to declare every apprentice a master;
in that whole machine of interrelated interests, which
kept literature, theater, learning, church, medicine, poli-

tics and law, all fixed in their mediocre functions, all constrained by the fear of their neighbors, all intent on their bank accounts—all that appalling susceptibility to regimentation by "business" and that incapacity for discipline of self, all that voracity for physical comfort, all that pervading commonness of mind, which, even in those sections of society from which Hugo's father had come and which had at least produced a few men like him, now debased their distinction to luxury and made cowards of their leaders. It was, perhaps, after all, hardly necessary to find special explanations for Hugo's fear of committing himself, of giving hostages to any group—which moved beside him like Pascal's abyss. It was, perhaps, after all, not unnatural that there should come a moment, in every company, when Hugo would want to snatch his hat, to say good-bye and get away.

II

WE WORKED IN SILENCE, dismantling the walls and packing Rita's belongings.

Rita herself had left us: someone had knocked at the door, and she had gone into the front room. We had heard her receive a male caller and carry on a rapid decisive conversation. And she had now been away so long that, deprived of her peremptory commands and made uneasy by the presence of the visitor, we no longer spoke to one another. Duff Burdan, the young man whom at Ray Coleman's I had taken for a baseball player but who had turned out to be a painter, was laboring over Rita's suitcase, in the broken strap of which, with a great air of masculine effectiveness, he was gouging extra holes with a nail-file. The young Jew was taking down the pictures and wrapping them carefully in newspapers. We had only rarely seen him at Rita's and had not expected to see him today. He was very quiet, polite and well-dressed, and we resented as complacency his modest amiability. But Duff Burdan and I were also resenting each other.

And in the stillness which had ensued on hammering down the last boards of a packing-case, I heard the moaning of boat whistles from the harbor, and my heart

horribly sank. So we had used to hear them in summer
—their sobbing, remote and melodious—in the late afternoon shadow; or at night, when the rumorous hum of
summer came in through the open windows; their trom-
bone and oboe notes. So one night she had imagined
Stokowski conducting a symphony of river noises from
the top of the Singer Building.

I stood up and tried not to hear them—tried to level on
the objects about me a prosaic disenchanted gaze, as if
by force of will I could insulate them and, impervious to
the aromatic smell of perfume and cigarettes—the odor
of Rita's hair—so put myself out of reach of that current
which had charged them with feeling and which still
gave them the power to shock me. They were meager
and battered it was true; the damaged electric heater;
the day-bed, with the strip of batik above it; the
sewing machine; the potted cactus; the water-color of an
Indian corn dance, with its delicate red-and-black figures
distinct against egg-shell white (it had been sent her, like
the cactus, I never failed to remember, by an unforgotten
admirer who had gone for his health to New Mexico and
who was always on the point of coming back); the purple
abstract painting of an eggplant taking shape amid a
maelstrom of female membranes (which had been given
her by another admirer about whom I had always wondered, but whose identity she had never revealed); the
bookcase, with its rubbed and broken volumes, so fan-
tastically miscellaneous, in which one could read, as in
geological strata, the so various interests and tastes of the
men whom Rita had known.

I looked away, and my eyes involuntarily sought the
half-open door to the sitting-room. There I could see
them standing at last by the door which led out to the
staircase. Rita was half turned away, but I had a brief
glimpse of the face of her companion: he was a thin, un-

distinguished and dingy-eyed young man, very commonly dressed. I saw him take some bills from Rita and put them away in his pocket.

When she came back, she gave a sharp look around. "Where's my little Buddha?" she demanded. I told her I had packed it in the box. "Well, you just get it right out again! I didn't want it packed! It will be smashed to bits!" I assured her I had packed it carefully. "No: it'll be broken in that box, just as sure as sure! I think I'll take it with me—I'll carry it myself."

"I'll carry it over separately, when the other things go, if you want me to," Duff Burdan volunteered. "Will you promise not to break it? No, I think I'd better take it myself." "What do you think I am—a smasher of images?" She laughed on her precise little notes: "You promise not to let it get broken?—promise! If I come back and find that Buddha broken, I'll never speak to you again! Oh, don't pack that Indian corn dance with the other pictures!" she interrupted young Kaufmann. "I do want to take that with me! Can you get it in the suitcase, Duff—or couldn't you strap it some way on the outside?"

Duff Burdan dealt with this problem. "Everything here is to go, is it?" he asked, looking around. "Yes, everything," she replied. "Are you sure you'll have room for it all?" "Sure: I'm throwing out a whole lot of my own junk." "It's so sweet of you to offer to keep it for me! Don't let anybody borrow my books!" she admonished him, the moment after.

I looked at my watch and announced that it was time to get a taxi. Duff Burdan was storing her furniture, but I was to see her off.

Those stairs which I had climbed so many times to find, at the top, her little figure, intense and sharp even in the doorway and dark against the light of the door, so that it seemed sometimes like a knife on which I was running—those stairs where too often lately I had felt that, in answering the doorbell, she had been hoping for someone else. As I descended them this afternoon, it was not without relief at the thought that I should never have to climb them after today.

And was that he, that sloppily-dressed reporter, that fellow from some insurance office, to whom Rita had been giving money—was that the visitor she had been always expecting, whom she would rather have seen than myself? I was glad of a new reason for disgust, of a new pretext for hating those stairs—and yet that hatred, as I knew, was only fear, the fear of remembering how much I had loved them. And such bitterness was ignoble, I knew—for houses were things to put away, like worn-out clothes, with the phases of our life, with the emotions with which life was clothed. And was not emotion here worn out?— on my side as well as on Rita's—had I not come myself to dislike the cold house, the sordid staircase, the saloon with its hanging blinds, the oppressive tunnel of the El, the bleak stony waste of the docks, where late one night I had walked so leadenly, not finding Rita at home? Had I not said to myself that afternoon, on my way to Rita's house for the last time: "Well, thank God, I'll never have to come back to this damned address again! I'll be out of prison at last!"

And now I could see that the winter sun was bright on a colored cigarette poster, and that the schoolgirls returning from school were prettier than any schoolgirls had seemed to me for many months. I compared one of them with Rita, to the advantage of the schoolgirl—Rita had lately been looking rather badly. I should be free to love another girl now! I thought of Daisy, whom I had seen the night before and who had seemed to me unexpectedly desirable. If I could only keep up my spirit—if I could only play the game according to the sportsman's

code which Rita had been trying to teach me so gravely
and so sweetly—if I could only, I told myself, do that,
then in the long run, all might be right between us—because I had not nagged her or wearied her, because I had
proved myself her peer, as prompt to offer all for love and
as brave to bear its passing. If I could only remember that
the days were not bricks to be laid row on row, to be built
into a solid house, where one might dwell in safety and
peace, but only food for the fires of the heart, the fires
which keep the poet alive as the citizen never lives, but
which burn all the roofs of security! Be glad, be proud, to
end so well—before that music of the harbor—I could hear it
now again, as I came back to Rita's with the taxi—before
that music had lost its beauty—for so one could hear it
for ever!

When I returned to the apartment, I found that a new
visitor had arrived to say good-bye to Rita. It was a young
man from Columbus, Ohio, whom I remembered having
met with her one evening when we had gone to the theater. He was one of those curious Westerners who dress
like Westerners, but who speak like Philadelphians. The
night Rita had recognized him at the theater, she had
seemed disquietingly glad to see him, and my first instinct
had been to identify him as the admirer in Santa Fe who
had sent her the corn dance and the cactus, and of whose
arrival I had lived in dread. When he had turned out not
to be this person, I had been exceedingly relieved, and as
Rita had never afterwards mentioned him, I had forgotten
him completely. Now, however, his presence seemed ominous: it was evident that Rita had been seeing him. I remembered that, when we had met him at the theater, he
had said that he was soon going West, and that, I calcu-
lated now, had been at least a month ago. It had, it
seemed to me, been just about a month that things had
been going badly between Rita and me.

She was hurried but gay with the partings—I thought that she had become more good-natured since the arrival of the new admirer. Just before she got into the taxi, she kissed everybody good-bye. The Westerner, with unctuous heartiness, was all for seeing her off, but she explained that this was my prerogative—and she kissed him a second time. I felt suddenly that it was an impudence for Rita to have divided with such scrupulous fairness, between Duff Burdan and me, the honor of seeing her off and the honor of storing her furniture. Yes, I remembered now, she had certainly got out of an engagement with me very soon after that night at the theater when we had happened to run into the Ohian.

I saw, as I helped her into the taxi, that she was carrying the little potted cactus, to which I had taken an intense dislike: it had a stubby and prickled stalk, and it had with time come to wear to my eyes a significance all too plainly phallic.

In the taxi, I at first said nothing: we had both become, together, so tense. But when we had turned into Seventh Avenue, I looked at her and smiled and said, "Well!" She puckered her eyes and mouth in one of her ecstatic grins and spasmodically threw back her head in the movement which had once made me feel that she was lifting me into her ecstasy, but which now seemed to draw her away from me: "Oh, it's so *wonderful* to be going away where I won't have to see any more people!"

Yes, she had left me already—long ago. She would not let me come with her to that world. I must return to the common world—and what should I do there now? Those qualities of desperate independence and of intellectual passion which had once exalted me so, could only make me now terribly glum!

She had decided overnight to leave New York. One of her aunts, who still lived in the little upstate town where

Rita had been born, had lately fallen ill, and Rita's mother, with whom Rita shared her rooms, had gone to stay with her sister. One evening, when I came to get Rita to take her out to the opera, I had found her, not even dressed for dinner, but sitting among packets of old letters spread out around her on the day-bed passionately preoccupied with the idea of returning to her native place, taking care of her invalid aunt and consecrating herself in solitude to the writing of a play in verse. To my annoyance, I saw she had been crying. And at the *Rosenkavalier* she had relapsed into that punctual responsiveness, with its effect of polite deliberate effort, which I had noted in her the night I had met her first, but which she had dropped when I had got to know her better. She had intimated, on the way home in the taxi, that she considered the *Rosenkavalier* a little cheap. And I had expected her to like it so much!

I had hoped then that her intention to leave New York, which I had applauded with insincerity, would evaporate like any other of those suddenly excited desires—to go to the Coast, to go to Paris, to return to the stage—which she would as suddenly forget; and I was dismayed when I found that she persisted in it. She had sat down and written half a dozen stories for a popular magazine, and had got an advance from the editor (who was also wildly in love with her), on the strength of a promise of further stories. She had then paid her arrears of rent and had persuaded the Italian landlord to allow her to break her lease.

I had made to Rita's sigh of relief, in the taxi on our way to the station, some appropriately sympathetic reply. I saw now that we were already at the Waldorf, where, with the traffic cutting across us, we stopped.

I looked toward her and saw that her face, with her old fur collar close about her neck, was pale and demoralized and ill, pinched and staring. For the first time since that night in Bank Street, when her cheeks had flushed a hot pink and, leaning back against my couch, she had revealed her long Muse's throat, her face seemed sharp-featured and tarnished. And though I knew well enough, even then, that, if all I had once so adored in that face—passion, intelligence, daring—seemed now to have disappeared, it was strained nerves and hard living which had killed them—her poverty which had put her at the mercy of all that importunate pack—myself among them—who had been forever ringing her doorbell, and all that alien life of the city which had taxed her almost to dementia (the crosstown traffic stopped; our own commenced to move: she had told me once that traffic terrified her)—though all my conscious feelings were of horror that someone I so honored should be injured, that I should ever come to find unlovely a being I had once so loved; yet that savagery of the human animal which makes us fall upon our wounded fellows, especially those whom we have feared, impelled me to say cuttingly and abruptly: "You have no faith!"

"What do you mean—religious faith?" she asked, as if she had been talking to a stranger—but I cut her short with, "No: the other kind—good faith, I mean!"

"You know very well," she replied, suddenly speaking to me directly, "you know very well that I know what sort of person I am—but if I wasn't that sort of person, I shouldn't be the sort of person who would do what I did with you. . . . I was cruel to other people then."

"Yes," I said, "I know—but when I see some of the people you care about, you can't blame me if I take it a little hard!"

"What do you mean?" she demanded.

"I was thinking of this afternoon."

"Duff Burdan and Max Kaufman are both nice boys

—I thought you liked them. And I'm not in love with either of them, if that's what you mean!"

"I wasn't thinking about them—I think they're all right."

"I hadn't seen Max Kaufmann for months," she went on. "He came around to see me just because he heard that I was going away. It was nice of him to come."

"Who was that fellow who needed a shave?"

"Who do you mean?" Her wonder made me angry. "You don't mean my brother?" she added, after a moment.

"Was that your brother?" I pretended to be amused by my own jealous suspicions. I had forgotten she had a brother, though she had told me about him once.

"Yes," she answered. "My brother came in this afternoon."

"What does your brother do?" I inquired.

"He drinks," she said bitterly, without humor.

As I remembered the visitor's face, dim-eyed and devoid of personality, I could see now in it Rita's sharp nose and her eyes of indefinite color. And my first feeling was one of relief that the shabby nonentity I had seen, to whom Rita had given money, was merely Rita's brother. But the discovery, as I found in a moment, had the effect of increasing my resentment: if my worst suspicions had been justified, I could at least, to that extent, have despised her, could even perhaps have washed my hands of her. But now I knew that if it was not the unknown visitor, as unconsciously I must have hoped, with whom Rita had lately been preoccupied, it must have been the young man from Columbus, who was obviously attractive and eligible.

"At least," I brought out after a pause, "this big-hearted guy from the West isn't a relation of yours?"

She was silent. Then she began, with her effect of dramatic sincerity which I had come to resent and dread:

"It's so false of you to nag me and scold me like this. You ought to understand how I feel! You ought to be able to see what I've been going through. If you really loved me, you wouldn't want to say hateful things to me! But I don't care now—I don't care about any of you!"

"I know: I do understand," I replied. "I hope that you get a lot of work done." But I wanted to say, "That's nonsense, and disingenuous besides, to say that my being jealous means that I don't love you enough. And then you accuse me of being 'false'!"

I stared out at the motorcars and taxis which were mounting the enormous driveway of the viaduct that girds the Grand Central. They had still, I found, the power to stir in me, like those taxis I had heard from the window the night I had first met Rita, the excitement and hope of the city. They were urgent and expectant now, crowding uptown along their private gallery, to dinners in apartments and hotels, where romances and adventures were beginning, where people were drinking cocktails and becoming amusing and gay (as I had not been able to be for so long)—to parties, to night-clubs, to plays, to the theatrical iridescent Forties, which I had never really explored and where I knew that Daisy was living.

"Did you know Daisy had left Ray Coleman and gone back to the stage?" I asked.

"No," said Rita. I could see that her hands were quivering with tenseness.

"I think it's probably a darn good thing, don't you?" By approving of Daisy's vagaries, I perhaps hoped to make reparation for my harshness about her own.

"Yes," she answered, "I suppose it is."

"I like her so much," I continued. "I saw her at Sue Borglum's last night. She has a wonderful sort of good-natured frankness. I really think, in fact, that she's one of the girls I know that I like best."

I hoped, no doubt, to make Rita believe that I had been happy the night before without her. She had told me—what seemed to me improbable—that she wanted to be left alone, that it always made her nervous to have people around while she was packing. I tried to fix my mind on Daisy as I had seen her at Sue Borglum's party: with bare arms in a girlish black evening gown, with her candid American smile and her continual spark of wisecracks. And it occurred to me now in the taxi that, as soon as I had seen Rita off—I had never hitherto been able to think beyond that event—I should be free to cultivate Daisy. I could go straight to her place on Forty-fourth Street—I could ask her to dinner tonight! And this realization sustained me.

We had been silent, but now Rita began again: "It's so *false* of you to talk to me like that! You used to understand things so well! You know that the first time I met you, you said that Ray Coleman was bitter because he hated his newspaper work, and that that had made him harsh with Daisy. Well, don't you think that *my* life makes me bitter? Don't you think *I* hate the way I've been living?"

"I know: I'm sorry," I replied, and I took her hand and pressed it without tenderness or warmth.

We had stopped at the station door. I gave Rita's suitcase to a porter.

"Don't you want him to carry that?" I asked, nodding towards the cactus.

"Oh, no!" she guarded it, grinning. "I wouldn't trust it to anybody—I'm afraid that something might happen to it!"

All the rest was mechanical—when we kissed good-bye, most of all. I sat down in the train for a moment, and told her how exciting I thought it was for her to go away alone and write: I hoped that she would accomplish a great deal. "You must produce a masterpiece," I said. "Let me see it when it's done, won't you?"

I plunged out into the hurrying concourse and made straight for the door to Forty-fourth Street.

On my way—as I was passing a newsstand—at the sight of a bright red magazine cover, I found myself shocked by that terrible current of which the furniture and pictures of Twelfth Street, of which everything connected with Rita, had been for so long such active conductors. It was the second-rate fiction magazine for which Rita had written the stories that had enabled her to leave New York. She had never been willing to sign them—I remembered that now—though they were really not at all discreditable: she was incapable of writing badly. But as she had never taken them seriously, as she had written them merely to make money, she had hated them and had signed them with a pseudonym, though she could have gotten a far better price for them by publishing them over her own name.

I turned suddenly back toward the train, as if I could still have redeemed our farewell from the memory of my bitterness and spite—but the man was taking down the sign.

*   *   *

The news of her aunt's illness had deeply affected Rita; and though I was skeptical and suspicious at the time, I see now that it had really preoccupied her to the exclusion of everything else. Aunt Sarah, who was always called "Aunt Sadie," had been the artistic member of the family; and Rita had originally been named for her. But when Rita had first come to New York, and had acted for a short time on the stage, she had substituted "Rita" for her real name, and she had never afterwards been able to bring herself to be known as Sarah again. Her first poems had been published over her stage name. And now she tortured herself with the fear that this might have hurt Aunt Sadie's feelings. With her passionate concentration, she had talked to me of that extraordinary little woman with the birdlike nose and neck, and the square enormous brow, which Rita had inherited.

Aunt Sadie had, in her youth, been the organist in the church and the gay getter-up of church "sociables"; she had wanted to go to Paris to study music, and she had almost succeeded in this. but the men of Aunt Sadie's family—like Rita's brother—had not made life easy for the women: some drank; some had broken down; some had simply disappeared. When she had found she could not go to Paris, Aunt Sadie had moved to Watertown and taught music; but a last brother, who kept the general store in the little town where she had lived, had been disabled by a stroke, and Aunt Sadie had had to take care of him and help with the store, for which she presently found herself assuming the whole responsibility. But as she had always been hopelessly perplexed by the problems of supply and demand, she was gradually deprived of her trade by a newer and more modern store, which had a soda fountain with tables. Now, in one of their terrible winters, she had come down with a bad case of pleurisy, and, even after recovering from it, was no longer able to work at all.

And Rita, brooding now on the slow extinction of Aunt Sadie's personality, tragically reproached herself for having suppressed Aunt Sadie's name. She talked to me about Aunt Sadie till I could see the chipped and yellow keys of her little upright piano, and the elegantly engrossed scrolleries of the old-fashioned black and white music covers, more clearly than the objects in the room in which we were, and could hear those other scrolleries, both elegant and noble, of the voices of the fugue, interweaving a watermark of beauty in the air of the cramped little parlor above the general store. Aunt Sadie had taught Rita to play; and Rita still remembered some fragments of Handel and Bach, which sometimes tumbled out without warning when she found herself beside a piano, all rumpled, as it were, but still fresh, from the disordered wardrobe of her mind. These gusts of music surprised me at first: they were so spontaneous, light-hearted and lovely—so different from the sometimes tight, and nearly always sober, style of her poetry; and I have since thought that they were perhaps all I ever knew of Rita as she had been in her girlhood.

For Rita, too, had spent long years in the little upcountry town; had sung in the church choir and known all the hymns by heart; had studied French from the book, where there was no one to teach her to speak it, and had read Baudelaire and Rimbaud when she could not pronounce their names correctly. And before she had gone to college on the scholarship she had won by fierce solitary effort, she had almost, she told me, abandoned the hope of ever sloughing off that life of the small American town, which she had seemed to put on every morning, like some cursed indestructible dress of girlhood, too worn and too soiled and too small.

Yet, I never heard Rita speak with resentment of her early environment: it was herself, and not the place or its people, which, in telling of her youth, she had made me see. When Sinclair Lewis wrote his famous novel, in its different way so intense, he made one feel that the American small town had rendered the whole of our life unpalatable, had flavored it with a rank flat taste, like some minute organism which spoils the drinking water. But my impression of the town from which Rita had come was made up merely of those moments in Rita's life which she had told me of passing there and which seemed to me, like everything else about her, to have taken place in a world where there was nothing common. She had described to me once, for example, how, lying awake at night, she had heard some drunkard, returning from the town, singing clearly in the empty country road, dark and clear under the autumn moon:

"I wooed her in the summertime
    And in the winter, too;
And all night long I held her in my arms,
    Just to shield her from the foggy foggy dew!"

Today, when I can sort out the drunkard, the song which everyone knows, the little New York state town, the girl who wants to get away—though I summon all the drunkards, all the bawdy songs, all the discontented girls, all the towns, that I have ever known—I can see nothing but that moment of Rita's girlhood, of her girlhood too long detained, which seemed to hang half clear black and half turbid crystal, in the radiant-dark country night, like a drop of foggy dew—I see all through the eyes of the poet, to whom our social history is invisible.

I made differences between New York and Paris; between New Orleans and New York. I had wondered, at Ray Coleman's party, whether McIlvaine were a Scotchman or a Jew; I had insisted on finding out from Hugo in what city Daisy was born. And though I did not, like Hugo, compute incomes nor peg out the people I encountered in the economic web, I marked degrees of education and tried to identify accents. I had noted, in this way, in Rita, the Irish fickle-mindedness and sharpness; the signs of the superior person in the small provincial community; of the original and bold personality in the community of college girls, who had, however, learned the language of the rest—that savorless language of young

segregated women to whom older unmarried women
preach the loftier feminine ideals; the intonations of the
American actress of English light comedy; and, finally,
dominating all, her role of princess and rake of the Village. But it made no difference how she talked, where she
had been, what she wore, where she lived, what boors
she caught up in her life, what threadbare images she
used—the being who filled my mind had little relation to all this. I had first learned from Rita that the importance, the significance, of what we see, is supplied by
the mind which perceives them—that the power which
creates, through imagination and passion, never stops to
appraise the value of the materials with which it works,
but itself assigns them value.

And just as, despite the fact that Aunt Sadie presented
herself as an obstacle to my happiness, that I was by no
means, at the time of which I write, in a mood to share
Rita's anguish for the muted and dying vibrations of that
tight-strung steel-silver soul—so she had forced me, against
my taste and interest, to accept all her friends and admirers at the value she put upon them herself. These
friends, when I came to meet them, almost always impressed me at first as quite unlike what I had heard
about them from Rita—as insipid, ineffective or under-
bred. And I used at first to find my jealousy allayed at
discovering that Rita's swans were geese—though I
suppose that I still felt, in the case of the Greenwich
Villagers proper, a sort of jealousy at their having partici-
pated with Rita in the braver exploits of an earlier day—
a day that I myself had come too late for. I had the
sense that even the worst of Rita's friends had at least
"fired one ringing shot and passed." But young journalists cheapened by their work; pottering young writers,
like myself; debauched or epicene young poets, with
neither genius nor self-respect; mediocre middle-aged

literary men, with bald heads and stale reputations; and all that odd mixed company of lawyers, contractors and brokers—I was obliged to grant even to these each his gift or his special distinction—and, even then, I could never be sure how far they were distinctions or gifts which Rita herself had lent them. So constant and so acute was her need to intensify experience that, just as she would cherish the timbre of certain boat-whistles which she heard from her apartment in Twelfth Street, just as she would sometimes keep for days a tangerine or an apple which she had bought at the grocer's on the corner, but of which, when she had brought it home, she had become fascinated by the shape or the color—so she had the faculty of endowing her admirers with qualities which they themselves may hardly have hoped to possess. With Rita, the vagabond poet would prove to have an interesting temperament; the journalist, an honest conviction; the obsolete editor or essayist, something of the grace of a man of the world; and those bewitched business men and brokers who so furiously pursued her seemed to have caught from Rita's own imagination some disturbing conception of themselves which they were straining to realize—she told me once how a man who had seen her on but a single occasion and whom she had afterwards succeeded in evading had recognized her again, after years, merely from hearing her voice over the telephone, when he had by mistake been connected with a wire on which Rita was talking to someone else.

But it was not merely that Rita disregarded all those social and moral considerations which occupy so large a place in the minds of ordinary people. It was not merely that she was free from prejudices; but that character itself, in the sense in which it may amuse us, stimulate our curiosity or appear to us picturesque, did not interest her. She was not at all the sort of woman who enjoys collecting types or celebrities; gossip did not entertain her; she had little taste for novels. In her own stories and plays, there were no characters, but merely situations and emotions. And so, not seeing at all in her friends what most of them saw in each other, she made it possible for them, in their relation to her, to play roles for which the world would never have cast them. It was as if, in their contacts with Rita, they had become somehow facets of herself, as if their desires had been given body by Rita's imagination and their vitality doubled by her force. They had become aspects of her own personality; and so wear for me even today—the middle-western journalist with the Abraham Lincoln voice, the snow and quiet of the diamond winter night when she had spoken to me, after he had left, of the purity and peace of his spirit of which she suggested that the longings were yet so poignant; the international vagabond, the muffled vagueness of the August dusk when we had carried him part way up Fifth Avenue in the victoria in which we were riding, and she had afterwards, in Central Park, among the dark walls and asphalt windings, where the lovers embraced mute on their benches, sung some Spanish songs he had taught her; and the man in New Mexico, alas! the sweet pathos of the short days she had known him, of which she told me with her brief telling eloquence on the very afternoon in Bank Street when I had counted on finding eloquence myself in order to persuade her to marry me; and the bare two days and a half she had spent with that tubercular landscape painter whom she had loved, she said, the best of all!

I myself had good cause to be grateful: when I had read to Rita my indifferent poems, she would afterwards take them from me and go through them intently herself, reading aloud some line that pleased her, so that it

sounded, brought to life by her voice, a good deal better than it actually was; and, at the time, I would never
remember that she had also a knack of reading certain
poems by Coventry Patmore and Arthur Hugh Clough,
poets whom I detested, so that they sounded as if she
had written them herself.—Even during our last conversation when I had scolded and complained in the taxi,
she had appealed to a generosity for which I was by
no means remarkable by reminding me of those excuses,
perfunctory and largely hypocritical, which I had made
long ago for Ray Coleman.

In any case, we swarmed to her apartment, devoured
her time and her force, and finally, at the period of which
I write, had rendered her life intolerable. I had told her
once of something that Hugo had said of literary people
together, as one saw them in New York or Paris—that
they were like the leeches in a druggist's jar: dependent
for nourishment on blood, but reduced to the desperate
necessity of preying on one another. "Yes," said Rita.
"And I'm the druggist when he puts his hand in the jar!"

So I had learned in half a year from Rita that from
another point of view than Hugo's, the world may present
quite different values and give rise to quite different
problems. But I had learned something else from Rita,
which it had cost me more pain to learn. When I had
taken her to task in the taxi, reproaching her for lack of
"faith," she had forced me to confront a principle which,
since I had known her, had haunted and tormented me,
but which I had hitherto tried to evade; and even she,
who must have lived with it so long, was reluctant to
confess it to me: she had pretended for a moment to mistake what I meant. As Hugo had learned from his weeks
in the prison camp that men who are beaten become bru-
talized and that men without food starve; so I had had to

learn from Rita that any great strength or excellence of character must be, by its very nature, incompatible with qualities of other kinds—that it carries with it weaknesses and ignominies inseparable from excellence and strength. I should, I dare say, like everyone else, always have been willing to admit both these truths; they would, in fact, have seemed to me platitudes. But I had to come to both through experience and once I had felt their reality, it had seemed to me that all our social and moral conventions had been based on the opposite assumptions—that a person who had had either revelation—either Rita's revelation or Hugo's—and who uncompromisingly met life on that basis, must, like Hugo or Rita, be a rebel, and, in consequence, an enemy of society.

For Rita, who exalted every impulse and made every relation dramatic, neither happiness nor drama could endure. I taunted her once, in those later days, with Wilde's saying that, *"He who lives more lives than one, more deaths than one must die."* But it was not deaths of the body that she suffered: it was the deaths of all those human relations—it was her rejection, day after day and year after year, of all the natural bonds and understandings which make up the greater part of human life—comfort, security, children, the protection and devotion of a husband, even simple comradeship and affection—so that she was still, at the time of which I write, an outlaw living from hand to mouth, always poor and often ill, bedeviled day and night by all the persons she no longer had the energy to excite to her own pitch of incandescence. And even at the time I had taunted her in the cab, it was my consciousness of this strength that had continued to keep me in subjection. For I knew now, in spite of all my pain, in spite of all my complaints and indignation, that if we are moved to admire what is admirable, we must also maintain the courage, and must not rage against—nor even try to minimize—that which makes it possible and mars it.

*   *   *

Outside the light had grown cold; but the white and orange power of the lamps was beginning to dominate the town. The day seemed hardly now to have been serious: it was withdrawing, by arrangement with the city, which had so much to do at night. The taxis on Vanderbilt Avenue were wedging, honking and hitching, in their efforts to turn and to pass; but I dodged energetically through them and headed west.

If I could only find Daisy home! If only she were free tonight! I had refrained from telephoning on purpose: I wanted so desperately to see her, even if she were going out.

I could still feel the thrill of Fifth Avenue—I scarcely glanced a second time at a face which looked a little like Rita's. And that fascinating region of the Forties, where lately I had gone so rarely—I found that I could still peer with interest at the photographs in front of the theaters and at the faces of the passing women, who seemed sometimes, with their theatrical make-up, as miraculously, ideally pretty as the women one saw on the stage.

The apartment house where Daisy lived was narrow and very plain: there was merely a bare hall, with a telephone man, who also opened the door and ran the elevator.

He took me up to her floor, and I knocked at her room, but no one answered; then, as the door had been left half-open, I went inside. The lights had also been left on, and the chairs and the floor were littered with a debris of stockings and chemises, as surprisingly slight and as sordid as the shreds of exploded balloons. On the table stood an empty spaghetti can, two plates gummed with cold tomato sauce, an empty gin bottle and several tumblers with the stale remains of drinks. It seemed to me, from the contents of the tumblers, that they had begun by drinking gin and ginger ale, fallen back on gin and water, and probably ended up with raw gin.

It would be hours now, no doubt, before her rehearsal was over. I had come far too early, had better go away and come back. I looked about the room, and then searched in my pockets for paper to write her a note, but could find nothing except a letter from a distinguished professor of philosophy whom I had greatly admired at college and to whom I had sent a book of Rita's poems. He had written me, thanking me for the poems and inviting me to come to see him. I had thrown the envelope away, but my respect for the professor had been so strong that I had never destroyed his letter though my preoccupation with Rita had prevented my answering it.

But now, as I could find nothing else—finally reflecting that colleges, after all, were places where poets were put to sleep—tore off part of the back page of the letter, just below the signature, and sitting down in a mission morris chair, I wrote a note to Daisy.

When I had finished the note, however, I turned over the pages of the magazine—it was a movie magazine called *Photo-Life*—which I had picked up to back the paper. Suddenly becalmed in that abandoned apartment, high aloft on that inaccessible floor, with the elevator between me and the street, I found that I had dropped into a pocket of inertia and lassitude. When I had exhausted *Photo-Life*, I looked carefully, with the same serious interest, through *Zit's Weekly*, the *Cosmopolitan* and a tabloid of two days before. Then, with the magazines in my lap, I sat blank and incapable of rising. I apprehended the onset of despair. What motive had I for moving? I could no longer go to see Rita, and was there anyone else in New York whom I really desired to see? It was as if the emptiness of Daisy's room had represented the emptiness of the world in which I had been left by Rita's departure. I had not slept much for several nights, and I felt that my joints were heavy. The telephone rang: I did not answer it.

There was a phonograph beside me on the table: it was a small cheap portable one. I regarded it with hebetude. Without Daisy, it seemed as depressing as the glasses, as the garments, as the magazines. But involuntarily grasping at a last resource against despair, I picked up the heap of phonograph records, lying half-shuffled, like a battered pack of cards. Scrupulously I pushed them even and ran through them, reading all the titles: *With You in Paradise,* from *Pretty Kitty,* sung by Bee Brewster; *Ben Bolt,* by John McCormack; *Chanson Hindoue,* Saxophone Solo; *So's Your Old Man,* Fox Trot, by Fred Casey and His Burglar-Alarm Boys; *La Forza del Destino,* Red Seal, Duet by Caruso and Scotti; *Mamie Rose,* Fox Trot, by Jake King and His Eight Kentucky Mocking Birds. I remembered that *Mamie Rose* was the fox-trot which Daisy had so offended by playing, the night of Ray Coleman's party, when Rita had been reciting her poems. I got up and put it on the machine.

The record, I noted, as I wound the crank, had been made by the American Melody Company. It was a pale and unpleasant brown and seemed to have been molded in river mud. Remembering the handsome victrola which I had seen at Ray Coleman's apartment, I pitied Daisy a little; yet she had had the right sort of bravery, the bravery to go free when love had passed! The only needles I could find were buried in an ash-tray under cigarette butts and burnt matches, and it was impossible to tell the used from the new. The first I tried began with a blurt, a hideous stuttering blur. Still dominated by Rita's tastes, I felt that turning on the phonograph would be like drilling with a dental engine: Rita had not cared for popular music—had thought lightly of even the *Rosenkavalier!*

The second needle turned out no better, but I let it go; and presently *Mamie Rose* emerged as a kind of fiendish jig, running itself off at impossible speed: too fast, too nasal, too shrill. I made an effort to regulate it and only effected a harrowing descent of pitch, like the gasping and discordant howl of some demon inside the machine crying out in intolerable agony at being compressed from one tempo to another. I listened for the first night I had met Daisy, but merely succeeded in having my heart wrung by the first night I had heard Rita's poems. The spring of the little phonograph held only for a single winding, so that the record began too fast and was already running down before it came to the end; but, what was worse, it had no horn, so that the demon inside the box, beating in its cramped black prison like a panic-stricken bat, had to squeeze out, as it were, through a crack—the little aperture at the base of the "arm." No wonder it chittered and squealed so thinly, like an unwinding wire of sound, like a wire, rusted, wry and eaten, worn away so that it seemed almost snapping, or so rough that it would stick and stammer over some echolaliac phrase! So completely had the music been robbed of resonance that it seemed a mere memorandum of music, as if some writer in sound had scribbled down the skeleton of an orchestration, with the brasses brief tin-whistle blasts and raspings, the strings a jotted jingle of cicada chirpings, and the tympani scored as tiny explosions and echoless crashes of glass. And the "vocal refrain," when it suddenly began, had as little in common with the human voice as the noises of the instruments had with music: it gave the effect of some mere momentary modulation in the quick mechanical jigging of a railroad train—it was simply a sharper shrillness, a more insistent iteration: *There she goes—Mamie Rose—She—loves—me!—Don't seem to show it!—How do I know it?—It's A.B.C.!—She's—* a crackle of high-pitched syllables ending with *aggravatin'—But when I want a little lovin' she don't keep me waitin'!—She's proud and snooty—But she's my cutie!—She tells me—* a second slip of dulled and driven cogs—*That's how I knows—Mamie Rose!—She—loves—me!* The jazz departed, with redoubled violence and complexities of deformation, into a last frantic charivari—then, after a brief unpleasing flourish, was bitten off as abruptly as it had begun.

I lifted the needle, clicked the little catch and went over to the window. Outside gaped a blank abyss: several buildings had just been demolished and the vacuum of vacancy they had left seemed to be sucking with its blind raw walls for some structure to rush in and fill it. I felt again the horrible imminence of despair, and I tried to summon against that blank outlook and against the mechanical voice of the phonograph—those negations of flesh and blood—an intensified vision of Daisy: her alert little yellow head, with its deep staining of Irish rust, her lips still moist through carnation rouge, and the robust little organism of her body, which made its home among those stone and metal cells, not merely resilient to their surface, but making their grindings quicken and feed it.—Then a sudden voice said, "Hello!" and with a start I turned round and saw her.

I asked her to come to dinner with me. She had on a dark blue street dress, and she looked tired. I had been imagining her animated and hearty, but it seemed to me now that she was frail: her eyes, a lighter green than Rita's, looked colorless and dim.—"Why—I'd like to," she demurred, "but I've got a sort of a date."

The telephone rang again and she answered it. I heard her begging off with her little-girl-like "Well, I don't think I will—I'm so tired—I just got back from rehearsal—I think I'll go to bed—well, I don't think I will —you go—well, I don't want to—all right, see you tomorrow!"

And I felt not merely flattered, but also reassured, to find that Daisy seemed to think it natural to set aside her previous engagements in favor of those higher obligations —of which I had learned the importance from Rita—of following one's own inclination.

"I'm glad you came," she exclaimed. "I didn't want to go to that party and if you hadn't come, I would have gone." "Where was it?" I asked. "At Myra Busch's." "Are her parties any fun?" She shook her head contemptuously: "No: she just has a lot of twirps.—I can't stand 'em!"

"How cute you sounded talking over the telephone!" "Yes: strong men weep!" "No, really: you're awfully cute!" "You don't mean it really, do you? It's a panic, isn't it?" "No: I do mean it! You sounded cute." (Now that I had to renew my assurances, I began to feel insincere—I had so long praised no one but Rita, and had praised her with such passionate conviction, that I found now that it cost me an effort to compliment anyone else.) "Ray Coleman used to say that I had the world's worst voice on the telephone—he said I sounded like some awful whining cash-girl." Another proof of Ray's stupidity! I could see what he meant, but there was about Daisy's speech something finely chiseled like her features, so that I had scarcely been aware of her voice; and my resentment at Ray's stupid taste imparted to my compliments a new fervor.

"Shall I go out and get a drink?" I suggested. "That would be fine!" said Daisy, brightening, and with the humorous consciousness of brightening, that irony of the city I so liked in her. "As the English actor said, when the girl said, 'How about twenty-five dollars?'—'That would be a godsend!'—I'll be getting dressed while you're gone."

When I came back she was still in the bathroom, and called out to me: "You might pass me a drink in here, if you don't mind." I poured the dregs out of one of the glasses and handed in some gin and ginger ale: her little naked arm, reaching out from behind the door, had the prettiness of a child's. "Now, you turn on the phonograph," she called to me, "so you won't hear me use the what-not!" I started *Mamie Rose* again and poured out a drink for myself: the music seemed almost gay, and when the record had come to an end, I put on another record.

When she came out, she had a rosier color and looked extremely clean: she was dressed in a light blue dress, with a blue scarf dappled with white, and wore straw-colored stockings. "How nice you look in your blond clothes!" I told her. "Oh, this is just an old rag!" she squeaked in a burlesque hen's voice. "Well," I insisted, "you look sweet!" "I probably look like the Collapse of Western Civilization!" she replied—but with a particularly charming smile.

She turned off the phonograph, which had been gibbering like an imbecile over a single unintelligible phrase. "That phonograph's a delight, isn't it?" she said. "I took it with me when I left Ray, because it was one of the only things I had left that had belonged to me before I lived withum. Phil gave it to me on our honeymoon. Some of those records are Ray's, though, I guess." I remembered Rita's bookcase.

"Phil was your first husband, was he?" "Yes: he's my ex," she said. She went on, after a moment: "Did you think I was really married to Ray?" "Yes," I said, "I did." "I guess a good many people really did. But we weren't. It was a lucky thing, too; if I'd marriedum, it would have been harder to leavum." "Did you have a pretty trying time?" I asked. "He wouldn't let me do anything or go any place. If I went out with anybody else, he'd burn up one of my dresses—he was great on burning things up—I used to tellum that if he'd lived a little longer ago, he'd have been burning witches. He'd say that he didn't buy me clothes to have me go out with other men. And then when I did stay home withum, I'd just have to listen to-um read to me out of the *Oxford Book of English Verse.*—Finally, one night I got reckless and stayed out for two days with Pete Bird"—(Pete Bird was the little man with whom I had seen her talking at Ray Coleman's and in whose company I had found her the night before)—"and when I came back, he wouldn't let me in, so there was nothing to do but go looping again —I was plastered for a week. Finally Gus Dunbar offered to let me stay here—it was awfully decent ofum and he just did it out of friendliness. He helped me get a job, too. I understand that Myra Busch is telling it around the Village that I'm having a love-affair with Gus—but that's just absurd—he's my oldest friend in New York: I knew him back in Pittsburgh. He's just my yes-man. He lets me sleep in the bed and he sleeps on the couch. And besides, he's sick!—He's gone out of town and I'm going to get a good rest. Oh, how I'm going to rest!"

We continued the conversation in a chop house, with red-and-white checked tablecloths and the smell of a butcher shop, where very large sour pickles were served with every order.

"What sort of a fellow is Pete Bird?" I asked. "Isn't he more or less of a twirp?" "Well," she said, "he did pretty well the other night: he spent about a hundred and thirty dollars." Even allowing for the tremendous prestige which always attaches in New York to the spending of large sums of money, I felt that she was evading my question, but I did not pursue the matter further: I seemed to divine that Pete Bird was the man with whom she had broken her engagement to go to Myra Busch's that night.

I asked Daisy how she had ever happened to run away with Ray. "I mettum in the Ritz Bar in Paris," she explained. "Phil and I didn't care anything about each other, by that time—Phil was in love with a French girl. I didn't resent his having affairs with other women, but he used to give her my clothes. Besides, I didn't want to have people saying: 'That poor little Mrs. Meissner, sitting around crying her eyes out, while her husband goes with other women!' Besides, Phil and I had just been thrown out of our hotel. Phil had a lot of money when I marriedum, but we spent it all. Ray came along and he seemed to be pretty affluent at that time, and I was so tired of not paying any bills. I will say about Phil, though, that he did everything with a grand air. Ray would get worried if a bill ran for as much as a week—whereas Phil never thought of paying a bill, even if he had the money. It was funny: when you were with Phil, you felt that you were swell, even though you didn't have a cent—but when you were with Ray, even though everything was paid for and all the bell boys and everybody tipped, you felt you were only trying to be swell."

I asked what Phil did. "He was a photographer," she replied. "Not an ordinary photographer, but one of those super-photographers. He only took a picture about once every two months—he'd charge a hundred and fifty dollars for a sitting. At least that's what he did when he did anything. He had money—at least, he did till his family wouldn't givum any more—so he didn't really have to do anything. He composed songs, too. But what he really worked hardest at was getting up practical jokes. He'd spend hours sending out invitations to all the worst bums in Paris, asking them to come to dinner at the house of one of the social leaders of the American colony." "What happened?" I asked. "Well, they all showed up—all the dope fiends and dead-beats, and all the old drunken bozos that hang around the bars—all the most undesirable Americans in Paris—and Mrs. Tilford was furious and almost gottum arrested. Then another time, when he had to have lunch with some friends of his family's from Pittsburgh, he put camphorated oil on the seats of all their chairs— well, camphorated oil makes you feel as if you were freezing—so they all had to sit there at the table with their fannies freezing and not knowing what was the trouble."

I laughed. "Well, that sort of thing," she explained, "can get to be pretty tiresome, if you live with it all the time. And I was his wife, so I felt partly responsible. When some guest almost broke his back on a chair that flattened out when you sat on it, I'd feel pretty humiliated. And then he'd work his gags on me. One day he left a note for me, saying that he'd committed suicide. And I suppose he thought it was a joke when he took half my clothes away and told me he was sending them to the devastated regions, and then gave 'em to-uz little French twirp!"

We had ordered ginger ale, and had had some more gin: "You really look marvelous in blue!" I said. She knocked herself under the chin: "That sets me all up," she said, meeting my gaze without blinking. Then she dropped her eyes and added: "Phil really had a lot of charm, though."

"What shall we do after dinner?" I asked. "Take me to the movies!" she said, smiling. "I've had a yen to see some movies all day. I want to do something restful.—Take me to some picture that's funny.—I'm so glad you came to-night! I've been beginning to feel like a twirp. If I keep on getting plastered, I'll lose my job.—It's so long since I've been alone or had any place where I could go and be by myself. It seems to me I haven't done anything for weeks but sit around and be funny for people I didn't really care about.—Gee, I don't know what to do! When I begin to get paid, I can live on what I make. But I've been afraid to sober up, because then I'd have to face the future." (She always gave to all her clichés—"facing the future," etc.—a special ironic emphasis.) "I can't think of anybody I care about—I haven't even got a girl friend any more: all the ones that I had are off me now because Ray wouldn't let me have 'em around. So I haven't even got anybody to laugh about things with.—Business of twisting handkerchief.—Let's go, before I have you in tears!"

We had a reckless taxi-driver; but to me, strong now with accelerations of gin and with my normal masculine self-assurance, which Rita had done so much to demoral-ize, now gratifyingly reinforced by Daisy's feminine con-fession of helplessness and distress—I had the illusion at that moment that I occupied a position of unchallengeable supremacy—it seemed that it had now become possible for our taxi, at its exhilarating giddy speed, to plunge through every opposition, to make every obstruction give way. I marked with intensest vision the objects which we seemed to ride down: a Railway Express truck; a woman who was walking a German police dog; other scuttling and inferior taxis. Rita, when driving in taxis, had always been nervous about El posts; but, as we ripped our way through the traffic, Daisy merely remarked: "Madcap Joe, the Demon Driver!"—and as we erupted into Broadway: "You better stop him or he'll drive into the lobby!"

I thought scornfully of Duff Burdan, who had been

barking so long on Rita's doorstep, and who, for the privilege of storing Rita's furniture, for the certainty of seeing her again, had been willing to clutter up his studio.

In the darkened moving-picture house, we found the newsreel passing before us like a gray inconsecutive dream, and its images, as I watched them, seemed to swell with the significance of dreams. A buxom and good-looking Sixteen-Year-Old Girl winning a Florida yacht-race in a bathing suit to the blaring triumphant pace of a red-white-and-blue Sousa march. "She's cute," whispered Daisy, "isn't she?" Yes: there was the real native American poetry!—my spirit flashed again at the thought of it —it had the daring and excitement of a poem!—and such a spirit, which abandoned itself to the water and the wind, to the speed of the flying yacht, would she not give herself also to love under the soft nights of Southern waters! Mayor Hylan—*East Side, West Side*—making a speech in New York: the flat-faced official visage, the senseless savorless words of the American public figure— while the bravest spoke with words of fire or slashed with white sails and tanned arms the deep blue of Florida seas!—free America that flew above those drones, that never paused for a thought of Mayor Hylan and his imbecile servile speeches. In our eagerness, our taut attention, stimulated more by the drinks than the film, Daisy and I were sitting forward and our arms were pressing each other. An airplane wafted by a waltz—I had missed the title, my mind ablaze with the beauty of poetry and sportsmanship—below, the city, flat as a map, a plane shifted, not haphazardly, but with some underlying harmony and balance, to a jerky succession of angles.—Laddy Boy's Rival, a husky brought to Washington, to the gallop of some lolloping dog music, by one of Harding's Secret Service Men—I whispered, "I believe that that husky would make good presidential timber!" I glanced aside at Daisy and saw her profile pale and clear as porcelain in the pale light from the film, in which her pert little nose and chin showed a fineness and purity of outline —an outline prolonged by the frail little hand which, with the finger-tips lifted to the chin, received also, along fingers and wrist, a pale porcelain border of light.—Members of the Municipal Council at Baka, Japan, to the tune of *We're Gentlemen of Japan,* visit the city's reservoir; they jump in and catch carp with their hands: "I should think it would be bad enough," whispered Daisy, "to have to drink the carp, without drinking the municipal councilors," and I so threw myself forward in laughing at this that Daisy became self-conscious about the pressure of our arms on the seat, and drew a little away.—A slow-motion diving picture of champion women swimmers— they turned along the sweet lengthened rhythms of *All Alone with the Telephone,* curving wonderfully through the air in molded recumbent postures and sending up, when they had slipped into the water, a slowly condensing cloud of spray—how Rita would have loved those slow parabolas, stripped clean of the flashiness of speed, as tight-strung as the curve of a bow—she would have exclaimed of the cloud of spray, "It's like some lovely sort of punctuation—as if you could punctuate a statue with some solid effect of light!"—The Prince of Wales—*It's a Long Way to Tipperary*—joking with a paralyzed soldier —I wondered whether Rita would find the Prince of Wales attractive, then reflected that, on the contrary, she would probably be just perverse enough to prefer the paralyzed soldier—it occurred to me now to consider that I was becoming too much preoccupied with Rita and not paying enough attention to Daisy, so I moved my arm back against hers.—Joe LeBlanc, Head of the New Central Ticket Office, playing tennis to the jigging tune of *Tea for Two and Two for Tea,* to decide who shall pay the religious expenses of one hundred Jewish children to aid the Jewish Education Association Drive—"I bet the other man loses, don't you?" Daisy remarked. I wondered whether perhaps, after all, I hadn't been unfair to Max Kaufman—whether, perhaps, what I had taken for complacency hadn't been, after all, merely modesty—I had a pang as I was pricked by the feeling that I had behaved rather badly with Rita in the taxi.—Bishop Manning, to the *Pilgrim's Chorus,* receiving an emblematic pastoral staff, a huge encrusted crozier, from the Chaplain of the House of Commons—Daisy and I thought that Bishop Manning had the look of a priggish baby being handed an enormous rattle: I put my hand gently over Daisy's which lay beneath it friendly and cool.—A Chimpanzee Chauffeur: roguish monkey music: *Yes, We Have No Bananas;* but I had fallen to reflecting that, like some hero of a medieval legend—the *Pilgrim's Chorus* and the pastoral staff had made me see myself in that image—I had, for a dreamlike space escaping human measure, been shut away with Venus under the hill, or, like Oisin, with some goddess of fairyland—that I had been gone from the world of men, and only now, still blinking from the Venusberg, still with the music of fairyland in my ears, still knowing how the ache for the ideal may torture us like the ache for a drug of which we have been deprived, beheld with bewildered relief the vision of Senator Oscar W. Underwood, who—to the rousing music of *Dixie*—was making a speech at a Monster Barbecue in Montgomery, Alabama—and found myself almost safe again in that folksy familiar American world, heterogeneous and absurd, which had ceased for so long to seem real to me, of which I had never for so long been aware save to repudiate it with scorn and impatience.—The Oldest Human Remains, a Skeleton of the Stone Age Discovered in an Oyster Bed: black bones embedded in oysters:

dull somber chords—Rita could have done something with this—something bitter about the fatuity of the twentieth-century traveler who was pointing at the bones with his stick—or better—what I could never have done: it was I who would have made easy capital out of the traveler with the spectacles and the stick!—something simple, troubling and hard about the bare black bones themselves.

And the smoothly revolving globe, supported by a kneeling goddess and scrolling out suddenly and rapidly —as if in the burst of an exciting revelation—the title of the comedy that followed—affected me, in a drop equally sudden, as idiotic and insupportable. Now that I had been brooding on those blackened bones, I had become impatient with everything again—and I crushed my way across to the aisle, over overcoats, seats and knees. I got some wax-paper cups from the smoking-room, and Daisy and I, in the half-darkness, had a drink of water and gin. The paper cups leaked, and we had to get it down at a draught.

On the screen, a dough-faced comedian with goggling horn-rimmed glasses was enlisting in a fire-brigade.—An alarm!—he is the first to respond—he rushes headlong for the fire-house pole, slides down it headfirst and remains at the bottom stunned—the firemen who follow fall over him and pile up like a football scrimmage. We laughed at this. On the way to the fire, the long hook-and-ladder truck, whisking briskly around a corner with impossible nimbleness, caused Daisy to laugh so violently that I thought again, as I had done on the night when I had heard about her motorcycle honeymoon, of that American sense of motor traffic which we had developed to such an extraordinary degree—and which was now further played upon, in the film, when the hero, in horn-rimmed innocence, allowed his hook-and-ladder attachment to swing around at right-angles to the truck, so that it swept the boulevard like a scythe, mowing the tops off

all the Fords, and never failing at every disaster to make
Daisy laugh with delight.—On the scene of the burning
building, the hero was contending with the hose, which
enmeshed him like a boa-constrictor. The owner of the
building appeared, a pompous and imposing dignitary, in
a frock-coat and silk hat. "Oh, I hope he turns the hose
on his hat, don't you?" whispered Daisy. And in a moment, just as the dignitary was denouncing the clumsiness
of the hero, an unexpected leak in the hose cleanly
squirted off the silk hat, which landed on an organ-
grinder's monkey and gave rise to a fantastic chase.

Such was our wild exhilaration over this that I reflected
as the chase began to flag, how, only half a year ago, if I
had gone to the same film with Hugo, I should, in laughing at the ruin of the hat, have been moved by something more than the impulse, the mischievous impulse of
a child, which I shared tonight with Daisy. I should have
laughed with both savagery and zeal. I should, like Hugo,
have taken the silk hat as a symbol; I should have made
of its destruction an issue. And now at last I became
aware how completely my point of view had changed
since I had fallen in love with Rita and ceased to see
much of Hugo. Had I not myself, only a few days before,
taken out my own silk hat to go with Rita to the *Rosenkavalier*? I knew now that I no longer cared to imitate
the intransigence of Hugo in these matters, his rejection of all the amenities of that civilized life of which he
was himself the product; his fixed belief that society was
divided into two mutually hostile classes, a proletariat and
a bourgeoisie; his unquestioning acceptance of the catchwords of the social revolution, and his hostile and suspicious unwillingness to arrive at a human understanding
with people who lived by different catchwords—all this
seemed to me tonight the product of a superficial point
of view, or, almost, of an arrested development. For Rita,

despite the revolt against conventions which all her life implied, despite her long association with radicals, had had really but little interest in politics: her revolt was a revolt of the individual—and I had discovered to my surprise, when I had come to discuss with her the personalities of the Village, her complete lack of interest in, and, in some cases, her positive contempt for, certain of the radical leaders who most generally commanded admiration; and that, in spite of the atmosphere in which she lived, it was actually possible to strike fire from her mind by reactionary or conventional views, if they were delivered with the right ring of bravery. And I had myself now, oblivious of the film, taken to meditating so exaltedly on the vanity of people's opinions compared to the deeper realities of character, the insignificance of politics compared to clairvoyance and passion, that I began to laugh only belatedly when I had already become aware that Daisy was roaring over one of the captions. The hero with the horn-rimmed spectacles had just been bitten by a small bull-terrier he had picked it up and bitten back— the caption read, "See how you like it yourself!"

"Oh, I'm so glad you took me!" said Daisy. "I think it's swell! I just wanted to see something funny!" I slipped my hand over hers again with sympathetic affection, and watched the rest of the comedy, leaning toward her and paying closer attention. We followed the picture together, with a lively interchange of comment.

"Well, I suppose you want to go to bed," I said to Daisy as we walked out into Broadway. I suggested that we might stop at a restaurant and finish up the gin. "No," she said, "I'm too tired for a restaurant.—Why don't you come up to my place and we can drink it up there?— 'Should she ask him in?' If he's got anything to drink: Yes!"

When we reached the room, the telephone was ringing. Daisy answered it, speaking with some vehemence: "No: I don't want to come—I'm tired, I've gone to bed— well, I went out to get something to eat.—No, I *don't want* to come!"

She lay down upon the bed, propping her head on the pillow and crossing her feet: she was wearing lizard-skin shoes, light brown and very small, but quite different-looking, I reflected, from any shoes that Rita wore: Rita's feet, like everything about her, seemed to manage to be attractive in a curious personal way quite apart from current fashions of prettiness, whereas Daisy's feet were pretty in an almost perfect ideal way, like the small feet of the girls with slim ankles in the drawings in magazines.

"Well," yawned Daisy, "this is where Mother takes a long refreshing rest!" I handed her her gin and gingerale and sat down beside her, drinking mine. "But I'm afraid I'm not going to be able to," she added, after a moment. "That's why I want to drink."

"What's the matter?" I asked. "Are you worried?" "No," she replied. "I've just got the heeby-jeebies!" "What's the matter?" "I think everybody's a twirp!" "Are you in love?" "No: that's the trouble." "You ought to be glad you're not," I said. "You have been, haven't you?" she asked. "Yes." "You still are, aren't you?" "No." I answered— "not any more." She was trying to kick off her shoes without unbuttoning the straps, and I undid them and lifted them off. "Thanks," she said. "As soon as I lie down, I'm dead!"

I held her firm little insteps for a moment in my hands: in pale stockings, her tired and sweaty feet were like two little moist cream cheeses encased in covers of cloth. Her body, which seemed now so slight in its pale blue dress, lay as limp as a lettuce leaf soaked by the summer rain.

"No," I said. "You oughtn't to be sorry if you're not in love." "I know: that's what I keep saying to myself when

I think what damn fools people make of themselves. But
sometimes you feel the old aching in the armpits—and it's
not just because you want to sleep with somebody either.
—You know the real reason why I asked you to come up
here? It was because I knew it would give me the willies
to come back alone. As soon as I get alone, everything
seems so empty—I begin to get panicky. Of course, it's
just the heeby-jeebies, though—after I've had a good
night's sleep, I'll be all right again."

A deep tenderness of sympathy seemed to flush my very
mind, and I almost felt she must feel its warmth as it
brimmed from my soul and bathed her. I put one arm
about her shoulders and with the other hand covered her
breast—it was low and lapsed a little—Rita, for all her
small head, her small hands and feet, had had the bosom
of some divine being—and from Ray Coleman's gesture
at the party, when he had put his arms about Daisy, and
from McIlvaine's plump little Venus, I had been imagining Daisy's breasts as little firm globes. I kissed her on
the neck—which was round and short and had no sculp-
tural contours like Rita's—and she kissed me back on the
cheek. It was like the kiss of a little girl, some cousin or
playmate from next door, whom, at ten, one decides to
marry, and the relief of that human kiss, that embrace of
simple comradeship, soothed the strain with which my
spirit, with which my body itself, had ached.

I stretched myself beside her. If I had ever had any
idea—playing the part I had learned from Rita—of making love to Daisy that night, I knew now that it had
never been real, I could not now even conceive it—it was
so long since I had heard the boats as they moaned from
the harbor in Twelfth Street, and the thought of them
no longer moved me, yet to try to love another woman
on the day one had parted from Rita! . . . And there began to take music in my weary, in my half-drunken mind

the falling rhythm of a poem, the beginning of a sonnet of which, the night before in my wakefulness, I had with obstinacy fixed in their target the accurate shafts of the end. It took the form of an answer to Daisy, and I found now that what had then been unbearable, because written of myself for myself, now that I could write from the point of departure of another's fate than mine, now that I could dramatize my fate for another—dignifying, or rather creating, for another person's mind—another's mind which I merely imagined, since Daisy, it seemed, hated poetry—a romance which should somehow console me for the wreck and defilement of romance—now I could bear to return to the poem, and to the pain which had stamped its images, putting another between them and me—"*Ah, never sigh for love, for love is death!*" . . .

She was asleep—I could hear her breath: it seemed so slight to supply the fuel for that warm body I felt against my arm, that engine of activity and desire. I turned off the electric light, covered Daisy over with a blanket, and lay down myself on the couch—and with the silence of the mind, love was still.

III

III

I HAD MADE A DINNER ENGAGEMENT with Daisy for the next evening but one after the night when I had taken her to the movies; but the sudden death of one of my aunts, who had for many years lived with my mother, prevented my keeping it. I was obliged to go down to the country, and for several weeks I commuted between my mother's house and my work. Sustained by the vision of Rita renouncing the vanities of passion and dedicated in solitude to her tragic play, I applied myself to reading Sophocles, who at college had rather bored me, but of whom I had so often heard it said that he saw life steadily and saw it whole that I wondered whether, in my present situation, I might not perhaps benefit by his wisdom. Rather, however, than risk a first evening alone in my Bank Street apartment, where for so long I had seen no one but Rita, I had asked Daisy to have dinner with me the night of my return to town.

After dropping my suitcase in the darkened sitting-room, with its drawn blinds and its frigid radiator, I felt for a moment, with a shudder, the shock of that current of emotion which I had hoped had been forever disconnected when Rita had moved out of Twelfth Street, but which I now found that my own possessions, themselves saturated with Rita, had also the power of conducting. At the sight of the couch, the Leonardo (which Rita had admired), the Pernod peach brandy bottle on the little marble mantelpiece (I had kept it there ever since the night when Rita had spoken of the label)—my heart sank as it had done in Twelfth Street the day when I had heard the boat-whistles. But I resolutely thought of Daisy —and as gaily as I had ever done, it seemed to me, I took my bath, changed my clothes, picked out an appropriate tie. I threw away the peach-brandy bottle, which the last time I had looked at it on the mantel on the occasion of a ghastly scene with Rita, I had had a violent impulse to smash as an outlet for my exacerbated passion. The bottle fell into the wastebasket with a thud which astounded and routed my nerves. I was throwing in, as if to cover and conceal it, all the circulars which had accumulated during my absence when, on the tightened silence of the room, the telephone suddenly blazed.

It was somebody speaking for Daisy; I was to meet her now, not at Gus Dunbar's, but somewhere else—I couldn't make out where: the voice—it was a man's—kept instructing me just to walk right in and ask for Mr. Somebody's —he was at once so indistinct and so admirably polite that I concluded he must be drunk. I asked if I could speak to Daisy, and her voice was presently heard through the receiver—she seemed far away, facetious and vague. I tried to find out whether the place I was to go to were a speakeasy or a private apartment—but she only answered, "Yes," and laughed, and then insisted that I should walk right in and go right up to Somebody-or-other's. I begged her to spell out the name—and she began with loud-vibrating emphasis: "M for mother—I for 'ighball—C for seasick—K for—Oh, you know K!—L for laryngitis"—she began to laugh again, evidently at some suggestion from somebody else in the room. I tried to check up on the letters which I had already heard, but she broke in: "Just put them all together and they spell love!"—then, with no relation to my further questions: "Yes, 'Mick'—just ask for Mick! All right!—hurry up! Good-bye!" She hung the receiver up. I had, however, got the address.

The taxi carried me far, too far—beyond Lexington Avenue—along East Thirty-fourth Street. The neighborhood seemed to me sordid. I had hoped to find Daisy all clean from her bath and with her lovely candid smile, as on the night when I had taken her to the movies. I had looked forward to watching her in the light of the little pink table lamp, over the white cloth and yellow wine of a brisk and bright French restaurant.

We drew up at a narrow entrance which the driver located with difficulty between a manufacturer of nasal syphons and a merchant of rebuilt typewriters. It was the meagerest pretence of a doorway: a layer of livid imitation marble, a length of blue-and-white rubber tiles. I looked above the bells in vain for a name which began with Mick; but then, in spite of the grimy little frames, there were not even any cards. I rang one of the nameless bells—but it awakened no responsive click, and I rang another.

A man was coming out of the hallway, and I asked him whether he knew of a Mr. Mickle. I looked into dim and evasive eyes. I was appalled to see that he had no chin, that his nose was an almost elephantine proboscis and that his ears stood out from his head like those of an elephant listening; he wore an old shabby overcoat and a curious gray felt hat, which tended to be conical; his hands were non-prehensile, and trembled. He shook his head without a word, in answer to my question—and passed on like an apparition. I thought: He must live alone!—he must have lived alone for so long that he is numb and can no longer feel loneliness, can no longer feel even irritation at strangers who are looking for friends and who hurriedly break in on his solitude. And I resented such an existence, solitary, uncouth and dismal, resigned to drop out of the world, hoping only to be noticed by no one; and I was repelled by his strange trunk-like snout: my own nose, I feared, was rather bulbous, and, as I mounted the narrow staircase, it seemed to me more bulbous yet.

The stairs turned above the typewriter shop, and I was confronted by the cramped and crowded doors of cheap dentists and real estate offices. I explored the corridor, and found another staircase, and climbed to another and darker hall, where there were no longer, as below, any names painted on the doors. That was evidently where people lived. It was as if the occupants had made their homes in the chinks left by petty business; they seemed as narrowly confined, as discouragingly inaccessible, as the inhabitants of a jail—and they lacked even that common bond, that limited intercommunication; each had stowed himself dumbly away at the bottom of his little slot, in oblivion of the others; each asked only to be let alone at the end of the herded day—behind the locked and anonymous door, presenting a blank to all the rest, as they presented blanks to him.

At random, I rang a bell—and, as if in confutation of my vision of benumbed and sullen recluses, after shuffling precipitate noises within, the door was suddenly flung open and there appeared a lady with bright dyed red hair and a lacy dowdy dressing-gown who, at the barest suggestion of a name which began with M-i-c-k, seemed transported by enthusiasm. Yes: they lived just across the hall—just opposite her own apartment. "Yes: they're just in now," she ran on, slopping over with friendly helpfulness and with a simpering ladylike smile. "If you'd come a little later, I don't think you'd have found them home, because they most always go out to dinner about seven o'clock!" She eagerly crossed the hall in her voluminous *négligé* and rang the bell herself. I thanked her, but she did not withdraw. She waited, repeating herself and beaming. I thought her a little insane—from loneliness, I supposed.

Someone was hastening from the depths within. Then Pete Bird opened the door and confronted me with a goggling stare. The red-haired woman still lingered in the hall as if she hoped for a little general conversation, but Pete Bird merely asked me in, and shut the door behind us.

We passed through a little dark hallway and emerged into a narrow sitting-room. I saw Daisy in a morris chair with her legs dangling over one arm and her back against the other. She greeted me with an odd unsmiling gaze. And, still charmed by the memory of her paleness when she had lain along the bed like a moonbeam the night that I had taken her to the movies, I was horrified to find her now with touzled muddy hair and a sallow puffy visage, in which the nose was an ignoble little knob, blobbed in candle wax, and the eyes were two protruding gooseberries, scored about with discolored skin. She was wearing a greenish-blackish plaid. I took her hand: it was a cold little claw.

I remarked that she looked quite different, that having her hair done differently had transformed her. I saw now that the ragged effect had originally been intentional. She said: "Yes, and I suppose you're going to tell me that it looks terrible, too." "You look like a French whore!" said Pete. "Well, you know what you look like?" said Daisy. "You look like some kind of a goblin that's been drowned at the bottom of a well!" And it was true: with his gargoyle gaze, his haggard greenish cheeks, the deep furrows in his forehead and the ape-like lines to his wide mouth, he had an aspect half immature and half prematurely old, at once aghast and disaffected. There seemed to have occurred, since I had talked to them on the telephone, some abysmal lapse of hilarity. Yet Pete Bird's double-breasted jacket, his spats, the handkerchief sticking out of his pocket, and the collar of his blue shirt fastened together by a small gold pin, gave to his appearance and to the whole situation an odd indestructible note of urbanity.

In that atmosphere clouded by drunkenness, I glanced instinctively about for a drink, and saw nothing but empty bottles and debris of the enormous thick crusts of delicatessen sandwiches, with the oiled paper in which they had been wrapped. "There's nothing to drink," declared Daisy with what I thought was a note of asperity. "What *is* this place?" I asked. "Listen to-um!" said Daisy indignantly. "He expects us to tend bar for-um!"

"No," I explained, "I just meant, who lives here?" "It belongs to Larry Mickler," she replied, as if she had already, over the telephone, made all this quite clear enough. "Mr. and Mrs. Lawrence Mickler," said Pete, with the invincible gentlemanly instinct to be informative and agreeable from his grave at the bottom of the well.

I inquired where the host and hostess were. "Well," said Pete, as if his own extinction, though powerless to impair his politeness, had rendered him uncannily detached toward the catastrophic fates of others, "Mr. Mickler's in the bathroom, probably unconscious, and Mrs. Mickler's in the bedroom, sore as a crab." "I insulted the hostess," said Daisy. "Well, anyway," concluded Pete, "that leaves the drawing-room to us!"

The "drawing-room," like everything else in that place, cooped one up and made one uncomfortable. I saw, at the other end, a contracted fireplace, like a large square-cornered rat-hole, with above it, on the shallow mantel-piece, a plaster cast of the Winged Victory; and between two narrow windows, which looked down on the Thirty-fourth Street car tracks, a book case containing, I noted, volumes of D. H. Lawrence, Cabell, Dunsany, and Shaw; George Moore's *Memoirs of My Dead Life*; Freud's *Interpretation of Dreams*; Frank Harris's *Oscar Wilde*; several volumes of Levy's *Nietzsche* and a whole shelf's array of Dostoevsky.

"Come on," exclaimed Daisy abruptly, swinging out of the morris chair. "Let's get out of here right away!" I asked her where she wanted to dine, in the hope that we might now be able to effect a separation from Pete. "I don't want any dinner!" she replied, as if nothing could have seemed more revolting. "I've just had some sandwiches. What I want is a dirty big drink!"

"I'd better say good-bye to Larry," suggested Pete Bird. "I wouldn't say good-bye to-um," said Daisy, "after the way he acted with us."

Pete went into the little corridor and knocked on the bathroom door. "We had a fight," Daisy explained. "We would have left before, if we hadn't been waiting for you. Larry sent Pete to the delicatessen's to get some sandwiches for supper and gave him a ten-dollar bill—and Pete brought back six sandwiches and Larry didn't think that Pete had given-um back enough change and accused Pete of keeping the money—when they'd actually cost that much!" We could hear the voice of Pete in the bathroom, pleading with the host on a tone of gentlemanly reasonableness. I asked how the *Frolics* were going. "Oh, I got canned!" she replied, sullenly and shortly. "I stayed away from too many rehearsals."

Pete returned with Larry Mickler. He was a young man with dingy skin, a round head and a small dark mustache, very smartly and cockily waxed: he bent forward from the waist when he shook hands with me, and I took an almost immediate dislike to him. He was taller than Pete Bird, but not so tall as I.

Pete was urging Larry Mickler to come out with us, and I seconded him insincerely. "Get Alice out," Pete insisted, "and make her come along, too!" "Oh, she's tired," Larry Mickler perfunctorily assured him—"she doesn't want to come!"

"I'm not out for any looping," said Daisy, with what I thought—with what I hoped—was an intention of discouraging this idea. "I think I'll go home and go to bed." "You're not going home yet, little woman," Pete asserted, with a firm, though humorous, accent of masculine domination. "You're not going home to bed till you've had a little insomnia medicine, a little touch of the magic elixir that causes the lame to see and the tongue-tied to run like rabbits! The old miracle-scattering scamper-juice! Am I right?" he appealed to me.

"Let's go to Tony Scallopino's," suggested Larry Mickler. "Let's not!" said Daisy promptly. "You see," Pete Bird explained, with dignity, irony and ease, "Tony raised a check of mine once and I've never felt quite the same about him since." I proposed Harry Heinz's. "Well, Harry Heinz and I are not quite the best of friends either," Pete casually replied. "In my opinion, a restaurant is a place where the patrons are supposed to drink while the man who runs the place stays sober. When the guests have to take care of the proprietor and put him under the pump, I consider that the time has arrived to seek recreation elsewhere!"

"Let's go to Sue Borglum's!" said Daisy, with a sudden inspiration. "Tonight is Thursday night, and she has a party every Thursday. I saw her the other day and I promised that I'd come.—Oh, I'm so glad I thought of that!" she added, smiling for the first time. "I want to see Sue Borglum!"

"All right: Sue Borglum's it is!" Pete approved, with rollicking decisiveness. "Come: snap into your coats, ladies and gents! Let's be off to some place where there's stimulants!"

I helped Daisy on with her coat, and as I caught a momentary glimpse of her pale watery-yolked poached eyes, it seemed to me—(Rita and I had read some scientific books together: the vision of human futility which she derived from scientific ideas exercised upon her a strong fascination, and threw her back with an exacerbated appetite on the gratification of the moment—and tonight it was these scientific images which rose to my own imagination at the expense of both Sophocles and Rita's poems themselves)—it seemed to me as if the Daisy whose profile had appeared to me in the theater, so fragile, pale and chaste, whom almost with the tenderness of tears I had covered with a blanket in Forty-fourth Street—as if that Daisy had been merely the spray of which I had happened to catch a glimpse for a moment on a wave of common human colloids, the unstable fluids of the body, continually gluing and ungluing—or a cloud which had for a moment taken symmetry from those atoms of carbon and the other things, but which tonight had been blown awry. I turned Daisy's collar down carefully.

Larry Mickler had been getting into his coat, a garish rust-red ulster, and Pete Bird had been helping him on with it. Now Mickler pulled up his collar, which completely covered his ears, and slapped on a rakish felt hat, pulling the brim down over his eyes.

"You know that damn statue annoys me!"—he indicated the Winged Victory: I saw that he was drunk. "Alice's had that goddamn thing ever since we were married: she acquired it at college. It always reminds me of a chicken running around with its head cut off!"

He produced a revolver from his pocket and, almost before we saw it, had fired point-blank at the little plaster statue. It fell from the mantel and lay shattered in chalky fragments and flakes.

"Well," said Mickler, "so much for Nikky! Alice may miss her at first, but I'm sure it'll be a splendid thing for her to have to get along without her.—I feel almost," he added, grinning at us, "as if I'd committed a murder, though! 'Ad Writer Slays Phi Beta Kappa Girl!'—Well, let's go! The neighbors may be coming in to find out who's been shot!"

He turned to me, grinning, and explained, as if in friendly humorous confidence: "No disrespect to the Greeks! I'm a Dionysian myself!—sometimes a Dionysian and sometimes an Apollonian!—it all depends on metabolism!" He began to sing, parodying the popular song:

"Sometimes I'm Dionysian!—Sometimes I'm Apollonian!
 My disposition depends on metabolism!"

Then, finding me a little unresponsive, he changed his tone and addressed me more earnestly: "I just wanted you to know," he insisted, "that I don't mean any disrespect to the Greeks. The Greeks knew what it was all about: they danced with arms and legs—but we lock ourselves up in the bathroom because we're afraid to face life!"

"Say, listen," declared Daisy, "if you're going to go out with us, you've got to leave that thing behind! I can face life without it." "Take it along to protect you!" said Mickler. "Never know who's going to stick you up nowadays!" "Don't be a fool," said Daisy. "I won't, sweetheart," he retorted. "Never you worry about that!"

"I'm going to say good-bye to Alice!" said Daisy, as if with a sudden resurgence of sympathy. She went out into the little hallway and knocked at the bedroom door, but there was no reply. "Oh, she's all right!" insisted Larry Mickler. "She probably thinks I've shot myself—let her enjoy a few minutes' happiness!" Pete and Mickler put their arms around Daisy, propelled her along the little hallway and pushed her out through the apartment door.

Outside, we found the lady in the dressing-gown, who giggled ingratiatingly: "I thought I heard a shot." "I was just shooting a cat," said Larry Mickler. "It was keeping my wife awake!"

I finally, standing in the slush, succeeded in capturing a taxi. It couldn't draw up to the curb, and Daisy got her feet wet. She seemed worried and morose.

"That old hag'll lie awake all night," remarked Larry Mickler, with a chuckle, "thinking that I've killed Alice!" "Well," said Pete, "it will doubtless afford her a great deal of entertainment. I'm sure her life is far too tame!" "Yes," said Mickler, "how they lick their chops in vicarious enjoyment over other people's murders! How all the world loves a murderer!" "It would take more than that," said Daisy, "to make me love you!"

"I hear," said Larry Mickler, changing the subject and evidently attempting to talk more soberly—"I hear that Bobby McIlvaine has given Sue Borglum the air. Is that true?" he inquired of Daisy. "Guess so," said Daisy. "I don't know." "I guess he decided that she'd done all she could for him," Larry Mickler continued, "and that it was time to move farther uptown!" Sue Borglum, who knew everyone more or less, had taken Bobby McIlvaine up soon after the night that I had met them at Ray Coleman's, and had done much to smooth his way among the managers and the dramatists. I remarked that I considered Bobby McIlvaine a very gifted fellow, none the less, and that I admired his designs for Homer. "Yes," said Mickler, "but why not make designs for Wells's *Outline of His-*

tory? Why not try to produce the *World Almanac?*—Bobby McIlvaine's all right on paper, but did you ever see a show that he'd staged that was worth its space in the storehouse? Look at *April Showers,* for instance. Fritz Fishbein, Al Leiper's publicity man, blames Bobby for the show being a flop. It seems that Bobby insisted on putting in a trick ballet, where the chorus had to wear papier mâché bodies. Al Leiper wanted to throw it out at dress rehearsal, because the papier mâché bodies took up too much room behind—they could hardly change the scenery. But Bobby hit on the brilliant idea of sending them downstairs in an elevator—it seems they use elevators in Berlin. The first night, the elevator got stuck just before the second act and they couldn't ring the curtain up—they had to hold it twenty minutes. Finally, Al Leiper sent some stagehands down with great big mallets and zongo! zongo! zongo!—they just smashed in the elevator doors and threw all the papier mâché bodies out in the alley—and then, when that was full, they threw them into Beattie's drugstore. There were all those pop-eyed dummies which Bobby had been working on for God knows how long lying around Beattie's—though I don't suppose you could have told them from the customers!—What a civilization, eh?" he turned again to me. "Bring slavery back, I say—it never should have been abolished! Bring slavery back and make nine-tenths of the people slaves! Then the superior man would be free to live life like it ought to be lived! As it is, the civilized man has got to black the peasant's boots!"

We had come to the end of Fifth Avenue, and Daisy, sliding back the glass panel that opened in the front of the cab, directed the driver to turn to the right.

Among those tangled irregular streets to the west of Washington Square, I caught occasionally, from the taxi, a glimpse, almost eighteenth century, of a lampless black-

windowed street-end where the street urchins, shrieking
in the silence, were stacking up bonfires in the snow—
those lost corners of the old provincial city, where the
traffic of the upper metropolis no longer gnashed iron
teeth, no longer oppressed the pavements with its grindings and its groans—where those soft moans and hoots of
the shipping washed the island from the western shore.
There they had come, those heroes of my youth, the artists and the prophets of the Village, from the American
factories and farms, from the farthest towns and prairies
—there they had found it possible to leave behind them
the constraints and self-consciousness of their homes, the
shame of not making money—there they had lived with
their own imaginations and followed their own thought.
I did not know that, with the coming of a second race,
of which Ray Coleman, without my divining it, had already appeared as one of the forerunners—a mere miscellaneous hiving of New Yorkers like those in any other
part of town, with no leisure and no beliefs—I did not
know that I was soon to see the whole quarter fall a
victim to the landlords and the real estate speculators,
who would raise the rents and wreck the old houses—till
the sooty peeling fronts of the south side of Washington
Square, to whose mysterious studios, when I had first
come to live in the Village, I had so much longed some
day to be admitted, should be replaced by fresh arty pinks
—till the very guardian façades of the north side should
be gutted of their ancient grandeurs and crammed tight
with economized cells—till the very configuration of the
streets should be wiped out, during a few summer months
when I had been out of New York on vacation, by the
obliteration of whole blocks, whole familiar neighbor-
hoods—and till finally the beauty of the Square, the pattern of the park and the arch, the proportions of everything, should be spoiled by the first peaks of a mountain

range of modern apartment houses (with electric refrigerators, uniformed elevator boys and, on the street level, those smartly furnished restaurants in which Hugo was soon to be horrified at finding copies of *Town and Country*), dominating and crushing the Village, so that at last it seemed to survive as a base for those gigantic featureless mounds, swollen, clumsy, blunt, bleaching dismally with sandy yellow walls that sunlight which once, in the autumn, on the old fronts of the northern side, still the masters of their open plaza—when the shadows of the leafless trees seemed to drift across them like clouds—had warmed their roses to red.

Sue Borglum, at any rate, at the time of which I am writing, had rented the whole of a large old house (of which she sublet the top floor and the basement) in one of the oldest obscurest streets, where the children, deserting their bonfire, came clamoring to open our door, and where the lights and sounds of the party seemed incongruously bright and loud amid the darkness and silence around. There were dark double ogival outer doors and, inside them, another pair of doors, with a design in frosted glass of sphinx-heads and vine-leaf scrolleries.

We pulled a bell, and a Jap let us in. Sue Borglum rushed up boisterously to greet us: she seemed high-keyed and overwrought, and embraced Daisy with cries of *"Darling!"* In her blatant green evening gown, with a rhinestone aigrette in her hair and on her fingers a large scarab and some diamonds, she seemed to me uglier than ever. Her cheeks were beginning to hang in jowls, her wide mouth was a grotesque gash of lipstick, and the pouches under her eyes were as distinctly shaded off from her cheeks as if they had been drawn by a caricaturist. Behind her, rose the hubbub of the party: the hallway and the rooms were full of people.

We had started upstairs to put our things away when

Sue Borglum, gesticulating frantically toward a water cooler in the hall near the staircase, shouted after us: "Cocktails!—Cocktails!—That water cooler's full of cocktails.—Yes! Isn't it a grand idea?"

Pete and Daisy came down first, and Sue had already swept them off by the time Larry Mickler and I arrived at the foot of the stairs. We stopped at the water cooler and drew our drinks. Larry Mickler swallowed his at a gulp. "That little bastard, Pete Bird!" he complained. "I gave him ten dollars at my house to get some sandwiches for supper and what do you think he did? He went out and got liverwurst—the cheapest kind there is!—and then had the Christ-Almighty nerve to bring me back four dollars change—six dollars for six sandwiches!" I asked whether he thought that Daisy was pretty fond of Pete. "She hasn't got the capacity for love," he replied, shaking his head with a sneer and turning the spigot for another cocktail. "But they're two of a kind—out for what they can do you for! She's a cold little proposition that calculates every kiss—and he owes money or he's passed bad checks in every joint below Fourteenth Street. It's wonderful how he's able to get away with it even where they're cagy! He's got this soft-spoken wide-eyed way with him. —Well, *he* can have her!"

We moved on to the door of the front room. Sue Borglum's front room was spacious and not without a certain grandeur. I could see, above a marble fireplace, the wide sheet of a gilt-framed mirror, which doubled the high white moldings and the somber maroon wallpaper.—Such a house as I had once imagined for Rita and myself to live in! Ah, I should have asked nothing better of life than to have fitted up such a house, to have passed my days alone with Rita in those high quiet rooms, hidden away among those crooked streets, with poetry and love!— But these fancies now seemed to me naïve, and I was ashamed of ever having had them. I stoically dismissed them from my mind, and could still, I found, feel hope and excitement in the variety and gaiety of the Village, so densely intermingling, so vivaciously chattering about me: the Italian and Russian painters; the intelligent amateur actors; the mad baroness who kept a restaurant; the radical journalists and agitators, who, despite the homely forthright style of their writings, not infrequently turned out, when one met them, engagingly shy young men of a personal charm almost cloying; the pretty Jewesses with thick red lips and glossy black bobbed hair; the austere and handsome woman managers of theaters and magazines, with their dignity of Mother Superiors; and the megalomaniac lunatics whom it was the thing rather to like.

Larry Mickler and I, in the doorway, did not at first encounter anyone we knew. "Well," said Mickler, lifting his cocktail, "here's to the Seven Deadly Sins! May they never perish from the earth!—Let's drink to the memory of Dostoevsky—the only goddam genius," he added, "who ever understood the human soul!" I drank with him to Dostoevsky. "The Seven Deadly Sins!" said Larry Mickler scornfully. "What chance have they got today when everybody wears these horn-rimmed glasses!"

I wondered whether it might not be true that a novelist like Dostoevsky was greater than any lyric poet, even so great a one as Rita—but suppose the play on which Rita was working should turn out to reveal wider gifts?—And, stimulated by my cocktail, I asked myself whether, in spite of everything, I shouldn't go to see her again, when she eventually came back from her aunt's: I had behaved so horribly when we had parted, and we had exchanged no letters since she left.

A man who had been leaning over the back of a couch that faced the marble fireplace moved away and let me see the head and neck of a woman who was sitting on the couch and whose bobbed and coppery hair reminded me of Rita's. What a comfort that it could not be she! Then the woman, turning her head with a staccato bird-like movement, in some gay interchange with the man sitting next to her, revealed her profile and I saw that it was Rita. I could see also that the man was Ray Coleman.

My companion recognized him at the same time: "There's Ray Coleman over there!" he exclaimed. "He's just got a new job on the *Record*!" Larry Mickler made his way across the room. I followed him, and spoke to Rita over the back of the couch, taking care to betray no surprise.

"How long have you been back?" I inquired. "Since last Friday—last Friday night," she replied, as if by frankness and accuracy to fend off my disapproval.

I asked about her aunt. "She's much better," she assured me, smoothing out the creases of her smile and making her eyes, which looked to me now like little hard green pebbles of glass, serious and blank. "The doctor said that she was simply tired out, that all she needed was to rest. My mother is still up there with her.—Do come around and sit down!" I sat down, not beside her on the couch, but on a stool at one side of the fireplace.

"You know, I was thinking about you," she said, "just before I left!" "What made you do that?" I asked. "I went wading in Stony River one day—in the cold, and everything!—and I thought about you then—because you liked the poem, you know!—You know, it was freezing cold: I almost froze my feet off—but somehow I wanted to do it!"

I asked how she'd got on with her play. She dropped her eyes, which had girlishly puckered over her wading in Stony River: "Well, I haven't actually written very much, but I've thought about it a lot. I know just what I *want* to write—I've got it all blocked out, you know!" And sus-

tained by this triumphant phrase, she lifted earnest eyes
to mine.

I said that she looked awfully well—and it was true: she
had already been flushed by the excitement of conversation, and when I spoke to her, she had flushed more
deeply, so that she burned like a little furnace, as she had
done that first night in Bank Street when she and I talked
about poetry. She had brought back from the country a
complexion refreshed from the tarnish of the city, and the
contours of her face had filled out again: again she could
challenge the world from the tower of her lovely throat,
which gave to her little figure a dignity almost extra-hu-
man, like the dignity of a great work of art. "And I *feel* so
well," she replied. "I went tramping and sleighing and
skating! I did all the things that I hadn't done since I was
a little girl! And I tell you, I went wading!—you don't
seem impressed by that, but I assure you it was no tame
experience: the water was so cold that it burned! The snow
is still on the ground up there, two feet deep—the river
banks were all crusted with ice—in some places there were
little fragile translucent ledges of ice that came out over
the water—just like blades of swords made of ice! You
know, I'm going to have a sword that's made of ice in my
play—don't you think that's a wonderful idea?" "I should
think it would break off easily." "Not if it was sharp
enough!" "Perhaps not." "Mine will be!" she held her
own, grinning briefly. "Well, anyway, I went wading
—and it was so *thrilling!* You haven't any idea how beautiful a river is in winter till you get right out in the
middle of it and see the water still alive like quicksilver
in the midst of the dead frozen landscape—running away
between the wicked jagged edges! It's as if the tighter
other things froze, the faster the river ran—like a live
vein in a paralyzed body!"

Her feeling for Stony River, which had once so completely enchanted me, now irritated me profoundly. I could see plainly in imagination some tall young country boy, panting with desire and only too happy to accompany her on her uncomfortable escapade. He would have carried her, of course, over the bad spots—would, in fact, probably have carried her most of the time—he had ended no doubt by chafing her feet.

"It must have been wonderful." I turned away to listen to Ray Coleman. Lina Lemberg, the young Polish girl who had been convicted of murdering her husband, had just been sentenced to death; and Ray was describing with enthusiasm how he had pursued the car which was taking her to Sing Sing, and had succeeded in having her photographed from the taxi. (He had just left the *Telegram-Dispatch* for the city desk of the *Daily Record,* the most important of the new tabloids.) "I see," said Larry Mickler, showing small white even teeth, "that she says she wishes Nicky were back with her." "She's going to get half her wish," said Ray—"She's going to get it fifty-fifty: she's not going to get Nicky back, but she's going to go to join him!" Larry Mickler laughed with loud appreciation. "Well," he remarked, "the murderer has his fun, and he ought to be willing to pay for it! True, he has to pay dearer than most people—but then he has more fun!"

Ray presented Larry Mickler to Rita. He did so with obvious pride—with, it seemed to my jealous eye, something akin to an air of proprietorship. She invited Larry Mickler to sit down, and he took the place on her other side. Ray Coleman inquired affably how Mickler's own work was going. "It's just the same old hick-diddling game!" he replied, leaning forward, his hands clasped between his knees. "We still manage to land the suckers!" I thought that he was ashamed of the advertizing business, and was being contemptuous about it for Rita's benefit. "Our latest masterpiece was putting over Marona—'Makes the Mouth Safe for Teeth!' was a product of our fly-paper factory." "You don't say!" Ray Coleman exclaimed, raising his almost continuous eyebrows, as if this feat commanded respect. "Is that so?" "You know what it's made of, don't you?" "No," admitted Ray Coleman, "what?" "Horse chestnuts! Nothing but horse chestnuts! Just nothing in the world but plain old buckeyes! Can you beat it? A million and a half people every morning, sitting down to a breakfast of buckeyes, with sugar and cream!" "Don't you do anything to them?" asked Ray. "Not a blessed thing!—just chop 'em up. We've struck such terror into the hearts of the boobs by telling them that ordinary food was soft and ruined their teeth, and that in a few more generations the human race would be toothless, that now there are a million and a half people breaking their jaws every morning over horse chestnuts! 'Makes the Mouth Safe for Teeth'—they find it irresistible!"

"Say," said Coleman, humorously, "isn't it about time that the Osage orange got a break?" "You might sell them for their perfume," said Rita. "They have a marvelous smell, you know!" "By Jove, that's a good idea!" said Coleman. "You might have all the women carrying them around!" I doubted whether on ordinary occasions he would have considered this a particularly good idea—it seemed to me all too plain that he had fallen under the spell of Rita and that he thought only of playing up to her. I remembered the night when I had first met them and when Rita had agreed with me that Ray was poisonous. "They'd be a little heavy, I'm afraid, to carry around," said Rita. "And they wouldn't be becoming to many people. I might wear one, though—a very little one —on account of the color of my eyes!"

She was gay, and seemed to me so pleased with herself, so sufficient to herself, so remote from me; and I reflected that, while she had been speaking, I had been aware, for the first time since the earliest days of our acquaintance, of her acquired British accent. Not that she always spoke in this way: she had the accent in which she recited her poems and the accent of the Village gamin —nor did she hesitate to bite down on a hard upcountry *r,* when some special situation—a sundae at the soda fountain or a hammock on a porch—had suggested to her versatile spirit the role of a girl in a small town; but, coming in contact with English actresses during the days when she had been on the stage, her natural disposition toward brittleness and briskness had found their accent a congenial modification, and it was this accent which usually predominated on occasions when she was meeting strangers. Yet how many times since that first night I must have heard her drop into this manner, without ever having been aware of it! And I was sharply forced to take account of the distance between the present and the days when I had first known Rita. Then, I had been in love— and that was what it meant to be in love: so to surround, so to devour, another human being with tenderness, passion, admiration, that their very absurdities and perversities were fused with the rest in the furnace till there was nothing but a white molten glow—till one resented, not merely the hostility, but even the critical detachment of others, because the point of view of a critic was unimaginable from one's own. But that critical detachment, today it was I who exercised it—and at the thought that I could now meet Rita with a mind which had become so cold that I could note her little affectations. I was now filled, not with the relief I had hoped for and in which I had tried to believe, but with a new kind of horror and fear. She had gone, the creature who had summoned my love—or whom my love itself had created, I hardly now knew which—the being who had commanded the allegiance of mind, imagination and desire—and could I never rejoin her again? Was it true that my love had been destroyed? Could I never retrace my way? Could I never get back across that chasm?

"I declare," Larry Mickler was saying, "I don't know where a civilized man can find more hilarious entertainment than in the advertizing game. You'd never believe what the boobs will consume till you actually commence to feed 'em! You can make 'em do anything, buy anything! All you need is a gaudy picture and an idiotic phrase and you can make them do themselves an actual injury! Now, of course, in the case of Marona, for example, horse chestnuts are indigestible—they make the mouth safe for teeth but they ruin the digestion. But that doesn't discourage the suckers for a minute. If they get sick, it would never occur to them to blame it on the Marona, because Marona, according to the ads, has been endorsed by eminent dentists. Nothing was said about stomach specialists. But then I suppose it's a desirable thing to provide the peritonitis surgeons with work—they're usually civilized fellows, the surgeons, and, if they prosper at the expense of the peasantry, that's quite as it ought to be. —You must have a lot of fun yourself"—he addressed himself to Ray Coleman—"in the newspaper game."

"Yes," said Ray. "It's amazing really. You can't lay it on too thick—the more maudlin and preposterous it is, the better they seem to like it. Have you been reading Lina Lemberg's confessions in the *Record*? They're written by Ted Mahony in the office—you know Ted, a big husky Irishman who's always half-stewed. You know that instalment where she tells about the birth of little Annie—well, when he read that aloud in the office just after he'd written it, the other day, he almost broke up the shop!"

I asked Rita where she was living. "Well, I'm not liv-

ing anywhere exactly," she answered. "I've just been visiting around." She lifted her eyes quickly. "I'll let you
know when I'm settled." "You must let me see your play
when it's finished," I said.

"Don't you think it's going to be fine?" Ray Coleman
demanded eagerly. "Have you heard about the idea?" I
assured him that I had. He turned to Larry Mickler:
"She's got the swellest idea. It's about this old woman
who lives in a tower——"

Larry Mickler leaned forward to listen, with a polite
appreciative leer; and Ray Coleman described Rita's play
with an enthusiasm even more emphatic than he had
brought to his previous account of the photographing of
Lina Lemberg. And it seemed to me that Rita herself was
gratified by this enthusiasm.

It had already occurred to me that Coleman must be in
love with Rita: everybody, more or less, was. But now,
with horror, I remembered that, since Daisy had left him,
he must be living alone in his apartment, and that Rita,
when I had asked her where she was staying, had seemed
evasive about her address. I watched Ray Coleman telling
the plot of Rita's play, and Rita herself, following intently
and occasionally prompting or checking up—lifting her
eyes briefly to smile or to put in a quick supplementary
word when Larry Mickler expressed appreciation, and
punctuating the pauses with whiffs at her cigarette.

I felt an urgent need to get away, and, looking up, I
saw Hugo Bamman, standing alone like a heron, just back
of Rita's couch, his head thrust forward, his shoulders
hunched up, his long arms hugged to his sides and his
hands in his trousers pockets, staring out, as I supposed,
half-blindly at the people moving about him.

I got up and went around to speak to him: I was glad
of a pretext for leaving in the middle of Ray Coleman's
recital.

When Hugo turned at my greeting, I was astounded to find his appearance completely transformed. Instead of regarding me at first for a moment with dubious unrecognizing lenses, he fixed upon me a naked gaze of deep-sunken but piercing black eyes. I asked him what had become of his spectacles, and he explained that he had been going to a different oculist, who had discovered a revolutionary method of treating myopic vision. This oculist made his patients go without glasses and had them exercise the muscles of their eyes. Hugo's father, to his dying hour, when he had lain sick in his Adirondack camp, had refused to summon a doctor; and Hugo himself was suspicious of doctors, as of all the respectable professions. But in this case, the doctor was himself a heretic and an outlaw; the fact that his methods had been denounced by all the other oculists was enough to convince Hugo of their value. The immediate effects of the treatment were in appearance certainly remarkable: Hugo had now unsheathed from behind his mild round blinders a darkly burning and eagle-like glance, beneath a steep and sharp-jutting brow which reminded me for the first time of his father's.

And, despite my present scornful point of view toward Hugo's political opinions, despite the fact that it was so many months since I had made any effort to look him up, I had never been so glad to see him. For one thing, without his glasses, he seemed to have become a more interesting person and a person with whom it was easier to communicate; but for another, I found it somehow a relief to be talking again with someone whom I had known before I had come to Greenwich Village. As there was no place to sit down where we were, and as the back room, where we found a large table with a punch bowl and sandwiches, was crowded even more densely, we made our way on through into the kitchen—which, by

one of those freaks of old houses renovated and rented out
for apartments, had been installed in a former hallway
and was thus located between the dining-room and a
bathroom (Sue Borglum had sublet the basement, where
the original kitchen had been), so that, in the absence of
any other hallway, it had become a thoroughfare for people passing back and forth between the two.

In the kitchen, I was surprised to find Pete Bird, who
such a short time before had been displaying so invincible
an *élan,* sitting alone, with his elbow on the sink and his
hand propping up his head, his visage chopfallen and
greenish almost with the mask of death, and his eyelids
as if sealed.

Our entrance did not disturb him, and we perched on
the drawers of a china cupboard on the other side of the
long narrow room. I spoke to Hugo of a school-friend of
ours who had just produced a successful play; and though
Hugo's friendly interest was largely superficial—since he
disapproved on principle both of everything connected
with his schooldays and of everything connected with
Broadway success—I found an unexpected pleasure in returning thus for a moment to that world of our early
years upon which we had both turned our backs, a world
where, for all its limitations, the ordinary contacts of life
had been easier and more agreeable than one usually
found them in New York: that world had been conventional, but a common understanding had at least meant
a mutual confidence. In the Village, I had felt less and
less confidence in the people with whom I came in contact and, what was worse, since my difficulties with Rita,
less confidence in myself. And I found now that—in spite
of Hugo's stern rejection of everything he had been
taught in his youth—I was aware tonight mainly of his
decency, his good manners, his cultivated intelligence. He
had been the first of the boys I had known at school who

had really interested me, and he had remained almost the
only one.

I remembered now how, once in our school days,
Hugo's father had come to see him and had sat down
on the bed and talked. I had heard something about
Mr. Bamman and, although Hugo rarely spoke of him,
I had always been conscious of him, in the background
of Hugo's life, as an important and formidable person.
But Mr. Bamman, though his dignity was regal and
his Olympian brow and beard almost those of the
schoolroom Zeus, had turned out unexpectedly agreeable.
He asked me questions about my studies and my reading quite as if I had been a grown-up person, and had
listened to my opinions with a deference to which I
was entirely unaccustomed. When he had learned that,
in our English course, we had been studying *Julius
Caesar,* he had embarked upon a discussion of Shakespeare very different from any that I had heard in my
English classes. What especially impressed me was a
certain respectful but urbane familiarity with which he
dealt with that great name—as if Shakespeare were a
man like himself, as if he were, in some sense, Shakespeare's equal. He spoke of Shakespeare's comprehension,
in his English and Roman historical plays, of the eternal
official and political types; to my surprise, he compared
Benedict Arnold to Coriolanus; then in a manner both
ironic and serious went on to speak of the Senate and
the White House, as he had known them in his time.
I had never heard anyone talk so before: it was as if the
world of Benedict Arnold had for him the same sort of
reality as the world of McKinley and Cleveland; and,
what was more surprising still, as if Shakespeare belonged to the same world as the United States; as if he,
John Ellison Bamman, belonged to the world of history
and of literature, and as if he took it for granted that

we, since he talked to us as equals, might hope to belong to it, too; as if, in fact, that world were our world! For the first time, I had had the sense of a reality—soon, at that age, to coagulate from what we see, what we read about, what we are told, and what we experience within ourselves—which finally supplies a connection between the private thoughts and emotions, and the names and legends, of youth.

I reminded Hugo now of this incident, and was going on to tell him of my great admiration for his father, when he broke in: "Yes, Shakespeare and Milton: he used to read them to us every night till I got so I hated them like poison! I never really got to like Shakespeare till I read him during the War—and I can't stand Milton to this day! I dare say it's not Milton's fault: it's probably simply due to the fact that Father and I antagonized each other so."

This frankness on Hugo's part surprised me: I had always found him rather reticent about both his family and himself. Whenever he had happened to mention his father since the days when we had been at school together, it had been always with affection and respect, and even sometimes as if with a sense of failure at not having lived up to his father's standard. But now it was as if Hugo's liberated gaze had been accompanied by some new freedom to express himself. I was sorry, however, and a little shocked, to hear that his relations with his father had been difficult, and I asked him what had been the matter.

"I don't know exactly," he replied, "but we never got along. He was pretty impossible at home, and I suppose I sided with Mother against him. He was nervous and hypochondriacal, and used to shut himself up for days in his room, and refuse to see anybody. Then he would suddenly appear in his dressing-gown and freeze us with

wild prophetic looks and announce that the household
was 'hurtling to ruin!' because he'd just gotten a caterer's
bill or something. He finally reduced the whole household to the state of a sanitarium—the doors were all muffled with felt, and he couldn't stand to have a light burning or to hear a sound after he'd gone to bed himself.
He was never rude or domineering about it, but he
would nag us to go to bed in an insincerely amiable
way that used to make me furious. Of course, he could
be charming and sympathetic when any emergency or
crisis arose, and he was able to embarrass us and disarm
us so by having recourse to sympathy and charm just
when we'd been resenting him at our sourest, that when
it actually came to a showdown, we were never able to
stand up to him. In any case, he had the effect on me of
making me adopt the opposite opinion to whatever his
opinion was. We used to have furious arguments about
Socrates and Christ: I used to back Socrates. I must have
been an unbearable little kid myself. I never really liked
him or appreciated him until after he was dead. The trouble was, I suppose, that he'd identified the household
with everything that was stodgy and deadly that he'd
been coming to loathe more and more as the years
went on.

"He'd had a sort of a crush on Adelina Patti, before
he married Mother, and I think that somehow all his
life, in spite of the fact that he enjoyed Washington for
awhile, he was worried by the feeling that he'd really
left the great world behind. I remember he got a phonograph record made by Adelina Patti just about the time
she was passing out, and when he heard it, he flew into
a rage and said it wasn't like her at all, that it was outrageous to allow such a record to be sold—and then he
shut himself up in his room and wrote at something or
other for days.

"I think he'd really wanted to be an artist—he had a very fine voice, you know, and loved to sing—but the 1880's got him—and then, when he found himself snowed under by American respectability, he tried to be a saint. Even before Mother died and he went to live in the Adirondacks, he wanted to carry us all away to the wilderness with him—but Mother wouldn't let him."

I had drawn Hugo out about his father with an interest all the more intent because I was trying to keep my mind closed to Rita; but Mr. Bamman and Adelina Patti had opened the fatal abyss, and as Hugo saw me becoming abstracted, he stopped talking and, looking around with eyes which could now see so much farther, he remarked that Pete Bird, who had not moved but was still posed against the sink, looked exactly like a waxwork. "Who is he, anyway?" I inquired. "What does he do?" "Why, I don't think he does anything," said Hugo. "He's just a bum like another. He writes some rather nice little poems occasionally!"

"Yes," said Pete, not opening his eyes, but speaking with perfect self-possession: "A bum like another—but a poet, nevertheless!" "Have you written anything lately?" asked Hugo, with one of those veritable hemorrhages of kindliness which, when he feared he had hurt someone's feelings, often followed his bitterest strictures. "I thought that some of your things in *Sedition* were weally awfully nice!" "I'm not a poet!" said Pete Bird, still without opening his eyes. "Ask Giovanni Squarcialuppi!—ask Mike Kraus!—ask Miriam Fotherwell Finck!"

"You haven't any manuscripts about you at this moment, have you?" inquired Hugo, who, despite his harsh and contemptuous judgments, had a secret sympathetic instinct for the vanities and aspirations of others. "I feel that I could read a little poetry. These parties seem to be getting less and less stimulating—Sue is getting to be more and more like a wegular Philadelphia hostess!"

Pete fumbled with one hand in his pocket, partially opening his eyes, but still supporting his head on his hand. He finally produced a cough drop: "Here's a cough drop," he announced, "if that would do just as well. Eases irritation, just like a poem. Of course, the cough drop's a little bit fuzzy, but then the poems are a little bit lousy!" "I know," said Hugo sympathetically, "when you try to find anything in your pocket, you always fish up cough drops and unpaid bills and things!" "Bills!" said Pete Bird. "They don't even send me bills any more! —I've gotten long past that stage!—Here's a villanelle,"— he said at length—"a little toy of a villanelle!—and here's an experimental poem—an experiment in multiple metaphors—all of my metaphors are multiple—they have an infinite number of facets—like the eye of a fly!"

He handed the verses to Hugo: "You read them yourself," he said—"My eyes are not very good tonight," and lapsed back into immobility.

The poems were on creased and dog-eared paper, typed in very small type with rather a wavering touch, but, to my surprise, they had a certain charm, in a rose-petally snow-flaky way. I could not, to be sure, distinguish very much difference between the sonnets and villanelles, on the one hand, and the "experimental" poems on the other: Pete Bird's "multiple metaphors" turned out to be quite easy and mild—his description, for example, of his mistress's hands as "little surprising moonbeam violins."

The door into the dining room opened, and Larry Mickler and Daisy appeared.

"Come on, yuh dope!" said Daisy to Pete Bird. "What d'ye thing yuh are, brooding around the kitchen?—a cockroach?" "Get away, yuh dumb cluck!" replied Pete,

reluctantly opening his eyes, "and leave me to my meditations!"

"Let's leave him to his slumbers," said Larry Mickler,
who was evidently drunker than ever. "The boyfriend's
passed out! Too many of those rich liverwurst sandwiches!"

"Come on, Mr. Zilch," said Daisy, still addressing Pete.
"The little woman wants to go home!" "Leave me alone
for three minutes!" said Pete Bird,—"only three minutes!
—and I'll rejoin you in the drawing room!" Though he
talked quietly and sensibly, he was evidently incapable of
moving. "Well, all right," she replied, with some sharpness. "But if you don't make it pretty snappy, you'll find
me gone!"

"Come on back and let him have his sleep out," Larry
Mickler pressed her, pulling at her arm.

But Daisy, ignoring Mickler's importunities as well as
Pete's mildly aggrieved remonstrances, turned to me:
"Take me in," she demanded, "and get me a drink and
dance with me!" She had made up again since I had seen
her: her eyebrows had been heavily penciled to an effect
of moth's antennæ and her mouth had been heavily
rouged, so that her sallow and waxen complexion merely
contributed a morbid paleness to an effect of provocative
luridity; and as I found myself responding to her make-
up, after my lapse of enthusiasm in the earlier evening, I
reflected, with dismay rather than cynicism, upon the
purely biological basis of the interest which we feel in
women, simple animals like ourselves, produced upon a
similar model, monotonous and banal, to which only the
recurrent brimming over of accumulating spermatozoa
imparts a recurrent attraction.

"Very good!" assented Larry Mickler, with a playfulness
distinctly malignant. "Then I'll just practice a little
marksmanship!" He retreated to the end of the kitchen

and, taking up a stand near the bathroom door, he aimed his revolver at a row of plates: "I wonder if I could pick those off in order!"

"Why don't you break them with the butt of the gun?" asked Daisy. "This long range marksmanship of yours burns me up! You've already won the barbed wire garters for shooting plaster statues at two yards!"

"Listen, Pete," insisted Larry Mickler, disregarding Daisy, "you go over to the far end of the room and throw up the plates one by one—and we'll see how many I can pot—like clay pigeons!" "All right!" responded Pete, not moving or opening his eyes. "Oh, don't be *dull!*" cried Daisy with disgust.

Sue Borglum burst in with the Jap butler, who produced, at her direction, from the icebox, a glass gallon container of cocktails. She threw an arm around Daisy's shoulder, and exclaimed in a strained excited shriek which she seemed to have become incapable of moderating: "Oh, you dear child! You were an angel to come! Everybody's deserted me! Bobby said he'd be here at ten, and it's almost midnight now. I suppose he's gone out with his little cutie. I don't mind his keeping a girl—if he'd only get one that was intelligent, or attractive, or something!—but she's just a dumb little wench out of the chorus—she can't even dance!" "I think all chorus girls are dumb," said Daisy. "I've just lost my job, that's why." "Stand 'em on their heads and they're all alike!" said Pete Bird, without opening his eyes. Sue squawked with delighted laughter.

Larry Mickler, since Sue's arrival, had been amusing himself at a distance by drawing his revolver on an imaginary foe: he would whip it out, declaring loudly: "I'll teach those damn goldfish to snap at me!"—then leer humorously in our direction; but as nobody paid any attention to him, he finally came over to the group and

poured himself a drink of Scotch from a bottle standing
on the table. "No wonder there are so many holdups!" he
contemptuously remarked to me. "These dubs that we live
among are just asking to be knocked on the head and
have their pennies taken away from them!" He proposed
drinking to Dostoevsky. "We've done that already," I
said. "Let's do it again," he insisted, with a suggestion of
becoming quarrelsome. "Drinking to Dostoevsky is always in order!" bubbled Hugo, with a tiresome recru-
descence of his gushing undergraduate enthusiasm.

"Are you going to take me in to dance or aren't you?"
demanded Daisy, turning to me, as Sue Borglum plunged
toward the bathroom to greet with effusion another guest
who was just emerging from there and whom she seemed
not previously to have seen.

Daisy and I left the kitchen together. As we went,
Larry Mickler called after me: "So twice is too many
times to drink to Dostoevsky, is it?" Pete Bird was still
sitting as before, his eyelids dropped in their death-mask
and his head propped upon his hand—which, I observed,
now that I had read his verses, was finely articulated and
long.

"Isn't it wonderful," Daisy observed, as we made our
way through the dining room, "how clean Sue Borglum
keeps her kitchen! Most kitchens would have an awful
hangover after a party like this—but I bet hers will be
neat as a pin!"

I avoided the large front room and led Daisy around by
way of the hall, through a door that opened out of the
dining room, to the room on the other side of the house
where people were dancing to the phonograph.

Daisy danced well: she was light; and the responsive
alacrity of her straight little legs walking backward in the
fox-trot had the same prosaic charm as her speech.

"Say, just do me a favor," she said. "Don't leave me

with Larry Mickler. If he tries to cut in on you, don't lettum—I'll just tellum, no soap!" I asked her what sort of fellow Larry Mickler was. "Oh, he's just a fool," she replied.

"I'm sorry about tonight," she went on. "I wanted to have dinner with you, but a whole lot of things happened. I'm awfully sorry." I told her that her touzled hoodlum haircut went beautifully with her plaid dress, and that the green in the plaid dress went beautifully with the green of her eyes. She said, "Yes, and the green of my eyes goes beautifully with the green of my complexion!"

I held her close. Her lips were slightly open, her eyes partly closed. I wondered whether she were really lapsing into a voluptuous languorous dream or whether she were merely very tired. It occurred to me, as I looked at Daisy's fingers, pale, brittle-looking and thin, that her hands, which I had never considered among her prettiest features, might very well be the "little surprising moonbeam violins" of Pete Bird's multiple metaphor.

But now I could stave it off no longer; I could talk no longer against time; I had to think about Rita and Ray! My first feeling had been one of horror that Rita should have been capable of betraying, not another, not me—but herself; then I had made, in my mind, as I quitted the pair, a movement of repudiation which passed even beyond anger; and, at the time I had been talking to Hugo and after, this had lifted me to a sudden elation of lucidity and freedom. But now my need to love and believe in Rita, even stronger than my impulse to reject her, reasserted itself. She must have found, I saw now, in Ray Coleman, with her confounded perverse generosity, some fineness, some crippled aspiration, which she had been able to cherish and feed. Was there not in his persistent desire to meet and entertain artists the inveterate ungratified longing to think and to feel like them? Had I not noted in him an unexpected deference, even in his face something gentle and abashed, when, after he had advanced with his usual assurance some opinion on art or literature, a critic or artist present had expressed contradictory views? And as I had watched him just now, in front of the fire, describing Rita's play, he had seemed to me more nearly amiable that I had ever known him before. He was happy because he felt himself on intimate terms with Rita—because she had told him about her play, and had allowed him to tell others. That was his destiny, perhaps—his salvation: to praise her, to care for her, to soothe her, to guard her from the pack of suitors who came baying after her like dogs—and so, at last, he might be useful and happy—even, perhaps, likable! So he might finally justify his calling by providing security and comfort to Rita!

As we danced past the door into the hall, I glanced across to the couch where I had left her, and the sight of the group which thronged there suddenly exasperated me as one is annoyed by the pathetic exasperating obstinacy of phototropic bugs. "Well," I said to Daisy, smiling, "Ray seems to be having himself a time with Rita!" "Yes," she replied; "I noticed that! He was trying to tell me last week that he was all to pieces about my leavingum—but it doesn't look much like it!"

I remembered how Daisy had complained of Ray Coleman's making her stay home and listen to his reading aloud from the *Oxford Book of English Verse;* and I imagined what a sympathetic audience he must now be finding in Rita: I could see how she would take the book from him and begin to read the poems herself, and how he would then make her recite her own poems—poems, no doubt, which she had written lately, and which I had never heard. He would flatter her without discrimination: I scorned her for accepting such praise!

"I suppose he's pleased with his new job," I remarked, "but a promotion from the *Dispatch* to the *Record* seems almost like a promotion from the morgue to the pound!" "If the boys on the *Record*," replied Daisy, "are any worse than the boys on the *Dispatch*, I'm glad I made my getaway in time!"

"Let's go upstairs for a minute, shall we?" Daisy suggested, as a record ended. "I want to give the old cuckoo's nest a comb."

On the stairs, I took her arm and steered her up toward the somber upper reaches, through the couples who were sitting on the steps. I gripped her firmly in my preoccupation, as if I had been guiding a child. "The trouble about having your hair done this way," she remarked, as if talking for other ears, "is that you have to keep fixing it all the time or people think it's just mussed up!" As we arrived at the top of the stairs, I found that I had gone suddenly hollow, and I remembered that I had eaten no dinner.

Instead of heading, as I expected, for the bedroom where the coats and hats had been left, Daisy went on along the dark upstairs hallway—she seemed to know the house well—to a door at the further end.

It was dark inside. By the light that came in through a single window from the house across the scanty backyard, I could see a cot and a simple bureau—the Jap servant's room, no doubt. I clawed the air for the chain of a shadeless electric bulb which was hanging above our heads. "Why don't you try the bathroom?" I suggested. "I don't see any comb on that bureau." "Never mind about that comb!" she replied.

I embraced her and pasted my lips on her half-opened mouth. I thought about the mouth and moth's eyebrows which had aroused me for a moment in the kitchen, but which I could not see now in the dark—and I tried to make up for my stupidity and tardiness by holding Daisy against me very tightly and kissing her again and again—but it was an assault of which I found myself conscious chiefly as a determined physical pressure and a deliberate application of the lips. I felt my arms crushing cartilage and flesh, and my mouth missing its goal against her teeth. It occurred to me that Daisy's lips were really, despite her make-up, not particularly well-adapted to passionate kissing of this kind. I still thought of them as cool-looking and childlike, as they had seemed to me the night of the movies. And I became aware of the succession of my kisses as something repetitive and tediously mechanical. Fearing Daisy might notice this, too, I broke it up by making her sit down on the bed. I had desired her, and there we were at last! I found myself representing the long stupefied embrace of passion by sheer immobility and weight. I was all too far from being stupefied, I reflected, during the moments when I relaxed my ministrations. Some obstinate unconscious loyalty, in spite of all my efforts, kept me cold. And I was distracted by a variety of ideas. I had a vision of the pilloried frog of a behaviorist moving picture which I had gone to see with Rita. The frog, with its brain removed, had responded with an automatic kick when an acidulated pad had been applied to one of its legs.—And the consciousness that the little bedroom belonged to the Japanese servant reminded me that the Japs did not kiss, that they did not know what kissing was—and I wondered whether they tried to learn kissing when they set out to become Americanized, and whether it took long. I murmured, "Daisy darling!" in a low and secret voice.

We became aware that the door was open: I looked around and saw a small spare figure. His face was half in shadow, and I could not see his eyes. I quickly sat up on the cot, and he suddenly withdrew and slammed the door.

"Who was it?" Daisy asked in a whisper. "It was Pete!" I replied.

She got up. "I don't care," she said. "A great help *he* turned out to be!" She pulled on the electric bulb, went over to the mirror on the bureau, and applied her powder and rouge. When she had finished, she said, without looking at me, putting her powder away in the vanity case, "Take me home, will you?"

We went out and extricated our coats—it was a little like a search in a bad dream—from the avalanche of wraps on the beds; and in silence descended the stairs, looking solemn and matter-of-fact, as we threaded our way through the couples.

So, I told myself, I had not hesitated to wound Pete in his love for Daisy, even after he had shown me his poems, such poems as I had written to Rita, in which his tenderness and his longing had, as it were, been confessed and entrusted to me—to me, another poet! In my glimpse of his face in the doorway, dimly lit by the light from the hall, his pale cheeks and his eyes large with shadow had seemed sensitive and even handsome. Was it Daisy's indifference, I asked myself, was it jealous suspicions like my own, which had given him that gargoyle's mask? Yet one had to be hard about these things: love and poetry, as I myself knew, were paid for with danger and pain!

Sue Borglum protested wildly and loudly against Daisy's leaving so early, and begged me, at any rate, to come back when I had taken Daisy home: she had evidently a morbid fear that her parties were becoming less popular—I felt the cold taste of winter in the vestibule.

After splashing about in the slush of the dark and de-

serted streets, I finally brought back a taxi. Hugo Bamman came down the steps with Daisy. He was wearing
his old limp felt hat, but no overcoat; and he was carrying
over his shoulder the musette bag he had had in the
Army.

We invited him to come with us in the taxi. When I
got in after Hugo and Daisy, I found Hugo planted on
one of the little turn-down seats, and it was only with
considerable difficulty that Daisy persuaded him to sit beside her.

"The tone of Sue Borglum's parties," Hugo began at
once to complain, "is certainly getting more and more
respectable!—she'll soon be sending out engwaved invitations!" I asked him what he meant. "Why, you just go
and meet people now, and talk to them a little, politely—
just like a Washington reception. Things used to be so
much fwanker and fweer at Sue Borglum's! I remember
one night when Leo Shatov got up and did a Cossack
dance on the dining-room table—and the Baroness von
Samstag-Solferino always used to appear wearing a coal
scuttle on her head!—And she has these little thin sandwiches, now, made of chopped olives and spiced ham and
things. There used to be just a great big cheese, and you
gouged out what you wanted with your pocket knife!"

We were about to drop Hugo off at his house, only a
block or two from Sue Borglum's, but he announced that
he was sailing at midnight and would, therefore, go further uptown. I forbore to show surprise, but asked him
where he was bound for. He explained, with his self-
conscious giggle, that he was sailing for Smyrna on a
fruit steamer: his ultimate goal was Afghanistan.

We asked why he was going to Afghanistan. "Well, I
think that it must really be an awfully fine place!" he
replied. "You know, it's one of the only places in the
world that hasn't been Europeanized—it's all a European

can do to get into Cabul at all. Not a trace of a business
man or a missionary or a newspaper! The Amir has electric lighting and European plumbing in his palace, but,
instead of sending for European plumbers and electricians
to put them in for him, he sends Afghans to Europe to
learn how to do it themselves. When they come back,
they're searched for Bibles.—At the same time, they go in
for witchcraft and all kinds of entertaining magic!"

He was bubbling now just as he had done at college
over the little pastry shop in the sidestreet where he and
his friends had bought cinnamon buns.

"Is that where the Afghans come from?" asked Daisy.
"Yes: I suppose so," chortled Hugo. "I suppose that, even
though it's forbidden to bring in any modern textile
machinery, a smart Europeanized Afghan might be able
to do a little profitable sweating in the Afghan business!"

I asked Hugo what his literary plans were and he explained that, when he came back from Afghanistan, he
was going out to the American West to write a novel
about one of the big Western cities, either Pittsburgh or
Detroit. (He had already done Boston and New York,
though he refused to pay Philadelphia even the compliment of exposing it.) "Oh, God!" Daisy exclaimed. "What
do you want to go to Pittsburgh for? I spent the best years
of my life trying to get away from there!" "Why, I've
always wanted to see a Pittsburgh millionaire," Hugo explained, gaily, mildly, sweetly. "Wasn't it you who were
telling me about the man from Pittsburgh who bought
ten thousand dollars worth of fireworks and set them off
in the Bois de Boulogne, and then committed suicide?"
"Yes," said Daisy, "that was Phil Meissner's uncle." "I
think Detroit must be awfully fine, too!" Hugo continued. "I've always wanted to see a Ford put together.
I've always thought it must be wather like one of those
things in the movies, don't you know, where the man

draws a cat, stwoke by stwoke, and then it suddenly comes alive!"

As I listened to Hugo's prattle, it occurred to me to suspect for the first time that he was allowing himself to prattle on purpose. His spectacles had had the effect of making him look owlish and juvenile; but now that he no longer wore them, his intent deep-sunken gaze betrayed the silliness of what he said—betrayed, I mean, that he himself was not silly. I became aware that the undergraduate patter from which, formerly and while still an undergraduate, he had so desperately strained to escape by harsh paradoxes and flat contradictions, was now a habit which he had accepted, partly no doubt because it was difficult to break, but also partly because he found it useful as a screen for his real purposes and ideas. His real purposes and ideas, it seemed to me, as I watched him in the taxi tonight, had by this time completely matured and stood firmly on their own feet; and a certain amount of success, which he had never aimed at or expected, had given him a new assurance. Hugo's novels on the American cities had become almost best-sellers; and he was no longer spurred by the painful necessity of asserting his views in ordinary conversation, but was content to chatter on like a schoolboy: it saved tedious contentious explanations.

There was no chatter about what he wrote: Hugo's novels were sober, even morose, and were built with a solidity of cement. They were comprehensive reports on human society, industriously and conscientiously drawn up. And as I thought tonight of Hugo's assiduity, his independence and his sense of responsibility, I seemed to recognize in them those qualities which had for so many years made his father a respected public servant. The son had cut himself off from his family; had even sold, piece by piece, all the furniture and family silver which he had inherited from his mother, and, set by set, his father's library; and he had done this—to the great consternation of his cousins and his aunts, to whom the sale of mahogany and silver was like a massacre of kin—all in order that he might live poorly in Patchin Place, writing appeals for political prisoners, making speeches for striking garment workers and composing those encyclopedic novels from which he had never hoped to make money. Yet, by the sacrifice of property and family, he had saved the honor of a family tradition which was otherwise largely moribund; he had truly assumed the responsibilities of leadership and shown the disinterestedness of public spirit, in the only fields in which, in our generation, he had found it possible to work.

I seemed to see that, behind the mask of the outlaw, he had finally arrived at a position very similar to that of his father, before his father, in his later erratic years, had withdrawn from public life. For Hugo had applied himself to literature as to one of the old-fashioned professions, Medicine, Law or the Church; and, in spite of his role of eccentric and rebel, had taken on—what set him off at that time from most of the other literary men of the Village—the solid and honorable character of a first-rate professional man. Through the late escapades of the father and the early extravagances of the son, the curve had come round again.

And I envied Hugo tonight: I could think only of his established position as a writer, of the security and the freedom of movement which his royalties had finally brought him, at the same time that he had earned the satisfaction of serious work well done. I myself felt disgusted and gloomy over the aimlessness and uselessness of my life. I had seen clearly, at the funeral of my aunt, that my relations did not think me a success. I was still an underling in a publisher's office, with no great enthusiasm for my work and with no particular hopes of advancement. And, on the other hand, I was not a writer: I had not made Hugo's sacrifice and effort. No wonder I had never been able to persuade Rita Cavanagh to marry me! I had offered her merely the meager resources and the questionable future of a young man with vague literary ambitions; and she had already known many such young men—had already, on one or two occasions, embarked on such lives of cramped space and small comfort, without finding them magic carpets. What wonder that she should now prefer Ray Coleman, with his apartment that overlooked the Square, his lettuce-green cocktail glasses, his water-colors of the Russian ballet, and his rye whisky bottled in bond?

Hugo asked us to let him out at the corner of Seventh Avenue and one of the upper Twenties. I asked him where his baggage was. "I've got it all here!" he replied, indicating the musette bag on his shoulder. "Haven't you even got an overcoat?" asked Daisy. "Why, you know, I don't know why it is," he replied, with the bogus naïveté with which he masked his stubbornest manias, "but I can't seem to stand to wear overcoats. They always make me feel so loaded down and sewed up—and they always make me too hot! I always feel, when I get into them, that there isn't a pin to choose between the modern winter overcoat and the Iron Maiden at Nuremberg." "I should think you'd get your death!" protested Daisy. "If the people in New York," he replied, "didn't wear so many overcoats, they probably wouldn't catch so many colds! They bundle themselves up in winter overcoats and lower the resistance of their bodies so that the least little change in temperature brings them down with the grippe or the flu!"

"Gee," said Daisy, with admiration, rather to my surprise, "I wish I was going to Afghanistan! Take me along with you, won't you?" "I'd love to!" said Hugo. "Come on!"—but he began looking out anxiously for the street. "Oh, *will* you?" cried Daisy. "*Take me!* I'm so fed up with it here! I haven't got any belongings either! I left most of what I had at Ray's. I could walk right on the boat now and sacrifice practically nothing. You couldn't really take me, could you?" "Why, yes—come along!" said Hugo, smiling but, I could see, with some uneasiness: he shrank from the possibility of committing himself to a woman—even in gallantry, even in jest—and was nervously watching the street numbers—"if you wouldn't mind a few tarantulas and scorpions and things that go with the date and fig trade!" "Well, the fruit's all unloaded here, isn't it?" Daisy determinedly objected, with a strong grasp of commercial realities. "We don't export it over there, do we?" "No: of course—it's all unloaded on us—but the animals may stay behind! I dare say that some of them are regular passengers!" "Well," said Daisy, "I've fought fleas and rats and bedbugs in my time—and Greenwich Village bar-flies—so I guess I could cope with a tarantula!"

Hugo stopped the cab. We were all for taking him to his steamer and seeing him off; but he refused to let us. I think that he was honestly afraid that Daisy would insist upon sailing with him—for he leaped out almost before the taxi had stopped, and his leave-taking was abrupt and expeditious. He opened the door again a moment afterwards and tried to give me some money for the fare, but I pulled his hat down over his ears. He waved at us once with a long spasmodic arm, then marched off in the direction of the docks.

"Gee," said Daisy, as we drove away, "I'd like to go to Afghanistan!"

We fell silent. Yes, I reflected, Daisy admired Hugo,

just as Rita admired Ray—because he had made himself a place in the world, because he was successful and independent!

I was on the point of taking Daisy's hand when she suddenly snatched the driver's license out of its isinglass frame opposite her and, without a word of explanation, tore it up, photograph and all. "What made you do that?" I demanded. "I can't stand his face!" she said tartly. "I've been looking at it all the way, and if I had to look at it any more, I'd begin to go half-witted myself!"

I was irritated by Daisy's gesture: it jarred upon my mood of enthusiasm for Hugo's sense of social responsibility, and I felt against it the same sort of resentment that was provoked by the perversities and caprices of Rita. But I laughed—with a certain harshness, as if to mock at the respecters of property, and at the poets who succumbed to their bribes—as if Daisy and I alone, now, still stood together against Ray.

Yet, I was thinking the moment after, one couldn't really blame Ray Coleman for becoming infuriated with Daisy: hadn't she squandered all his money and then kept having C.O.D. packages sent home? Hadn't she even complained to me, the night that I had taken her to the movies, of Ray's too conscientious practice of paying all his bills? I thought of Daisy the night of the party, when I had first met her and Rita. Hadn't she behaved like a little fiend? Hadn't she turned on a phonograph record in the middle of Rita's poems? Hadn't she humiliated Ray by leaving the party with Pete Bird? I found that I forgave Ray more easily for his violent scene with Daisy, which Rita and I had overheard.

But now, when I recalled that detestable scene, it was no longer as it had seemed to me that evening. That night I had been a spectator looking on at a melodrama,

at a melodramatic tableau of jealousy: Ray pointing at
Pete's broken cane; Daisy abashed among the ruins of the
party; and I complacently and gallantly helping Rita on
with her wrap. Now I had myself played Ray Coleman's
part. I remembered the spiteful scene which I myself
had provoked with Rita in the taxi, and the scenes which
for weeks had preceded it. It was as if the roles had now
been reversed: it was I who was the jealous blackguard
and Ray Coleman who was the solid decent citizen!
And now those memories must perhaps always stand as a
barrier between Rita and me, as they had done at the
party tonight—a barrier of coldness and resentment which
could never be forgotten now and whose shadow must
lie, also, behind on all that had been beautiful before.
If I could only just now have said the word which would
have caused it to fall away!

"I don't want to go home!" said Daisy, as we were
crossing Forty-second Street. I suggested that we might
go to a night club. I did not, as I say, at that moment,
particularly care about Daisy, but then, there was nobody
else I liked better—least of all did I like myself or want
to be alone with myself. "All right. I can't go in this
plaid dress, though. I tell you: you go and get something
to drink, and I'll go and change my clothes." "I'll go and
change, too," I said.

The moment after, she had some sort of qualm: "Give
me a piece of paper," she said, "any kind of piece of paper
will do." The only paper I had in my pocket was the letter
from H. M. Grosbeake, the professor of philosophy at
college to whom I had sent Rita's poems and who had
invited me to come to see him, but to whose letter I had
never replied, though I had been carrying it around ever
since. I had torn off the blank part in Daisy's room, the
day I had written her the note, and now I gave her what

was left, the page with the letter itself. She stuck it into the driver's license frame behind the isinglass.

I left Daisy at her door.

*   *   *

Larry Mickler, with his revolver and his passion for Dostoevsky, had made upon me an unpleasant impression. I had come to connect him obscurely with my impulse to smash the peach-brandy bottle, when I had felt myself so helpless with Rita, and I found that I disliked Dostoevsky, because Larry Mickler admired him. I remembered—as I went back in the taxi to my own apartment in Bank Street—Dostoevsky's sadistic manias, his complaisance in self-degradation combined with extravagant vanity; I now felt, after meeting Mickler, that the masterpieces of such a man of genius were a doubtful compensation on paper for the moral bankruptcy of a life. Were not the purity of Dostoevsky's tenderness, the flights of his Christian idealism, counterbalanced by his cruel perversity, his almost sub-human depths of indifference? Were not the Svidrigaïlovs and Stavrogins in Dostoevsky's novels—those malignant growths which sprouted and seemed, almost without the author's intention, to swell to such monstrous proportions—were they not the price which one had to pay for the Myshkins and the Alyoshas?

True, it was quite unfair to Dostoevsky to identify him with Larry Mickler; it was the triumph, at least, of the great writer that, by dint of terrific effort, he had, if only in the world of his novels, succeeded in restoring a moral balance of that universe which he had once felt reeling with the world of his own soul; whereas, in the case of Larry Mickler, who had merely to read Dostoevsky's books, all that desperate idealism, that victory of moral passion, would, it seemed to me at that moment, go principally to give him a good conscience in licking his chops

over the cruelties and perversities, and to leave him with
the gratified conviction that there was no kind of discreditable behavior which imagination might not redeem.

And Pete Bird, with his charming wistful verses and
his swindle of the liverwurst sandwiches! And Rita—
without that mêlée in which her varying passions had
involved her, that possession by all the devils of all the
sensual desires at once, all that panic and anarchy and
anguish and deceit of her daily life, would she ever without all this have been compelled to the noble severity, the
firm and harmonious form, the bravery of candor, of her
verse?

And those poets of whom Rita and I had talked the
first night I had known her in Bank Street! Tonight, the
curses and groans of Catullus only filled me with
the same disgust for his abasement at the feet of Lesbia as
did my own preoccupation with Rita. And Verlaine, in
his prison cell, with his imbecile alternations between
piety and pornography—if he had published his religious
poems, as he had originally intended to do, sandwiched
in between his poems of lechery, he would have furnished a perfect example, an example forever ludicrous,
of the disorder of the poet's mind.

Even Dante, of whom I had once thought, of whom I
thought still, as the supreme poet of Europe, who had
possessed together the fiercest passion and the most powerful intellect, who had been able to apply to one work
all man's highest faculties at once—what stiff-necked,
what stupid obstinacy, what fanatic self-confidence, going
against all common sense, must have lain back of all that
subtlety and feeling! Had not Dante's indignation with
his neighbors, as Professor Grosbeake had once suggested,
been based upon an utter incapacity for understanding
the realties of his time? Yet he had been spurred by such
a passion to be *right*, that, balked and exiled in the real

world, he had gone to live in the world of his poem, where, passing over both Pope and Emperor, he had sat in the place of God himself!

And even the philosopher and the saint! When I thought now of Professor Grosbeake, it was with a certain sentiment of scorn for the domesticity in which he seemed buried, and with misgivings as to whether his metaphysics were not merely a monstrous hypertrophy, arising, first, from a certain ineptitude at dealing with the affairs of the practical world, and fostered, later, by his practical wife, who had taken possession of him and securely immured him in a life where nothing but contemplation was possible. And had I not just learned that Hugo's father, from whom I had caught for the first time in my boyhood the sense of the unity of life—had I not just heard that he had fed his vision with the dead wood of some area of his nature from the desolation of which he had never ceased to suffer, and that his ringing arraignment of the Congressmen for their failure to search their hearts in a spirit of Christian humility had been purchased at the expense of the tyrannic subjection of his household! And in the case of Hugo himself, it now appeared to me—what I had never understood before— that his ideas had been given their direction by his early revolt against his father, which had made him, not, as his father had been, the prophet of a new moral discipline, but primarily a champion of the oppressed who still feared and resented the oppressor.

But these reflections began to sicken me (I was at once hungry, nervous and weary). I had succeeded in accounting for all these people, who were precisely the people I most admired, as the victims of deficiencies and derangements; and I felt now that I had been deriving an ignoble satisfaction from knowing the secret of every one's disease. While I was changing my clothes in Bank Street, I began to remember Dostoevsky's miseries: the neurotic family given over to its manias and collapsing after the mother's death; the boy neglected by the drunken father and left without money at his school; the elder Dostoevsky murdered by his peasants; Dostoevsky sentenced to death for plotting against the Tsar—taken out and tied to a stake to be shot, and only reprieved at the last moment; his four years of imprisonment in Siberia, wearing the fetters with murderers and thieves, hauling bricks and pounding alabaster; his later years of servitude as a soldier; his persecution by his brother's creditors; and the epilepsy which had accompanied all from that first day, when, a boy at school, he had heard the news of the murder of his father. Where was there place for ironic patronage in the contemplation of such a life or of the writings which had been its products?

And I remembered how Hugo, too, had suffered in his prison camp in France. No wonder that he hated authority and discipline! It was true that prison had made of Hugo an uncompromising revolutionist, whereas it had made of Dostoevsky an equally uncompromising conservative. Hugo himself was naturally good, and it seemed to him, in consequence, that all the evil which he encountered must be the product of institutions somehow imposed on humanity against their wish; whereas, in Dostoevsky's case, his inescapable sense of his own guilt, of the evil in his own heart, seemed at last to have reduced him to feeling that, though he had been punished for a political offense only, his punishment had been somehow deserved, and that he had actually been expiating crimes of which he had never been accused. He had come to believe in the badness of humanity, and mere political readjustments, in consequence, no longer appeared to him important. Yet the effect of the ordeal in each case—in Hugo's and in Dostoevsky's—had been essentially the same: as Dostoevsky's years in Siberia had caused him so deeply to distrust even the liberalism of educated Russians, so Hugo's weeks in the prison camp had made it impossible for him to accept, even in their most genial guise, the complacency and comfort of America. Both had been forced to live at close quarters with the basic contentions and discords, the basic horrifying anomalies, of our common life. And both were always afterwards to look with the eyes of strangers and exiles upon even the most conscientious, even the most intelligent, even the most amiable of their fellows who had never recognized those realities.

Hugo and Dostoevsky alike had attempted to explain them, to resolve them, those contentions, anomalies and discords. And were not these the prime provokers of literature?—not encountered in prisons only, but in all treachery, violence, frustration, all the outbreaks of our barbarous nature and the unlooked-for disasters which befell us at the mercy of unknown forces. Such disasters and outbreaks alone could rouse us from our normal existence of non-thinking and non-feeling, the laziness of bodily processes inertly fulfilling their functions, of the consciousness inertly drifting among random and meaningless images—memories and anticipations—with unconscious but cunning instinct steering clear of problems and tasks. What were literature and art but the by-products of these collisions with the uncomprehended reality—collisions whose repercussions, when we had withdrawn into the shelter of ourselves, we attempted to palliate, to harmonize, to account for, to subdue to a smoother rhythm in the current of our thought, now resuming, which for a moment had been troubled or torn? And was it not true that the individual artist—the greatest master even: Dante himself—no matter how detached his intelligence, how rich his imagination, how

comprehensive his range, was never able to escape from
the instinct which made him justify his own life? If the
poet wrote about himself, or identified himself with his
hero, the hero must emerge victorious; or if the hero were
allowed to be beaten, he must at least be made to triumph morally; or if the writer confessed to sin or ig-
nominy, the confession itself must be a merit; or if he
wrote neither of himself nor of a hero, the historian, the
economist or the philosopher, in defending certain values,
made them play the hero's role. Like the instinct which
made us blink our eyes when anything was brought near
them, the instinct to produce a work of art (so I somberly
reflected tonight in that room where, so short a time before, as I had heard Rita reciting her poems, the language
of literature had seemed to me something at once natural
and noble)—the instinct to produce a work of art was
merely a self-protective reflex like another. Were not
imagination and reason like the phagocytes of our physical nature, which, as soon as an infection occurs, rush to
mass themselves at the breach, where they ingest the
disturbing intruders and put a stop to the progress of the
malady?—with this difference, that the work of art, unlike
the dead and discharged phagocytes, for some time and
under certain conditions, may retain a certain efficacy for
others.

For the harmony, the justification, provided by a successful piece of literature was accepted by the reader as
valid. Yet the writer had falsified life, because he had
pretended to harmonize something of which he was conscious chiefly as chaos, and to explain what he was aware,
all too well, he could not fully understand. So, when I
had written a sequence of sonnets about the night of my
first meeting with Rita, I had not mentioned, as I have
not mentioned in my description of that evening, the
drunken friend who had kept calling me up and inter-

rupting our conversation; the agonized cries of cats; the howling and sobbing of a baby; the sore throat which, toward the end of the evening, I had begun to find very uncomfortable and which, afterwards, during the days when I had been falling in love with Rita, had developed into a case of flu. So I had also deliberately left out all the egoistic and unreliable aspects of Rita's character, of which I had already become aware and which were already making me anxious.

A work of art was, then, an imposture. But the reader, himself balked and bewildered, received naïvely the artist's picture as a true diagram of the world. The artist who had been disconcerted and spurred to compose a work of art by his failure to discover in the universe either harmony or logic, supplied the logic and harmony himself; and the reader, who had also been hungering for harmony or logic, accepted with joyful reassurance what the artist gave him, and assumed that the artist's makeshift was a certified revelation, and the artist a kind of oracle. The reader leaned on the writer: what for the latter was a vague, a confused or an approximate form of expression, the former applied literally. All that part of literature which dealt directly with current events—editorial writing, pamphleteering, history, much novel and play writing—was but the painting of the thinnest varnish of a comforting reason and art over earthquakes which actually took place, not in the world of art and reason, but in the barbarous animal world, bloody, uncontrollable, ignoble—and all the writer could hope for, at best, was to divert the attention of his fellows, like a bystander at a street accident who, when the rest of the crowd are only gaping, insists upon the removal of the body, or like an actor in a burning theater who, by coolly addressing the audience, tries to avert a stampede and panic. Yet the public, remembering the catchwords, the

incantations, of their leaders, attempted to enforce them as
laws; and a flourish of rhetoric, under pressure of a desperate crisis, would be imposed as a practical program or
developed as a philosophic system.

Or the public got to the point of behaving as if every
feature of the artist's work were something premeditated
—writing, for example, after the author was dead, "It was
about this period that X, in his attempt to understand his
own time, decided that it would first be necessary to
understand the career of James G. Blaine, and, finding
no satisfactory book on the subject, he set out to write
one himself," or, "It was in the course of his travels in
the tropics that the necessity first appeared to Y of a new
and chaster form of expression"—when the truth was that
the life of Blaine had been merely a piece of hackwork
for a publisher, suggested by the publisher himself, and
that the baldness of Y's prose had been simply the result
of enervation caused by the tropical heat. Or some work
which had exacted from the writer a furious effort for
completeness of understanding, for impersonality of pro-
jection—an effort obstructed, to the writer's dismay, by
his personal obsessions and mannerisms, his family habits,
his organic defects, the limitations of his nation and race,
which pursued and exasperated him, like a tin can tied to
a dog's tail—for the public, who knew nothing of his aim,
it was precisely the writer's personality which they savored
and glorified, descending with gratified complacency those
very lines of least resistance against which the artist had
struggled to mount, and delighting in those very stigmata
which the artist had strained to efface. So posterity would
piously cherish a distinguished writer's roughest notes,
though these might merely be irrelevant excretions, under the pressure of emotions and interests not commemo-
rated in them at all—productions which drew their only
vividness from the acuteness of the writer's need to turn

his mind away from his troubles of the body, the heart or the purse, toward something remote and indifferent— or they might be meaningless mechanical notes, the merest rudimentary twitchings of the literary temperament, made in moments of drunkenness or fatigue, but hungrily saved by the writer's admirers for their infinitesimal drops of some peculiar personal color, no more interesting or precious in itself than the color of his eyes or his hair. From these notes, the writer's disciples might end by constructing a system which would have filled the writer with horror, but which now carried the credit of his name—just as in the case of ancient poetry, where the text was corrupt or fragmentary, Æschylus seemed to us all the more awful and all the more oracular because, not knowing precisely what he wrote, we did not know precisely what he meant; and Sappho all the more divine because there was so little of her left.

Nor were the public readers merely: they were also writers who imitated the author. One had had a vision of movements in literature sweeping over the minds of humanity like the wind that makes waves in the wheat; but would it not, I now reflected, be more accurate to liken such movements simply to the collapse of a row of dominoes, of which only the first has felt the shock, the shock from the unknown reality, and the others have merely toppled over, receiving it at second-hand? Till, at last, the original composer of the symphony, the original inventor of the system, would catch back from the minds of the public themselves (who had merely taken it from him), a new belief in the all-embracing, the all-satisfying character of that pattern, in the finality of those conclusions, which, at the time he had first conceived them, he had never himself regarded as quite satisfactory. Some day, like a fool, I should myself read those poems which I had written long ago about Rita, and I should be convinced that when we were young, it had actually been like that. Not content with deceiving others, I should finally deceive myself!

But then, in the long run, if my sonnets had become famous, the public—if not permanently bemused by them, as in the situation mentioned above, would have had time to find them out. When the readers have got used to a writer—when our first delight in his peculiar color, his peculiar music or flavor, has commenced to wear rather thin—then the familiar malaise assails us: we fatally begin to recognize, just under the novel or alluring surface, the presence of all those grievances, those diseases, those insane preoccupations of the straining incomplete human being—all those anomalies, discords and contentions from which, in seeking the support of literature, we had hoped to be set free. And in the end, the public of readers, when they had found out the weaknesses and falsities of the system which they had once accepted—when they had perhaps tried to put into practice some vision—the morality of Nietzsche (another favorite of Larry Mickler's)—which the invalid writer had imagined in his bed, they would turn against the writer and reject him.

Yet beyond the work of any individual artist, there was the general concerted effort, the gigantic universal imposture, of literature itself!

I remembered the dark volumes of Jebb in which, with the hope of tranquillizing my spirit, I had lately been reading Sophocles. *There* was perhaps the supreme achievement of the organized imposture of literature! How many times had one seen the calmness and the sobriety of Sophocles played off against the harshness or the cynicism of some modern tragic writer! These plays had become the unchallenged example of classic moderation and wisdom, the great corrective of modern turbulence. Yet in what work of a modern dramatist had the harshness of Sophocles been surpassed? I remembered the unruly tempers of the family of Œdipus: the foolish quarrel of Œdipus with his father over a casual encounter on the road; his asperity with Tiresias; the passionate directness of all his gestures. Did one find even in the *Œdipus at Colonus* that spirit of peace and resignation with which Victorian critics sometimes credited it? Was the exiled and embittered king a figure of mellow clemency? Surely the old man's cursing of his sons was one of the most shocking scenes in literature!—nor did the species of divine electrocution with which Sophocles finally disposed of him strike precisely a note of tranquillity. And those sons who quarrel for the kingdom and who finally slaughter each other! And the passionate obstinacy of Creon, so like the passionate obstinacy of Œdipus—and the passionate obstinacy of Antigone! The mother and daughter, in *Electra*, bandying the most brutal abuse! These people were, in their way, and even on the occasions when they were animated by some passionate fanatical loyalty, as narrowly egoistic as the characters of Ibsen, but more quarrelsome and more virulent!

Was there, indeed, I suddenly asked myself, from the point of view of barbarous behavior, very much to choose between Sophocles and Dostoevsky himself? There they were, the old hideous discords—Œdipus killing his father, the old Karamazov murdered by his sons—that cruel inevitable turning upon the beings who have given us life! I remembered how Hugo had just told me that, rebelling against his father, he had come to hate even those poets whom his father had most loved—and how Rita, in leaving behind her all that dull and homely little community which for so long had hobbled her youth, had discarded the name of Aunt Sadie, who had taught her to play Handel and Bach. And were not the horrors of Dostoevsky—Myshkin's epilepsy, Zossima's putrefaction and Stavrogin's gratuitous rape—quite matched by Philoctetes' ulcer, by the unburied corpse of Polyneices and by the incest of Œdipus? Though the form of Sophocles' tragedies was certainly more chastened than the tumult of Dostoevsky, his spirit was more astringent!

I remembered the story about Sophocles in Plato—how he had been asked whether old age had made him impotent, and how he had answered that growing old was like deliverance from a mad and cruel master. Was this the saying of a calm balanced nature? And what of the supposed tranquillity of even those later years? I remembered in the second Œdipus, the terrible description of old age—"unfriended, feeble, chided, unfit for company, the crowning ill of all—not to be born is best, but once we have seen the light it is better to go soon!" How did Matthew Arnold know that "from first youth tested up to extreme old age," "passion" had never made Sophocles "wild?"

Yet so great was the need of humanity to believe in a human intellect all-self-controlled and all-wise that there had been superimposed on the plays of that great master of hatred and horror a legend which now disguised them —and the solemn impassive don, laboring day after day at his desk, explaining, interpreting, translating, every word of the poet's text—if necessary, altering his words—had pared Sophocles down, had sapped his power, ironing out to marmoreal smoothness a style rather nodulous and tough, congealing angry cataracts of consonants to colorless pediments of prose and reducing the weighty rhythm, with its urgent pulse of blood that carries along from one line to another the contractions of swift-spoken speech, to a tongue which could never have been spoken—the British don, after centuries of critics, had supplied us with what men of letters, what all mankind, had desired: a writer superhuman and humanly impossible, a writer who could never have existed—a Master, of impeccable technique and imperturbable equanimity, a writer who could never be supplanted and never be left behind, a writer unassailable, a classic!

In this way we had established the myth of the classics. From the written remains of humanity, of beings outraged and bewildered like ourselves, we had created the illusion of a fortress of absolute beauty and wisdom in which men who had studied Greek could always take sanctuary, on whose invulnerable ramparts they might always rely.

And I thought, also, of those other efforts, those efforts more characteristic of our time, which aimed, also, at an absolute beauty, at an art wholly independent of the appetites and agonies of men—paintings that represented nothing, "pure poetry" devoid of ideas: both, in reality, mere assimilations on the part of literature and painting to the pattern and rhythm of music—which itself had been piously striving—in those composers who named their productions after trigonometrical figures and the integral calculus—to assimilate itself to mathematics.

How senseless such attempts seemed tonight! How could there be anything pure or absolute about such exercises as the arts, which were but pleasing arrangements of sensations, and which, therefore, were inextricably dependent on the senses we had clumsily evolved to meet our needs and to find our way through the jungle of nature! And if the art which derived from our hearing appeared to us purer than the others, it was merely because we experienced, in this region of sound disassociated from speech, sensations less complex and complete than are stimulated by images or words. These crude games, so much the play of our bodies, of our primary animal life, that neither stories, visions, drama nor music—not argumentation even, not Euclid's geometry itself, which comes to a climax, like a Greek play, with the proposition of the square on the hypotenuse—had been able to liberate themselves from the type of our reproductive processes —so that one had always either, as in Greek plays, to work up to a climax toward the end and then gently and briefly subside, or, as in our modern ones, to reach a climax and then abruptly cease. I thought of the heat of Catullus and Keats, of the mounting excitement of Dante; of the even unimpassioned glow of purely homosexual writers like Plato and André Gide; of the blank stretches where the climaxes should be in the novels of Henry James.

And I reflected that between the sexes—Rita's poetry and Catullus's—there was no real common norm of judgment in matters of literature or art—men and women were each tied to their stakes: they could only turn in circles about them. What critic could really pretend to judge the work of men and women side by side? or, for that matter, the work of different races, or even of different nations—of different periods, generations, each compelled to make its own adjustment to the world which pursued and pressed it, each with its own disasters, its own maladies and discords and conflicts, which, to be easy, it must resolve? Or even of different individuals!

What a discrepancy—worst of all—what a gulf between the self which experiences and the self which describes experience! What was the sense, I asked myself, in that room to which I had once brought Rita and in which we had talked the night through and seen the blue of June on the glass—what was the comfort of "moments of emotion recollected in tranquillity?" As if there could ever be a common denominator, as if there could ever be a fusion or union, between those moments of tranquillity and our moments of pain!

*   *   *

As I went out to buy a bottle of gin at a nearby Italian restaurant, I resolved to disgorge these ideas in a gigantic desolating essay. But I found now that I was getting a headache: my mind was still going on at a furious fatiguing rate—with slashed and deflated tires, running rackingly on its rims—and I wanted now to make it stop. I had been feeling rather faint with hunger, and, while the waiter was wrapping up the bottle, I ate some bread and drank a highball.

I tried to shift my thoughts to Daisy, as I expected to find her when I should call on her—in her pretty black evening gown, and much beautified and refreshed.—After the highball, and a second highball, I found myself full of enthusiasm for the night club.

When I arrived at Forty-fourth Street, however, the door of Daisy's apartment was opened by Pete Bird, and I saw Daisy sitting on the edge of the bed, with the same old rowdy plaid dress and the same demoralized countenance, now unnaturally pale. Pete said, "Oh, hello!" and both stared at me. I saw that Daisy had been crying: she had a bandage around her wrist.

I inquired what had happened. "Daisy cut her wrist," said Pete. "I was trying to open a spaghetti can," said Daisy, without expression. "Good Heavens!" I exclaimed. "Don't you think you ought to have a doctor?" "We've had one," said Pete. "He's just gone." Daisy continued to stare up at me, not speaking, with watery swollen eyes.

I felt a deep disgust with them both. I protested that she should have waited, that I had planned to get dinner at the night club. "Just didn't want to wait," she replied —then added, after a moment's pause: "I had some spaghetti here, and I thought I might as well eat it!"

"I don't suppose you want to do any more looping, then," I said. She answered shortly: "Not tonight."

Pete Bird had sat down on the bed beside her, and put

one arm around her: he looked like a faithful dog. She looked like a wounded owlet: I was astonished to observe that her nose, in the center of her pale round face, could appear like a little beak. She had, through fatigue and suffering, reached one of those moments when women seem completely dispossessed of their sex, and it occurs to us as a surprise that they probably resemble their fathers.

I asked whether she wouldn't like a drink. "You might leave some here," said Daisy. I felt that Pete regarded me with coldness, that he had assumed complete proprietorship of Daisy, so I gave them the bottle and took my leave. "I'm sorry," said Daisy, "that I couldn't go out."

I directed the taxi driver to take me to Sue Borglum's. —I was irritated by Daisy's clumsiness in cutting her wrist on the spaghetti can; and I resented the presence of Pete Bird. I did not particularly want to see any more of Sue Borglum's party—in fact, the thought of returning was repugnant to me. But I had got to the bottom of everything—nothing really mattered tonight. Going back to my apartment alone was the most intolerable prospect of all.

In the cab, I fell to wondering, in my discouragement with art and literature, whether it might not perhaps be possible to find a deeper, more austere satisfaction in scientific writing and research. My mind had been haunted that evening by ideas from my recent scientific reading. In the sciences, at least, one was dealing with ruthless reality itself: *there* one did not pretend to justify; *there* one's work was accomplished in indifference as to whether it solaced men's minds. I regretted that I had not had the foresight to study physics and biology at college. And in an attempt to exercise, at least, that gift of scientific observation upon which I had rather prided myself, I asked the taxi-driver, as I was paying him, whether he had not been born in Alabama. But he replied that he had been born in New York, and had lived there all his life.

I was struck, when I reëntered Sue Borglum's, by a certain demoralization which seemed to have taken place since I left. In the room where people were dancing, a little baldish man with spectacles was playing on a set of trap drums. He was apparently under the impression that he was contributing to the pleasure of the dancers; but as his drumming made the phonograph inaudible, they were trying to tone him down. He was complacently smiling to himself, and when anyone remonstrated with him, only glanced up and smiled more happily, deafened by his own drums. From time to time he blew a kazoo.

On the couch on which Rita had been sitting in the room across the hall, lay a man (though he might almost have been a woman of the taller more aquiline type) in a green and orange kimono, from which protruded lean bare shanks and feet. He made me pause in horror when I first saw him: his eyes, which had mascara on them, were cadaverously closed, and his unnaturally narrow face had almost the pinched look of the dead.

In the room where the refreshments had been served, there was nothing left now but a sandwich which someone had bitten into, and the purplish dregs of the punch. Bobby McIlvaine was leaning against the mantel: his straight mouth and his narrow eyes seemed to have shut themselves up, at the intimation of danger, like the shell of a turtle when one picks it up. Sue Borglum was vehemently haranguing him, while a girl with lusterless complexion and lips painted a heavy magenta was expostulating tearfully with Sue in an endeavor to justify herself for having just thrown a punch glass at another girl, who, in her turn, feminine and frail in a fashion rather wispy and washy, was half hiding, like a fright-

ened chick, behind a species of woman doctor. This last
person, who was broad and well-tailored, with white cuffs
and a black mannish dress, was herself defying and derid-
ing the girl who had thrown the glass with robustious
male taunts and chuckles which served to convey female
malice.

Sue received me with a violent gust of welcome, evidently forgetting that she had seen me before—no doubt
my changing my clothes had misled her—and immediately
called me as a witness against Bobby McIlvaine: "Now,
tell him—tell him frankly!" she shouted. "I want him to
know what people really think of his sets! Did you ever
see anything more terrible in your life than the first act
of *April Showers?* I tell him that as a snug little cottage
it would make a good annex to the Public Library!" I
said that it was a great pity that the scene hadn't taken
place in a palace, because Bobby was so good at palaces.
"It'll take place in Cain's Palace soon!" Sue Borglum
breathlessly went on. "Palace! The trouble with him is
that his style has gotten vulgar! It's vulgar, that's what it
is! Palace! It looks like a movie palace! It looks like some
movie man's idea of a palatial ladies' lavatory!"

I drifted on, after a little, to the kitchen. Perhaps I
wanted to be sure that Rita had really gone—perhaps I
still hoped to speak to her alone and to break down that
constraint between us of which I carried the consciousness everywhere, like an ache at the back of my head.

In the kitchen, I found a small group waiting around
the bathroom door. One of the men was remonstrating
with the others. In those days, in Greenwich Village,
there was always a man in a dinner jacket who was present on all major social occasions. He was some sort of
bond salesman or broker who took an interest in the arts.
When, as in the case of Sue Borglum's Thursday evenings, these occasions became a little more formal and

many people wore dinner jackets, he began to appear in a dress suit. Thus costumed, he was now leaning against the sink, with his hands in his trousers pockets—his regular equine face expressionless and almost distinguished— protesting with good-humored gentlemanliness against the vigorous measures proposed by certain other members of the group for inducing the occupants of the bathroom, who, it appeared, had been in there a very long time, to give somebody else a chance. It was also suggested that the people inside might actually be ill, that they might even have committed suicide, and that one really ought to find out. "No," said the gentleman in the dress suit. "I don't think they've bumped themselves off. A little while ago I heard somebody laughing." "Maybe one of them bumped the other off," suggested somebody in the group, "and it's the one that's alive that's laughing." "I don't think so," replied the arbiter. "I know them both. I want to get in," he added, "just as badly as you do, but I think we ought to be discreet."

"Well, I'm damned if I do!" declared a little chunky Hungarian, one of the editors of a Communist paper. "Whatever they've been doing in there, they've been doing it long enough!" "Yes," said a furtive-eyed poet, who wore a khaki shirt. "It's time the workers got a break!" The girl who accompanied the Hungarian, a chunky and pretty Jewess, smiled a little uneasily, in awe of the Communist, but impressed by the man in the dress suit.

The Hungarian marched to the door and knocked with aggressive loudness. "Look here, old chap!" said the man in the dress suit, going forward and taking him by the shoulder, though without any show of heat. "Better lay off! Let's be tactful!" "Get away, you animal cracker!" the Communist retorted. "Don't try to high-hat me! There are other human beings in the world besides you and your friends in the bathroom!"

The door opened suddenly, so violently that it hit the Hungarian in the face, and Larry Mickler came out. He was followed by a tall plain blonde, very much flushed and evidently angry. They made their way through the group at the doorway, looking fixedly straight ahead of them. But when Mickler came up to me—I was the farthest from the bathroom—he stopped and let the girl leave the kitchen alone.

"Well, old-timer!" he greeted me genially—with the exaggerated heartiness of one who has failed to commend himself elsewhere. Not knowing what else to say, I asked him if he knew whether Rita had left. "I don't know," —reaching for the bottle of Scotch. "She was in the other room a little while ago.—*There's* a woman who's not afraid to be herself! These women are all afraid of themselves—they're afraid to say *Yea* to life! Village and college girls, one's just as bad as the other in this goddam country of ours!—Like that rope-haired blond girl, for instance—she wants it and yet she's afraid of it—when it comes to the point she's afraid! She pretends to be scandalized when she's really only sore at herself!—Well, let's drink to Rita Cavanagh, the woman who's not afraid!"

"I'm all for Rita Cavanagh," I said, "but I've drunk enough toasts tonight!" "That's right!" replied Larry Mickler, immediately directing his resentment at me. "Say *Nay* like all the rest! I'm not surprised you're in the publishing business. The publishers are all *Nay-sayers!* I wouldn't be writing ads instead of novels if the publishers said *Yea* to life!—Why, if the whole tribe of publishers—and editors!—and critics!—were combined in one attack, they wouldn't amount to enough to make a Dostoevsky scratch the bite!" I repressed an impulse to answer, "To hell with Dostoevsky!"—but replied, "I never heard that Dostoevsky had any trouble getting published." I left him glaring, before he had retorted, and went back into the dining room.

In the dining room, the girl with the lusterless skin had broken down and was weeping on a chair, while Sue Borglum, her own eyes leaking tears, was making an effort to console her. Sue was saying: "Never mind, Claudette—you can't win! you can't win!" Bobby McIlvaine, who was standing alone, his face locked against the scene which confronted him, produced two theater ticket stubs from his pocket and dropped them into the dregs of the punch. He remarked: "That's a combination that I've always wanted to try in the theater—a blending of mauve and blue!"

In the front room, to which I immediately returned, I was just in time to witness an arrival which made upon me a curious impression. I could hardly at first believe my eyes. There had appeared, under the escort of Tony Scallopino, the proprietor of one of those Greenwich Village restaurants which were beginning, at that period, to be transformed into small but increasingly expensive night clubs, two young women who, even among that company where one was not ordinarily surprised at anything, astonished and jarred upon me like some incongruous image of a dream remembered after we wake, some image which owes its strangeness, its power obscurely to worry us, to the fact that it has been transferred from its surroundings in the waking world to surroundings in which we should not expect to find it. They were strangely conspicuous, these girls—more conspicuous, even, in their way, than the man in the orange kimono or the woman with the stiff white cuffs. In the first place, they were very brightly dressed, one in blue, the other in red—and I saw, at a second glance, that their dresses, although gay, almost smart, were also flimsy and cheap. Neither was bad-looking; and when they first came in, I thought they were attractive. The small one, the one in blue, had blue eyes and looked a little like a fish; but the other, the one in red, was quite handsome: she had rich brown hair, large brown eyes, full cheeks, fleshy lips, rather a creamy complexion and a nice thick nose. But their cheeks were aglow with a heightened color, and their eyes were starred with a black radiation, which, among all the varied make-ups, seemed improper and out of place. Such faces were not meant for the lighting of ordinary private houses but for the pink-shaded lights-in-darkness of Tony Scallopino's night club. And in their eyes I saw that public stare, the stare of the prostitute, which, like the jockey's bowed legs, the tailor's peering eyes, the court-room intonations of the lawyer, the military officer's curt-ness, is the universal sign of the profession—that stare which must be always watching, which must meet all the world without winking, without demurring or veiling it-self—that stare which sometimes looks amazed, sometimes panic-stricken, sometimes resentful and sullen, and some-times almost insane, but which seems always to have robbed the face of some essential element of personality, and therefore of humanity itself.

I gazed at these girls, and, in an instant, the brunette had become aware of my gaze and was welcoming it, with smiling eyes. I approached her, and she began at once, before I had even spoken: "I think this is the most delightful old house! What a lovely old mirror over the mantel!" We discussed the house, the weather, the the-ater. She had opinions about the plays that were being given in the little Village theaters: I was surprised to hear her make conversation so cleverly and with such a good manner, but I was shocked to see her ply her trade

—she made no pretense of anything else—so brazenly and so promptly.

It made me uneasy, as we talked, to meet nothing in her large fine eyes but a look of sly humorous complicity. Those eyes, despite a kind of intelligence, had been glazed against the warmth of frankness, the expression of personal feeling, as much as those of any streetwalker's who makes off to the streets again the moment her transaction is finished. And this troubled me—I hated and resented it: tonight I had felt myself estranged, first from Rita and then from Daisy—I felt cut off beyond even communication. And now I exerted myself to make a contact with the brown-eyed girl in red —to force her to meet my friendliness.

But as she saw that I declined to do business, she soon passed on to the gentleman in the dress suit, who happened to be standing near us. Without excuse or explanation, without hesitation or resentment, like some salesman of carpet-sweepers, who, rejected at one door at which he has knocked, immediately passes on to the next, she assailed him with her shameless patter.

I wondered how Tony Scallopino had ever dared to bring these women here, and I was roused to disgusted anger. (I found out afterwards that Sue herself, in her morbid and hysterical fear lest her party should be ill-attended, had telephoned to Tony to bring anyone still at his place—meaning, of course, his regular patrons.) I remembered how Tony Scallopino, in the days before his advent to the Village, had been an I.W.W. agitator and how, in the course of the long Italian dinners, in his former and cheaper restaurant, he had often sat down at our table and talked about politics with us. I had at that time always rather liked him, but it seemed to me tonight that Tony had become Manhattanized and cynical. It did not occur to me that, from Tony's point of view, the girls were working people like himself, and that in bringing them to Sue Borglum's party he might be merely endeavoring to make it up to them for a night of bad business at his night club; I might have guessed from their technique of hungry wolves that they were desperately in need of business. But I only felt that Tony had somehow become a traitor.

The fish-faced blonde now approached me, hoping to succeed where the other had failed. I let her see that she was wasting her time, and she passed on to the creature on the couch, the man in the orange kimono, and by some playful overture, woke him. But he, nervously starting up, regarded her with indignant surprise, and exclaimed in a high peevish voice: "I want to be left alone, please! I've got a perfectly terrible headache!"

Sue Borglum and Bobby McIlvaine had, in the meantime, appeared from the dining room; and Sue, beholding the girl in red, who had not long been detained by the dress suit, address herself immediately to Bobby as if she already knew him, had concluded at once that she was some flame of his, whom Bobby had invited without her approval. And, in a moment, on learning that Sue was the hostess, the newcomer had turned to her enthusiastically, exclaiming over the beauty of the old house, the old mirror, the quiet charm of the neighborhood, the delightfulness of the occasion: "But I'm so sorry to miss seeing Rita Cavanagh: I admire her poetry so much! I was so excited when Tony told me she was going to be here tonight, and then we missed her—she left before we came!"

I made my way to the hall again, where, in the manner of Larry Mickler, I drew and drank rapidly several cocktails from the lemon-cloudy lees of the water cooler. Then, feeling that these drinks were weak—they consisted mainly of melted ice—with a vision of a den of drug addicts gathered together, in gruesome merriment, to dose themselves with alcohol, I drank what was left of a bottle of whisky, which turned out to be excessively bad, stinging my tongue and constricting my gullet.

Now I began to ask myself whether it had been the revolver Larry Mickler was carrying which had made me break off with him so quickly and leave the room without waiting for his reply.

Through a door which led into the dining room and which opened behind me from the hall, I could hear Sue, who had left the sitting room—retreating, as was by no means characteristic of her, at the advance of the outrageous guests, whom she still believed to be friends of Bobby's—pouring out, to the equally unfortunate Claudette, in a shrill, strained and grating voice, her grievances against Bobby: "It isn't as if I'd ever been anything to him—I never was! I never wanted to do anything but help him. Some women would have tried to get a hold on him!" etc., etc. At that moment, it seemed to me that Sue—whom I found that I now somehow identified with the woman of the dyed red hair and the slatternly lacy dressing gown whom I had seen at the beginning of the evening in the house where Larry Mickler lived—that Sue Borglum was the ugliest and most odious woman whom I had ever known, and that she possessed the most horrible voice. Yet it was not really her voice which made me hate her, but the fact that she was lonely and in pain.

In the room where the phonograph was playing, the dancers had abandoned the floor, driven off by the man with the drums, who, however, still sat trancedly drumming. They sat or lay on the couches and chairs, which had been moved back against the sides of the room—as if washed up, I said to myself, in what I thought was a felicitous fancy, like driftwood, dead fish and seaweed left behind by the tide on the shore. Then I remembered

Rita's poem, the poem about the beach fire and the darkness: it seemed to me that my own image had been caught from it, and I felt that I had been travestying it foolishly.

With an impulse of irritation, I broke in upon the imbecile with the drums, interrupting him in a loud clear voice and inquiring whether he knew the time. "I don't know the time," he replied, with his abstracted fatuous smile. "But," he added, after a moment, when he had come to the end of a spasm of drumming, "I've got something else that's just as good!" He produced a pint flask from his back pocket: "And a darn sight better!" he added. He offered me a drink, which I accepted. I sat down on a chair beside him. "This is something," he further observed, after taking a swig himself, "that makes time unnecessary!" He had the conviction of quiet humor of a very stupid person. "If you carry a little flask," he continued, after a brief pause—he had begun softly drumming again—"you don't need to carry a watch!"

I asked him whether he knew Larry Mickler, and when he shook his head, always smiling, I expressed the extreme distaste I felt for the admirer of Nietzsche and Dostoevsky. "Why, he's a fellow," I protested, "who smashes the statue of the Winged Victory that his wife brings home from college—a perfectly nice little college girl! He tries to neck other girls in the Jap's room—in the bathroom! He threatens them with a gun! He's the most objectionable man I've ever known!"

And I reflected to the tune of the fox-trot and to the subdued rat-a-tat of the drum, that what I had said was literally true. Larry Mickler was, without any question, the most obnoxious man I had ever known—and I had failed to put him properly in his place! I had been afraid of his damned revolver! Here there had come to me an opportunity to stand up to Evil itself. It might be that such a moment as this, such a moment that tested a man, came but once to a man in his life! And I had quailed at the thought of a gun! Yet to stand up to Larry Mickler would be finally to vindicate one's honor against the shame, the despair, of Sue Borglum's terrible house! They themselves, I felt sure, would thank me for it!

I decided to seek him out. I should find him slinking about the rooms—I remembered his dirty complexion and his furtive ill-natured eye, his cockily waxed mustache. He would ask me to drink to Dostoevsky, and I should answer: "To hell with Dostoevsky! What's the good of a Dostoevsky to nourish such worms as you? The world would be more decent without him!—the world would be better off if it were rid of all the cripples and defectives who find their only justification in reading and writing books!"

And I was steadied with a deep satisfaction, a perfect self-assurance: I took on a new authority. With the most affable friendliness, I complimented the man with the spectacles on his mastery of the traps, and asked him whether he had taken lessons. He said, no: that he had just picked it up, and added some quiet pleasantry, at which I uproariously laughed, but to which I had paid no attention, as I had been thinking of the classical statue which Larry Mickler had smashed on the mantelpiece and which now appeared to my mind in the guise of a silver-gray Athena as slender as her spear—and this vision, in the glimpse of a second, had dragged with it all the fresh bright beauty of the portfolio of drawings for Homer which Bobby had shown Rita and me that May night in University Place.

I arose and thanked the drummer for his drink, which I extravagantly commended with a condescension almost regal. He offered me another, which I took.

Walking composedly from room to room, I began scouring the house for Larry Mickler. With a keen and arrogant glance, I scrutinized the groups one by one. I told myself that, once Mickler was disposed of, I should carry off the pretty brunette, who had now come to seem to me desirable. I should meet her at first on her professional basis, and then I should compel her to be human with me—she should drop that horrible manner and mask, she should share with me her thoughts and her feelings!—She should become my companion—she should love me!

But I could find Larry Mickler nowhere, and when at last I began to inquire, nobody seemed to know what had become of him. In the front room, I was taken aback to discover that the girl with the brown eyes had already reached an understanding with a clownish-looking elderly man, who wore a heavy black ribbon on his eye-glasses. He was pressing her to leave with him at once; and she was explaining that she would have to wait until her "girl-friend" was ready to go. The little fish-faced blonde, for her part, had, in the meantime, been taken in the toils of one of the licensed Greenwich Village lunatics, who, without a penny in his pocket, was exerting the active and ironic intelligence of which his derangement had never deprived him to convince her of the seriousness of his intentions.

I went up to Tony Scallopino, who greeted me with a broad sunny smile, and asked him whether he had seen Larry Mickler. "I just see him go," he replied.

I stood for a moment without speaking. Then, "What's the idea," I began, "of bringing these girls here tonight!" "They're just two little girls," he explained, "who come to my place to dance. They've had hard luck and they have to earn a little money. They're two very nice girls." He had said this with a smiling eye in which I thought I detected insolence. I found myself glaring at him. "Well,

I think it was a great mistake to bring them here to-night!" I declared.

His grin was for a second obscured by a blink, like the shutter of a camera. He began to say something more, I don't know what. I only stared into his face: his eyes were wide open but shrewd; he still smiled—he had the habitual tactfulness of the Italian restaurant proprietor, but his obsequiousness was gone: he was raising his heavy black eyebrows, as if in surprise and protest. I felt that he thought me drunk, that he considered my objections tactless. Was Tony Scallopino not himself an independent Villager? had he not been invited to the party? had he not sometimes loaned money to the lunatic who was attempting to impose on the blond girl? had he not talked like a brother to Hugo of the trials and aspirations of the workers? had he not sometimes cashed my checks?

My lips opened, without my having planned it, and, despite the gummy tongue of drunkenness, I heard myself suddenly interrupt him: "You used to be a Wobbly! You used to talk about justice to the workers! Well, it seems to me that now you're betraying the workers! You're trying to give the Greenwich Villagers a taste for leisure-class luxuries! You've turned your old Italian restaurant into an expensive uptown night club!—and you charge us high prices for bad liquor! And you have the nerve to bring these girls—" He tried to slip away, but I seized him by the arms and pinioned him against the wall: "You used to talk about the social revolution—well, if there's ever a social revolution, you proletarians who run night clubs will be the first to get the axe!—When I first came to Greenwich Village——"

He was angry and tried to pull away—I thought I heard him say, "You must be drunk!" and saw him give me a black malign look. With a powerful movement of his arms, he lifted them and pushed me away with such force that I staggered backward and almost fell. I struck him in the jaw with my fist—and the next moment was looking at the room from a different point of view, and knew that I was lying on the floor.

IV

In the bright warm room, so alive inside the bleak November dark, before the fire burning briskly and stoutly, Professor Grosbeake's three beautiful daughters gave me tea in their parents' absence. Among the elegant slender spindles of the legs and rungs of the English furniture, which seemed blacker and stronger-grained than American mahogany—which, as in the case of the Queen Anne secretary, with its narrow shape, its dark dense grain, its close-laid shelves above, hooded with a double-loaf top, and its close-packed drawers below, diminishing in thickness toward the bottom, its air of having always contained sealed letters and legal papers, all safely and neatly locked away, seemed designed for a tighter, compacter and more downright civilization; among the late pale autumnal flowers, the roses and the bowl of white cosmos; the white ruffle-bordered curtains against the black of the winter panes and the patches of confused pink and green touched in by mildly modernist paintings—in this setting, Magda, Frieda and Rosamond, themselves in fresh light frocks like the flowers, enchanted me with their loveliness and candor.

They were all very smooth and blond; they had never bobbed their hair, and Frieda and Magda wore theirs brushed abundantly down their backs, like Alice in the Alice books. Rosamond, who was older than the twins, had hers up; it was parted in the middle and tightly wound behind in a blond and young womanly knot, so that, if one thought only of her hair, she seemed like a young German fräulein (Mrs. Grosbeake was German), whereas, if one thought of her blue eyes, her straight nose, her long oval face and her long and graceful neck, she seemed like an English girl. She served tea with nice shy manners. Rosamond was dressed in pale blue; and one of the twins, Magda, wore white, and Frieda, a kind of lilac, with stockings a kind of lavender lighter than the frock. The twins seemed rather German than English: they had plump round cheeks and round noses, and were maturely developed for fourteen.

Frieda had golden-red hair, which gave a singular effect of richness as it came down over her purple dress; Magda was more heavily built and slower-moving and slower-thinking than her sister: she was the blondest of all—her hair was the palest purest flaxen I had ever seen. And her blondness made me think of Daisy, whom I expected to see the next day.

(I had lately come back from abroad. My aunt had left me a small legacy, and very soon after the night at Sue Borglum's, I had gone to Europe and had stayed there till fall. When I returned, I had been eager to see Grosbeake, one of whose books I had bought in England and had been reading on the boat, and in whom I now felt a new interest. I had also planned to visit Daisy and Pete Bird, who had left New York, even before I had, and were now living together in the country, not far out of my way back to town. Since I had been back, I had written to Daisy, and she had invited me to come to see them.)

I liked the English voices of the young Grosbeakes:

they had a soft flurried way of speaking and a maidenly innocence of timbre quite unlike young American girls (though the twins were beginning already to acquire American slang). "I don't like this kind of crackers," said Magda. "We couldn't get the regular biscuits," Rosamond explained. "The grocer's all out of them.—I'm sorry," she went on seriously to me. "I'm afraid they're not very good!" "You always say 'biscuits,'" said Frieda, "and Magda always says 'crackers.' I think we all ought to say the same thing!" "What do you say?" queried Magda. "Sometimes I say one," said Frieda, "and sometimes I say the other. But I like 'biscuits' best!" "I think these are really crackers," said Rosamond, who did not want my feelings hurt by a discrimination in favor of "biscuits," "because they crackle so when you break them." "That's why I think 'biscuits' is better," insisted Frieda, "—because 'crackers' sounds as if they *all* crackled—but *some* biscuits just bend, you know!" "They're not biscuits," said Rosamond. "They're cakes. Won't you have some more tea?" she urged me. "No," said Frieda, "you know those little soft ones that we had in the country last summer, that you can almost bend in two!" "They were little cakes," said Rosamond.—We heard someone come in at the front door. "There's Father," Magda announced.

I could see Grosbeake taking off his black coat and his low-crowned black hat and setting his stick in the stand, before he appeared in the doorway. He had the rounded back of the scholar, a back, indeed, almost humped—of which I always used to feel that the exceptional extent to which it was bowed was an index to the degree of the difficulty of his researches. But Grosbeake, beyond this, had nothing of the physical deficiency—the weak eyes or the feeble figure—ordinarily attributed to the scholar. On the contrary, he seemed to have sprung from some tough ruddy-cheeked English stock which not even a lifetime of universities could enervate or fade. Despite the fineness of his features, he had something of Mr. Pickwick and even something of Mr. Punch. And on an American who had been living in New York he produced a special impression: it was as if one were surprised and rejoiced, after seeing a horde of depersonalized masks, at finding someone who possessed a face. With his fair cheeks flushed rosy by the cold, his salient nose and chin, his slanting Henry VIII eyes and his look of having been carved by hand out of some very sound kind of wood by a woodcarver of the days before machinery, he had the look of being a product, by way of past generations, of a constant hand-to-hand encounter with the turbulence of the elements and with the occasions of human life. He wore black English clothes and his stiff cuffs were very white. His collar and his cravat, and his white locks which came down over his collar, seemed to me extremely old-fashioned. He always carried a thickish dark stick, with a brass top of interlocked apes, which a brother had brought him from India.

He greeted me with his charming courtesy and peered up at me with wise and subtle bird-lidded eyes. "I'm sorry," he explained, "not to have been able to be here for tea. But there was a meeting of the examination committee at precisely a quarter to five—something which would be unthinkable in England, you know." He lifted sparse old eyebrows in a smile. "Rather than make the dons miss their tea, they'd allow the examination to be prepared without adequate consultation! I had proposed holding the meeting in a tea-room, but they didn't seem to care for the suggestion—or to take the hint!" He spoke slowly and very deliberately, and his voice had fine up-and-down inflections of sweetness and humor; his nostrils had inflections, too, and vibrated while he spoke.

"I'm afraid the tea's cold," said Rosamond. "I'll have

some fresh made." "No: never mind!" said Grosbeake. He stood before the fire, his hands clasped just above his stomach. "I think we shall have snow," he announced. "I think we shall have snow! The Dean was very sure we shouldn't—but I believe that we shall!" I remarked that we had had no frost and that the afternoon had been warm. "That was what the Dean pointed out," he replied. "He even insisted on making a bet with me. He bet me a bottle of Scotch whisky against a bottle of my sherry. I think he'll get the better of the bargain: the sherry is very good—it was given me by a friend in the Embassy, who had the privilege of bringing it in!"

He took the cup of tepid tea from Rosamond and sat down in an armchair before the fire. He asked me about myself and what I had been writing. I was ashamed to be obliged to tell him that, even while I had been abroad, I had really not written anything. I said that my literary morale had been low, or something equally silly.

"I was just thinking," he replied, "in the Dean's room, in looking at the portraits of the college presidents there —that it may be from certain points of view as much of a misfortune to have too much character, too well-sustained a morale, as to have too little. When I looked at the early presidents, especially the seventeenth-century ones, I said to myself, 'There are men whose character has been overdeveloped! It's a very special combination of qualities, you know, that's required for a mind capable of original work. A man mustn't have his character too vigorously developed, because he must be able to experiment with ideas. It's like going to buy a hat, you know— first you try one on and wear it for a bit to see how it goes, and then you try on another. But a man with a strongly developed character is unable to do that.—Yet, on the other hand he must, of course, have character enough not simply to drift about without preferring one idea to another."

Grosbeake had a curious irony, which was always at the same time benign. It was the irony—one sees it seldom —of a mind which is at once innocent and subtle, and which has, in consequence, something divine about it: an irony without malice. He had a touch perhaps of the vanity, or rather, of the dandyism, of the modern mathematical philosopher, who finds himself provided with paradoxes at once so surprising, so attractive and so sound. I have heard him comment with his calm amusement on the mistakes of unmathematical philosophers when they attempted to invoke mathematics: "It's curious," he would say, "how peculiarly unfortunate they are in their choice of mathematical examples! They always seem to hit upon something which isn't necessarily true at all—which might as well be the other way, you know! Bradley, for example, in his *Logic*, when he wants to give an illustration of a particularly indisputable truth—something we must accept as self-evident—that, if B is to the left of C, and if A is to the left of B, then A must be to the left of C, also—when, of course, that's not true at all!—if you prolong a straight line indefinitely, you come back on the other side!" Though, I reflected, when Bradley wrote, the new non-Euclidean geometry could hardly have been widely known. There may have entered, also, into Grosbeake's attitude, in this particular instance, some element of the opposition between the points of view of mathematical Cambridge and humanistic Oxford.

But no one could have been farther than Grosbeake from the essential triviality of mind which academic arrogance or complacency so often attempts to disguise. For if Hugo Bamman and his father were the modern type of saints, Grosbeake was a modern type of sage, who taught wisdom in casual conversation and virtue only by example. I had felt his influence even in college, at a time when I as yet knew nothing of his philosophical ideas. For Grosbeake had the most comprehensive mind, at home in the most varied fields, with which I had ever come in contact. Philosophy for him meant the striving to take account of all the aspects of the universe, and to find in them coherence and a meaning, so that his comment on any subject had a special significance and value, and in spite of the fact that he never made an effort to expostulate or convert, was likely to present itself long afterwards as something to be seriously considered in making up one's mind on the subject. And though he detested every sort of preaching (Mr. Bamman had been a born preacher), and though even the study of Ethics was inconceivable to him, he had the effect, more than anyone else I had known, of making moral distinction attractive. I remember his saying once of some student, a student of whose abilities he thought well, but who, as punishment for some escapade, had had his chapel cuts taken away from him, so that he could not go out of town over Sundays, that this privation would "do him good" because he would now do some work during the week-ends. "So you do believe in doing people good!" someone present had caught him up. "I thought you didn't believe in that!" "That's an object," Grosbeake had answered, a little taken aback, "which I believe is best promoted indirectly."

Mrs. Grosbeake came in before dinner. She was a broad, handsome, placid German woman, very thoroughly educated but extremely practical. One always felt that she was a kind of base upon which Grosbeake's metaphysics rested; for he was more high-strung and sensitive than he seemed, and, although intellectually imperturbable, was in other ways easily disorganized.

We had dinner in the white-walled dining room—it

was a solid and attractive colonial house. The Grosbeakes had brought over their own silver, as well as their own furniture, and the pieces had always seemed to me to possess personal physiognomies. There was a squarish silver teapot which squatted flat on the table and had a very sharp emphatic spout that jutted straight out from the base and was balanced on the other side by a long straight high-cocked handle; and the cream pitcher, the sauce boat and even the little salt cellars straddled sturdily on three tiny legs, like some sort of blunt-beaked beetles, or rather, it occurred to me tonight, like the spouted and pot-bellied demons of Bruegel or Callot. Even the color and substance of the food seemed to have a special richness and density, as if they had been painted in a still-life. The bread and the boiled potatoes looked particularly white and firm, the mound of currant jelly particularly lucent and red, and the beefsteak particularly vivid in its contrasts of red and brown. The Ambassador's sherry was delicious. In spite, however, of the relish with which Grosbeake had spoken of it, his epicurean tastes were really indulged almost exclusively in the things of the intellect, so that I have heard him relish a page of Hume as if it had been a wine, whereas food and drink themselves, as well as other material comforts, he usually disregarded. Now he dominated the table, talking tranquilly and blandly; and in the presence of their father and mother, the three lovely Grosbeake girls—unlike young American girls, who often interrupt their parents —were respectfully in abeyance. The twins, who were sitting together had an occasional low rapid interchange.

"I've been reading Sinclair Lewis's *Babbitt*," said Grosbeake. I asked him what he thought of it. "Oh, very good," he replied. "Though a little unfair to Babbitt, I think. Of course, I know very little about the American cities of the Middle West—I can't pretend to speak. But from the students from the West that I've had in my courses, I get rather a different impression. They're very alert, you know—very eager to learn. And they do well: they grasp things very quickly. So I don't think that the families they come from can be quite so uniformly benighted as Lewis represents them in *Babbitt*.—And I feel, in reading your friend Hugo Bamman, that he paints, in much the same way, perhaps too somber a picture of the business men and their families.

"It seems to me rather a mistake, you know, to hold the business men up to ridicule for their Rotary Clubs and their fraternal organizations. Under conditions of that kind, where the city is quite new and the people have no institutions, they have to create some sort of institutions in order to hold the community together. Rotary Clubs and societies of that sort, imperfect as they may be, fulfil a very necessary function.

"It seems to me that, from some points of view, the most unfortunate feature of American business is its failure to provide real leaders. Professor Pittinger, who has been making a study of the subject, tells me that it has become impossible, for example, for the president or one of the directors of a large corporation to leave a controlling interest to his son. He can only leave him an investment, and the son can spend the money as he pleases; but he inherits no power and no responsibility, and the surviving officers of the company don't recognize his right to any. That seems to me unfortunate, because after the father has had to make his own way, largely without advantages, to a position of importance, the son, who has had the advantages, is left without any power. You often find in England that the squire who has lived in the country and has had to deal at first-hand with his tenants, and with his animals and his property, has a far stronger sense of realities than the more enlightened Londoner."

"But he sometimes mistreats his tenants and misman-
ages his estate abominably," Mrs. Grosbeake interjected.

"If he does," continued Grosbeake, "he knows better
what he's doing, nevertheless, than the average Liberal
member of Parliament, say, who has the best intentions
in the world, but who lives between his club and the
House of Commons and certain houses to which he goes—
always seeing the same people, who are all people of precisely his way of thinking, who are living in precisely the
same way—so that he never at any point really comes into
contact with realities—and so never really knows what he
is talking about. Even Morley was a little like that.

"I wonder whether it mightn't be an advantage, both
for the sons of business men and for the businesses themselves, if the second generation could take over some
responsibility in connection with their fathers' work.
They seem to me very intelligent—so far as I've been able
to judge from those I meet in my classes—and the effect
on trade and industry of even one generation of such men
might, I should think, be enormous. In that event, the
Rotary Clubs might become very important institutions—
they might provide the moral leadership for business."

I had so long been taking it for granted that no good
could come out of business, that this idea of Grosbeake's
seemed to me a very queer and foreign one; but I reflected
on what he had said.

I always listened with interest and respect to Grosbeake's opinions on American matters. He had studied
American affairs with the attention, at once sympathetic
and detached, which he applied to everything, and he
often succeeded in illumining them with that uncanny
divination which he displayed in all sorts of fields quite
outside his special province. At that time, it had become
the custom for Englishmen who visited America—we
encouraged it, of course, ourselves—to edify us with gen-

eralizations about American life and institutions—general-
izations often based on a round of cocktail parties in New
York, or, at most, on a lecture tour. So many of the prizes
in America always went to the third- and second-rate that
we had become, especially since the War, a paradise for
British mediocrities—poets, novelists and universal critics,
who had often great success as lecturers. They went about
patronizing the Americans with a gusto and a giddy elation which suggested that they might themselves have
been patronized at home; and they would sometimes tour
the country from coast to coast and return again and
again. It was, therefore, peculiarly gratifying for an American to discover in Grosbeake those qualities of toughness,
richness, eccentricity and independence which one had
admired in English literature and history, but of which
one had so often been disappointed in the English celebrities who visited us.

After dinner, we sat before the fire. Mrs. Grosbeake
seemed to contribute a ground-tone of reassurance: she
made one feel that the body of humanity was invulner-
ably solid and sound, and that it was deep and contained
many treasures which had not yet been brought to birth.
She sat with her feet side by side, resting squarely on
the floor, and she wore some sort of leather sandals with
very wide blunt toes. These sandals, like the modernist
paintings—which Grosbeake had bought from a former
student, who was having financial difficulties—were one
of the odd notes of unconventionality in the tranquil conventional household; and they surprised me in the same
unwarranted way as when one found Grosbeake, in certain of his writings, carrying his philosophical principles
through morals into the field of political criticism and
expounding an indictment against nationalism or capital-
ism.

I had never, as an undergraduate, read anything that

Grosbeake had written, and I had never taken any of his courses. I had, however, in my senior year, occasionally gone to his house. After meeting him once or twice at teas, I had run into him one day in the hallway of one of the recitation buildings. He had recognized me and stopped to talk to me about an article which I had written for the college magazine and which had aroused a certain amount of controversy. I had attacked, as a sinister conspiracy against freedom of action and thought, the policy of the English Department, the administration of the Dean's office, football mass meetings, compulsory chapel and the custom of making freshmen wear little black caps; and I was surprised and rather embarrassed by Grosbeake's expression of friendly interest. I replied almost apologetically—I had been somewhat dismayed by the rumpus I had roused—that I seemed to have laid myself open to a good deal of adverse criticism. "Ah, well," Grosbeake had reassured me, "one can't take up any position, can one? without doing that." My complaints had been made in resentment, and they had been answered with resentment by the faculty, the alumni, the editors of the college daily, the officers of the athletic association and some of the more ardent and articulate freshmen, who insisted that they asked nothing better than to pay homage to the college tradition by continuing to wear their little black caps. It had never occurred to me, at the time, that I was engaged in doing anything so dignified as taking up a position, and I had felt I must be careful, in future, to carry the controversy with the utmost fairness and sobriety, that I must keep firmly in mind my intellectual responsibilities. And half my bitterness and indignation against the college authorities disappeared from the moment when I realized that an elderly and important professor would consider without heat what I had said.

He had invited me then to his house, and I went afterwards on Sunday evenings, when the Grosbeakes received faculty and students. I rarely heard him talk about his subject, and did not understand him when he did: I had only the vaguest notion what this subject was. I figured him as eternally occupied with solving the same sort of problems with which I had struggled in trigonometry and coördinate geometry. I did not know that those strings of puzzles were not the whole of mathematics, but merely multiplied illustrations of general mathematical laws, in which no one had attempted to interest me. And still less did I realize that Grosbeake had passed beyond mathematics proper to symbolic logic (it was mainly the fact that we had in the faculty another symbolic logician —a man with whom he wished to collaborate—which had brought him to the United States and which had kept him here so long). I did not know that symbolic logic was an attempt to provide a universal language for all the branches of science, and that this attempt to formulate relations common to different departments of thought was itself a deeper expression of the same genius which had given rise to Grosbeake's interest in such varied fields of human activity and of his extraordinary instinct for tracing their interrelations. Aside from his personal distinction and charm, it was this gift which had fascinated me: he had usually talked to me about literature, but, aside from his appreciation of poetry, plays and novels as such—which was in itself remarkable—he had also a brilliant faculty for reading into them social and moral history and revealing their philosophic implications. He was the first person, since Hugo's father, who had helped me toward the kind of education which began for me when Mr. Bamman had talked to me at school about Shakespeare.

I had, however, never guessed at Grosbeake's real importance—and indeed his importance outside his special field had never really appeared until a year or two before the War, when he had turned from mathematics to philosophy. I was astonished when I read his books. First of all, Grosbeake's tone and style, in his philosophical writings, were not at all what I should have expected. His manner in conversation was rather urbane, dispassionate and dry; he seemed, as I have said, to approach ideas with a certain epicureanism of the intellect. But his writing had a close tough grain; it was crystalline in the sense that it gave an effect of the hardness and clarity of crystals rather than of the limpidity of crystal; it had a peculiar earnestness and intensity, and a kind of incandescence. But what had surprised me most—I had already had some idea of the universal scope of his mind— were the power of his imagination and the boldness and stoutness of his spirit.

Grosbeake was one of the first modern philosophers, really competent to understand the new physics of relativity and quantum theory, who had made an attempt, on the full scale, to trace the consequences of these discoveries for the concepts of general philosophy and to construct a system which should admit them. This had brought him to a drastic rejection of the philosophical assumptions of old-fashioned mechanistic science.

Since my recent encounters with the world in New York, which had made me feel my own weakness and baseness, I had myself been haunted and oppressed, as on the night of Sue Borglum's party, by the thought that humanity, after all, was merely another race of animals, whose behavior was fixed by their environment, and by the cells which they had had from their parents, and that the earth with all its creatures was only a complicated interaction of hard little particles like bullets. I now learned that it had lately become possible, in the light of

scientific research—that it had even become inevitable
(though I was far from being able to follow all Grosbeake's arguments)—to conceive of the universe as not a
machine, which had once been wound up and was still
running but as an organism in course of development.
The unit was no longer a bullet, but something called an
event; and the world was a flux of events. The relativity
of time and space and the anomalous behavior of elec-
trons, in undermining the "iron laws" of nature, had
opened floodgates of speculation that the ordinary rea-
sonable mind, the kind of mind which respected science
without examining its assumptions or attempting to force
them to their consequences, had long tended to regard
as closed. And unabashed by the surprised disapproval of
other mathematicians who, capable of practicing only one
trade, prided themselves on sticking to their lasts, Professor Grosbeake had late in his career emerged as a
metaphysician.

I wanted to make him talk on this subject, and I
asked vaguely about the congress of a scientific association which he had attended the summer before. He told
me briefly of some of its proceedings, then added, after a
pause, with his bland and serious irony: "If you want to
see the sort of men that the medieval church must have
been made up of, you should study an assemblage of
modern scientists. I thought about them last summer that
they must be very like the medieval doctors. They're all
more or less internationally minded, you know, and
they're men of strong character and conviction—and
they're all authoritarians: they subscribe to a body of
dogma and they won't countenance any heresy. If a sci-
entist has evolved an hypothesis which runs counter to
the established hypothesis, they won't give it a serious
hearing—if he's performed an experiment, you know,

which conflicts with accepted experiments, they refuse
to look at it!"

At this point in the conversation, Magda and Frieda,
who had to go to bed, came in to say good night. They
kissed their mother, who spoke to them in a low voice,
but they hesitated about kissing their father—in the midst
of solemn discourse and with a visitor present. Magda
hung back by her mother's couch, but Frieda cut the knot
by dashing forward, diving for his bald brow—I saw her
own beautiful hair over her shoulders, like some spilling
of gold by the gods—and abruptly running out of the
room. "Oh, good night, my dear!" said Grosbeake.—"They
have never executed anyone," he continued—Magda
kissed him on the cheek, more diffidently: "Good night,
my dear!—But there are other methods of suppression
even more expedient and effective, for burning calls attention to the victim."

His criticism of contemporary science soon led him into
metaphysics.—The entrance of those gold and white girls
—the offspring, so late in life, of that old bald round-
shouldered man who had spent long years in the obstinate plumbing—by means of formulas so abstract and
difficult that they excluded even ideas of number, so far
beyond the ordinary reaches of even scientific minds that
they dismayed even mathematicians—in exploring that
mysterious reality which is at once what we find outside
us and what we think about it—the entrance of Grosbeake's lovely daughters had had the effect on me of a
revelation of the human vitality, the creative force of
flesh and blood, which may be embodied in abstract
thought. It was as if my imagination had fully conceived
for the first time that the logician's chain of propositions,
no less than the astronomer's systems and the physicist's
analysis of the invisible, could be as much the ripened
fruit of rich natures as the poetry of Shakespeare and

Dante, or as those beautiful long-limbed children, the breed of the Kentish seas and of the forests of the Rhineland, who had brusquely embraced their father.

He talked to me about the book he was writing. All that I had ever learned at college of philosophy had been a conception of the external world as a colorless and soundless wilderness whose true nature one could never know, which one could not even imagine—but which I did, none the less, imagine as a vast landscape of polar spaces in whose eternal twilight one wandered, preoccupied and deluded by a flicker of magic-lantern pictures which danced inside one's mind and forever remained private to oneself. I had now learned, however, from Grosbeake that since, for example, the high flush of Rita's cheeks and the sound of her voice reciting poetry had so radically affected my behavior, they must belong as much to reality, to that Nature which was no longer outside one, as the blood corpuscles and the light waves, the sound waves and the vocal organs which were assumed to have produced these. And I now found that Grosbeake admitted as belonging, also, to reality those aesthetic values which, for example, had made Rita, when she wrote her poems, declare that the pavements of the Village were harsh and that the sound of the river was musical. And so, finally, he told me, moral values, which he identified with aesthetic values, must be equally a part of that reality which he found it impossible to split into two divisions of mind and matter, body and soul. Those moral judgments, then, I reflected, which had given rise to my disgust and despair the night of Sue Borglum's party had been, after all, as real, as much to be taken seriously, as the biological and neurological processes to which I had tended to reduce them.

What astonished me most, however, was that Grosbeake now crowned his system with a new conception of God. He brought God back into the universe of science, under what appeared to me at first an unfamiliar form. For Grosbeake's God was as different as possible from the tolerant and moderate Great Spirit, the enlightened parliamentary monarch, of the modern liberal theologian. God, for Grosbeake, was the ultimate harmony implied by the aesthetic and moral values of which men were aware in the universe; and our moments of divine revelation were simply those when we recognized most indubitably the necessity of this harmony and order, when we became most acutely conscious of this creative purpose of God. And it was, then, this creative purpose which, in the interest of the ultimate harmony, determined which possibilities, among the infinite possibilities of the constant flux of events—the development of the universal organism—should make themselves actualities.

I listened to Grosbeake with excitement. He seemed to me at that moment to justify those instincts and beliefs which—suspicious of all the world and uncertain of myself most of all—I had lately come to doubt. And I was moved by what seemed to me the greatness of his mind and the boldness of his spirit within the modesty and mildness of his home. I mustn't keep him up, then, and tire him. Mrs. Grosbeake had already gone to bed.

I said that I must go, and he got up and brought a bowl of nuts, which we cracked in front of the fire. He told me some Victorian anecdote about Gladstone and Disraeli, whom he always called "Dizzy."

As I finally came out of the warm house into the white-framed, glass-sided porch which enclosed the front door, I felt a tinge of crispness in the air, as when the first ice-splinters web a pond, and I caught the chilly fragrance of the roses and the white and daisylike cosmos, which had been set out in vases for the night; and as I took leave of Grosbeake—gazing out through the glass at the pavement lightly dappled with leaves and the dark grass glittering with wet, my mind bemused with a vision of God as a vast crystal fixing its symmetry from a liquefied universe—I felt a delicious delicacy of iciness, glossy fall-leaf slivers and black rain-glinting glass.

"It's beginning to snow," said Grosbeake. It was true: it was not raining, but snowing. A great flake alighted on my sleeve. "So I win my bet with the Dean," he said. "I shall have his Scotch whisky and not he my sherry!— You know, the weather's the only subject on which I really regard myself as infallible. It comes from being bred on the Kentish coast—learning about one's weather from the 'narrow seas'! What does Dean Mosley know of the weather?—coming from an inland city like Indian-apolis!"

Grosbeake stood in the outside door and regarded the large flakes with satisfaction. "Dean Mosley kept insist-ing," he continued, "that there were none of the signs of snow—and when he came to enumerate them, I saw that it was true: there were none of the signs. But I knew it was going to snow!"

*   *   *

It was a heavy snowstorm for November. It had snowed, and then rained, and then frozen. On the train, the next afternoon, when I scraped a peephole in the frost-glazed window, I disclosed a vignette of fences, strung with wires of ice, and tree branches decked with crystals, like glittering chandeliers.

But it was late when I arrived at my station. The cold and the falling darkness lay heavy on the little town. I finally succeeded in getting a taxi, which had no cushions on the seat and which bucked over the frozen ruts. There were nice white houses on the road and all the people seemed to be inside them: the windows were orange against the snow, which was blueing and graying with the night.

To the east, when we had left the town, an army of corn-stalks in the grayness were frozen to their posts; and to the west, the skies were split across with the tragic gold and black of a late November sunset. The grandeur of the winter landscape—since Grosbeake had predicted the snowfall—had associated itself in my mind with the grandeur of the philosophic mind; and as I gazed at those gigantic cracks of what seemed to be a light beyond human skies, I remembered the fiery walls of the world of which Lucretius had said that the thinker, in sending his intellect beyond them, had broken Nature's locks and won the freedom of the universe: they seemed to speak to me of bold and lonely thought.

The house, when we finally pulled in to it, was so low that it looked sunk in the snow—deep-embedded in the winter ground, which held it fast. There was a single yellow square of light.

Pete Bird hurried cordially out—I could see Daisy standing in the doorway. Pete insisted on my not paying for the taxi: "Just put it on my bill!" he told the man.

Inside, I found Daisy transformed. She greeted me with her frank American smile, but it was this time unmistakably the smile of the young American girls of my boyhood who had never used lipstick or rouge. I was surprised to see her wholly without make-up: her lips were a pale coral-pink and her hair, which at Sue Borglum's party had been mongrel, muddy and dull, was now an even flaxen yellow. She was wearing a neat white apron over a pretty blue dress, and looked exactly like some model little housewife in a bright-colored American advertizement, smiling happily over the lightness of a new kind of pancake flour or the flavor of a can of baked beans.

She apologized for the apron—she was just getting dinner, she said—and I thought that she knew she looked well in it. I told her how healthy and lovely she looked. "Just feel this!" she invited me, hooking up her little short-sleeved elbow. I found it studded with solid bulging muscles. "Good Heavens!" I exclaimed. "How did you ever get like that?" "Just working!" Daisy explained. "We fixed the place all up ourselves. When we came, it was just a dump!"

Pete himself, to my surprise, with his slight erect figure, seemed wiry, effective and hardy. He wore a khaki shirt with a smartly tied navy-blue tie, which gave to his old gray trousers and his old Norfolk jacket which did not match them, a gentlemanly air of roughing it.

Daisy amiably excused herself and went to attend to the dinner on the stove. Pete Bird—a casual and cordial host—invited me in before the fire.

The hall had been a little nondescript, a cross between a workshed and a hall closet; but the living room was orderly and cheerful. There was a bright rag rug on the floor, and on the walls were colored prints and maps—Pete was a great hand at map-making. There were lamps with warmly glowing shades, also the work of Pete. In a large old-fashioned fireplace, big logs were roaring and snapping on tall black old-fashioned andirons, still stiff-necked, though lame and leaning.

I expressed my enthusiasm for the fire, and admired the fireplace and the room. Pete received my compliments with the easy nod and brief word of the owner of an Adirondack camp. He made one feel that the spacious fireplace was something he had had specially built—he seemed to imply snarling bear heads, moose antlers and other trophies under heavy and darkling rafters.

"That black log's not burning well," he announced. "Either it's frozen in the cracks or it's cranky!" He hooked it and wrenched it with a poker and an old rickety pair of tongs which did not come together. He had a master's way with the logs: "Get over there, you old alligator! You *will* be hard-boiled, *will* you!"

"I'm sorry," he remarked, as he stood up in front of the mantelpiece, which was almost as high as his head, and invited me to sit down before the fire—"I'm sorry that I can't offer you a drink—but the only things you can get around here are apple and alcohol, and both of them are vile. We've finally come to the conclusion that it's really more considerate to the guests not to offer them anything at all!"—"We hoped you might bring something with you," said Daisy, looking up with her sweet candid smile. She was dealing out white plates around a table in the middle of the room. I apologized for not having thought of it. "We never think of it ourselves—if you can believe me," Pete insisted. "It's almost impossible now to get any kind of decent liquor—in New York or anywhere else—and the kind of drinks that you can get just don't interest me!" I agreed with him heartily and added that the trouble with New York was that everybody there drank far too much bad liquor. "That's why we came to the country," said Daisy. "We decided that it was that or the drunkards' home!"

"Now, good people!" Daisy invited us, mimicking the kind of women who say, "Now, good people!"—"The dinner is all ready!—if you'll just sit down and fly at it!"

The dinner was an admirable pot roast, with onions, potatoes and carrots. We all ate a great deal and did very little talking while we ate.

The table was thick-legged and long. It seemed that Pete had made it himself—and that he had also made or made over most of the other pieces of furniture. When they had moved in, the place had been desolate—full of rubbish, mold and rats. It had taken them all summer to make it habitable. Pete had rummaged in old barns and houses and unearthed many mutilated antiques, which he had then, with great patience, repaired. He seemed to know a good deal about antiques. The principal prize was a comb-backed rocking chair, for which Pete had himself supplied new rockers; but they warned me not to try to sit in it because it always went over backwards. I told Pete about the Grosbeakes' furniture, and he remembered that there was a Queen Anne secretary something like the one I was describing, in the Metropolitan Museum.

For dessert we ate golden canned peaches, and we drank a great deal of black coffee. "Now, don't worry about the dishes," said Pete to Daisy. "Just stack them in the kitchen, and I'll do them later myself!" "If that doesn't mean," replied Daisy, "that I'll have to do them in the morning, when they're all greasy and cold." "Don't be silly!" said Pete, indignantly.

After dinner, we sat around the fire. I asked them what they did in the evenings. "We just do this!" said Pete. "We read aloud," supplemented Daisy. "We've read Bulwer Lytton's novels almost entirely through." "Is he any good?" I inquired. "Fine," said Daisy. "Besides, he's the only novelist that they've got in the village library." I was amazed at the idea of Daisy spending long winter evenings over Bulwer Lytton; but as I had talked to her, I soon discovered that she had always been addicted to novel-reading and had very good sense and taste—it had apparently been only Ray Coleman's reading aloud to her out of the Oxford Book of English Verse that she hadn't been able to stand.

I saw now that her ordinary vocabulary was partly literary, and that it was the combination of literate words with slang which gave her speech its peculiar charm—as when she had said, at the time I had first talked to her, that her nightmare horse had been "leering" at her or when she had told me that Ray Coleman in Paris had seemed "pretty affluent."

I asked her what writers she liked best. "Well," she said, "when I was a girl at school, I used to think that Compton Mackenzie was the swellest thing in the world —I thought that that was what life ought to be like— that was what I thought Phil and I were like when we ran away from Pittsburgh. But I soon found out that the old routine was more like a Russian novel!"

Russian novels reminded me of Larry Mickler, and I asked Pete and Daisy about him. I had never seen him before or since the night of Sue Borglum's party, and I had never been able to explain him: he had come to seem to me—like the man with a proboscis whom I had met in the doorway on Thirty-fourth Street—a sort of demon who had fleetingly materialized out of the infernal fumes of the evening. "Oh," said Daisy, "he's perfectly harmless—he's just a fool, that's all. He's usually controlled by Alice, his wife. He was just acting up that night because Alice wasn't along. He's always threatening to do something desperate, but he usually ends up with Alice administering triple-bromides." I asked what Alice was like. "She's just a clean stalwart college girl," said Daisy. "She doesn't know quite what a genius is," contributed Pete, "but she thinks that Larry is a genius. He wrote a novel once which he was never able to get published, and he's always threatening to write another. In the meantime, he's in the advertizing business, which he says he can never respect."

"I don't like Larry Mickler," Pete added, after a pause. "He cheats at limericks!" I asked him what he meant. "Why, he gets you to play this game where you both have to take the same first line and make up a limerick to fit it. But he's got the limericks all made up beforehand. When

I finally got wise and supplied the first line myself, he couldn't do a thing—he got sullen and wouldn't play. Our relations have never been cordial since.— That's why he tried to make out that I gypped him on those liverwurst sandwiches."

I had been watching Daisy follow the talk with a child-like seriousness and candor. Though it was cold, she wore no stockings—for reasons of economy, she said—and she lifted her slim and pretty legs, with their straw-colored sharp-toed slippers, in the movements of a good little girl listening restlessly but attentively to the conversation of her elders. As we joked or talked seriously, told limericks or deplored the demoralizing effects of the city, she would respond with gravity or humor, turning her eyes from one speaker to the other. She seemed sober-minded, shy and nice: I felt that some of the limericks embarrassed her. I came to think of her almost as a proper young wife and vaguely confused her in my mind with Grosbeake's golden-haired daughters.

Like all people who live in the country, they commenced about at ten to yawn. When I suggested that they must be tired, they confessed it with little pretence.

"Now," said Pete, "we have a guest-room which is always at the disposal of our guests—but it's as cold as a fiddler's bitch tonight, and if you really want to keep warm, you'd better sleep here on the couch." "But what about you?" I asked. "If you can stand the cold, I can." "Oh, we sleep in here!" replied Pete—and opening the door into the next room, which was barren as an attic and littered with all kinds of junk, he produced a gigantic set of bedsprings, which he maneuvered through the door with nonchalance and set out on a pair of trestles.

I explored the regions beyond. There was a bedroom behind the living-room, like a plunge into a cold black lake. Through the little, low, square-paned window, I saw

the moon, cut in brightest coldest silver over the lonely
and frozen fields. There had been something almost
miraculous about Grosbeake's predicting the snowfall—as
if Nature had admitted him to her secrets!

I returned to the smell of wood smoke and the yellow-
shaded lamps of the living-room, and announced that I
would sleep on the couch.

How jolly it was, I reflected, back amid the warmth
again, to go to bed in front of a fire, in the country, in the
winter time, in the house of friends! And as I undressed
in the dark and grisly storeroom, which evidently represented the house as they had originally found it—before
they had taken it in hand—I was moved by admiration for
what seemed to me their pioneering heroism. They had
established, with no help and little money, in the midst
of that hard rural wilderness—if but in a single room—
these decencies and amenities, this hearthstone of civilized living.

And they were right! Who should know it by this time
—all the more since my visit to Grosbeake!—better than I?
All that dignified mankind, all that kept us from the
bawling and the squalor which, the night of Sue Borglum's party, had seemed to me the universal fate, had
been built up through endurance and patience, through
good faith and steadiness of purpose, through property
well administered, through families standing together,
through lovers true to their pledges! Why had I ever been
taken in by that foolish and shallow philosophy of living
only for the moment?—that philosophy I had learned
from a woman, which was possible only for a woman,
given up, by her woman's nature, to her impulses, passions and moods! I remembered how I had once used to
wonder at Rita's preoccupation with death, both in her
poems and in conversation, and I saw now that such a
life as Rita's, looking always on the image of itself, must

be ridden by the terror of death, because death meant for it the end of the world.

When Daisy was in bed, Pete Bird summoned me back into the living room, and I wrapped myself up in blankets and lay down before the fire on the couch. But the coffee had made us wakeful and we went on talking in bed. At first, we told funny stories, till we had obviously exhausted our best and had begun to fall back on second-rate ones. Then Pete regaled me with reminiscences of eccentric Greenwich Village characters who had flourished before my day—there had been one uncompromising idealist who had made a practice of robbing fur-stores. He would hide himself among the furs at the back, till the shop had been closed for the night, then climb out with his booty, through a window. He never profited, however, by these thefts, but gave everything he stole to the poor, himself lived in direst privation.

We agreed that the great days were passing. I tried to remember some of the songs which Bobby Edwards had once sung in the restaurants. Pete, it turned out, knew them all by heart and could sing them from beginning to end. We agreed that there had been something special about Bobby Edwards. I said it was the curious prestige which very clever people may acquire by pretending to be very stupid. Pete said that this was not quite it, because Bobby Edwards did not look stupid: the thing was that he never changed his face and consequently had everybody buffaloed.

These songs led to other songs. Pete and I finally got to the point of singing *My Bonnie Lies Over the Ocean* and *There Is a Tavern in the Town.* "I suppose this burns you up," I said to Daisy, who had for some time been lying silent, "I suppose you want to go to sleep." "Oh, I guess I can bear it!" she answered—then added, after a pause: *"My Bonnie Lies Over the Ocean* always reminds

me of when I was a girl in Yarmouth—in Canada. My
uncle used to sing it.—And he used to sing *The Girl I
Left Behind Me*, too. I used to love to hearum sing that!"
Her voice, as she lay in the darkness, divested of the emphasis of day, had almost the timbre of a child's—and it
moved me with the charming pathos of young girls'
voices, the pathos of frailness and freshness. "Did you
come from Canada?" I asked. "I thought you came from
Pittsburgh!" "My mother came from there," she explained. "My aunt still lives up there. When I was a kid,
I used to go there quite a lot. Yes, I'm really just a country girl!" she said, burlesquing herself. "That's why I
take so easily to living out here. My other aunt," she went
on, after a moment's recollection, "married some kind of
a nobleman.—I always thought there must have been
something wrong withum—he must have had syphilis or
something. But he was a real nobleman, it seemed!"

When we were tired of singing ballads, we experi-
mented with hymns. I rendered, with what I felt at the
time was an impressive solemnity and resonance, *Oh God,
Our Help in Ages Past* and *The Starry Firmament on
High*. But the second of these was met by silence—I received no response from the bed. And when Pete and
Daisy replied to my good night, it was plain they had
been asleep.

Those magnificent hymns! I went on thinking. What a
fine poet Watts had been! And that grandeur of the universe which gave us faith and imposed moral principles—
did one not feel it, also, even, in the calm complacent
firmament of Addison?

In the bitterness and disgust of the winter before,
when Larry Mickler had seemed to me a hobgoblin, I had
begun a corrosive satire, which my conversation with
Pete and Daisy now brought back into my mind. I recalled what I had already written and began framing

further paragraphs: "The attitude of the demons toward each other is entirely devoid of the amenity and dignity characteristic of human behavior. In their amorous relations, they are neither romantic nor faithful. Many of the demons do not function sexually, but among those that do—notably the succubæ and incubi—their matings are wholly physical and transient, and involve neither affection nor responsibility. A human being who has seen the demons at close range is not perhaps disposed to consider this unnatural. The more hideous and monstrous types have died out, like the larger and more powerful: the bat's ears, pig's snout and ape's mug appear only in modified forms; and such a bestial and complex mask as that worn, for example, by Dürer's Satan would probably be impossible today. Yet the devils which have endured to our own time are still sufficiently unsightly and grotesque, and in a sufficient variety of ways, to appear repulsive to human taste as objects of amorous desire, and impracticable even for each other. We do not wonder when a female demon, coming straight from the embraces of a male, makes no scruple of spitting and jeering at him in the presence of other female demons, or in the presence of another male; or when a male who has been mating with a female makes her the victim of one of those practical jokes to which the devils are so inveterately addicted—impaling her in a public place or hacking off her arms and legs and leaving her on a crowded thoroughfare. We should, however, be quite wrong in supposing that the devils resent each other's ugliness: being entirely without ideas of beauty, they are, in consequence, impervious to ugliness, and do not even, as has sometimes been supposed, esteem it for its own sake. The demons exchange, in their amorous intercourse, in a manner not unlike ours, pledges of lasting affection and epithets of tender endearment; but these expressions are simple reflexes involved in the physical process itself and as involuntary as it; they attach no significance to them and we should wrong them in supposing they do. The devils have no offspring: they are unable, or unwilling, to reproduce their kind.

"These beings have a highly developed literature, which reflects their ideas and habits. It is mostly printed on crude loose sheets which are passed around from hand to hand; and it mostly consists of obscene anecdotes and stories of atrocious crime. We must, however, bear in mind, in connection with this literature, that to the demons, whose point of view is so incomprehensible from our own, a scandal is not a scandal, nor a crime a crime. The former they enjoy as a farce and the latter as a practical joke. They have an interesting school of poetry, of which the leader is Blashtalatshk. I have met Blashtalatshk and found him a devil of high intelligence. His horns are rudimentary and his lower jaw is lacking: but his enormous dark eyes are among the most sensitive and glowing that I have ever seen. His poetry and that of his fellows is, of course, devoid of the moral ideas and the ennobling emotions which distinguish human poetry today: it is exclusively occupied with the mere representation of sights, sounds, smells and other sensations, which the demons have a genius for recreating with vividness and precision, though occasionally with so much complexity as to produce an effect of incoherence". . . .

At this point, however, I dropped it. I found that my satire was boring me, and that it also went against my conscience. My portrait of the demon poet had been a caricature of Pete Bird, and I had now no real desire to caricature Pete. On the contrary, I liked him. I found that I did not want to write a satire: to satirize humanity was to slander it, and I no longer thought so ill of humanity. Pete and Daisy and the rest, after all—even Larry

Mickler himself—were not really base: they had disliked their lives as much as I had. If I had disliked them and found them base, it was because I myself had been tarred with the same stick. Moral problems, I now saw, were too complicated, and human nature too delicate a matter, to be hacked by the axe of satire. So, regretting the emphatic prose style with which a simple moral conviction may equip us and which I now found myself obliged to sacrifice, I decided to be scrupulous of the truth.

But I still lay awake. I sat up, with my back against the arm of the couch, and saw the round cold winter moon, of which I had before had a glimpse on the other side of the house, now studding the pane with its white blinding pearl. When had I seen it before, setting so, but the moon of summer then, embedded in the morning glass? I thought of Rita, in Paris now. I had been wrong about her and Ray Coleman: Rita had merely, at the time when I had seen her and she had seemed to me evasive about her address, gone to stay at Duff Burdan's studio— all the rest had been a gruesome fantasy of my jealous imagination and my shaken self-confidence. She had gone abroad, alone, for the first time in her life just when I was returning, and I had had a letter from her the day before. It had reached me the morning I left town for the country. She was staying, she wrote me, in a little Left Bank hotel, and had as yet seen nobody. But the early morning market trucks, she said, which rumbled through the Rue du Four and caused the walls of her bedroom to vibrate, though they kept her awake after midnight, made her feel that she was "really part of Paris." I seemed to divine behind her letter an aching loneliness—the loneliness of all Americans when they first try to live in Europe; and I imagined about her, as she wrote, the dark brownish walls of the room, the dispiriting wash basin and the slop jar, the stuffy and musty French bed. It was partly the fact that I could pity Rita, and that at last she had written to me, as well as the spectacle of Grosbeake's equanimity, which made it possible for me to think well of humanity.

Not that her letter was plaintive or effusive. On the contrary, it was brief and dry; but the fact that she had written me at all—she very rarely wrote letters—seemed to me to imply, on her part, an unusual degree of desolation; and the two poems which she enclosed in her letter —she told me she had composed them at night when she was kept awake by the trucks—were the palest things of hers I had seen. The first was meager, terse and wistful; it ticked off, in three brief stanzas, three images from that countryside of her youth—a lone elm, a gray stone fence, a pond athrob with frogs at nightfall; and I recognized in their phantom faintness—so unlike the stinging actuality that she usually gave to such things —that dim aspect which, to the traveller abroad, even the best loved and known sights of home come to wear in alien places, as if perhaps they had never existed, but were the receding images of a dream.

The other poem was a sonnet; and when I first saw it, I did not know what to make of it. It seemed very unlike Rita. In the first place, she never wrote sonnets; and my first thought, when I commenced to read it, was one of solicitude. I felt distressed that her isolation should so disastrously have affected her poetry. Then it dawned on me, after I had finished it, that it was supposed to be addressed to myself. I reread it with attention: it was the first time she had ever written me a poem. Then I became aware of what had happened: the trouble here with Rita's style was simply that, for the moment, she had become infected with mine. It was I who was addicted to sonnets; and I could recognize in this one of Rita's my own forcible-feeble rhetoric and my adjectives in monotonous pairs—all those unavailing devices with which I had muffed the kind of effects that she would clinch with a single short verb or a commonplace idiom. I had never thought myself much of a poet, but now that Rita seemed to be talking my jargon, seemed to be trying to reply to me in the language in which I had been apostrophizing her, I found that I was sickened by it. And I was horrified to observe that even the banal imagery with which Rita could usually perform miracles remained, in this ill-inspired sonnet, irredeemably banal.

My first feeling had been one of depression, the result partly of wounded *amour-propre*—because Rita, having written me a poem, should have written me such an indifferent one—and partly of pained concern that she for my sake should have let down her art. I had been embarrassed as to what I should write her: I wanted to urge her to suppress the poem, but, since the sonnet had been written in an effort to be nice to me, it was impossible to be so ungracious.

Now, as I lay staring into the fire, I thought of the sonnet again, and ran over it in my mind. It was a memory of our first days together, when we had sat up late talking about poetry; and now suddenly, for the first time, I was touched that she should have remembered those days and should have tried to let me know it. I had thought only of the artistic sincerity which she had sacrificed for her subject! Now I was able to take account of the sincerity of some personal sort which must, after all, have come into play to induce her to sacrifice it. In her dismal Paris hotel—so cold and dark in November—had she been trying to recall, to reaffirm, in spite of all our quarrels and failures (and she had known then, as I had not known, how life undoes the soundest of our reasons and depreciates the dearest of our hopes), those moments of common understanding and common enthusiasm of the days when we had first talked freely together—when we had both, for that moment, found a language for those deepest unspoken convictions, for those deepest realities, of such different lives!—And I began even to wonder at last—a possibility I had never admitted—whether, that night at Sue Borglum's house, when I had met Rita with my freezing blank looks and my tiresome disapproval and when, reminding me of the poem which I had so loved when I had been in love with her, she had tried to describe to me the river all lined with sword-blades of ice— and when I had listened only with contempt—I wondered now whether, after all, she had not herself been glad to think of the hours—how rare in the world they must be!—when poetry had burned with love. Had not the river itself been the symbol of the breaking and fraying of passion, of the dispersal of the torrents of the heart?—and had she not, when she had told me, at Sue Borglum's, of the river alive in winter, for all the frozen countryside about it and though cramped by the ice of its banks—had she not tried to tell me something more, to speak again to the old comrade and admirer, over the head of the angry lover—to establish again that contact— which I now chose to make impossible—but which had brought once, if only for those moments, that common light into a world which, for her as well as for me—it occurred to me now for the first time—must be chiefly a world of darkness? And was the sonnet really so bad?

The last log had a comforting beauty—all woody rosy luminosity—but I saw that it must soon crumble. I put on another log, trying not to wake Pete and Daisy. I glanced over toward their bed—they had turned to each other in sleep. The log smoked, and then caught fire: it sent up little tongues of flame. What a pity that I couldn't write a satire for lack of misanthropic conviction! The log began to crackle and blaze.

I looked for the moon, but it was gone. I craned around the side of the couch and saw it low, vaporish and gray, as if dissolving in the ichor of dawn. So I had watched it set so many times, on guard at night, in France—in that terrible, dull, dead hour when night is over and day not begun, when one must either make verses or be dull, be dead, as the earth and sky, as the soldiers in their deepest sleep—I had run into Hugo in Toul—I had not seen him since the beginning of the War and we had only had a chance for half an hour's talk in a café—he had been so funny about his unit, so funny and so good-natured, that unit which was soon to condemn him to the horrors of the prison camp—what a great fellow he really was, in spite of the fact that, as Grosbeake said, he did caricature American business men too grimly—how few there were like him!—that France where Rita had never been till she arrived in that dreary hotel, where the market trucks kept her awake! I rolled over and went to sleep.

But I had scarcely closed my eyes, it seemed, when persistent coughs, steps and bumpings compelled me to open them again. It was Pete, in the gray early light, getting into his khaki shirt and his pants; he was rolling up his sleeves at the window.

I tore myself out of my blanket-cocoon and—though he begged me not to get up—I blinkingly pulled on my clothes, and followed him out into the cold undersea of the early morning ocean. He had gone into the shed to chop some wood: I had used up the last log during the night, and he wanted to make the room warm for Daisy. He begged me again not to bother; but with eager, if incompetent, helpfulness, I hacked up a large crooked limb, as well as several of the planks of the floor.

After this, we went in and had coffee—Daisy was still asleep. We talked about literature and drinks: Pete had volumes of Shelley and Keats, and a treatise on

French wines, which he said were the only books he had not sold when he had come away to the country. Sitting close against the stove, I examined the wine book with interest. "Never buy 1916 Burgundy," Pete admonished me, with an air of independent knowledge. "From 1910 to 1914 are all good years—and 1915 is fair. But you have to go back to 1904 to get really A-1 Burgundy!"

I had to leave before noon—it was a long way into the town and a long way back to New York. We talked a little about a taxi; but as it was already growing late and as the nearest telephone was at a farm some distance away, I decided that I would undertake to walk, and Daisy offered to go with me. Pete had promised to call on a farmer and examine his grandfather's clock—putting clocks in order, it seemed, was one of his curious useless aptitudes—in return for which service, he explained to us, he hoped to be able to induce the farmer to make him a present of a crippled lowboy which was being used as a kitchen table.

"I can supply the handles," he assured us. "Nothing easier in the world! Just take them off that old bureau in the storeroom. But I don't see how I can supply that missing leg without a lathe.—But, after all, why not have a lathe?" he went on, with the liberal enthusiasm of a thoroughly practical man. "Think of all we could do with one! We could make regular tables and chairs!—Why, I'd be turning out table legs so voluptuous that all the local oafs would be trampling over one another to buy them!" "I suppose," said Daisy, "that you're going to buy the lathe with the money we owe the grocer." "My dear child," Pete retorted, like a millionaire who takes pleasure in explaining that he always saves money on his clothes by having them made while he is in London, "you can get a lathe from Sears Roebuck for ten dollars! You simply say that you want to buy it on installments, and they send you the lathe. Then you don't pay them anything more—and by the time they've sent a man for the money and he's gotten way out here, you've had time to turn out a whole dining-room set, enough legs and rungs for several dining-room sets, and you've sold the sets and ordered another lathe from another mail-order company, paying the first installment out of what you get for the sets—so that by the time the first lathe is taken away, another one is just arriving, and the work goes merrily on!"

We set out—Daisy and I—on a hard crust of frozen snow, which broke through at every step and let us down into powdered depths. Daisy was dressed in high laced leather boots, a white sweater under a tan leather jacket and a round knitted white cap. I had never liked her so much: a certain strength and independence of character, which I had felt in her even at the period when she had seemed most demoralized, had now fully come into its own. Her frankness and her common-sense jokes, which I had once thought the typical products of Pittsburgh and New York, now seemed to me the wisdom of the country, which the false values of the city couldn't fool. I began to think—it had already occurred to me—how delightful it would be to live with Daisy in a solitary farmhouse in the country, to chop wood to keep her warm, to sit with her at night in front of the fire, to read Bulwer Lytton's novels aloud. I thought wistfully of Bulwer Lytton, whom it seemed to me I should like to read.

I congratulated her on leaving New York. "I began to feel before I left," I said, "as if the Village were a cage of wild animals—I began to feel that it might be just as well to make good your escape in time." "I certainly felt that way," said Daisy, "but I didn't know anybody else did. I thought everybody ate it up but me. I got so I felt that I couldn't trust anybody!"

We strode, plodding, through the snow. "You know, Pete and I," she went on, "just after that last time I saw you—we got on a train with our last money"—(the money, no doubt, from Pete's books)—"and got off at the first town that looked good to us out of the train window. We went to the real estate office and asked for the cheapest thing there was—and we finally got this old hell-hole. The owner said that, if we'd fix it up, they'd give it to us free." The idea of this exploit enchanted me, and I envied Pete more than ever.

I told Daisy how much I liked Pete—what a relief I thought she must find him after living with Ray Coleman. "To tell the truth," she replied, "I don't notice much difference. The only thing is that I get along much better with Pete. We can sit around and wisecrack for hours. The time that we had that party—the first time that I ever met you—I'd only seenum a few times, but I said to-um, 'I get along with you better than with anybody else I know.'" "What did he say?" I inquired. "He just grinned," said Daisy. I remembered how I had felt myself when it had burst upon me that Rita, instead of scorning my apartment, enjoyed it. "So," Daisy continued, "we went out and went to Julius's bar together—and here we are now!"

I told her again how wise they had been to have left New York for the country—how glad I had been to go abroad—what a fool I had made of myself the night of Sue Borglum's party. "As far as I'm concerned," she replied, "that night was about the worst I remember— about the worst sunk I've even been."

"You know," she added, after a pause, "I cut my wrist that night—you knew that, didn't you!" "Good Heavens!" I exclaimed, "Why did you do that?" "Why, because I'd lost my job, I suppose," she said, "—and because I got tired of the traffic going in and out of Gus Dunbar's rooms—and I'd been drinking so much that I didn't know what I was doing anyway. I felt like such a tramp—that I'd been so inconsiderate of other people, and just gotten myself into a worse mess than before. I cut my wrist," she went on, "with Gus Dunbar's razor blade. I never saw anything spurt the way the blood did—it seemed as if all the blood in my body must be right in my wrist—it spurted clear across the bathroom. I just stood there and looked at it—the only thing I could think of was the leak in the hose in that movie that you and I went to—don't you remember?—a little while before. If Pete hadn't come in just then, I'd probably have bled to death. But he arrived and called a doctor and put a tourniquet on my wrist. He certainly stopped it in short order—it seems he knows all about tourniquets."

"Oh, my dear," I said, "did you do that? Is it really all right now?" "Yes: the doctor said that I ought to have an operation, but I'm almost all right again now."

I made her take off her gauntlet: I saw that she could hardly move the fingers of that hand which Pete had once described as a "little surprising moonbeam violin"— they were as stiff as the fingers of a doll which a child tries to make hold a broom. "Why don't you get them operated on?" I asked. "It probably isn't a very serious operation." "Can't afford to," she replied.

"What had happened, anyway," I asked, "before I came to get you that night?" "Oh, it was horrible!" said Daisy. "I'd gone around to Larry Mickler's to see Larry about getting Pete a job—he was a friend of Gus Dunbar's.—When I'd called him up on the telephone and suggested sending Pete around, he'd said for me to come —but I told Pete to drop in after I'd been there awhile. I could see what Larry wanted, but I thought that I'd jolly him along a little if Pete could get anything out of it. I thought that I could fix it all up and get back in time to have dinner with you. Well, when I got there, he made me drink and then he tried to grab me. And then before Pete arrived, his wife came in. It was awful: that was really one reason that I cut my wrist, I guess—I was so disgusted with everybody!"

I thought with pitying superiority of Larry Mickler. I felt today that I myself was so very far from being capable of behaving in such a way as to make a young girl lose her faith in life!

We marched on—we were in wagon ruts now. There was a long rising road before us, with a straight row of trees on each side. We climbed the hill—there was a farmhouse at the top—we started down the slope of snow.

"Our favorite yokels live in there," she said. "You ought to see me giving parties for the yokels—I have the time of my life—and so do they: they think I'm swell—they never saw anything like me before!" "It must be nice to live in the country," I said—I felt envious of the yokels. "It must be nice to know your neighbors—which you never do in New York." "Yes," said Daisy. "I get to take positive pride in competing with the other housewives to see who can have the best-looking kitchen. You know how sloppy Gus Dunbar's looked?—I think it was that as much as anything that discouraged me with life that time—well, when I came down here to the country, the first farmhouse kitchen that I saw brought out a suppressed housewife's complex"—I remembered her remark, at Sue Borglum's, on the neatness of Sue Borglum's kitchen—"and I used to feel ashamed unless our kitchen was just shining!"

There was still a stretch at the bottom of the hill. What a marvelous walker she was! And she had felt, as I had done, that life without honor was horrible! But where Rita could save her self-respect with a poem, where even I could write part of a satire, Daisy could only cut her wrist!

We walked on for a time in silence. I could be so happy with Daisy, I thought—taking long walks in the snow in silence!

"I was in a pretty bad way myself," I presently remarked. "That night that we went to the movies—you really saved my life! You don't know how sweet you were!" "Well," she answered with amiability, "you weren't so sour yourself!"

We were coming now into the town; we had reached the first white houses. I was cheered by a sudden inspiration: "Look," I said, "we couldn't get a drink, could we? Isn't there some kind of a bootlegger in town? I've got plenty of time before the train." "We might go to Ned Lovejoy's," she said thoughtfully.

It was just a room in a private house: there was an oilcloth-covered table; a stove—which was pleasant after the cold; some "cabinet-size" photographs of members of the family, paralyzed in family groups; and an old-fashioned tinted picture of a little beribboned girl, smiling innocently and sweetly upon a sweet-natured cat and dog who ate amicably out of the same bowl. I don't know which was worse—the gin or the ginger ale. Ned Lovejoy was inclined to converse, but we discouraged him and he left.

"You don't think that Pete and I are getting to look alike, do you?" asked Daisy. I assured her that they weren't in the least. "That's what Gus Dunbar said when he was out here a couple of weeks ago: he said we were getting alike. They say that people who live together do get to look alike."

I began telling her yet again how much I approved of her course; how I had come to detest New York. I explained that I was going away, and intended to stay away as long as I possibly could. When I had returned in the fall from Europe, I hadn't been able to get back my job; and I had decided that, before looking for another, I might as well go on squandering my legacy, to the extent of a trip to New Orleans. I wanted to be there for the Mardi Gras.

Against the cold sunny light of the window, her sharp nose, pale eyes and blond hair looked almost Scandinavian. I told her how much I had enjoyed myself—how fine it was to have seen her again—how much I wished I were living in the country. "Why do you go to New Orleans, then?" she asked. I replied, not without a touch of wistfulness, that I had no place in the country to go to. I tried to summon another drink; but Ned Lovejoy was absorbed by his radio, of which we could hear the sepulchral buzzing—and there was a long, rather stupid silence. I went and found him, and got him to bring us some more ginger ale and gin, of which I had almost ceased to notice the taste.

I told her how splendid she looked with her outdoor complexion and clothes; and how much I liked and admired her. She said suddenly: "Take me to New Orleans!" "Come along!" I replied. "I'm sailing just after Christmas." "Take me away from all this!" she went on, burlesquing a woman in a play saying "Take me away from all this!"—but it seemed to me, and shocked me a little, that she was partly in earnest. "Pete can't go on like this!" she said. "He'll have to go back to the city and get some kind of a job. We owe everybody in town! I get panicky about it sometimes. Living with Pete like this is just like living with another woman—you have to live on your own wits from day to day—you don't dare to think ahead. You know: you can keep yourself on the go and keep using your vitality up, just so you won't mind things so much—but every now and then I begin to think about the situation and then I don't know what to do! I never thought I'd be living like this—I never thought I'd be with anybody the way I've been with Pete and Ray!" . . .

I remembered how, suddenly one night, she had left Ray Coleman and had never come back—and I remembered how she had begged Hugo to take her to Afghanistan. What if I could really get her away from Pete! I wanted a mistress now, and I liked Daisy so much —I desired her so much. But I couldn't flatter myself that she cared about me, she merely wanted to get away —and all that treachery, that promiscuity, that stealing of other men's girls, had come by this time to seem to me detestable. I had known Pete Bird through his poems, and had stayed in his house and read his books, drunk his coffee and eaten his food—and I remembered how bitter I had been when Rita had not scrupled to betray me, poetry, devotion and all, for that fellow from Columbus (or whoever it had been: I never knew; if it had not been merely some image of herself, that self which could not mate with others, because it held already, in one body, a union of female with male). Pete Bird had, as it were, built his house with his own hands, and he had not had the advantage of legacy.

The cold light on the cold road which I was looking at out the window, early as it was in the day, was already beginning to darken; and I had a feeling of stoic fortitude at the thought that, if the sun was short, I could endure the closing down of night. I spoke to Daisy of the sad imperfection inherent in all human relations, and of the necessity for loyalty and faith in a world where love was sure to fail us. "But," I warmly and earnestly broke off, "you know all about everything better than anybody! You're one of the most intelligent girls I know!" And I told her again how much I liked her and how well she deserved of life.—It was time for me to go.

At the station, I tried to get some gum for her out of a solitary slot-machine, but it was apparently frozen up. There were some country people standing about, and I was a little shy of kissing her good-bye; but we kissed, as I was getting on the train: I touched her coral lips for an instant. It was deliciously cold, moist and light, like that moment of ice and winter flowers inside the glass of Grosbeake's porch.

V

IN THAT ASPHALT SKY OF AUGUST, the summer sun burnt a blunt point of light, like the blinding violet-livid torch with which a worker on city mains gashes through a tough piece of pipe. A gray haze blurred the vistas of Fifth Avenue and dulled the too full-blown bushes and trees which one saw beyond Washington Arch, as if the buildings and pavements themselves, under the action of the terrible heat, were vaporizing and fogging the air.

Down a side street, an old white truck-horse stood sleeping and stupefied, its head lowered like a lizard's and its eyelids closed, while the driver, sluggish and sweating, piled a mountain of boxes on the dray. And farther over, on Seventh Avenue, I saw a barefoot ragged boy, who had flung himself down on his stomach above the grating that ventilates the subway, and whose coat was blown up violently behind him, like the streamers of an electric fan, by the warm sudden gust from the trains.

My handkerchief was sopped with sweat, and I was refreshed by an unexpected breeze which washed over the butt of the island the hot bilgy river smell, as if, now that the people of the Village had abandoned the Village for the summer, the waterside were invading the town. I saw nobody anywhere that I knew. On the cor-

ner of Twelfth Street, where Rita had lived, the obsolete
beer saloon still bore its discolored blue Pilsner sign.

It occurred to me to examine, as I passed them, those
landmarks of Abingdon Square which, the morning of
my first meeting with Rita, when I had been drunk with
peach brandy and poetry, had seemed to me impressive
and romantic, but which I had afterwards passed so many
times without ever observing them closely. I now found
that what I had taken for a statue of some interesting
celebrity of the quarter was merely a monument to the
soldiers of the ward who had died in the European War;
and that the object which had figured to my fancy as a
temple or a tomb was simply a disused bandstand.

Daisy and Pete had come recently to town. Gus Dunbar, who was now in Boston, had, at Daisy's instigation,
taken steps toward getting Pete a job there; and Pete had
gone on to see about it, leaving Daisy for a few days in
New York. She had called me up the day before, and,
with the idea of getting away from the heat, I had suggested our going to Coney Island.

She was to meet me at the pier. I had not been to
Coney Island since my childhood, and for some reason,
I supposed that the boat left from the foot of Christopher
Street. At the docks, I learned otherwise, and took a taxi
down to the Battery, along the wide cobbled avenue that
runs along beside the wharves.

There was a funny high yellow façade, built of wood
but with an aspect of pasteboard: it had precisely, I
remembered, the quality of the amusement places of my
boyhood, and it looked faded and flimsy now.

Daisy was waiting in the cavernous anteroom. In a
corner of the high darkish space, she showed charmingly
neat, small and clear. In spite of the roundness of her
hips and the smartness of her clothes—her white dress
and her tight *cloche* hat—she might almost have been

mistaken for a child. How cute and how chic she looked in those short tight skirts that cut off her slim legs just above the knees! "Well," she greeted me with her unblinking smile, "the first twenty years of my life I spent waiting for the Coney Island boat!" I apologized and explained. "But why didn't you find out first?" she protested. "It's a good thing you didn't think it left from the foot of Forty-second Street!"

"Well, how do you feel?" I inquired, as we climbed the flight of steps. "I feel pretty sassy!" she said.

I had of course missed the four o'clock boat, and now we should have to wait for the five o'clock one. But upstairs, the gray-timbered shadow of the low-roofed leaving-place was tranquillizing and cool. Through a low narrow opening that ran along the side, one had a glimpse of the crude unshadowed blocks of the enormous downtown buildings, where only one sheer green roof and a steep crane on a float that was green broke the cliffs of colorlessness.

I had brought along some gin, and I bought ginger ale at the refreshment stand. "I must tell you my joke," she said, as we drank that impossible concoction—at once too bitter and too sickeningly sweet—for which I had acquired a certain affection because I had come to associate it with Daisy. "I've made up an idea for a joke. There'll be a caption that says 'Striking a Happy Medum'—and then there'll be a picture of a medium—you know, a spiritualistic medium—with a big piece of bogus ectoplasm coming out of her mouth and a grin of satisfaction on her face, and a man with his arm all raised, just ready to smack her down.—Don't you think that's pretty good?" I told her that I thought it was terrible.

There was a large old slot-machine phonograph standing against the wall: it was lyre-shaped and had a mirror in its belly, and seemed stationed as an outpost and siren for the frivolities and gaieties beyond. We put a nickel in and started it playing an antiquated xylophone record of the *American Patrol*: its patriotic gallop, half-stifled behind the glass and losing itself in the wide gray waiting-room, woke in my heart a happy response as if to Fourth of July bands of my boyhood.

Then the boat was in; the doors were opened; we went down and stepped over the side. Assailed by the sunlight, we were dazed: in the brightness, we seemed merely to enter a smell of white boat-paint and to ascend to a brisk and merry tinkling of some pretty antique tune.

I pulled two camp-stools up beside a rail on an upper deck.—Sea and shore were rawest gray and the sky a raw pale blue—it was not that the blue was pale, but rather that blue was lacking. The sun streaked the water to the west with a bright glaze of zinc.—I got some more ginger ale and a couple of paper cups from the little soft-drink bar below.

On one side, as we left the dock, we looked out at the Statue of Liberty, a solid dull slug of gray against a colorless burning sky; and on the other, at the old red fort, round and full of holes like a mouse trap, with its rusty and abandoned barracks.

The thin strains of linkèd sweetness, with now and then a note frailly sour, of the harp and violin—some old musical comedy tune I remembered from my college days—seemed even in this false and elfin echo to keep more that was human and charming than the pace of the newer dance music had ever allowed it to suggest; and as I glanced at Daisy, now gazing out like a charming good-natured child at the sights of the passing shore, I was touched with sentimental revery.

Then the music was blotted out by the vehement snoring of a steamer and the pert sput-sputtering of a tug.

She seemed unusually carefree today, and I saw that

her lips were rouged an unusually pretty mauve. I told her how pretty she looked, and she replied by complimenting me on the harmony of my clothes: "With most people," she said, "their socks, for instance, haven't anything to do with the rest of their clothes—but your socks match your suit." My socks, which were a grayish blue, had been given me as a Christmas present and I had worn them only by accident on the same day as a gray summer suit. "But you have the worst-looking nails I ever saw!" she went on. "They look just like mechanics' nails, except that mechanics' nails are dirty." I explained that I always cut them with a pair of library shears.

I now decided to speak to Daisy of a matter which had been worrying me since I had met her at the pier. I said, "I think you've got some egg or something on this cheek." She took out her little mirror: "That's just a streak of cold cream," she replied. "It always does that when I leave some on and the powder sticks." She rubbed it off. In the stunning sun of that windless unshaded day, we were both dumb for a time.

Governor's Island, the harbor in summer, the old patriotic tune, the statue of the soldier in the park, had brought back to me another vision which for some moments loomed bright in my mind.

Once—it seemed to me long ago—on a morning in early July, I had come back to Governor's Island when it had been green with trees and grass, and when the barracks had been low white houses. There had been soldiers in khaki grooming horses or standing at the water's edge, in white shirts.

I remembered how, the afternoon before, though we had not yet been in sight of land, the empty horizons of those waters had held already the presence of home. The hours had seemed to pass more smoothly with the run of the homing ship—and in that calm summer evening the sea had scarcely breathed. The silver sun had dipped, had sent its silver path along the blue, and had sunk at the end of its path—spreading yellows and reds, which the night took.

Then at last the yellow star of a lighthouse had been winking in the black—it did not seem like the play of a machine, but a deliberate human signal; and then a lightship spangled with stars. A quarantine tug had presently come toward us from the still invisible shore, and had sent out some men in a boat. They transacted their business quickly, rowed quickly back to the launch and were pulled up in their boat with such promptness that it seemed to leap over the side. One had heard American voices: that was the American way of doing things!

Then a bed of lights on the water: after nearly two years of France, Coney Island had seemed incredible!

Then land on either side: there had been trees and lawns on the shore, and large white American houses, with here and there a lighted window, set along on a hill that sloped down to the water—and each of the houses was provided with its boathouse and its little pier. Now soon one was to walk in such houses!—to play one's part again in that life hidden there behind those lighted windows, in that life now somehow grown strange and yet the life of home!

There had come to us a sudden sweet smell through the quiet summer night: trees and flowers; the summer grass; the luxuriance and rankness of America. And then, as the ship passed on, a smell even more unmistakable, a smell even more of home, surrounded and saturated us. It was the rotten smell of the river, which, when today I had smelt it again in the Greenwich Village streets, had made me think of the salt bilge-water of the harbor, but which had breathed then the grease, the sour heat and the smoke of the factories, of the city. Dark chimneys were disturbing the darkness with their noiseless eruptions of red. That evening, on Riverside Drive, the benches would be full of couples, and all would be soaked from the Jersey bank by the hot heavy fumes of the glue factories.

Then suddenly I had almost caught my breath—I had been curiously moved by the sight of a single solitary street-lamp on the Staten Island shore. It had merely shed a loose and whitish radiance over a patch of the balding road of some dark thinly-settled suburb. Above it had loomed an abundant and rather messy summer tree. But there was America, I had felt with emotion—there under that lonely suburban street-lamp, in that raw and livid light!

Then, from somewhere behind those shadowy lawns, one heard the moan of an American train, and then its faint bell, and the swift shuffling sounds of its progress. It was speeding away with eagerness and sureness to American cities at night—far, perhaps—to the farthest reaches of a continent without frontiers! There had been a petulance and a sadness in the piping of the French locomotives—they had spoken always of the dead hours of dawn and the carloads of wounded men. But these trains were bringing soldiers home—and far away from Europe at night!

In the morning, off South Brooklyn, at anchor, we had seen the smoky rose of dawn come up over the black roofs of the city, and we had listened to the river traffic waking with soft puffs and toots. The colors had begun to come out on the vermilion smokestacks of steamers. The gray sides of a battleship were clear; it was soon trimmed with live figures in white suits. We had put down a motorboat, which sprang away, when it touched the water, as if the water had given it life; a blue sailor, standing at the tiller, and negligently and gracefully leaning to balance the tilt of the boat, was guiding it in bold easy curves.

Now the varied craft of the harbor were coughing and sneezing all about us, fully waked up for the day: squat shouldering ferryboats and tugs; a tiny motorboat darting like a waterbug; railroad barges floating freight cars —Delaware and Lackawanna; New York, New Haven and Hartford—all those dear, square names of home!

Then the shore was moving. To the left, the docks had begun to bristle with the first thickets of the forest of masts. In a moment, the sky would be crowded, and one would behold, above the docks and the shipping, the tremendous towers of the town!

At that moment, on our way to Coney Island, the freshness of that other summer day, when I had come back to the United States with what seemed infinite freedom before me, was recreated in my mind so vividly that I tried to describe it to Daisy. But for Daisy, the things which had delighted me—the boat leaping into the tug, the sound of the train in the dark, the sailor guiding the boat, had no special significance or point, because they were things which she took for granted, and which seemed perfectly commonplace. I felt that she kept waiting for these incidents to develop into anecdotes in which something entertaining would happen.

When I had finally given it up, she put her hand over the middle of my face and regarded me attentively. "You'd be very good-looking," she said, "if it wasn't for your nose." I said, "I know I've got a terrible nose!" "No," she reassured me. "It's cute. But it interferes with any Adonis-like beauty that you might otherwise have had."

In the harbor, the harbor of the August day which was actually about us, the lowering of the zinc-bright colorless sun had made of the water to the west a gleaming sheet of zinc; and to the east, it had begun to blue. A bell buoy clanged and bathed. Before us, we could see the steamers moving out toward the open sea, their smoke trailing back from seaward. A fresh easier breezy sea smell reached us—it was a lightening of the load of life.

"Doesn't that feel nice, though!" said Daisy. "I think I'm going to enjoy this trip!"

I asked her about Pete and his job. "I'm so glad we're going to Boston," she said. "I'm tired of the country, but I don't want to live in New York! I think New York is terrible!"

Sea Gate—and beaches rank with bathers; little brummagen summer bungalows with green or red roofs.

Then a monumental buff hotel with a blunt obelisk tower rose alone from a level shore—where, however, we could presently make out the skeletons of roller coasters and the squirrel cages of ferris wheels.

Now, more quickly than in our daze we had expected, the boat was pulling in toward the boardwalk: we could see a row of improbable objects—the sails of a bright red Dutch windmill; the teeth of a gigantic grinning mask; a rocking full-size Noah's Ark, with animals sticking their heads out of the windows and with curious half-clownlike figures, which made the spasmodic movements of automata and which seemed the true unearthly inhabitants of that city of enormous toys.

When the boat stopped, we stood on deck, waiting to disembark and we suddenly again felt the heat. "The sun makes me reel!" said Daisy. We walked, dazed, up a little gangplank and down a very long white pier. The hotel, which rose now to our left, against the dazzling zinc of the sky, was a dull and solid slug, as the Statue of Liberty had been. The sea was now quite blue.

I was enchanted by the Noah's Ark: there were an ostrich, a giraffe and an elephant, wagging their heads out the portholes; a Noah, who, at regular intervals,

threw back his Uncle Josh beard and took a swig from a
bottle of whiskey; and a fisherman who, at similar intervals, jerked up an old shoe on his hook. There was also
a mysterious monster, labeled "Hank," half-human and
half-brute, who in paroxysms shook his window bars. An
urgent and ominous foghorn sounded at the same short
intervals. I was all for going inside.

"Let's go in swimming first," said Daisy, "while we've
still got the sun—then we'll feel fine—then we'll have
another drink. Then we can go and do things, huh?"
She squeezed my arm; she seemed happy.

We floated, on our way, through warm currents: the
balm of hot buttered popcorn; the fragrance of burnt
molasses; the sweet-acrid odor of orange peel.

And then, after the close musky smell, human and
marine, of the damp-and-dry gray boards of the bath-
house, I met Daisy in my hired bathing suit, and we
walked out under the boardwalk to the beach.

She had brought an old bathing suit of Pete's, which
had enormous brown and white stripes and which was
in places much too tight for her. With her fair skin
among the tanned bathers and her hair tucked behind
her ears, she looked like one of the Mack Sennett bathing
girls in the old-fashioned movie comedies. "I know it
looks awful," she said, when I kidded her about this,
"but I thought it didn't matter at Coney Island—and I
couldn't afford to get a new one."

There were tiny children playing in the surf, in little
slips of bathing suits of yellow, pale green and red, like
the various flavored fruit drops—orange, raspberry and
lime—in the glass jars we had passed on a candy counter;
or like the bottles of colored soft drinks—cherry, orange
and lemon soda—which we had seen at a soft drink stand.
The children were splashing in wild delight or fleeing
from the sea with squeals.

Daisy worked for a few minutes, squinting, in an ineffective underwater side-stroke. I, still partly bemused by my drinks, flung myself with abandon to the waves, and swam around a small stone breakwater in what—although I ran into the breakwater—I thought was pretty good order.

"That was a marvellous wallow of yours!" said Daisy. "I thought you were trying to push the breakwater over! I was just going to yell out and tell you to stop, it was built there on purpose!"

She had brought out of the surf, about her shoulders, a great strip of glossy gold-brown seaweed, and she wore it as a boa. It went beautifully with her hair and with the taffy-colored stripes of Pete's bathing suit, both darkened by the wet. Her slim legs below her full hips looked almost like the legs of a bird.

We lay on the sand for awhile. "Your hair seems a different color," I said. "In fact—I don't know whether it's just my imagination or not—but it always seems a different color every time that I see you." "It is, I guess," she replied. "They put white henna on it when they bleached it for the *Gambols*—and I always used to put peroxide and lemon juice on it every so often, but I haven't been able to lately. That's why it's pink, I guess." I asked what color it had originally been. "Oh, Gee: I don't know," she said. "It's so long ago!—Mouse color, I guess!"

I inquired about a system of vivid blue veins on her thigh. "That's my charley horse," she explained; "I got it in the first *Gambols*." I asked her why she didn't go back on the stage. "I'm too short," she replied, "and my feet are too small for me to dance well—and I don't like it, anyway: I always get independent and cut too many rehearsals. That was why I got fired the last time."

Beside us, a brown young man had his arm about the

shoulders of a young woman in an old-rose bathing suit,
with large carpet-like flower patterns, which richly harmonized with the purple tan of her skin. She presently
slipped a hand beneath the top of her companion's bathing suit and affectionately rubbed his back. A handsome
blond girl in blue, who seemed to have two men in attendance, was pawing the sand with one foot. Another,
in a turquoise costume, had stretched out on her back
on the sand, with her shoulders between a man's knees;
he was passionately stroking her arm.

I watched one really beautiful woman, very blond and
rather Germanic: she wore a pair of red bathing trunks
with an orange stripe down the side, belted and athlet-
ically faded, and a plain white bathing shirt. She lay
voluptuously, with one knee up and her head on the
knees of a barrel-shaped man in horn-rimmed spectacles.
Her skin was extremely white, only toasted a little about
the shoulders; and she had smiling darkish brown eyes.
I watched her as, presently, she got up and walked over
to the water, and—while her companion bobbed in the
surf—with an easy and graceful crawl, lay voluptuously
along the swell.

"This is all artificial sand, you know," said Daisy—
"Oh, yes: they spent half a million dollars fixing up this
beach. There didn't used to be any beach at all. That was
the same time they put up the hotel. I wonder if they're
making money."

Gray steamers were passing quite close along the gray
line of the water—they made me think of summers in
Europe, of coming back from abroad in the fall—at the
age when I had last visited Coney Island, there had always been uncles and aunts sailing to or from France—
there had been an uncle who brought home from Paris
silk stockings for my cousins and aunts—he had had a
bluff and ironical way of retorting, "You don't say!" which

was precisely the way Daisy said things—it was a characteristic American way. The Americans went to Paris, and then they came back again with silk stockings and things they had bought, and that frank American smile, and that straightforward way of speaking. The people who interested me most were, almost all, I reflected, now abroad: Grosbeake was in England for the summer; Hugo, in spite of his enthusiasm for the American Middle Western cities, was still in Afghanistan; and Rita was still in Paris —yet I did not at the moment seem to miss them and did not want to go abroad myself. What fun we had had together after all—Rita and I—though we had never been quite easy and friendly together, as Daisy and I were today. There had been one evening—we had been drinking raw gin—Rita would never have drunk the gin and ginger ale to which Daisy was addicted—when we had told one another intimate things—I couldn't remember it all, but she had told me something about her girlhood, it was that night she had sung me the song about the *foggy, foggy dew*—and I had told her then how my father had died of tuberculosis—and what a rotten time I had had at boarding school, and how I intended to write a novel about it. Those nocturnal drunken conversations which seemed to mean so much!—which did, no doubt, mean so much. All literature, perhaps—and not poetry alone, but even the systematized facts of Hugo's documented novels, even the formulas of Grosbeake's logic—was in the nature of a drunken language, expressing, by certain symbols, sensations and emotions merely—the readjustments, that would be, of our little corner of nature to the universe of which we were part—which was forever passing into new phases and where each phase meant a new adjustment for every part—where, then, a new idea or a new kind of art was something more than the mere compensation for an individual weakness or disaster, it was a necessity of universal development—I would think it all out sometime—the sun was hot on the sand.

"Well," said Daisy, "now that we've earned that other drink, how about going in?"

Hot dogs were being roasted twenty at a time, on wide polished iron slabs: they were crisp, with a delicious stink. At an oilcloth-covered table, Daisy and I ate one apiece, dabbing them gamboge with a long-handled wooden spoon from the common mustard pot.

"I'm ravenous!" said Daisy, biting into the pulp of her roll.

Dim and languid from the swim, I was watching the reflections of girls, in wide hats and bright summer colors, shine briefly in the high silver myriad-paned mirror, in the sun that was bleaching whites whiter and blues and yellows white.

"Do you want another?" I asked, when she had bolted the last morsel. "Not now—maybe later," she said.

We did the shooting galleries after this, and the ring-throwing and ball-rolling games. We were both quite good: we knocked over any number of moving ducks, which was what we had decided to concentrate on; and we won a baby doll in a chemise, a miniature roulette wheel, a harmonica, an atomizer and a trick pistol which shot off a snake. Daisy was so delighted with the snake that she kept shooting it down the ball-rolling table, so that the Jap had to find it and bring it back. Every time, with oriental patience, he would stuff it into the pistol, hand it back to Daisy, and caution her politely with a smile, as he indicated the trigger: "Now don't put your finger on that!"—whereupon Daisy would shoot it off again. I was somehow obscurely reminded of that horrible night at Sue Borglum's, and I began to dislike the Jap and made Daisy move on.

"Let's send some goofy postcards," said Daisy, in front

of a postcard store. We went inside and chose several with fastidious care. I sent cards to Hugo and Rita; and Daisy sent cards to Gus Dunbar and Sue Borglum. "I'm going to be dirty," she said, putting a cross on a bathing beauty, and writing, "X marks my room."

I asked her if she would care for a pin-cushion heavily encrusted with sea shells and inscribed, "Souvenir of Coney Island," or if there were anything else she would like. "I'd like some moccasins," she said. "Very well," I replied. "Will you really buy me some?" she asked eagerly. "You great big munificent old thing! I haven't got any slippers now, and I used to keep getting my feet full of splinters and thumb-tacks in the country."

It turned out that her feet were so small that the man had to get a special size out of the stockroom at the back. The woman in the shop, fat and sharp-eyed, became very friendly with Daisy and, while the man was looking for the moccasins, tried to engage her in conversation. "Do you mind my asking what kind of lipstick that is?" the woman inquired with interest. Rather to my surprise, this seemed to embarrass Daisy: she explained that it was called "carnation," but when the woman asked her how much it cost, Daisy said that she had forgotten, and became markedly unresponsive. "If they can't find the right size," she presently remarked to me pointedly, "we might as well go!" The moccasins, however, were forthcoming: they were moccasins for a child and I did not suppose they could fit her; but they did. She looked down at her little blunt-toed foot with its border, at the throat, of gray fur: "That's all right," she said shortly.

"That woman certainly took a friendly interest," I remarked, when we were out on the boardwalk. "Yes," said Daisy. "I never know what to do when people like that get chummy."

I had been surprised at Daisy's shrinking from the

familiarity of the woman in the shop, and I was now to be surprised again. I had lingered in front of a sideshow, where there were posters of a Hula-Hula Dancer, a Dog-faced Boy, a Mermaid, an Hermaphrodite and a Magician, and I suggested going in. But Daisy evidently did not care to. "My mother would never let me see any freaks," she said. "They're all fakes, aren't they?" she asked a little timidly.

As we walked on, she shot the snake off again, and I had to go and get it out of an umbrella-stand bristling with pennants and canes.

Then I discovered the Éden Musée—I had forgotten that it had moved to Coney Island and had thought of it as having perished. I had not visited it since my child-hood, when, coming up to New York with my father, he used to take me to see it in the days when it had still been on Twenty-third Street. There I had seen for the first time moving pictures, along with the automatic chess player and the manipulator of liquid air. And now here was the same old policeman in his high obsolete helmet; the same refined widow in black, with the tight waist of the early nineteen-hundreds; the same old hay-seed with his spectacles, his flopping wide-brimmed straw hat and his flaccid carpet-bag—but now no longer posed inside, where they could no longer be mistaken for real people, but set out in front as a guarantee of the authentic antiquity of the exhibition.

I induced Daisy to go in. There they were, that spooky group of my youth, though it seemed to me their number was diminished: Jenny Lind, Mary Queen of Scots, Anna Held, Oliver Cromwell, Beethoven, Brigham Young, General Grant, Napoleon and Booker T. Washington. I was sorry to see that Marshall P. Wilder, the hunchback comedian of vaudeville, no longer had a place among them.

I did not examine them closely, however, for Daisy, who seemed never to have seen waxworks before, hurried on to the more dramatic tableaux set back in compartments along the side. She passed before them, gazing in silence. The groups were not particularly interesting, but they presently led us to the "Crypt." We entered a darkened curving passage. I was delighted: it was the old "Chamber of Horrors," for which in the Twenty-third Street days one had had to go downstairs to the basement. We gazed at the Opium Den; the Execution of a Burmese Criminal (it seemed to me now that the elephant who steps on the criminal's head had shrunk since I was a boy); the Cannibal Feast; the Whipping Post, "still in use in the State of Delaware"; and, the electrocution of poor Lina Lemberg, who had finally, a few weeks before, been executed for the murder of her husband. The witnesses, in the Death Chamber, were regarding the proceedings with simpers, and I thought that they had been borrowed from an old tableau of a lobster-and-champagne supper, with Mephistopheles in the background, of which this personnel of revellers seemed to me, like the Burmese elephant, to have dwindled since the Twenty-third Street days. I suggested this to Daisy. "I don't think this is very exciting," she said. She seemed to look at everything so perfunctorily that I was afraid she was being bored. Since she had never seen the Musée in her childhood, I could not expect her to share my interest in it.

Several tableaux farther on, I found that I had turned a corner and left Daisy behind—still staring, no doubt, at Lina Lemberg. I was standing before a group of the Spanish Inquisition, and I had a sudden happy inspiration for enlivening the entertainment for Daisy. I climbed quickly over the railing, put my straw hat on the head of the presiding inquisitor—he had a lean and sallow face, and the hat came down over his eyes—and, with my back to the railing, struck an energetic pose among the torturers with red-hot irons, myself applying to the victim's blood-streaked shoulders the corkscrew I had bought for the gin. In a moment, I heard distinct light steps, which stopped—then, after an instant's pause: "Come on out of there, you old cut-up!" I climbed back over the railing. "I thought you were real at first," she said, as we reached the exit. "You gave me quite a turn!"

On our way out, I caught a glimpse of Roosevelt, the Teddy Roosevelt of San Juan Hill, who, with his hand-kerchief knotted about his neck, his Rough-Rider puttees, his felt hat, his mustache, his glaring teeth and his eye-glasses, made me think of that younger America which I had assumed we had forever left behind, but which today seemed quite close to me again. It had been a boy's America—and not merely because it had been the America of my boyhood. The Roosevelt who had always been so charming with his children had become the idol of the public for very much the same reason—he had been everything that a boy could imagine: Dan Beard, Old and Young King Brady, Frank Merriwell and Stanley in Africa, all rolled into one. I asked Daisy whether she remembered the time when Roosevelt had been a great hero. She said, "No"—and showed so little interest that for a time I relapsed into silence. Then I learned what she was thinking about: "I've never seen a dead person," she said.

"By the way," I asked, after a moment, "what became of that thief that Ray Coleman caught—the one that didn't steal anything of yours but stole the bathrobe of the man next door or something?" She was silent. "Don't you remember?" "Yes, I remember," she replied. "But I don't know what became of him. I was thinking too much about myself at that time to pay much attention to anything else."

"Would you mind taking me to dinner?" she said presently. "I'm absolutely starved!" I asked her where she wanted to go. "I'd like to go to the old Seaview, if you don't mind. I don't know how the food there is now—but I'd just like to see the place. I stayed there with Phil Meissner," she added, "when we first came on from Pittsburgh."

The Seaview was quite remote—beyond a kind of grassy common, criss-crossed with bald paths. It was an old-fashioned summer hotel, of the cupolaed and pillared design of the days before concrete and brick. Like all wooden hotels by the shore, it had a flimsy discolored look and seemed peculiarly desolate and dry. The dining room was entirely empty: only a few of the tables were set. One side was all high narrow windows, separated by thin wooden frames, which looked out on the boardwalk and the sea; and on the other, an old closed piano stood against the wall, and space had been left for a dance floor; slim pillars from floor to roof at intervals threaded the room. We waited, but no one came. I finally hallo'd; and a waiter appeared from the pantry. He came forward without inspiration, as if he expected to be asked for cigarettes or to direct us to Luna Park. When he learned that we wanted dinner, his eagerness to serve us was extreme.

"Well," said Daisy, as we sat down, "the table linen's nice and clean, anyway." It was true: large white napkins had been folded into angles and stuck into large clear goblets.

"I'm going to have clams," said Daisy. "They used to have the most wonderful clam cocktails here." I ordered a melon for myself, and blue fish for both of us afterwards. I also ordered some ginger ale and poured out what was left of the gin. "I don't think I'll have any," said Daisy, "until after I've had something to eat." She looked a little pale and was silent for some time, and I hoped that the Chamber of Horrors hadn't upset her. She smiled broadly, however, at last, and proclaimed: "Look out, Food: I'm coming!"

I asked her how she and Phil had ever happened to stay at the Seaview. "Phil knew the manager," she explained. "The manager gave a party in my honor—just some of his men friends. We had champagne, and I'd never had anything to drink before—I was awfully young —I was only seventeen. I thought it was swell, and I got lit. They kept filling up my glass with champagne. You know how men are when they've got a girl that's young and kind of cute, and they're trying to get her tight. I had on a little black dress like they wore then, that buttoned up the back, and the bottom buttons got unbuttoned—and then every man that danced with me would unbutton another button—so that pretty soon it was unbuttoned all the way up to the waist. I didn't know anything about it and just went on smiling and dancing, and thinking I was cutting quite a figure, with my legs hanging out all the time!"

I laughed about this.

"I certainly enjoyed those clams!" she said, when all the little hollows in her plate were empty around the red-splashed glass of sauce. She smiled: "After all," she declared, "say what you please—there's nothing like a good plate of food!" I asked her if she would like some more clams. "Yes," she answered, after a moment's thought, "I believe I would." I ordered another clam cocktail.

I asked if it weren't true, as I had heard from Hugo Bamman, the night of Ray Coleman's party, that she and her husband, on their honeymoon, had ridden on a motorcycle all the way from Pittsburgh to Atlantic City. This had seemed to me tremendously romantic. "It wasn't Atlantic City," Daisy explained. "It was here."

"What was Phil Meissner like?" I asked. "He had a lot of charm," said Daisy, "and a lot of brains, too—he never did anything with them except perfectly foolish things. For instance, he'd spend days inventing something that worked by electricity to make the blinds open in the morning—he could lie in bed and press a button and make the water basin fill, and when it was full, the faucet would turn itself off and everything!"

"Were you very much in love with him?" I asked. She shook her head, as if in scorn. "I didn't know anything about anything then. He was the first regular beau I'd ever had: my father wouldn't let me go with the boys. I was all excited aboutum at first. I was so much impressed withum when I first marriedum that it was just ridiculous! I couldn't even go to the drug store to get a tube of toothpaste without askingum what kind to buy. But I wasn't really in love withum—I didn't know what it was all about—and then, by the time I might have been in love, everything was pretty well wrecked. My father followed us here and burst in on us with a detective at four o'clock in the morning. He made us get up and get married then and there—we hadn't gotten married before we left because Phil didn't want to attract attention. Dad said I'd either have to marry Phil or go back to Pittsburgh. So we got up and got married at four o'clock in the morning—it was the night after the champagne party and we both felt like nobody's business. Phil was sore as a crab, because Dad had a Catholic priest marry us, and Phil wasn't a Catholic—but Dad threatened to havum arrested for abducting a minor, and he had the detective right there.

"Things were never quite the same after that. I don't blame Phil for being sore: nobody likes to be forced into a thing like that—especially with a hangover, at four o'clock in the morning!"

I had been thinking: her father from Pittsburgh—why had they named her Daisy? I remembered that old song of my boyhood.

> "Daisy! Daisy!
> Give me your answer true—
> I'm half crazy!
> All for the love of you!
> It won't be a stylish marriage—
> I can't afford a carriage!
> But you'll look sweet, upon the seat
> Of a bicycle built for two!"

—that old song of an earlier time to which Daisy's name seemed to relate her—and her large hips, too—I had never been aware how round they were till I had seen her in her bathing suit—they were the kind that had been admired at the time when the song had been new—they went in for slender hips today—but I liked Daisy's none the less—how bicycles had gone out, too—but she and Phil, appropriately enough, had spent their honeymoon on a motorcycle.

"Are you happy now with Pete?" I asked. She shook her head: "I don't know if I've really ever been happy—but I've sworn to go through with this with Pete. I'm tired of leaving people." "Are you and Pete married now?" She shook her head again and grunted negatively "uh-uh!"

"I know I'm not happy now," she went on, "because I keep having these dreams where some kind of a great piece of good fortune is just about to befall me—and they're the goofiest dreams!—When Prince Charming comes along, he's always just a great, big, strong, clean-limbed American who gathers me up in his arms. It's so silly! I feel ashamed of myself after I wake up.—And I'm always dressed in the costume that I wore in the first *Gambols,* when I came out in a white old-fashioned dress, with curls and pantalettes and everything. I loved it —Gus Dunbar used to say that I looked so sweet and dewy that he wanted to smack me down. But you know one night the boys from Notre Dame came and stole my picture in that costume that was on show in front of the theater—and they published it in the college paper. They sent me a copy of the paper: I was tickled to death. That was the only one they stole!"

I had been watching, through the tall open windows, the double, white, pearly globes of the boardwalk lamps, so pale, so chaste and so bright, hanging gracefully, like lilies-of-the-valley, from their straight slender stalks, against the background of the paler blue, now the cooler blue, of the sea, where a bell buoy shone like a ruby.

When we came down the steps of the hotel, all was in deep blue dusk, with the lamps a double rope of moons. "Have you noticed this?" I asked, waving my hand toward the lamps.—"I suppose the last time I was happy," she said, "was back there in the old Seaview dining room!"

We were confronted, when we turned back toward the amusements, by a large and very garish electric sign in the form of a gigantic human foot, on which a red Mephistopheles was standing. By means of alternating systems of bulbs, the arm of the Mephistopheles was made to jerk back and forth, energetically prodding with a spear an illuminated corn on the big toe, which at each jab changed the color of its light, first blue, then purple, then green. The legend, which flashed on and off, proclaimed, in contorted striking letters: "Take a walk with Clancy's Corn Fix. Knocks the Devil Out of Sore Feet."

"Oh, do you see that sign?" said Daisy. "That was Larry Mickler's idea. He's making a lot of money out of it.

They've got them all over the country." I was glad to know that Larry Mickler, through a truly Dostoevskian device, had constrained his sadistic instincts to serve this beneficent end.

"I hope we get somewhere soon!" said Daisy presently. "I've got to go to about eighteen ladies' rooms!" We had been walking along the boardwalk and were only just reaching the shops again. Daisy presently disappeared into a small and rather sordid-looking restaurant.

There was a penny-in-the-slot place next door, and as I walked back and forth in front of the restaurant, I stopped and looked in. I saw, standing before me in the doorway, a tall young man with a stoop, who had a darkish toothbrush mustache which I considered a little silly, and rather large brown eyes of the kind usually described as spaniel-like. He was wearing, like everybody else, a straw hat with a black band, which, it seemed to me, he had pulled too far down on his forehead. I had a feeling of mild irritation that he should be standing and staring so innocently, so well-meaningly and so lackadaisically, square in the middle of the doorway, where he was making it difficult for people to pass. He was laden down, I saw, with packages: no doubt some woman had made him carry them.—Then sharply I pulled myself up from that vague and absent moment: the man was my own reflection in a mirror opposite the door. On either side were other mirrors which distorted people's shapes.

I continued to gaze at myself: how had I ever failed to recognize—especially after Daisy had remarked on it— my ridiculous bulbous nose? My eyes, which I had hoped were intelligent, had only appeared to me canine—and my mustache was unsuccessful. My pockets were bulging with the atomizer, the mouth organ, the baby doll and the pistol with the snake; and I was carrying the roulette wheel and the moccasins, which had been put into pasteboard boxes. I seemed to myself a figure from the funny papers: Mr. Suburban American, at the seaside, with packages and a straw hat.

I went to the door of the restaurant. Daisy had not yet emerged. There was a radio playing outside, and for some reason the program included some vaudeville or night club woman soloist singing *Mamie Rose,* that popular song of several years ago which Daisy had started on the phonograph when Rita had been reading her poems and which had desolated me so on the day when I had seen Rita off at the station and had been waiting for Daisy in her rooms. Now I listened idly for the words, parts of which, on that horrible record, I had never been able to catch. The contralto, whose voice was rich and deep, delivered them with a masterly casual emphasis, in that nondescript dialect—perhaps the result of Irish actors learning from Jewish comedians how to sing Negro songs —which has become the language of American jazz:

> "There she goes,
> Mamie Rose!
> She—loves—me!
> Don't seem to show it!
> How do I know it?
> It's A B C!
> She's smart as Satan—
> She's aggravatin'—
> But when I want a little lovin',
> She don't keep me waitin'—
> She's proud and snooty,
> But she's my cutie—
> She tells me, Fireman, do your duty!"

That was the line that I'd never been able to hear!—That song, but a few years old, seemed already to belong to the past, like *Daisy* and the *American Patrol,* and the old musical comedy tune which the musicians had played on the boat, and I found that I had at last come to feel for it a certain familiar affection. Furthermore, I now thought it quite good. There was something rather unexpected, something even quite original about the manipulation of the tune. What was original and unexpected was the repetition, in some sort of minor, of the pattern which had just gone before—recommencing, with *She's proud and snooty,* what one had thought was entirely finished—and recommencing it agreeably and queerly, so that for a moment one always paused to listen. I wondered how the composer had arrived at it. He was a man named Harry Hirsch, I remembered. I imagined him: a small, young Jew with very large, intense black eyes, like motor headlights; after the success of the musical comedy in which *Mamie Rose* had been sung, he had probably taken to wearing spats. He was no doubt the son of a rabbi or of the cantor in a synagogue. The base of his music was German, and I imagined some dark room of a stifling apartment on the East Side, in which his youth had been fed on Schubert and on the light opera of Vienna and Berlin, cities which his eyes had never seen. But what had he done to this music?—what had made him repeat those bars of the sweet German melody with which he had begun, but transforming them abruptly by daring what any hack worker in the field would have told him *a priori* was impossible, what would have lasted in commonplace hands impossibly too long? By carrying us beyond expectation, by breaking into that new accent, half agonized and half thrilling, he had enchanted the public so completely that not merely had *Mamie Rose* turned out to be one of the principal factors in the success of the musical comedy in which it had first appeared (and in which, as a matter of fact, the director had been afraid to feature it), but it had been heard on every radio and phonograph; at every college prom, at every Greenwich Village ball; from the most perfunctory chirpings of the orchestras of restaurants to the jazz bands de luxe of roof gardens; on the vaudeville circuits of small towns and in the scores of feature moving pictures; worked up for the Elks' summer fair; struck up, with words thrown on a screen, during the intermissions of burlesque shows; ground out at the "dancing academies" in which, from New York to Los Angeles, inarticulate and clumsy young men pushed wary and inarticulate girls about a crowded monotonous floor—and as I had heard it once, late at night, sung strangely from a summer street by a child's voice, nasal and shrill, following subtly and with marvellous accuracy the deviating minor strain, and repeating it again and again.

Where had he got it?—from the sounds of the streets? the taxis creaking to a stop? the interrogatory squeak of a streetcar? some distant and obscure city sound in which a plaintive high note, bitten sharp, follows a lower note, strongly clanged and solidly based? Or had he got it from Schoenberg or Stravinsky?—or simply from his own nostalgia, among the dark cells and the raspings of New York, for those orchestras and open squares which his parents had left behind?—or from the cadences, half-chanted and despairing, of the tongue which the father had known, but which the child had now forgotten and was never to know again?

But the relations between Schoenberg and the taxi brakes and the synagogue resisted further speculation. And, in any case, what charmed and surprised one, in this as in all works of art, was no mere combination of elements, however picturesque or novel, but some distinctive individual quality which the artist himself supplied. Of all the young Jews in New York who had listened to the service in the synagogue or who had been kept awake at night by taxis, how many had written good music, even good popular music? I thought of that personal color or rhythm which, the night when I had been dressing in Bank Street to take Daisy out to a night club, had seemed to me, in the work of an artist, as little important or interesting as the color of his hair or eyes, or his way of mispronouncing certain words; but I could recognize now that it was precious. And as I recalled my gloomy meditations of the night of Sue Borglum's party, I remembered how the Greeks had given Sophocles the name of "the Attic Bee."

Yes: I saw it. There it was: it was acrid, but still honey; and it was something more than beauty of verse. The Greeks' idea of sweetness had been as different as possible from Robert Louis Stevenson and the "honey-dripping style." I saw it now—not merely in the nightingales and the ivy of that chorus at Colonus for which the jury had applauded Sophocles, when his competence to dispose of his property had been called in question by his son, but in the passionate frankness of Antigone, even in the asperity of Oedipus, even in the guile of Odysseus. I thought now of the exquisite proportion, of the style with its unique combination of modulation and pith, of the strong and sensitive hand placing with so light yet firm an emphasis those culminating scenes in which the nobler instincts of humanity reassert or declare themselves: Electra when she speaks to the urn which she believes contains her brother's ashes, Neoptolemus confessing at last that he cannot act against his nature to deceive even an outcast who has trusted him—as, in the case of Dostoevsky, I remembered, no longer the contention and the horror, but the brightness of the high comic sense which interpenetrates all that is turbid, which flowers constantly in such charming passages as that in *The Idiot,* for example, in which the young girl buys the hedgehog from the boys and sends it to the Prince as a peace-offering, and which makes even of *Crime and Punishment* a comedy rather than a tragedy. It was not that the Athenian jury had merely demonstrated their gratitude for—that the crowds at Dostoevsky's funeral had merely regretted being deprived of—a sedative to which they had become addicted; but that both had been ravished by the taste—and by it had been partly repaid for the harshness of the common life—the taste of that miraculous secretion of the mind which there was only one man to supply. And so every sort of good literature, so every sort of good art, provided an aliment, a stimulant, as natural and necessary as food and drink themselves! Even the tannic tincture of Poe, which seemed to turn the throat to leather and almost to petrify the taste, had its own peculiar tonic value, and even from the coarse used mash of Byron it was possible to extract a strong brandy—even the writer of popular music.—The radio was hawking and halting; I had already been waiting a long time—much too long, I began to think. And I suddenly remembered how Daisy had slit her wrist on the night when I left her at Gus Dunbar's apartment.

I was on the point of going in to look for her when she finally appeared. I was so much relieved to see her that I did not at first notice how pale she was. She said that she was sorry to have kept me waiting, and we walked on for a moment in silence; then I asked her whether she had been ill. "No: I'm all right," she replied. "You were such a long time in there," I said.—"Are you sure that you're all right?" "Yes, I'm all right," she said again. "You were sick in there," I challenged her, stopping. "Did you throw up?" "I'm all right!" she repeated. "It was just the smell of that place, I guess!"

I made her sit down on a bench. She would not let me get her anything, and neither of us spoke for a time. A fresh fishy breeze was blowing in: I hoped that it would make her feel better. A lighthouse was winking punctually; the ocean was grayest blue, and the low waves were pale as porcelain on the sands of palest buff; the late bathers were coral limbs. Some children, still playing on the beach, were holding out into the ocean and the night the brass-bristling frost-crystals of sparklers.

I asked Daisy presently how she felt. "All right: fine!" she replied. I tried to find out whether there were anything seriously wrong with her. "No," she said. "To tell the truth, we haven't had very much to eat out in the country lately: the grocer and the butcher in the village wouldn't give us any more credit, and we had to live on the things that we already had in the house—which were mostly corn flakes—corn flakes without cream or anything —that was about all we'd had for a week before we came in. I guess I overdid it with those clams."

I said I thought that the gin had been rotten and that the ginger ale had been inferior. I began to produce the toys from my pockets. She took a sudden interest in the harmonica and amused herself by working out tunes on it: her most conspicuous success, from which she seemed to derive a good deal of satisfaction, was *Nearer My God to Thee*. After a while, she said: "Well, let's go on!" I asked her whether she wanted to go home. "No," she declared, "not yet. I want to do some more things!—don't you?"

We explored Luna Park—all bright minarets and festoons of white imitation pearls. I offered to take her on the "Thunderbolt"; the "Shoot-the-Chutes"; the "Dragon's Gorge"; but she did not seem very eager. "Why don't we try that Noah's Ark thing?" she suggested, as we were wandering a little aimlessly, "that thing that you wanted to go into when we first came."

We went back to the steamboat pier and found the

Noah's Ark still rocking and sounding its somber fog horn. It was lighted up now with green ship's lanterns, which revealed the elephant, the ostrich, and the giraffe, the fisherman pulling up the shoe, the old patriarch hitting his bottle, and the monster shaking his bars. "Do you think you can stand it?" I asked. "Oh, yes," insisted Daisy, smiling. "I want to go in, don't you?"

We bought tickets and mounted the gangplank. Inside, the Ark was rather a sell, as there was nothing amusing to see—the animals and the monster turned out to have been constructed so as to be visible merely from the outside. We found that we had been let in for an assortment of banal and disconcerting sensations. We had to walk on a shifting platform—pass along a wobbly corridor—climb a flight of quaking stairs. Our hats were almost blown off by a violent blast of air and when we tried to catch hold of the railing, we received an electric shock. I was afraid that it might make Daisy sick again, and asked her whether she wanted to go back: "No, I'm all right," she replied. We went through with it to the end, in silence and rather solemnly. I felt protective and tender toward Daisy, and contrite at having brought her in. I was only just beginning to realize that she had probably, when we first started out, been faint for lack of food; that she had been drinking on an empty stomach; that she had been sickened by the Éden Musée and upset by my stupid joke; and that revisiting the Seaview Hotel, which had brought back her first days with Phil Meissner, had finally overcome her. I became acutely aware, too late, that if she had insisted on going in for the Noah's Ark, it had been entirely because she thought I wanted to. The last stunt was a spiral slide which landed us on a whirling platform. In my efforts to rescue Daisy, I fell on the roulette wheel and broke it.

It was now time to go home, we decided—but as it

turned out that the last boat had left, we were obliged to go back by the bus.

On our way to the place where the buses stopped, we passed the poster of a spiritualist fortune teller. "Did I tell you my joke?" asked Daisy. "About 'Striking a Happy Medium?'" "Yes," I said. "I think it's fine!"

As the bus left Coney Island behind, a cluster of bright pearly globes among the vivid red pumps of a filling station repeated the pearls of Luna Park and the drooping white lamps of the boardwalk.

Along the boulevard to New York were aligned little sections of shops, bright-windowed and built in new concrete: drug stores; grocery stores; automobile showrooms; a bank.

There were girls in summer dresses, hatless, with bobbed heads and pink or tan stockings, strolling out, alone or in couples. Down side streets, I could see little houses with compact and screened porches giving way to the wastes of building lots, where a lonely and random street lamp would light untidy bushes and trees. That was the America to which I had returned when, coming back after the War from France, I had been greeted by that other suburban street lamp on the Staten Island shore! That was the America to which tonight I felt myself returning again—those neat and new little shops, those girls wandering out in the evening between the drug store and the building lots—hardly knowing what they expected but half hoping for some new turn to their lives! Had not Daisy been once such a girl, walking out in the streets of Pittsburgh—had not Rita, in her upstate town?

I asked Daisy about her father, of whom she had told me at dinner that he had not let her go out with boys. "He was Irish," she explained. "He lost all his money when we were just kids. But he was determined that the

fact that he'd lost his money shouldn't make any difference about our being well brought up—I guess it did all
right, though." She smiled her candid smile. "That's one
reason they used to send me to my aunt's in Nova Scotia
so much." I remembered her timidity about the freaks,
her "independence" about rehearsals, and her coldness
with the woman in the store. "That was one trouble
about Phil and me," she went on. "Phil's father and my
father had known each other very well when they first
came to Pittsburgh. We used to live next door to the
Meissners, before they made money and moved. And in
those days, Dad had a much more important position
than Mr. Meissner: he was one of the principal men in
the Billings Company and Mr. Meissner was just a clerk
in a bank. Then when the Meissners made money and
Dad was down and out, they got snooty about us—and
Dad didn't want me to go with Phil—Phil had the reputation of being the wildest boy in Pittsburgh. Dad was
fit to be tied when I ran away withum!"

I marked another filling station: a crowd of great white
stars, which seemed uttered by a rocket's detonation.

Now we were passing a row of small houses with
tapestry-brick façades and, in front of them, little green
lawns enclosed by little hedges.

"Dad was really a bright man, though," Daisy presently went on. "He was one of the first people in the
country to design certain kinds of trucks. He invented
all kinds of things—he invented a kind of siren."

A filling station where the lights were dimmer and
the pumps a duller red was outshone by the lunar beauty
of the radiant white pergola which followed it.

"Did you ever hear them talk about auto horns—in a
store or anywhere, I mean?" she asked. "It's a shout.
There's a *toot-toot* and a *beep-beep*—and an *oorah*—and
a *blah-blah* and a *burp-burp.*—Dad's was a kind of a

oorah—and it was a humdinger, too!—it had an authoritative sound and it wasn't ugly like most sirens."

In the showrooms on either side appeared the present-
day glories of the motor industry: the Lancerd was cele-
brating its "Silver Anniversary" with a new model in
"distinctive" apple-green, posed with dignity behind its
plate-glass pane, in a white-balconied colonial salon.

"It was getting indicted for manslaughter," Daisy went
on, "that really ruined Dad: he and another man ran
into each other as Dad was coming out of a garage. It
was really both's fault—but the man was killed and they
indicted Dad—though he'd been a month in the hospital
himself. They made him pay a big fine and he lost his
job—and he never could get back after that. He used
to come home drunk and sit down on the edge of my
bed and hold directors' meetings all by himself—I used
to think it was funny, but my mother used to be so
worried!"

I had been brooding on the name of Meissner, which
seemed to raise for me vague associations. "Did they ever
call Phil Meissner, 'Junior'?" I finally asked. "The family always calledum that," she answered. "Why?—did you
ever knowum?" "Did they live in a great big house with
green and blue stained-glass windows?" "Yes," said Daisy.
"Why? Did you ever knowum? They lived at Aylesworth
Avenue. That was where they moved to after they lived
next door to us."

Phil and his family were the people, then, whom I had
visited as a child, when I had gone to Pittsburgh with
my mother, and who had been evoked in my mind when
Hugo, at Ray Coleman's party, had said that Daisy came
from Pittsburgh! I told Daisy how much I had envied
Phil Meissner's elaborate toy railroad and his device for
making dinner plates jump, but how obnoxious, on the
whole, I had thought him. "He was spoiled to death,"

said Daisy. "That was what was the trouble withum, I guess."

And this discovery that Daisy had married a boy I had known in my childhood had an effect out of all proportion to its apparent importance or interest. Hitherto, I now fully took account, I had regarded Daisy as an alien —first, as a denizen of Broadway, and afterwards, as a product of the Village. But she seemed now to have taken her place in the world which I had always known. She was no longer of a different race—of an exotic glamor or guile: she was simply an American girl, who had grown up in an American town like other American towns, lived in a house like other houses, gone to a school like other schools. I seemed to have been given a new vision of the fluidity of manners in America, the plasticity of social position—of the swiftness and adventitiousness of the way in which such things changed. If Daisy's family had gone down in the world, the Meissners had obviously come up. But the human material was the same; and in the face of its constant fluctuations, attempts to fix social differences came to seem ludicrous and futile. Americans might turn into anything!

What, for example, might not be made of Daisy? At each of the times we had been together, I had seen in her something different, as my own mind had been differently disposed by my personal situation at the time and by the influences by which I had been affected—by Hugo, first; then, by Rita; then, by my disgust and disillusion the night of Sue Borglum's party; then, by my evening with the Grosbeakes. And I could see how she herself had taken the color of each of the men with whom she had lived since she left Pittsburgh: Phil Meissner's extravagant tastes; Ray Coleman's constrained correctitude; and Pete Bird's engaging humor. She had even, I noted, begun lately to talk exactly like Pete. She had been eager to accept whatever they gave, and how little they had had to give her! Phil with his inherited money, his egoism and his silly jokes; Ray with his substantial salary, his ignoble employment and his meanness; and Pete with his pennilessness and uselessness, his gentlemanly hobbies and his charm—they seemed now to me like figures of comedy for familiar American types.—But what hope was there for Daisy with any of them?

"I declare," I said finally aloud, "I don't see why you haven't been able to do better than Pete and Ray! Haven't you ever found anybody in the Village that really amounted to something and that you liked at the same time?" She shook her head, not turning from the window. Then, after a moment, she turned: "You know the only person," she said, "that I ever thought I could get a real crush on was your friend Hugo Bamman. I actually got all hopped up, that night he was sailing for Egypt or wherever it was, about the idea of going away withum. I think he's good-looking, too—especially since he's stopped wearing spectacles. Some people think that scar spoils his face, but I think it's smart-looking.—But he's certainly cagey about women—Myra Busch was crazy aboutum, you know. Either that or he's afraid of them. —He's so sure of himself, too—he knows what he wants to do.—None of the men I've ever lived with were sure of themselves.—You know what you told me out in the country about my knowing about everything better than anybody—well, I wanted to say at the time that that isn't true at all. That's just the trouble: I don't know what it's all about. I want somebody to tell me!"

Daisy's mentioning Hugo reminded me of the world as I had seen it through his eyes when I had first come down to Greenwich Village. Then, like him, I had thought myself a rebel against the standards of a bourgeoisie— that is, in a country like America, where there was really only one class, or rather, as I had just been reflecting, no classes, properly speaking, at all, against an abstraction of all the worst qualities attributable to respectable Americans; then later, when I had been in love with Rita, all the interests and occupations of the common life had seemed to me on so low a plane and of so lax an impulse, that I could feel for them nothing but contempt. Now my trip to Europe since the War had had the effect of making me more content with America even at her worst; and my conversation with Grosbeake *à propos* of Lewis's *Babbitt,* though Grosbeake's opinions had surprised me at the time, had in the long run had the effect of helping me to approach America from a different point of view than that which, at the time when I had been influenced by Hugo, had allowed me to take account only of American mediocrity and timidity. Today I seemed to have reëntered that world and to find myself perfectly at home there; now I found that it no longer inspired either hatred, apprehension or scorn.

"By the way," I presently asked, "where did you get that line about 'the downfall of western civilization'?— You know, that night I took you to the movies, you said that you probably looked like the downfall of western civilization." "Oh," she said, "that was just something I picked up in the Ritz Bar in Paris!"

The little tapestry-brick houses had been supplanted by apartment buildings, also in tapestry-brick, and with attractive green or brown awnings at the doorways and windows; but now the awnings came closer together and the crowded house fronts were laced by zigzagging fire-escapes; they got dingier, balder, denser. We were in Brooklyn, and now Brooklyn Bridge repeated the fire-escape zigzags.

Delancey Street, with its car tracks and hooded subway entrances; the Bowery, with its El.

We got out at Astor Place. I asked Daisy what she wanted to do. "I think I'd like a drink," she said. "It's so long since I've been absolutely free, without any house-work or anything, that I feel like making the most of it!" "Have you gotten over your sinking spell?" I asked. "Sure," she replied with conviction. "I feel fine!"

The oppression of summer, again, hung over and hushed the city streets: the very taxi horns seemed muted. The greenery in Washington Square, behind the arc lights, looked heavy and dark; and the benches overflowed with Italians, dirty and sweaty, swarming to the air, giving out the sounds of life, but heavy-footed, slowed down and subdued.

My rooms in Bank Street were stuffy and messy. The colored woman who took care of them had abandoned me without warning, and they had not been cleaned for a week. I threw open all the windows. In the house across the court, the people were sitting on the fire-escape in their undershirts. A baby was howling and sobbing.

I had brought in some ice from a drug store, and this time we had Scotch instead of gin. It was pretty good Scotch, as it went, and we had highballs with mineral water. It was pleasant to relax on the couch, with the cold misted glasses in our hands, alone, with nowhere to go, with no buses or boats to catch.

"Who did you say you were staying with?" I asked.

"Sue Borglum," Daisy replied—and added: "I think she's going nuts. Have you seen her lately? She's turned green! She's turned absolutely green! But I can't worry about her! I've got all the worrying I can do with Pete and myself!"

"Did you ever know Peter Kester?" I asked. "No," said Daisy. "Who is he?" "He's a great friend of Rita Cavanagh's—she always used to be telling me about him. I met him yesterday for the first time—he's just come back from New Mexico. He's just a nice old bozo, who paints rather mediocre landscapes. He's just like all the American painters of that generation that you meet at the Washington Irving Club. He wears tortoise-shell-rimmed eyeglasses with a big black ribbon—and he thinks that Picasso is a clown!"

The electric lights were hot, and I got up to turn one out. "Why don't you turn them all out," said Daisy, "and just turn on that lamp in the alcove? It would be a lot cooler." I turned on the table lamp in my study and put the others out. I was glad that the things in the room were obscured by the shadow now: I had been feeling that that Leonardo was not a particularly suitable picture for New York in the summer time.

When I came back, she had stretched out along the couch, with her head propped up on a pillow against the arm and her highball clasped in her hand. "I hope you don't mind my lying down," she said. I sat down on the edge of the couch beside her.

The voice of a radio, dimly muttering or hoarsely warbling, came in to us from across the back yard. I was reminded of my recent meditations while I had been waiting for Daisy in front of the restaurant, and I told her now about looking in the mirror and mistaking myself for someone else.

"You're not so bad!" said Daisy. "I think your mustache is all right. In fact, I've always liked the way you look." I replied, "Well, I've often told you how much I like the way *you* look!"

Encouraged, I began to describe to her my consoling aesthetic revelations in connection with the popular song. —I had always thought of her, I told her, ever since that first night I had met her, whenever I had heard

Mamie Rose.—I talked on, and even got as far as the Attic Bee.

But all the time that I was talking, she was looking at me, serious and flushed, as if I had been making love to her. At last I stopped and said, "You're such a darling!" and kissed her. We said almost nothing after that. . . .

When, from the profuse delight of that love, hot, moist, mucilaginous and melting, I found my thoughts springing up again, they seemed unfolding like fresh new leaves in an atmosphere of peace and gentleness.

I thought of Daisy under her different aspects, as she had seemed to me at different times—and I remembered the literary productions which at one time or another she had inspired—all so different from my present vision of her, from the reality of our present relation: first, the night that I had met her at Ray Coleman's, the cool Gallic short story I had fancied, with its humanitarian irony —then, the night that we had gone to the movies, the romantic apostrophe of the sonnet—then, the night that I was to take her to a night club, when my alienation from Rita had had the effect of thrusting away from me all the rest of the world as well, Daisy along with the others, the desperate exposure of literature itself, on which my mind had run so furiously and interminably—then, when I had visited Pete and Daisy in the country, the savage moralistic satire which the letter I had received from Rita and the spectacle of Grosbeake's equanimity had prevented me from continuing. I had, in fact, rejected all these projects, as I had outgrown those phases of myself of which my successive conceptions of Daisy had been merely the reflections in another.

And now I felt that I should be content if I could only make some sketches of Daisy, as I remembered her at different times and places—if I could only hit off, in prose, her attitudes, her gestures, her expressions, the intonations of her voice—preserve them so they should not vanish, as Degas had done for his dancers, as Toulouse-Lautrec had done for the women of the cabarets. . . . I dreamed a whole series of Daisy. . . .

So I should perhaps save myself at last from that dreadful isolation of the artist which had appalled me in Hugo and Rita—both forever, it seemed to me now, occupying impregnable solitudes with the creation of impossible worlds—so, by the way of literature itself, I should break through into the real world—just as tonight I had seemed at last, with Daisy, as if by a quite simple mutual transfusion, to come so naturally into contact with life. Such pictures as I imagined of Daisy would grow directly and freshly from life. And it seemed to me tonight that literature was as amiable as writing ballads, as necessary as making tables—and indeed that, when one came right down to it, there was really no difference in kind between carpentry and literature.

I bent over Daisy—her head on the pillow had that look—the little soft round chin and the soft bare throat—of women in those moments when they have dropped off, along with their garments, all the ruses and resolutions with which they meet the world—when we see them just awakened or lying thinking at night, with wide eyes and anxious mouth, and we realize how gentle they are, how much they wonder, and how tender toward them we must be. . . . I wondered whether she would leave Pete for me. . . .

"Let's run away together!" I suggested.

"Oh, I couldn't—now," she replied. "I told Pete that if he got a job, I'd stay withum."

It seemed to me now that I wanted above everything to go away somewhere with Daisy.

"I'll take you on a motorcycle!" I proposed.

"No, you won't!" she promptly replied. "I've done my last motorcycle elopement!"

"Still you must have had a lot of fun!"

"I didn't know whether I was ever going to get there alive. We had about six accidents. . . . The real reason for the motorcycle, I found out afterwards, was that I was afraid I was pregnant and Phil wanted to bring me around. He thought that a motorcycle trip would be just the thing. . . . There! I'd told you that we weren't married! Oh, well—never mind!" She was silent a moment, then went on: "That's something that nobody but Phil would think of—taking a girl on a motorcycle trip to bring her around! . . . He wouldn't even let me ride in a side-car—he carried me all the way on the handle-bars!"

I made her turn and embraced her anew, kissing her with pleasure and compassion. When she told me of the rejection and death of her love, I recognized the fate of my own. And it was sweet to include in my arms that warmth, that solidity, that slenderness—and to feel that she followed me! . . .

In the peace and silence again, I could hear that poor child still crying, and I remembered how once, as a child, I myself had lain awake with the heat, and suffered and complained.—Then, in a moment, I remembered, also, how those same children of the Village had figured in the poem which Rita had recited the night of Ray Coleman's party and which she told us she had written that day. On that very day when she had filled my imagination with the splendor of her genius and her beauty, when she had seemed to me a goddess or a muse—on that day, her own mind had been haunted by visions of imbecility and deformity—she had seen only, among those children of the streets, the most wretched and the most afflicted, and she had seen in them only the crippling of the spirit and the clouding of the mind by unhappy love. . . .

What relief and what a rebirth, our only real birth into this world, when from the fears and snobberies of youth, from all our preconceived ideas, from all those foolish abstractions we learn, all those things that we think we think, we find at last in these beings who have crowded, offended, disgusted or fought us, that interest and that value which we have found only in a few or in one—when, youth's passion and anguish spent, we see rising about us that reality of those we have looked on as strangers, and know that it is our reality—that what is strange to us is strange to them, that what hurts them hurts us, that what is good for them is good for us—when we no longer dread the fool nor hate the one who wounds us, but sleep in our beds in peace and in peace face the waking world! . . .

I kept telling Daisy how smooth her skin was, and she was finally moved to retort: "Are you used to women with scales?"

"I suppose I ought to go," she said presently. "I don't want Sue Borglum to have it on me that I stayed out all night."

"I've been so happy with you today," I said, "and I'm afraid that you haven't been happy."

"Oh, yes, I have," she replied. "But I've been depressed about the Boston business. I don't want to go to Boston, damn it!"

She sat up on the edge of the bed. "Now you go into the other room while I put on my dress!"

When she came back, her dress wasn't hung very well, and her lipstick, newly applied, had a look of fresh paint.

"I don't care about any of those things," she said, "except the mouth-organ and the pistol."

I wasn't able to find the mouth-organ. I looked for it

all over in vain. "Confound it!" I exclaimed, "I must have left the mouth-organ in the taxi!"

"Oh," she said, "I wanted to show Pete how I could play *Nearer My God to Thee!* But I guess that the snake will amuse him!"